UNDER THE *Lies*

SARAH E. GREEN

To Jessica and Lacey.
Who rode out this novel with me from the very first (painful)
draft to the one in your hands.
Who kept me strong when I felt like breaking.
I'm so thankful for them. Forever and always.

one

Sayer

"To my Sayer! For moving back home to be closer to me so I'd miss her less!" my best friend, Brin, shouts over the pounding music in the club. She shoves a tall, skinny shot glass in my limp hand.

"And not at all because I came back to finish grad school," I add dryly.

Among other things…

"Grad school, smad school." Brin waves away my words, not seeing the lackluster shine in my eyes. She can't, not when she's well on her way to drunktown.

Clinking our glasses together, she tosses hers back and her delicate face pinches in a grimace. "Gah!"

I follow suit, wincing from the burn and chase it with my watered down soda. *God, shots.* Of all the ways to consume alcohol, shots, by far, are my least favorite.

Taking the empty glass from my hand, Brin drops it on a nearby, *occupied* table, ignoring the nasty and confused looks from the people sitting there, before pulling me into a bone-crushing hug. "I'm so glad you're back!"

I can hear it. The excitement and the happiness and the love in her voice. Brin's thankful I'm home.

My arms wrap tight around her and my eyes close in relief. It's been a long time since I've been hugged by a friend. So long tears prick my eyes as I whisper with words too low to be heard, "Me, too."

It's a half-lie bitter on my tongue.

We break apart and I study our surroundings. Call it growing up with a paranoid granddad but it's ingrained in me to always be aware of where I am. Unfortunately for me, that currently happens to be the last place I ever wanted to visit in this forsaken city.

Heathen's Hell.

A den of debauchery. A place for sinners and dealers.

I mean, they even have cages.

Metal and ornate and structured like birdcages, they dangle from the ceiling with men and women in elaborate masks dancing in them. My gaze keeps straying up, unable to look away.

It honestly might be the safest place to look. At least when I stare at them, I don't find myself looking between the sea of people on the crowded dance floor or around the lounge where Brin and I are loitering.

I keep telling myself I'm not looking for him, convincing myself that my heart isn't skipping at the sight of every tall man with broad shoulders and dirty blonde hair that my gaze locks on.

I'm trying to pretend I don't care if I see him when that's the only reason why I came here.

Even if I don't talk to him, I have to see him.

Noah Kincaid.

My tormentor, my first crush. My devil.

His name haunts the streets of this city, half the buildings are plastered with it, but it's not just his money that makes people stand at attention, it's the way he holds himself. With authority and arrogance, like he's better than you and wants to make sure you know it.

He's the unofficial ruler, this city is his kingdom and I'm on the hunt for his throne.

Merely out of curiosity. To see if my memories of him match up or if he's evolved into something worse.

At least, that's what I've been telling myself since we walked in here.

My fluttering stomach says otherwise. I ignore it.

Brin grabs my shoulders, giving me a shake. "Get out of your head, Say. Let's go dance!"

I let her pull me to the dance floor. There was a time where I would've been the one pulling Brin, and just like the hug that feels like a different time. I used to love dancing, I used to love a lot of things, but like so many things that have brought me joy, it's on pause and I don't know if I'll ever hit play again.

But I try. As my body sways and thrusts to the beat, I dig down deep into myself where a light once shone. I dig and dig and dig only to find cold, vicious darkness.

I stop moving. Dancing no longer holds an appeal.

Brin's oblivious, finding entertainment in a man who's slid up behind her. I motion to her that I'm going to get a drink, she nods before twisting around in her partner's arms.

I'm about halfway to the bar when my phone starts to vibrate in my bra—this dress is too tight for pockets. I deflate at the caller I.D. when I wrangle it out, the screen smudged with boob sweat.

Mother

I don't move to answer right away. It buzzes in my hand, a bomb racing toward detonation. Should I answer? Should I let it go to voicemail?

I sigh, knowing if I don't answer she'll only keep calling. I head for the exit, to the cold street where she'll be able to hear me. She probably just wants to tell me about her upcoming vacation to Europe with my father, they're leaving tomorrow, and how I have to attend a function in their honor while they're away.

Whatever the reason for her call, I don't get to find out.

A man with a neck tattoo steps in front of me. I skid to a stop, narrowly stopping myself from smacking into his broad, muscular chest.

"Excuse me," I say, sidestepping him, phone violently shaking in my tight fist.

He mirrors my step. A neutral, if not, cruel face stares down at me.

"Excuse me," I try again, louder and with the authority of a Brooks, only to get the same results.

With a deep, frustrated sigh, I stare into his dull, dreary eyes. The phone in my hand now silent. "Typically when someone says excuse me, the other person lets them pass."

He doesn't say anything, doesn't blink, but his hand darts out with viper-like speed and grips my arm.

I slap him with my free hand. He retaliates by tightening his hold. "You're not going anywhere, sweets."

I recoil, my face pinched in disgust while my heart beats wildly in my chest. I try to break his hold but the man has a grip of iron. "Nice try, darling, but I was given orders not to let you leave."

His words cause a ruckus in my chest. "Ordered by who?" There's an inkling of who coiled inside me.

"Let's go, doll face." He smirks, ignoring my question and jerks my feet into motion.

Three nicknames. Three condescending pet names this stranger has called me in all of our five-minute interaction. It wracks against my skin. I have a name. It's Sayer. And if someone told him not to let me leave, I bet damn good money he knows it too.

He's *choosing* not to use it.

Just like I'm choosing not to be cooperative. As he drags me to the bar, I dig my heels into the ground, my nails into his skin. I try to pull away.

It does nothing. He doesn't so much as glance my way.

In fact, he doesn't show my struggling inconveniences him at all until I'm shoved none-to-gently onto one of the barstools. I glare at him and he gives me one right back.

Watching us with intense interest from behind the bar is a bartender with salt and pepper hair and aged eyes. He places a dainty martini glass in front of me. Bright, citrusy liquid fills it to the rim.

A lemon drop.

My favorite.

Unease wraps around me as I push off my stool. I don't get far. Mr. Neck Tattoo Man moves behind me to grip my shoulders, holding me in place.

"Stay," he hisses in my ear.

"I'm not a dog, you oaf!" I snap, trying to shake him off.

It doesn't work. His grip is as tight as his stare is cold. He shoves me into the wood, my nose inches from the bar top while my sternum is rammed with enough force my breath catches.

"Don't hurt her," the bartender warns. "Boss won't like that when he gets here."

Noah.

Alarmed, my eyes snap to his as my stomach tightens. Noah's coming. I know I've been spending the night hopelessly searching for him but now that the reality is happening, my palms start to sweat.

Do I really want to see him?

I don't think I have a choice.

Finally, reluctantly, Mr. Neck Tattoo lets go of my shoulders. He doesn't back away, though. His rancid breath brushes my skin as he reaches around to slide the lemon drop closer to me. Liquid splashes onto the bar. "Drink," he orders.

"No." Defiance chills my tone. I don't accept drinks I don't order myself, especially not when one is being shoved in my face by a bruising asshole.

Mr. Neck Tattoo is quiet behind me. Tense, but silent. I can still feel his warm, stale cigarette-coated breath on the back of my neck.

Until I don't.

He moves away and I slump down in my stool in relief. A relief that doesn't last long as another set of hands curve around my shoulders.

These hands are different—larger, broader, rougher. Commanding to the touch.

My insides trip over themselves as a shiver glides down my spine.

Six years and I still recognize his touch.

It's hard to forget the way my body ignites with a trail of heat that settles between my legs, the way my heart feels too large to be contained in the cage of my ribs when one particular person is around and his touch is branded on my skin.

Noah.

He's close, so close I can feel his chest, which is pressed against my back, still chilly from the frigid winter outside.

Cold or not, it does nothing to quench my torrid flesh as his unshaved cheek brushes against the shell of my ear. "Don't like your drink?"

His voice is poison coated in sugar. Sweetly hiding what lies beneath. Temptation. A shiver slithers along my spine.

It's a fight to keep my voice steady. Unaffected. "Not a fan of drinks from strangers."

Noah chuckles against my ear. "I'd hardly call us strangers, Sayer Brooks."

I would. Spinning around in my stool, I stare into the harsh, chiseled features of a man who radiates power and can, in fact, attest that we're nothing but strangers.

I no longer know what haunts the depths of his eyes. And he no longer is responsible for mine.

The club is packed around us but everything gets drowned out, the music, the people, as I study Noah.

His face is a beautiful nightmare. Cruel by design. Perfection that only ever seems to unfairly grace someone so wicked. There's no warmth in his stare as it pierces me, making me want to look anywhere but into those wolf-blue eyes behind his thick, black-framed glasses.

A predator's gaze and a cold, dark heart.

Why couldn't he have boils? Boils on his cheeks, above his eyebrows. I'd take the boils anywhere, not greedy with the placement. Just something, anything, that'll make looking at him easier and not like I'm back in high school where watching my sister's boyfriend leaves me flustered with a single stare.

But aside from a freckle that sits above his eyebrow, his face is blemish free.

I grew up seeing some of the most remarkable art the world has to offer thanks to my granddad being an art buyer but no piece he ever brought home had ever been as exquisite as Noah, who has the face of an old time star with a jaw carved from marble and an attitude as welcoming as an iceberg.

"Miss me?" Smirking, he watches as I continue to drink in his face, his features, his presence.

Miss me?

Does one miss the Devil after they've found salvation?

Does one miss the darkness when they've stumbled into the light?

Crossing my legs, I give him a blank stare. "You'd be surprised how little I've thought about you."

His hand covers his chest, mock hurt on his face. "You wound me."

"I wound your worshipped ego." I roll my eyes. "You could benefit from getting knocked down a peg or two."

He chuckles again, but he watches me with keen, alert eyes. "No one dares to do it but you."

"That's because you have the whole city afraid of you."

"Except for you."

Especially me.

I'm not afraid of Noah in the same sense as everyone else in town. I'm afraid of him because he makes me feel things I shouldn't.

Noah reaches around me for the lemon drop and brings the glass to his lips, downing it in a swallow. His arm brushes mine as he places it back on the bar. "What brings you to my club, Baby Brooks?"

Whatever tingling feelings I feel from his touch get snuffed with that name.

Baby Brooks.

That's all it takes for my teeth to clench and my irritation to rise. I push against him, jumping off the stool, stabbing a finger into his chest. "Don't call me that. You know what my name is."

Noah laughs, completely unbothered. As he should be since he's the one that came up that god-awful nickname to begin with.

What started out as a name for Noah to call me when he was visiting my sister at our house quickly became the name everyone at our prep school adopted. I was always Baby Brooks, never Sayer and I *hated* it.

As much as I hate hearing it six years later.

"My apologies." He sounds anything but apologetic.

"What're you doing here, *Sayer?*" he asks again and I don't miss the mocking emphasis he puts behind my name.

Looking past Noah and out into the dancing crowd, I try and fail to find Brin.

"Sayer." Noah draws me back to him.

"I'm here to have fun." *I'm here to remember* how *to have fun.*

Noah pulls me away from the bar. "Then let's go have fun."

I swallow, but don't fight him—too curious to know what he has in mind.

Our ideas of fun are on opposite ends of the spectrum. I like to stay firmly within the law while to Noah and his friends, the law is nothing more than guidelines on how to break them.

So, I let him lead me onto the dance floor, almost in a trance.

Noah is touching me.

Noah is touching me.

Noah is definitely touching me, my mind screams when his hands fit to my hips, moving them to the beat of the music. Slowly, rhythmically, Noah's hips move against mine, rolling in sensual, heart-stopping thrusts.

Fun isn't the right word for this. My skin feels charged, my blood humming. *Alive.* I feel alive. Noah is making me feel alive. My lungs are tight, my palms tingling as my hands entwine around his neck. Holding him close. Wanting to chase the feeling he's created inside me.

We dance and dance, exploring not only the music but each other. His hands leave my hips only to roam my sides, my breasts, squeezing them as we move to a rhythm that makes me want the clothes separating us to disappear.

My hands leave his neck, going to his hair and pulling at the strands that sit longer on top than the sides.

The teenager in me, hell the current twenty-four-year-old

me, is dying over having an all-access pass to feeling Noah up, to feel his muscles constrict under my passing palms. To feel his steady heartbeat pressed against my erratic one.

His touch passion. His stare hungry.

There's something about being this close, around all these strangers, and still feel like we're alone as we explore. As we feed the hunger growing in every touch.

I feel myself melting against him, wanting more. Noah sees the desire in my eyes as he pushes the hair off my neck, gracing my skin with a hard, possessive kiss.

"Noah," I breathe. My body ignites, tension and need building inside.

His name is all it takes for the cord holding his restraint to snap. Noah makes a noise of impatience in the back of his throat as he quickly pulls me off the dance floor and into a cramped, dark closet behind the bar that isn't made for two people.

"What are we doing in here?"

Noah's scent invades my senses, evergreens, spiced cloves, and worn leather, as his husky voice whispers in my ear, "Let's play a game."

"What kind of game?" I whisper back, excitement racing inside me. One that revolves around removing clothes?

Noah smiles against my skin. "Think of it like strip twenty questions. But for every question you don't answer I get to take something off you."

His sharp gaze rolls down my body while his finger traces a line of beadwork on my dress. "Maybe I'll start by taking this."

When I came here tonight, I felt numb and dreadful. But now, I can't imagine leaving. Not while I'm trying to chase this moment of *feeling*. "What do I get to take?"

One of his knees knocks my legs apart, backing me up until I'm plastered to the wall. "Whatever you want."

Pants. I want to start with his pants.

No, his shirt. My hands wander to the buttons of his crisp white shirt, feeling the muscles that lay beneath.

Yes, definitely his shirt.

"Sayer," he practically purrs, soft but seductive.

"Hmm?" My eyes flutter shut while my hands still move up and down his chest.

"What happened when your sister came to visit you?"

My eyes snap back open. Hands freeze.

A different Noah stares back at me.

Gone is the man from the dance floor, even the bar, and in his place is the one people know to fear. Cold and ruthless eyes stare down at me, his words singed with controlled anger.

Did I hear him right? Did he just ask me about…Harlow?

Five days ago, just as I was getting settled in my new apartment after a long day of moving boxes, my sister showed up.

To some having their sibling show up might have been a welcomed surprise but for me, seeing Harlow was worse than being trapped in a room full of poisonous snakes. She's much more unpredictable.

"Nothing happened." Unless you count all the ways she verbally bashed me, which I'm not telling him. "She just came over to catch up—whoa! Hey! What're you doing?"

Noah moves like lightning as he makes a displeasured sound in the back of his throat, hands gliding down my body, over my hips and thighs.

"I warned you," he growls, grabbing my ankle.

This isn't like when we were dancing and his hands were on an exploration, now they feel like a restraint, holding me in place.

"Noah…" I warn as he undoes the strap of my heel, slips it off my foot, and tosses it over his shoulder.

It hits the wall with a hard thud.

As it lands, Noah looks up at me with wicked eyes. "Now. Let's try that again."

He grabs my other ankle, looking up at me beneath his thick, dark lashes that frame those hypnotizing blue eyes. "What did your sister want?"

His grip on my ankle is a shackle I want to be freed from.

I could kick him in the face. A spiked heel to the nose wouldn't feel good.

"Don't even think about it," he warns, reading the intent on my face.

"You don't know what I'm thinking."

"Oh, I think I do." His chuckle is far from humorous. "If you try to hurt me, you'll find out what an unforgiving man I can be."

"I think you're all talk." I know he's not all talk. One time in prep school I saw him beat a kid to the point of hospitalization with only a lacrosse stick.

His lips curl. "That right?"

I want to yank my challenging words back, but another part wants to push even more. So I do.

"You act all big and bad, but what do you really do? I bet you sit behind your desk all day—"

While I ramble and have him distracted, I use the foot Noah is holding and dig the heel of my shoe into his shoulder.

He hisses in pain, but doesn't loosen his grip. "Mistake."

Yeah, my rampant heartbeat is agreeing with that.

Noah twists my foot and spins me around so my face is to the wall.

Quickly, he yanks off the shoe before towering over me.

"You don't want to push me, Baby Brooks. When I bite, I'm not gentle."

His words cause a flurry of warring emotions to erupt inside me, my body running both hot and cold as the door to the closet opens.

"Boss." The bartender from earlier looks between us with some sort of humor. "You have visitors."

Noah stiffens at my backside, mumbling something I don't catch. He pulls away but not before pointing two fingers at me. "Don't think we're done here, Baby Brooks. You'll be seeing me again."

My mouth feels too dry as I watch him retrieve my shoes before walking out of the room, leaving me alone. And barefoot.

I don't know how long I stay in the closet.

All I know is by the time Brin and I get back to my apartment, I can still feel Noah's body against mine.

Two

Sayer

WHAT HAPPENED WHEN YOUR SISTER CAME TO VISIT *you?*

Noah's question follows me into the next day.

As I ate my sad breakfast of plain toast since I forgot to pick up butter when I did my first and only grocery run.

As I walked across campus to each of my classes.

As the professors went over their syllabus.

I should've been focusing on that, this is my last semester of my Master's in Art Conservation before I start my internship in the fall, but my professors were the last thing on my mind.

I tried and tried to kick the blue-eyed devil out of my head, to forget the husky and enticing sound of his voice. Tried and failed every time.

His words are a phantom I can't escape.

I wasn't lying last night when I told him nothing happened. Nothing that would interest him, unless he took pleasure in all the ways Harlow tried to put me down…which knowing Noah he might. Other people's pain is his pleasure.

He doesn't need to know any of that.

Though, something doesn't sit right about my sister's visit the more I find myself thinking about it. Little details of that night surface each time Noah's question runs through my head.

Harlow wasn't quite…Harlow. She's usually as recklessly carefree as they come and up until that night I don't think I'd ever seen her rattled. Not even when she got into a fight in prep school, bleeding from a broken nose, but that night it was like she was possessed by violent nerves, on edge and vicious.

At the time, I didn't question it. I stopped concerning myself with my sister's problems around the same time she held a knife to my neck when I was seventeen.

But after my encounter with Noah yesterday, I can't stop wondering what happened and why Noah cares.

With my mind preoccupied, the majority of my day has passed in a daze. My body might be present but my mind is not.

It's not until I'm walking to my final class of the day, Technology and Conservation of Art, that I feel myself snap out of the foggy haze that's consumed me. And it's only because I spy a familiar figure leaning against a light pole with carefree arrogance.

My steps slow but it's futile. I can't avoid him. He's strategically placed himself in the direct path to my next class. It'd be stupid to turn around and go the long way around to the back entrance.

I'm not fourteen anymore. I can handle Noah Kincaid. So I swallow the groan that's built in my throat and raise my chin, conjuring confidence I don't feel as I stroll up to him.

He smirks around the cigarette between his lips as I near.

I study him, taking in his black on black suit sitting beneath the steel gray pea coat. All articles of clothing tailored to perfection.

The arrogant smirk grows as the distance depletes between us. He stubs out his cigarette on the light pole, flicking it to the ground as he pushes off it and meets me halfway, bringing us almost toe-to-toe.

"What're you doing here?" My arms cross over my chest, a barrier, a shield between us.

"Just passing through." He slides his hands into his pockets, looking as innocent as the wolf who ate the lamb.

"Bullshit."

A brow peaks up from behind the mirrored aviators he wears. "My, my, Baby Brooks what a filthy mouth you have."

"All the better to sass you with."

Amusement twists his lips. "The last time I saw you, you still blushed when saying darn."

"A lot has changed, Noah." My crossed arms tighten. More than I want to admit.

He takes off his glasses, sliding them into his coat pocket as his eyes roam over my body. "Clearly," he murmurs, taking in my curves, my attitude. I see the appreciation on his face, the mask he usually dons slips, revealing a glimmer into his thoughts. *Baby Brooks is all grown up.* A part of me hums under his sweeping gaze.

In a louder voice he adds, "But that sharp tongue you've grown isn't going to save you today, Brooks."

"You don't know the things this tongue can do."

Time freezes as my words hang between us, as my eyes widen and heat blooms across my neck and up my cheeks.

Noah's face piques with interest and that perfectly manicured brow of his raises again. "There she is." His words are innocent but spoken with heavy meaning, no doubt thinking of much dirtier uses for my tongue than I can imagine. "There's the Sayer Brooks I know."

There was a time when I would've never been so mouthy to Noah. Where forming a sentence past a couple syllables was a challenge. Back when he was the bad boy in a beat up leather jacket who was four years older than me. He simultaneously terrified yet sent thrills through me every time I saw him.

He still does.

"What're you *really* doing here?" I ignore the way my body hums with him so near. There should be a switch to turn this reaction off.

"I told you last night we weren't done."

Unease courses through me, but I keep my face blank. "I already gave you my answer."

"I don't believe you."

"Well that's too bad," I shoot back. I glance down at my phone, I have less than five minutes to get to class. Time to end this conversation. "Have a good day now."

I spin on my heels and am about to walk away when he calls out, "She's missing, Sayer. She ran away."

I stop, mid-step. *Missing?* Turning around I meet his eyes, they smolder in anger. "What do you mean?"

"She ran away. After she paid you a visit," he speaks slowly, condescendingly.

"I got that. Thank you." I bristle, eyes narrow. "And what? You think I helped her?"

"The day Harlow goes to you for help is the day hell freezes over. No, I don't think you helped her. But that doesn't mean you don't know something. Think hard, Sayer. What happened when she stopped by your place?"

I've been thinking about it all day! I want to shout. I swallow them instead. "You can keep asking, Noah, it's not going to change my answer."

The frustration grows on his face, tension lining his eyes.

A small, satisfied smile tugs at the corner of my mouth.

"Sayer," he growls in a deep timbre. "You're not the only nuisance I have to see today."

My fist clench. The way he says it...putting the blame on me. Like any of this is my fault. Yeah, I don't think so. Despite the chilly January air, I feel warm all over. Heated with anger.

"Oh, I'm sorry, did I make you come here?" I snap, earning a few curious glances from students passing by. They quickly divert their gaze when they see Noah. We both ignore them. "Did I hunt you down to waste time going in circles when not liking the answer you've already been given? No! That was all" —I poke his chest— "*you.*"

Not amused with my smart mouth, Noah takes a step toward me with a deep frown, seizing my wrist. He's quiet, the only sound between us is my deep, irritated breathing, but his jaw clenches.

"Have you had enough, yet?" I ask, quietly. "Enough of wasting both our times?"

He's so close that his scent is invading my senses. The richest amber, the deepest mahogany with hints of tobacco.

A pressure presses down on my chest. I want to lean in, knowing I should push away.

"No," he answers, matching my tone as he stretches out a hand to grab the end of my scarf. He tugs on it, pulling me close. "Not until I know where your sister went." Said like a man on revenge.

A chill unrelated to the weather slides down my spine.

What did my sister do?

When she was at my apartment she kept glancing out the windows, shifting the bag from her lap to the floor back to her lap. Unable to stop fidgeting. Restless.

I didn't think anything of it, chalking it up to Harlow being her normal self, but what if it wasn't?

Looking at Noah, I'm afraid to ask. This close, I can feel how tight his body is wound. Whatever Harlow did it's not anything I want to get mixed up in. Not anything I want to have a kernel of knowledge of.

Knowledge is power, my granddad always said, and with knowledge came burdens.

I have enough of my own burdens, I don't need to bear any of my sister's. Not anymore. "I wasn't lying when I told you I don't know where she is."

"But you know something."

It wasn't a question.

I don't have a chance to deny it, either. With my silence, Noah pounces, pulling me so there's no space between us. My palms flat on his pecs. "Play this game all you want, Baby Brooks, but we're going to find her, and if I find out you're doing anything to help her I'm coming for you, too."

My skin blazes with the feel of his lips brushing against my cheek, to my ear. "And when I do," he whispers in a low, gruff voice. "I'm going to make you pay."

I don't move. I don't blink. I don't even breathe. I can't, not when my lungs are seized in a tight, painful grip.

It's not until he lets me go that I collapse into myself, palm pressed to my chest, over my thundering heart.

Noah walks away without another word and my eyes are glued to his back. He doesn't look back, except once. Catching my eye, he smirks. An unspoken promise sits on those lips. *This isn't over.*

"What did you get me into, Harlow?" I whisper when Noah disappears from my sight completely.

As I walk to class, several minutes late, I fear it won't be long until I have my answer.

The rest of the week passes in mundane normalcy. Or as normal as it gets being a socialite's daughter in Haven Harbor. With my parents in Europe, I keep getting invites to go to this gala, that charity auction, and whatever insert-business-here opening. I've turned them all down. Instead, I've holed up in my quaint apartment in a not-so safe building with my snow-white cat, Pan.

Thank God for takeout delivery.

Haven Harbor, and the world occupying it, has never felt like my home, but my prison. Moving back I made a promise to myself that I wouldn't get locked away in their games.

So the best way to do that is avoid, avoid, avoid. A skill set I've since mastered.

The only bright spot this week has been not seeing Noah. He hasn't made an appearance since that day on campus. As bright as that is, I know it won't last long. The determination that filled his eyes that day, the silent promise he gave as he sauntered away were reminders that I'd be seeing him again.

It's the *when* that's tarnished my week. Set me on edge whenever I bump into someone in a nice suit. Has had me looking over my shoulder as I walked the streets.

I feel like bait on a line. Waiting and waiting for him to make good on his promise.

Part of me wishes he would just get it over with.

But that's why he's waiting, letting me get wound up for the perfect moment to strike. Noah lives for the surprise.

Shaking Noah from my thoughts, at least for the time being, I focus on the boxes still stacked along the hall wall.

Moving is stressful but unpacking is a bitch. I feel like it's never ending. I empty one box and two more surface. So this is how I'm spending my Saturday night.

Except, I don't want to finish. I don't want to empty the last box and feel a sense of satisfaction. Because it won't come.

Being done means my move is official, I'm truly back in Haven Harbor. The very place I swore to never return too when I was eighteen and kissed the skyline goodbye in my review mirror the second I had my diploma in hand.

I don't hate my city, per se. I hate what it does to people.

Haven Harbor rivals New York for all things on the East Coast, food, fashion, art. Just a couple hours north, on an island much like Manhattan, you'll find Haven Harbor.

It's a city of opulent wealth. Where old money is celebrated and your last name is everything. It matters who your parents are, who your grandparents were, and how many zeroes are attached to your bank account.

Where you walk a minefield of hidden bombs never knowing if a single move will set off a cataclysmic disaster.

Gossip is traded like currency and scandals define your family.

My family has had a lot of scandals thanks to Harlow, who never fit the traditional mold of what the upper-crust society of Haven Harbor was looking for. Which is why my parents had me, their second chance at the perfect daughter.

And perfect I was, playing the part to a T. I got the grades, had the manners and poise. My schedule was filled with social obligations, cheerleading, and volunteering for various charities.

I was everything my parents wanted. So much so they didn't care they stripped me of all things *me*.

I wasn't a person, but a portrait, only showing the surface level.

Lost in my thoughts, I'm able to make it through one box on autopilot. I don't even know what was in it. Glancing down at the cardboard in my hand, my handwriting spells out KITCHEN in black marker.

Hmm, okay then.

After breaking down the box, I move on to the next. Dropping to my knees, I peel off the tape. This one isn't labeled so it's kind of like Christmas, seeing what's inside. Is it one of the many boxes full of shoes? Or maybe a box of my favorite historical romances?

I open it up and immediately suck in a tight breath. Jumping away with frantic steps, I put some distance between me and the box. I eye it wearily, like it's holding poisonous spiders rather than what's actually inside.

I close my eyes, counting to ten. I wasn't prepared.

I'm okay I'm okay I'm okay.

Of course I'm okay. I want to shake myself to calm down. It's not like I've seen a ghost.

Except, in a way…I kind of have.

With unsteady steps and shaking hands I move back toward the box, reaching for the contents inside. Fingers closing around the first object they brush against, I pull it out.

The well-loved paintbrush feels heavy in my hand.

Twirling it in the light I stare at it, trying to remember the last time I held it.

Too long, my mind whispers.

What was once an extension of my body feels foreign, intimidating. Forgotten.

I've forgotten how to hold it. I stare at the brush. It feels wrong and uncomfortable when it used to feel comfortable and grounding.

My parents might've made me into a portrait of shallow perfection, but it was through painting that I found my depth.

What would my granddad say if he knew it's been over a year since I picked up a brush, mixed together paints? That I hadn't touched a canvas since he died a year ago?

He'd be disappointed. He showed me painting could be an escape.

For years, it saved me. Rooted me to the Earth.

But the desire to create left me when he took his last breath.

His death left me numb. My best friend, here one day and gone the next. I wasn't ready to lose him and now I don't know how to move on. I still wait for his phone calls, I still wait for the letters he used to write me.

Each day is supposed to get easier, right? Then how come every day I find myself missing him more and more?

I moved back for a person long since gone. To be closer to the memories, to him.

I'm rolling the paintbrush between my palms when a sharp knock breaks the silence in the apartment. Startled, I drop it back in the box.

The knock comes again. More urgent than the last.

A pair of icy blue eyes and a tailored suit flash in my mind. *Noah.*

He's come to collect.

Walking to the door, I curse my sister.

Ba-bump, Ba-bump, the beating of my heart fills my ears as my hand tightens around the knob.

Resting my head against the cool metal, I count to three.

And count to three two more times before I'm able to open the door.

When I do, the face staring back at me almost makes my knees buckle.

"Oh, Brin, thank God!" I collapse against the door.

Her wide grin shrinks with concern. "Are you okay? You're pale. Paler than usual."

"Yeah, I'm fine," I reassure her, motioning for her to come in. She does and I shut the door. "You just scared me. I wasn't expecting you."

Brin's smile is back to full wattage. "Keeping a secret lover from me?" She makes a show of looking around the apartment.

I snort, leaning against the door. "Yeah if I had a guy sharing my bed, he wouldn't be a secret." I'd be shouting it from my balcony. It's been that long.

"Who said anything about a bed?" Brin wiggles her eyebrows.

"Ooo, you bad!" I laugh, pushing off the door to walk into the living room. I smack my friend's butt as I pass.

I'm about to collapse onto the couch when Brin says, "Don't get comfortable, Sayer. We have plans."

"We do?" I don't remember that. "Here I thought you wanted to get drunk on fine wine and watch old 90s movies." It's what we did my first night back in town.

"We do." She digs in her purse and pulls out two black envelopes with gold lettering. Brin fans her face with them.

"What is that?"

"It's a surprise."

Her coy answer stirs up unease. I don't like surprises. I like straight forward. "Brin…" My warning trails off, taking in her attire as she slips off her coat.

She's definitely not dressed like we're going out for a night in the clubs. Brin's in a gown. A long and elegant pale pink dress that hugs the curves around her hips, the skirt touching the floor. Her midnight hair is twisted up in an elegant updo while the only makeup she has on is a simple winged liner on the lids of her dark brown eyes.

Simple elegance and way too much effort for what I feel like putting in right now.

Seeing the answer on my face Brin pouts. "You'd make me go alone?"

"I don't even know where you're going!"

She hesitates, knowing she's going to have to really sell it for me to be enticed enough to put a bra back on. "It's super exclusive" -aka snobby—seeing that she's already losing me, Brin backtracks— "but it's not a party or a charity auction or any of the boring things you hate. It's something else entirely. Something fun."

"Like what?" My interest is mildly piqued just from hearing it's none of the things I've turned down this week. "What is it?"

Brin bites her lip, thinking.

"Brin, if you don't tell me I'm not going."

"Fine," she sighs. "It's a gambling hall."

That has me sitting forward. "A gambling hall?"

Seeing she has me hooked, she nods. "Yeah, except there're no slots, just tables. I know how much you love blackjack."

I do love blackjack. In college I was the blackjack (and strip poker) queen.

"Okay," I sigh, more from the effort of getting off the comfy couch than anything else. "I'll go."

"Really? Omg yay!" She squeals, jumping as high as the dress will let her. Once she's done with her mini celebration, she clears her throat. "Let's get you changed. There's a dress code after all."

Of course there is. It wouldn't be in Haven Harbor if you weren't required to dress to the nines. But even that can't suffocate the small feeling of exhilaration as I slide into one of the many gowns I still have, thankful the one Brin's helping me zip up still fits, if not a little tight.

As Brin tames my dirty blonde hair into something passable and not a nest for woodland creatures, I stare at my reflection in a total not-a-narcissist kind of way.

I look exhausted. My gray eyes empty.

At least my dress looks pretty. Midnight blue with flecks of silver woven into the fabric, I feel like the endless night sky.

Done with my hair, Brin shoves a pair of shoes on my feet before yanking me out of the room and out of my apartment. "C'mon, we're going to be late!"

Late for what? I want to ask but my lungs are struggling for air by the time we reach the sidewalk.

It's not until we're at the crosswalk, waiting for the signal to change that I ask, "What's this place called?"

I don't think she mentioned it before.

Brin looks at me, tension in her eyes as she hesitates. "The Underground."

My eyes widen. Now I understand why she didn't say anything.

The light changes but I'm rooted in place.

three

Sawyer

The Underground.

A renovated mansion turned gambling hall with a 1920s style. Polished and elegant, the gambling hall is dolled up with elaborate chandeliers that drip from the ballroom's ceiling. Blacks and golds, that shine when they catch the light, decorate the space.

It's hypnotizing. It's beautiful. It's alluring. It's opulent. Jazz music mixes with the chatter and poker chips falling onto the tables.

I can't believe I'm here.

A cigarette girl in an all black dress walks by and Brin snags two champagne flutes off her passing tray.

I take it, knowing I'm going to need more than champagne to get through the night.

Brin, unknowingly, has brought me to the den of anxiety. The Underground belongs to Noah Kincaid, stamped with the Kincaid Enterprises vintage feel.

This ballroom, the mansion, is like stepping back in time.

"I feel severely improperly dressed," I tell Brin as she links our arms together. "I should've at least worn my beaded shift dress."

"The one from Halloween five years ago?"

I nod.

"Lucky bitch," she murmurs with love in her words. "I

don't think I've been able to wear a single thing from when I was eighteen."

"You still look fabulous."

"Of course I do. I just had some really amazing pieces I wish still fit. Screw what's hot this season, I hear vintage is in."

I laugh, taking a sip of the fine bubbly. Only in this city can five years be considered vintage.

"Can you believe we're here?" she asks, her grip tightening around my arm.

No. "No." I can't. "Your parents actually bought memberships?" The monthly fee for one person is basically a year at an Ivy League, let alone two.

Brin shrugs, not concerned in the slightest. "It was Mom's gift to Dad for their wedding anniversary two years ago, but really I think it's because Dad was having too much fun at their swingers club so Mom wanted to find them a new hobby."

I stare a Brin for a beat, unblinking. I don't even notice I stopped walking until Brin tugs on my arm again, walking us in the direction of the closest card game. Sometimes I forget that I'm from this world and that the news of a swingers club shouldn't be shocking to me. It totally is, though. My six years away opened my eyes to how closed off our little city actually is.

It's a whole great and messy world out there that makes this place look like a different planet.

"I just can't believe your parents still refuse to get a membership." Brin takes a dainty sip from her flute. She's barely touched hers while I'm almost done with mine. One more sip and I'll be ready for my next one.

"Really? You can't think of one glaringly obvious reason?" I give Brin a look over the top of my glass. "I can give you a hint. It rhymes with Snoah Mincaid."

"More like Mclaid." She snickers. In a more serious, but

not quite serious, tone Brin adds, "But they're still holding grudges? They're missing out on all this."

She waves a hand in front of her with a wild flourish, her eyes glued to the poker game. More specifically the lean and dapper player with the dark hair and even darker eyes.

He glances at us, sending her a wink.

"What can I say." Reluctantly, Brin looks at me, forgetting her next sexual victim for the moment. "My parents operate on levels of petty and when it comes to Noah there is no tier high enough to hold the amount of spite they'll sling his way."

My mother's words float back to me. *Just because we can afford a membership, doesn't mean we should. I mean, it's more exclusive that we don't. We don't want to do what everyone else is doing. The Brooks family strives to stand out.*

And by stand out she meant being exactly the same.

Despite my parents' sheer refusal to join The Underground, I had always wondered what made it so special.

It couldn't only be the price tag to join, or that the pots to win went astronomically high. Everyone knows the house always wins, right?

As if on cue, the sounds of dismayed and disgruntled groans hit my ears.

Apparently not.

The curious cat that lives inside me has always wanted to know. There had to be something else. Something more. Special.

And now that I'm here, I don't get it.

Maybe it *is* the membership fee, the exclusivity and anonymity of the place, thanks to the NDA they have you sign when you first arrive.

Whatever it is, I find myself wanting to explore more of this place rather than play a game of cards. At least for right now. My fingers still twitch in eager anticipation to play. The house might be conned to win, but they never had a grand-dad like Jack Brooks, card shark extraordinaire. Just one of my grandfather's many talents.

My eyes continue to absorb what's before me. "It's like we're back at Winter Formal. You know, if it had a theme other than virginal." I still have nightmares of the white dress my mother forced me to wear. Horrendous doesn't even cover it.

My gaze devours the fancy tuxes and gowns at the card tables, leaning against the bar, and simply floating across the floor. At the diamonds that sparkle in the light and the crystal champagne flutes that wink by me on passing trays.

Add in a fountain and braces and you have my debut into society.

It's been so long since I've been to a gathering of this taste that I feel like an outsider peering in to a secret world that only comes from a birthright. A birthright I have but no longer feel like a member of.

"Bite your fucking tongue." Brin smacks my arm. "That is one day I do *not* want to relive."

"Why? It's not like you fell into the fountain with your all white gown." Because that was me. And who was the first people I saw when I resurfaced? Noah Kincaid, of course. Staring at my soaked form, laughing.

I shudder at the memory. I can still hear the sound of his twisted delight all these years later.

"What do you want to play first?"

I don't. I want to explore. To not only see what else this club has to offer, but to see if the owner is home as well. I've spent all week hoping to not see him and now that I'm in one of his places of business, I can't help but want to get it over with.

This extra tension under my skin isn't worth the stress.

I don't tell Brin any of that, she doesn't even know that

Noah and I had a run-in the night at Heathen's Hell, so when she starts to pull me in the direction of the winking, dark featured poker player, I let her.

Standing among the small crowd that has gathered around, I recognize some faces, mostly friends of my parents but also a few people who went to prep school with me. None of them meet my eyes and if they happen to glance in my direction, it's with a look of tolerance and disdain.

Confirming what I haven't really let myself acknowledge… I don't belong here anymore. And not just at the casino, but around these people. This world. The wealthy elite. The privileged top tier.

Thanks to college, I now know what it's like to live paycheck to paycheck instead of wiping my booty with hundred-dollar bills. And if it wasn't for the money I inherited with my granddad's death I'd still be working now. I don't touch the trust my parents set up for me.

But money or not, one fact remains true.

This world isn't mine anymore.

I'm the outsider.

And I don't know what to make of that.

How to feel.

Do I still want to belong in a place I hate so much?

I just want to find out where I belong.

If it's not in the place where I was born, then where is it?

A commotion at a nearby table draws my attention away from such a lackluster poker game.

Shouts ring out, chairs clamor to the floor.

"Ohmygod. They're here!" Brin whisper-shouts in my ear.

What? Who?

"Look!"

I follow where her finger is pointing and feel my eyes bulge, my skin grow cold.

Greeeaaat. On the journey here I was mentally preparing myself to see Noah, a small, sick part was even hoping, but in all my prepping I hadn't thought to account for the others.

His friends.

Reeve, Thea, and Gabe are surrounding the nearby table that's playing baccarat. Casually I slip behind Brin, like her small frame can hide me. Several inches separate us in height, even in heels.

Three out of the Fearsome Fivesome—a nickname I coined for them back in prep school—are present.

There's Reeve Morgan with the top hat, no shirt and purple paisley pants, he's easily the most chaotic of the group. An artist soul and fighter's temper, spilled gasoline waiting for a match. He holds a cane with a hawk's head handle like a weapon as he stares down a younger man.

Next to him is Gabriel Ruiz, quiet and reserved. Understated. Always with a novel or book of poetry in his hand. The thinker. Rumor is he collects just as many virginities as he does first editions. Like Reeve, Gabe watches the younger man with a glare.

He cracks his neck and I can hear the pop from here. I recoil, always hating that sound.

On the other side of Gabe stands Thea le Veck, a boisterous free spirit and unapologetically herself. The youngest of the group, she's often underestimated when her wit and brain is sharper than any weapon. She smiles at the man, but it's not sweet as she runs the back of one of her fingers down his cheek.

What is happening?

I recognize the man they stand in front of. His name is Henry Porter and he was in the same year as me in school. He was always the runt, the outsider. He floated under everyone's radar.

Until now.

The whole casino falls quiet. Waiting, watching.

But the three of them remain silent.

Henry does nothing. He doesn't cower, he doesn't tremble, he faces them head on. A bead of sweat trickles down from his temple, the only sign of his nerves.

They haven't even glanced my way and *I'm* nervous. Nervous for what they can do.

"What do you think he did?" I whisper to Brin.

I feel more than see her shrug. "Nothing good."

Well obviously, Brin.

Reeve tears his gaze away from the frozen man to stare across the room. I follow and see where the ruthless leader of the Fearsome Fivesome is stationed.

Noah sits in the middle, a neat glass of amber gold in hand, watching his friends intensely.

And he's not alone.

A woman straddles his lap, lips roaming over his neck and along his jaw. She molds into his body while he sits board stiff. She's the only one in the room not paying attention to what's going on. She's too focused on attacking Noah's throat, his chin, the peeking of his chest beneath his unbuttoned collared.

He seems wholly unaffected by her. It brings a cynical smile to my face. I wipe it away immediately.

The temperature in the room drops, the air is tight as people stare. Reeve raises a single brow and Noah nods.

And with that nod action snaps into place.

Gabe snatches Henry's arms and pulls him off his chair only to slam his chest on the card table, his face smashed against the black felt as he shouts to be let go.

Gabe does nothing but smile. One that promises pain and blood. Chills wrack my body at the sight. With one hand pinning Henry down by the neck, Gabe shoves his other hand into the other man's pockets.

"Hey what—what are you doing!" Henry shouts, bucking his hips to shake Gabe off. Gabe's grip tightens as he pulls his out of one of Henry's pockets, fist clenched.

"Weeding out a rat," he whispers, full of venom.

He lets go of Henry, moving to his side, and Henry uses that as an opportunity to get up. Reeve stops him with a whack to his spine, his cane resting like an iron bar on Henry's back.

A smile stretches Reeve's face. Relishing in the ripples of pain that wrack Henry's body as he brings down his cane again, the sound piercing the room. It's gone deathly quiet. Not even a breath stirs the charged air.

I chance a glance at Noah but he is no longer in the booth. He's striding to his friends with unhurried steps. His face remains impassive while his blue eyes flare with wanton rage.

When he nears, Gabe opens his hand and poker chips fall from his palm, between his finger, to their feet. Almost in slow motion one rolls on the ground, stopping before Noah's shoes.

He steps on it, continuing his march to Henry. Brin and I share a look of worry, of fear and the unknown, as he bends at the waist to meet Henry's eyes.

"Trying to steal from me, Porter?" Noah's whisper reaches my ears. There is no promise of salvation in it. "You should know I don't take kindly to people stealing from me."

Henry doesn't answer. I see the back of his legs shake uncontrollably.

Noah sounds *pissed* beneath the calm and control he's wielding over his body. I hold my breath as he waves Reeve away. He helps Henry stand up, holding on to his arm.

"Do you know what happens when people try to steal from me?" Noah still has a hand on Henry's arm.

Henry hesitantly shakes his head.

A crack, then a scream fills the room.

Henry collapses to the floor, his arm still in Noah's grip

though it's bent at an awkward angle between them. A piece of bone protrudes and I have to force myself not to gag.

Noah broke Henry's arm. He broke his arm and he's wearing a smile.

They all are. Reeve, Thea, and Gabe are grinning ear to ear. Enjoying this.

My stomach churns. Noah drops the arm and Henry howls out in anguish.

"Get him out of here," he growls. Thea skips over to the body and hauls him up. Noah gives her a look and in a hushed tone that my ears strain to hear he says, "You know what to do."

With a smile too sweet for the circumstances, she nods and leads him out of the ballroom. Gabe and Reeve, who's whistling, stroll out leisurely behind her.

At first, there is only silence as the door shuts behind them.

Then, Noah shatters it.

"Let this be a lesson to everyone here." Noah doesn't shout. Doesn't yell. His voice is steady. A lethal quiet that causes everyone in the room to lean forward to hear what he has to say. He holds the room on a precipice, antsy with anticipation and fear. We just saw him break the arm of a thief. "Anyone who tries to cheat or steal at The Underground will be caught and dealt with." A pause. "By me." One hand slips into his pocket, his body still tight with tension. "And next time I won't stop at a warning."

He is the judge. The jury. And the executioner.

Noah's voice grows colder with every sentence. Angry. I can feel the anger pouring from him. Even when he's silent. It fills the room.

You don't try and cheat the Devil. He'll always win.

He snaps his fingers and a cigarette girl walks to him, her tray full of champagne. He picks up a flute, holding the delicate glass between two fingers, raising it above his head. A toast. "Now." He smiles, dark delight brightens his harsh features. "Let's get back to why you came here. To drink and give me your money!"

As the crowd cheers with him, I scrunch my face.

Seriously?

Noah tips his drink back, christening his words.

When he places his empty glass on the tray, he's not paying attention to the crowd as they walk around him, going back to their table of choice.

He can't.

Not when his eyes are on me.

If he looked intense before, it has nothing with the fervor that burns behind his eyes.

A fire erupts in my stomach under his stare. Starting from the top of my head, his penetrating eyes drink me in. They feel like a caress reaching all the way to my bones. Sensual and commanding, calling me to attention. Everything else fades to the background.

My memories of him, even from earlier this week, haven't done him justice as I take him in. Dressed in another black on black suit, he's as polished as they come. Except for his hair, it's a wild mess on top of his head.

A flash of that woman on his lap burns through my mind. She knows what I've always wondered. What'd it'd be like to feel Noah in the palm of my hand. To come undone and lose control with me.

A sea of people walk between us but it's like we're the only two in the room. I hear nothing, see nothing except him. Until someone knocks into me, jostling my shoulder, the connection between us is broken.

I lose him to the crowd. He left the safety of his booth and has made himself approachable to everyone who wants a piece of him.

Everyone except me.

Feeling warm and overwhelmed as the noise of the room comes rushing back to me, I need a drink. A large, stiff drink.

Before turning my sights on the bar, I turn to Brin to ask if she wants anything but I see she's already preoccupied with the poker player from earlier. When I reach the bar, the tall bartender with peppered hair from Heathen's Hell appears as I slide into a stool.

What's he doing here?

He winks. "Lemon drop, right?"

Slowly, I nod.

The bartender walks away and I feel a body slide behind me.

A sense of déjà vu washes over me as I keep my gaze trained on the shelves upon shelves of liquor.

Without looking, I know who it is. There's an energy around him that's charged and always has been, only to be amplified with time.

"You look lonely."

I shift in my seat at the sound of his voice.

Smooth and rich, the finest liquor on the top shelf. *Intoxicating.* It warms me and chills my bones at the same time.

He followed me over.

The little kernel of knowledge does nothing to help the flutters and nerves twisting my stomach. Thank God the bartender returns with my drink. I take a healthy sip as he nods to Noah.

"Maybe I like to be alone," I tell him.

"Oh I remember." The husky quality of his voice makes

it sound scandalous. "But maybe you might want some company. Just this once."

"You mean so you can question me endlessly about my sister? No thanks." I start to turn the stool around when Noah's hand shoots out, holding my thigh.

I stare at it, my breath slowing. Gradually, my eyes meet his.

"Perhaps I want to talk about you." His eyes are honed on my lips.

Noah's not the only one with eyes on me. Over his shoulder the woman from earlier glares at me, still seated in the booth.

"Looks like your friend is missing you."

A wolfish grin appears. "Want to join us? She always does better with two people."

"Tempting." I take a sip of my drink, licking the excess liquid off my lips. "But no."

His eyes flash, locked on my lips.

Feeling bold, I dart my tongue out, licking them again.

Noah's hooked on the movement.

He takes a step closer as I say, "Go back to your lady-friend, Noah. I'm not here for you."

He tilts his head to the side. It must be baffling to his ego that my being here has nothing to do with him.

"I'm here as a guest with a friend," I continue when he doesn't say anything.

Noah stares at me and I stare back until he shakes his head at my naiveté. "You shouldn't have come here, guest or not" — he snatches the martini glass out of my hand and downs the rest— "But now that you have, I'm not letting you get away."

I swallow as a wicked gleam brightens those frosty eyes.

A dark chuckle fills my ears. "Ready to play, Baby Brooks?"

four

Sayer

"What's your poison?" Noah asks, shuffling a deck of cards between us.

We're sitting around a poker table in a private room that's hidden behind a locked door.

Me, and the most powerful man in town.

"You're letting me decide?" Disbelief colors my tone.

He clicks his tongue. "Always thinking the worst of me."

"Do you blame me?" I can't help but ask. "I just saw you break a man's arm."

Noah's hands stop middle shuffle. "Are you afraid to be alone with me, Sayer?"

Am I afraid to be alone with him? Did he ever care before? All the times he sought me out when I was a teenager? "No."

"Liar," he challenges with narrow eyes. "I terrified you as a teenager."

I was afraid with how you made me feel. I bite the inside of my cheek to keep from answering.

Noah goes back to shuffling the cards and I watch them blur between his hands.

"What's your game?" he asks again.

"Blackjack."

He nods, starting to deal out the cards. One card face down for each of us.

I stare at the card. "I'm not giving you any money."

"I don't want your money."

"Then what do you want?"

"You."

My arms drop from my chest. Is my mouth open? It feels open.

I wait for him to crack a smile or laugh, to show any sign that he's joking. Until I remember who's sitting across from me. Noah Kincaid doesn't joke. Not about debts and sex.

"I'm not on the table."

"You could be." His eyes dance when I shift in my seat.

I stop, pushing away from the table instead. "Noah, be serious or I'm leaving."

"You're not going anywhere, Sayer. Sit down." His tone brooks no argument and I'm wise enough to listen.

Slowly, I sit down. "I'm not playing strip poker."

"Tempting." Noah smirks. "But too frat house for me. I was thinking of something a little different."

"Which is?" I ask when he doesn't elaborate.

"Favors."

I don't like the smile he gives me. A predator closing in on his prey.

Sitting here, I feel like an idiot. Of course he doesn't want my money. He has more than enough.

Noah lives for a challenge.

Too bad for him, I don't. "There's nothing that I want from you," I say.

"You sure about that?" he asks, heavy with implication.

I raise a brow. "Positive."

He plays with the collar of his shirt, still exposing part of his chest. My eyes hone in on it. On his neck, watching it constrict as he swallows. Masculine and sharp, he's honed into a weapon.

A weapon set out to distract me. *Entice me.*

Noah's chuckle crashes into me and my eyes meet his. "Yeah. You don't want anything."

He flicks a card in my direction.

Four of hearts.

Silence settles between us.

I came tonight to sit at a table and play a game or two of cards. To see the mysterious Underground. Now I'm sitting at a table playing a game of cards with someone even more mysterious than The Underground itself.

For the past week I've been on edge, not wanting to see him, thinking he'd collect on the promise of whatever he has going on with my sister not being over, but here we are now and he hasn't so much as brought her up.

There was a brief moment, years ago, when he felt more like mine than hers.

And maybe it's the drink from earlier or the quietness of the room that feels so small but is not, whatever it is, I want to get to know that person again.

"What did you have in mind?" I ask when the stillness of the room becomes too much. "What kind of favors?"

I don't get an answer.

Across the table Noah studies his cards. What's there to study? You get two cards in blackjack.

I clear my throat.

Still nothing. Not even a twitch of a brow.

Well, fine then.

If he's going to ignore me, I'm going to give him something he can't ignore.

My butt is barely in the air when, without looking up, Noah growls, "Sit."

I narrow my eyes at his authoritative tone. "I'm not a dog.

Commands don't work on me." I hop off the chair. Marching right to him.

He still won't look at me. It grates on my skin. *He* dragged me into the room. *He* wanted to play this game. *He* unbuttoned his shirt. Now, he's ignoring me.

My fingers wrap around his chin. I ignore the wave of electricity that ignites inside me as I force his gaze to meet mine. "If you're going to invite me to play a game, I expect your undivided attention."

"Oh, you do now?" Low and husky, his words brush against my skin. "My apologies, my lady. Let me rectify that."

His hands shoot out, sinking into my hips, pulling me close. Right onto his lap.

"How's this?" he whispers in my ear. The arms around me feel like steel bands, keeping me secure against his body. Slow, methodic strokes move in circles along my skin, hypnotizing me, holding me in place.

Fire blazes in the wake of his touch.

Noah Kincaid has always felt larger than life, the kind of person that makes everything else fade away when his sole focus is on you, and right now he's pressed mute on the rest of the world.

All from a caress of his thumb.

Wonder what he could do if more than his thumb was involved...

Stop it. Stop it right now, Sayer Brooks. We do not have these thoughts about our sister's ex-boyfriend.

Except we are totally having these thoughts about our sister's ex-boyfriend.

"How are we playing?" I ask softly as I stare at our forgotten cards, needing the distraction from the growing need inside me.

"One round," Noah says, the words shooting down my spine like an arrow. "Pick your favor."

"And keep it in my head?" My voice is low and packed with sass.

"Smartass," he chuckles, shifting behind me to reach into his jacket. Something brushes against my backside and my eyes widen a fraction.

I'm not the only one affected by our closeness.

Seconds later, pen and paper are placed in front of me. "Write it."

I look at him. "How do I know you won't peek while I write?"

"You don't," he answers.

I frown. "Have you always been so insufferable?"

How did I have a crush on him?

Noah reaches into his jacket *again*—Jesus, is a man's suit jacket lined with a million secret pockets?—and pulls out a vape pen.

Putting it to his lips, I'm reminded why.

Because my clichéd teenage heart loved the idea of a bad boy. And a bad boy he was. And if my treacherous heart doesn't flutter at the sight of him taking a hit from his pen, smoke leaving out of his nose.

Dang.

It's hot when he does that.

He smirks, tapping his finger on the paper. "Write what you want, Sayer."

With a resigned sigh, I do.

Leaning over the table as much as I'm able with Noah's arm still around my waist, I write the first thing to pop into my head and before I can second guess myself, I fold up the paper and leave it on the table.

I start to sit back up when Noah's palm presses into the middle of my back, keeping me curled over the table.

Removing his hand, a piece of paper takes his place. Sharp

and purposeful strokes from a pen follow, just deep enough that I can feel them through my dress. The letters, though I can't make them out, feel etched on my skin.

Noah folds the paper up and flicks it over my shoulder.

Still bent over the table, I feel his body stretch out above me to bring my forgotten cards closer. Yet the cards are the farthest thing from my mind feeling his weight press against me.

It's gone all too quickly as he sits back. The spell broken.

I have to focus on the cards, the game. Not just to stop focusing on Noah and how it feels to be so close to him, but because I don't want him to win. Whatever he wrote down is going to take me out of my comfort zone.

I bite my cheek to hold in a curse as I peek at my bottom card. A nine. A freaking nine!

I try to glance at Noah's bottom card but he barely peels up a corner. On top sits a king.

"What's it going to be, Sayer?" His words soft in my ear, despite the challenge they hold. "Hit or stay?"

I tap the table with two fingers, afraid how my voice will sound if I try to speak right now. I take a hit.

And bust.

Noah's hand tightens on my thigh.

Crap. "Crap," I whisper, eyeing our bets. The only way I'm saved is if Noah busts too. Which seems unlikely.

The house always wins.

Muscles I never knew I had are tense as he chuckles, shaking my body.

Almost in slow motion he reaches for his cards.

I don't breathe.

I don't blink.

Noah flips his card.

Noah won.

And he's cashing in on it now.

A favor disguised as a dare.

"No," I whisper as we stand on the roof of the building. "I'm not doing this."

Standing a few paces behind me, Noah is unfazed by my refusal. Letting me deny, deny, deny while he watches with his hands in his pant pockets.

Of course *he's* relaxed. He's all cool, calm, and collected in his comfortable position of being the winner.

After showing his hand of twenty-one, Noah gave me the piece of paper he wrote on. Then he reached for mine. I tried to snatch it back but he swiftly put it in his pant pocket. I wasn't bold enough to retrieve it.

"Heard you the first twenty-five times, but really, it was this time that has made your point perfectly clear."

I shoot him a nasty glare.

Noah speaks four languages, his most fluent?

Sarcasm.

The cherry on top of his asshole.

He glares back.

We're locked in a stalemate until Noah grows bored and marches over to me, grabbing my arm and guides me to the roof's ledge.

"Dance," he instructs, low and commanding. Dark as the night with no stars in the sky.

He brought me up here and wants me to dance on the building's ledge. He wants me to dance on the edge of the roof.

The thought alone has my muscles seizing.

"Sayer," Noah calls when I don't move.

"Stop talking, Noah."

He raises a brow. Not happy.

A small, sassy smile pulls at my mouth as I see him clench and unclench his hands.

Getting under Noah's skin is quickly becoming my new favorite hobby.

"Get up there, Sayer."

I shake my head, the smile growing, aware that I'm walking a thin line taunting the king of the city. I can't stop though. It might not be under my touch, but it's liberating watching Noah come undone before me.

"It is an honor, you know. To play against one of us. You saw the crowd downstairs, they would love to lose to me. Be up here with me."

"So go grab one of them." I cross my arms, partly in defiance, partly for warmth. It's freezing tonight and here we are without our coats.

"Can't do that, Baby Brooks," he taunts, not at all bothered by the cold.

"And why not?"

"Because I enjoy your company more." He takes a step toward me. "How you try and fight me." Another step. And another, until he's right here in front of me. "It's cute that you think you can win against me."

I don't remind him I already lost because I don't think he's talking about the poker game. There's so much heat in his features, something wild in his eyes. A chill unrelated to the cold goes down my spine.

Noah wraps a strand of my hair around his finger, slowly. We stand so close as he rests his forehead against mine. I feel my heart go wild with how close we are and I pray that he doesn't hear it. I don't know what he's doing but I don't want to stop it. There's something intimate about how we stand. Locked in this embrace, forehead to forehead.

I close my eyes, breathing in mahogany and amber. Breathing in Noah, getting lost in him as his thumb traces my cheekbone. With every stroke my chest feels heavier, beats wilder.

My eyes snap open, wide, feeling his lips brush against my skin on their journey to my ear. In a soft, sensual whisper Noah says, "Get on the ledge, Sayer."

I pull away. He doesn't let me go. And maybe it's because I still feel the high of his touch or the altitude from being up this high is getting to me but my fate is sealed the second I open my mouth. "Make me."

A dare wrapped in a pretty bow. Noah seizes it with an iron grip on my hips. He carries me to the edge and as he does he whispers in my ear, "There's a lot I want to make you do, princess, but I'll settle on this." He puts me down and backs away. "For now."

I make the mistake of looking down and wish I hadn't. My throat works with difficulty to swallow. I don't move. I've forgotten how.

Noah doesn't pay attention to the turmoil that's frozen my body. He doesn't care.

"Go on." He crosses his arms. "Dance for me."

He practically purrs the words. *Dance for me.*

I used to love to dance. I grew up taking classes, it was the one thing my parents forced me into that I actually enjoyed. Maybe that's why they ripped me out of them two years later.

I can't even force myself to shift an inch, though. Heights are a foe I have no courage to squander but Noah waits. A knowing gleam rests in his eyes.

He knows.

He knows I'm afraid of heights despite me never telling him.

It's been a fear that's only lived inside me.

Surprise should come but it doesn't. *Of course* Noah knows.

This is his kingdom and I am a lowly subject.

He knows all. Sees all.

And he looks ready to stay up here all night.

I'm not. Too bad my body is still locked in fear. To get out of it I have to channel a person I probably shouldn't.

What would Harlow do?

The answer comes immediately.

She'd do anything, fear nothing and go after whatever she wants. Harlow would play this game while inventing her own.

And that's what I need to do.

Confident. *I need to be confident.*

So I dance. I dance to no music, hips swaying with the wind.

After several unheard beats of awkwardness, my body loosens up and I dare to meet Noah's eyes.

They flare when we connect.

A jolt stuns me.

Power shifting in the air.

Power directed at me, solely me. Noah's undivided attention. He follows my movements, my hips rolling, hands exploring.

I'm out on display but only he's watching.

And that does something to me.

Never have I felt the heat of a stare or seen anything as intense in his eyes. They ignite a revolution in me. No one's ever looked at me like this, like he's assessing me while drinking me in.

If I thought he made me feel alive at his club, what he stirred up downstairs, it was child's play compared to this.

His attention feeds me, my moves becoming more daring. My wandering hands become bolder as they glide over my hips.

The air outside is tortuous and I should be freezing, but everything melts under Noah's stare.

He's fire. He's fury.

I spin around, smiling coyly over my shoulder and that's when everything goes wrong.

Balance—I've lost it and my eyes widen in horror as I feel my footing slip, finding ice concealed by the night.

A scream tears my throat.

And I'm falling

Falling

Falling.

My life flashes in short clips.

Moments with my parents. My friends. With my sister. The tears and laughter.

The memories of my granddad and the lurid thought that I'm about to be reunited with him.

Time stops and I scream for I don't know how long until I realize I'm not falling, but dangling.

Noah.

He's staring down at me like an avenging angel, determination on his face as he pulls me up like a rag doll.

Once I'm back on the roof, I crumple to the ground. The biting cold pierces past my clothes and I don't care. I don't care about anything but the air in my lungs.

I'm alive. I'm alive. I'm alive.

And I'm shaking.

Cold, strong fingers grip my chin, forcing me to look up at him.

Part of me expects some empathy, some compassion but instead his expression is as cold as his frozen fingers. "How do you feel?"

"What?"

"How do you feel?" he repeats.

Alive. "I feel alive." As strange as that may sound to my ears, I feel awakened.

Noah lets go of my jaw and steps back.

I push myself up, pulling my coat close. He smirks.

"Why?" I ask him. "Why did you make me do this?"

He doesn't answer as the distance closes between us.

My body trembles. Only this time my reaction isn't toward anything but him. I'm not like this.

I like rules and everything Noah stands against. I'm always careful and conscious of everything. So why is there a tightness encasing my chest, my lungs?

I shouldn't like this feeling—this humming in my veins, jolting and waking me up. And yet, as he closes the space between us, I find myself leaning toward him.

With ice-like hands, Noah cups my cheeks, leaning in close.

He's going to kiss me—

And I'm going to let him.

Noah Kincaid's nose traces my cheek as his hands move to my throat.

My breath catches as he squeezes, just a little, and I close my eyes.

Only for them to snap back open.

"I'm going to break you."

five

Sayer

Tucked between the bookshelves of the school's library, I sit at a table with a large stack of books, along with a few empty coffee cups from the little cafe downstairs scattered around me. Wireless earbuds sit in my ear, blaring a 90s grunge song with my pen softly tapping to the beat of the music as I turn the page to the text I'm reading.

It's after eleven at night and with barely a dent in my to-do list, I'm thankful the library is open until three in the morning. My productivity is crap when I'm at home. But it seems tonight, no matter where I work I'm destined to be distracted.

My mind keeps slipping back to two nights ago when I was on the roof with Noah.

How charged I felt with his stare attached to me. I don't know what it is about him that is able to tap into a well inside me, bringing out a side I haven't seen in who knows how long.

I didn't feel like a void taking up space. I felt daring and bold.

Almost falling was terrifying, but in a way, it was the wake-up call that I needed.

For an entire year, I've been feeding the loss of my grandpa, letting it control me instead of allowing myself to mourn. It's been holding me back when that's the last thing my grandfather would've wanted.

He wanted me to live in all the colors life had to offer, to not be as cold and distant as my parents.

"Your life is a masterpiece forever in progress," he used to say. "So go make something grand out of it."

I haven't.

But I need to.

Noah's displeasured face pops up in my mind.

He could show me, help me. He already brings out a change in me.

I want to chase the high only danger can provide. The kind only Noah can provide.

The other night on the roof, when he held me in his arms, our faces inches apart, I thought he was going to kiss me.

An absurd concept. Me. Noah. Kissing.

We live in the same world, but we're on two different planes.

I probably don't bring out any of the feelings he stirs up for me in him. I'm not even sure he's capable of feeling anything beyond stubborn annoyance and dark amusement when it comes to me. If it's possible to reach past his icy exterior.

I want to find out.

I can't stop thinking about what it would be like to feel his lips move against mine. Is he as aggressive with a kiss as he is in business?

To have his body pressed against me without the barrier of clothes between us. Would he take control over me and render me to a drunken mess at his feet?

All these questions that will never find their answers.

I can't do anything with Noah.

Not just because he dated my sister and Harlow is the definition of a possessive and vindictive ex-girlfriend.

He'd ruin me before I'd even realized it.

And I'm already broken enough. Lost with no destination in mind.

I haven't forgotten his promise either.

I'm going to break you.

Break me how? Break the shell I'm hiding behind or break my hidden spirit?

I should probably be scared, I should probably already be running. I'm not. I won't. I want to find out what he means.

I remember the hungry look in his eyes as I danced for him on the roof, how he fisted his hands at his sides as if that was enough restraint to keep him going after what he wanted.

Me.

I shift in my seat, squeezing my thighs together.

I'm in the middle of taking down notes of a painting when my ears are no longer full of angry, angst screams. Only the silence of an empty library.

Glancing up, my pen falls from my hand and rolls off the table.

I make no move to retrieve it.

I'm too busy staring at who's sitting across from me.

Noah lounges in the vacant seat opposite of mine, with a leather jacket around his shoulders and a beanie pulled low over his head and a grin designed to melt panties.

Perfect.

He always looks perfect. Even his glasses sit aligned on the bridge of his nose.

Meanwhile, my hair is pulled up in a messy bun because it hasn't been washed in two days and I'm pretty sure I have flecks of croissant from the pastry I ate earlier around the corners of my mouth.

All aboard the hot mess express, passengers: me.

"I've been looking for you." Noah pulls me out of self-deprecating thoughts.

"I've been here." I reach down to pick up my pen, ignoring his eyes following me as I do.

When I sit back up, it's to see Noah's putting one of my earbuds in his ear. A brow quirks up when he hears what's playing.

"Interesting." He drops the pod between us.

"Not what you expected?" I ask, reaching for it.

"I took you for a bubble-gum pop kind of girl."

Now it's me who raises a brow. "There's a lot of things you don't know about me."

He mulls over the words, a curious expression on his face. The intensity of the stare has me shifting in my seat. "I'm starting to see that."

I don't like how it feels as if he's stripping me away piece by piece.

"What're you doing here, Noah?"

"I came to see you," he says it like it should be obvious.

"Why?" I ignore the thrill that shoots through me.

"We have unfinished business."

My mind immediately goes to the roof. To the night I can't get out of my head. "We do?"

Is it naive to think maybe he did feel something akin to what I did?

"Your sister is still gone."

Apparently yes, it is.

Of course it's about Harlow. That's the only tie knotting Noah and me together. "I've already told you, Noah. I don't know where my sister is."

He doesn't believe me. I see the disbelief in his hard face.

"I can promise you, whatever you think I know, I don't." My arms wrap around my waist.

"Just tell me what you know. It could be important."

I stare at him. "Why?"

"Because your sister took something important from me and I need to get it back."

"What is it?"

He tsks. "That's not how this game works, Sayer."

My head tilts in response. "I didn't know we were playing a game. I thought you were here to disrupt my study time."

"Just tell me what you know."

"Why?"

"Why are you protecting her?" Add another emotion I bring out in Noah to the list. Frustration.

"Because I'm having fun riling you up." I smile, feeling bold.

"That so?" His jaw ticks.

Almost in slow motion, Noah leans over the table, dropping a neatly folded piece of paper on top of my notebook.

He watches me expectantly when I don't make a move to grab it.

"What's that?" I ask, even though I have a pretty strong inclination.

"You have hands. Use them." Noah leans back in his seat.

I press my lips into a thin line, keeping the words that I want to spit out at bay. "The last time I opened one of those from you, I almost fell off the roof. I don't want a repeat of that."

"It's not a dare." A pause. "Well, not exactly."

That does nothing to soothe my worry. "Not exactly a ringing endorsement to get me to open it."

"Just do it."

I don't. I flick it back to him. "Go home, Noah. Go anywhere that isn't here and just leave me alone, please."

"Can't." He leans back in the chair, hands fanned behind his head. "I need you."

My thighs clench at his words, not understanding he

doesn't mean them in the way my libido wants. He needs me for information. Nothing more.

"You're turning me into a broken record left on repeat. I don't understand why you aren't listening to me."

A dark look crosses his face. "Forgive me for having a hard time trusting the Brooks family."

His words are a reminder of the past. A past I've long since separated from. "You know I had nothing to do with that."

He shrugs. "Maybe, but I don't trust anyone in your family."

"It was my dad's doing. I was still in high school!"

Slowly, like an idle cat, he unwinds from his relaxed position to lean across the table. "Doesn't matter. You knew something then just like you know something now."

"Just because my father kept you from buying a piece of property on the outskirts of town *years* ago doesn't mean I knew about it. Or that I know anything now."

A flicker of emotion dances across Noah's face. Surprise. He looks perplexed. An emotion I'm sure that rarely finds a home on his striking features.

For a man who is always prepared, he seems at a loss of words right now. "That's what they told you?"

"That's what happened." Now it's my turn to be confused. "You guys were in court for months."

Noah shakes his head with a curse under his breath. He looks back at me and gives a sharp nod. And without any hint of emotion. Back to the cool and indifferent steel of a man.

"I have a proposition for you."

Curiosity has always been my downfall and I feel myself slipping now. "What exactly are you offering?"

"Help me drag out your sister."

"Why?"

He stares at me like I'm an idiot. "I already told you, Sayer.

And I really hate repeating myself, but for your small addled brain" —I glare at his insult— "allow me to remind you, she stole some very important documents from me that I need to get back. Quickly."

"And how am I supposed to help?"

"What has always been Harlow's downfall?"

"Uh." It takes me a minute. She has a few. "Spite and jealousy?" I guess.

He jerks his chin, nodding. "I need to drag her out. And you're the key to do that."

Key. An interesting word when he's really asking me to be his pawn.

"How?" I question cautiously. "How am I going to help you find my sister?" I know what this means, if I agree to help him I'm basically signing my sister's death warrant.

"With what you said. Spite and jealousy, BB," he said simply. Plainly. "We're going to drive her crazy with thinking you've replaced her."

"What do you mean replace her?"

"I'm in need of some new arm candy."

My ears must be full of wax because they're deceiving me. "What?" I choke out.

"If we're going to get your sister to come back, we're going to have to give her a reason. You, Sayer, are that reason. And that means we need to appear together. In public."

"And why would I help you?"

"I can give you what you want."

"And what do you think I want?"

"To live without expectations. To be alive."

I press my lips together, not denying it. He's right, it's like he was in my head earlier. He's not just asking me to help him find my sister. He's giving me an opportunity to seize. He could help me be alive, take away the sting of being numb.

Still, I can't give in that easy. I have to make him work for it a little more. "I don't have time to run around the city with you doing God knows what. In case you didn't know I'm about to graduate with my master's."

"I'll work with your schedule." He makes it sound so easy. That I'm not about to sign my life away to him for an unpredictable amount of time.

No matter how tempting Noah's smoldering eyes are behind those glasses, this is going to end badly.

Either by his hands, my hands, or worse—my sister's.

I bite my lip and ever the opportunist, Noah jumps on it.

"Think about this, Sayer. Of all the times your sister made your life miserable."

I do and it's not a pleasant trip down memory lane.

She might not be the best sister, but we were always taught by our grandfather that family matters.

Conflicting emotions grip me as Noah waits for my answer.

I shouldn't want what he's offered, but I do. With an unsteady breath, I nod. "I'll help you. On two conditions."

He snorts. "What makes you think you're in any position to negotiate?"

"Because I'm the only shot to finding my sister, right?"

He doesn't say anything but the tick in his jaw speaks volumes.

I'm right.

"This is only going to work if I'm cooperative. Which is only going to happen one way."

"Well, please. Don't hold me in suspense any longer." Sarcasm. "Tell me what these *conditions* are."

Ass. "I want your word that you'll protect me from her when she comes back to town." Because if I do this and it works, my sister won't be coming for Noah. She'll be gunning for me.

I need an insurance policy.

"Fine." He gives a clipped nod. "What else?"

"You don't hurt her."

He sits up. "You don't get to make that call."

"I do when I'm the bait you're using." I grab my notebook and rip out a piece of paper. "You're not going to hurt my sister. You're going to get what she took from you and that's it. No vendettas, no torturing. If she wants to walk after, then she does."

I'm not going to willingly throw my sister to the wolves. Not when I love her in that ingrained family way even if I don't like her.

Noah watches me for a moment. "You know she wouldn't do this for you, right?"

I do, but the roles aren't reversed and my conscience won't let me do this any other way.

He regards me in a thoughtful manner and I'm trying to make sense of it when he nods. "Okay."

Two syllables. One word.

Okay.

"Just like that?"

He nods.

Just like that, I have the word of a dangerous man on my side.

"How do I know you're not going to screw me over?"

Noah leans across the table. "Are you planning on screwing me over, Sayer?"

"No."

After what feels like an eternity of me staring into the dark depths of Noah's nonexistent soul, he nods. "Then you have my word I'll protect you from your sister when she comes back."

If I've learned anything from my father, a prominent law-yer, it's that verbal contracts only last as long as the time it takes to say them. Uncapping my pen, I furiously scribble on the paper I ripped out.

By the time I'm done writing the most pathetic contract in the history of ever, making the details of our arrangement clear, I slide it to Noah, who takes his time reading over it.

"Would you prefer I sign this with my blood?" he asks when he's finished.

"That's not necessary," I tell him. "A simple pen will do."

He reaches over to my side of the table and takes the pen from my hand. His fingers brush against mine and leave an electrical current in their wake, shooting up my arm.

After it's signed, he slides it back over to me.

"Now what?" I ask while I fold the contract up and stuff it in my bag.

He pushes away from the chair. "Let's go."

"Where are we going?"

Noah extends a hand toward me. "To get started on draw-ing your sister out."

I should be worried, maybe even scared. But I'm not. And that's what scares me the most as I place my hand in his, giving myself over to the unknown.

six

Noah

SAYER BROOKS.

Blonde hair. Gray eyes. Five foot seven.

And that's it. Those three facts are the only things that have stayed the same with her in the last six years.

Where did the fifteen-year-old wallflower go?

In her place is a twenty-four-year-old sharped tongue woman.

As she walks next to me, with her shoulders back and confidence in her steps, it becomes clear. Sayer Brooks isn't the same little girl she was when she left.

I spent a lot of time in the Brooks' mansion as a teenager. Dating the delinquent daughter, nothing pissed Harlow's parents off more than seeing me hang around the pool smoking a joint or with Harlow lounging between my legs.

It was fun back then. When nothing mattered and Harlow and I were a means to an end.

Users, we relied on each other. Harlow wanted to keep her reign of being the bad Brooks and I wanted a distraction from the growing numbness inside of me.

But somewhere along the way, Harlow started to want more. More of my time, more of me. More than I was willing to give her. I broke things off around the time Sayer was sixteen, but I still kept coming around.

Harlow didn't mind. As long as I hung out with her, she

was content, but if she caught me in a room with Perfect Sayer, as Harlow liked to refer to the younger Brooks, she'd go ballistic.

Possessive and jealous even though we weren't together anymore. I was Harlow's, not Sayer's. She wanted Sayer to have nothing she did.

And suddenly, I had another way to fight the numbness.

I started to play a game. A game where I'd actively search out Sayer, hunting her down in her own house.

Sometimes I'd find her in the kitchen in her prep school uniform drinking sparkling water, her plaid skirt an inch or two shorter than what was permitted on campus with her knee-high socks askew.

Sometimes I'd find her in the pool house wearing a barely-there bikini. She was still a minor, but her body was anything but childish. It took everything I had in those moments to hold myself back.

I knew she had a crush on me. It would've been so easy to walk up to her and take what I wanted, knowing she'd give herself over to me without a clue of what that really meant.

But no matter what bullshit truth is spewed about me around this gossip whore of a city, I don't have any jailbait tendencies. I never laid a hand on Sayer, but Harlow never knew that.

She'd find us and start screaming her head off. One time she even broke a priceless crystal vase in a fit of anger.

Messing with Harlow always distracted me from all the shit that swam around in my head. But what distracted me even more was Sayer. The innocence in her gray eyes as she stared up at me, the way she clung to my every word like I was her salvation. And maybe I was. I knew she didn't have that many friends.

Somewhere along the way, I stopped seeking out Sayer to

mess with Harlow and started going to her for me. To hear her laugh, they sounded like little bells that made me feel a little lighter. To talk about her day, how empty she felt on the inside. It mirrored what lived in me.

What we had was simple. It was mundane. It was enough.

Sayer wasn't the sun brightening my day, she was the stars that hung around the moon. The night sky was dull without her. I felt dull without her.

And then she left. Leaving me with Harlow.

For six long years. Now that she's home, I want her back.

Harlow leaving is a pain in my ass, the ledger she stole can ruin me. Ruin all that I've built, all that was left to me. But it's the perfect excuse to get close to Sayer.

She was right when she said she was the only person able to help me do this. There's no one that gets under Harlow's skin like her sister.

"Where are we going?" Sayer asks as we walk the streets of the city.

I don't answer. She can find out when we get there.

Apparently, that doesn't work for her.

After a couple feet of us walking without me acknowledging her, Sayer stops, making me as well.

We're still holding hands.

If I let go, I have a suspicion she's going to bolt and I'm not in the mood for any chasing tonight.

"We need to lay down some ground rules."

I only raise one eyebrow, knowing it annoys her when I do.

Case in point, she glares, squeezing my hand. It's kind of cute she thinks that could hurt me. "I'm serious, Noah."

"The floor is yours, Brooks."

"You have to be honest with me."

Am I missing something here? "I've been pretty straight forward with you thus far."

"But when I ask you a question about where you're taking me and you don't answer, it's hiding something from me."

Well someone tightened her morality compass this morning.

"That it?" I ask.

"No. I've been making a list in my head of all the things we need to iron out that I think we should discuss."

Of course she has.

Bored with just standing on the street, I tug on her hand and set off for our intended destination. She can talk as she walks.

Sayer digs her heels on the sidewalk. Dig all she wants, the only thing she's going to achieve by doing that is ruining her shoes.

"Would you just walk for fuck's sake," I growl, growing annoyed from dragging her dead weight behind me. "We're going to a restaurant, nothing scandalous is going to happen." I give her a look. "Unless you want it to."

She huffs, falling in step behind me.

When we get to the restaurant, the maître d' is waiting for us.

"This way, Mr. Kincaid." She leads us through an empty restaurant until we're at the best table in the place. Which is always reserved for me.

As Sayer sits down, she watches the maître d' as she checks me out. But what Sayer doesn't understand, it's not in a way that speaks of appreciation, attraction. It's a look that searches for opportunity. People always want something from me.

I chuckle as she walks away, liking the way Sayer's so easily riled up. "Jealous, Baby Brooks?"

"No." She rolls her eyes in an exaggerated flourish. "More annoyed that anything. What if we were on an actual date?"

I grin. "This isn't an actual date?"

She levels me a flat look. "We both know this is a business arrangement."

"That doesn't mean we can't have a little fun."

"That" —she points at me— "is exactly what I'm talking about. None of that."

"None of what?"

"That" —the finger is now moving in circles in front of my face— "flirting you're throwing my way."

I lean across the table and in a filthy, hushed tone I tell her, "Oh you innocent little thing. This isn't flirting. I haven't even gotten started."

A blush dusts the tops of her cheeks as I move to recline in the seat. Satisfied.

Before Sayer can find words for a retort, our waiter comes over to pour us a glass of their finest wine. He leaves the bottle in an ice bucket on the table.

When he walks away, I raise my glass to Sayer.

Skeptically, she raises hers. "What're we toasting?"

"Us."

Her eyes widen.

I add, "And our agreement."

Her eyes go back to their regular size. "You brought me here to celebrate?"

"I brought you here because I'm hungry. Now, I know your mother taught you proper etiquette, Sayer. Clink your glass with mine."

She does, hesitating before taking a small sip. Keeping my eyes locked on hers, I down half the glass.

Sayer looks at everything but me. From the menu to

around the empty restaurant. "Why is there no one else?" she mumbles, as if to herself.

I answer anyway. "Because they're technically closed. They stayed open for me."

She digests the words. "How does it feel?"

"How does what feel?"

"Having the entire city ready to do your bidding?"

"Powerful." I think she asked not expecting an answer, so I shock the hell out of her by doing just that.

Her mouth parts, making me hone in on the plumpness of them. Little pillows waiting to be used.

I can think of a few things I'd like to do with them.

Not yet, I remind myself. I have to ease her into that, which if her words from earlier are any indication, she's drawing the line there. Lucky for me, I'm very persuasive. Even when pitted against the stubborn will that is installed in all Brooks members.

I've waited a long time to have Sayer Brooks tied to me, I have to be smart about this.

Shifting in the chair, I clear my throat. "What stipulations did you want to add to our agreement?"

I don't bother to point out if she had more to add, she shouldn't have written the bullshit "contract."

Folding her hands on top of the table, Sayer sits up straighter. "I have two."

I hold back a groan. If Harlow was the slacker in the family, Sayer is the overachiever. "Well, go on, Brooks."

"First, I need you to be upfront with me. On everything. If I'm going to help you, I don't want to be blindsided."

Amending her speech in my head to: "she can know whatever benefits her." She doesn't get to know everything. She can't.

But I can tell her enough to keep her satisfied without jeopardizing everything else.

"Okay." I nod. "What's the next."

She blinks. "What?"

I smirk, enjoying that I keep surprising her. It's only fair. Since she's been doing the same to me from the moment I found her at my club.

"Your second stipulation." I tilt my head. "Actually, this is your fourth. You're being greedy with my generosity."

"This is you being generous?"

"Would you rather I not give you anything you're demanding?"

"My second requirement. Right." She nods. "Absolutely no touching. No flirting. I know we're going to have to pretend in public for people to see, but I'd like to request we keep the physical contact to the bare minimum."

I take a sip of wine. "If I was a more sensitive man, I'd be heartbroken that you don't like me."

"Then it's a good thing you're a heartless man," she says. "Do we have a deal?"

I'm not a PDA person. But with Sayer I find myself wanting to touch her, to be near her. She's so soft and full of light, a stark contrast to my dark.

"We have a deal," I tell her when the waiter shows up to take our order.

She might want this now, but I've seen the covert looks she gives me when she thinks I'm not looking. She still wants me.

And I want her.

By the time Harlow comes back, mark my words, I will know what it feels like to be between the legs of her little sister.

After dinner, my watch goes off with a text. Reading what Reeve sent, I frown.

"Something wrong?" Sayer asks. Her tone is almost hopeful, like if I have to duck out she can go home.

Typing out my reply, an idea forms.

Smirking, I look at her. "C'mon, we're going to stop number two of the night."

She watches warily as I get up from my chair and walk to her side of the table. With my fingers wrapped around the top of her chair, I pull it out.

"Where are we going?" she asks when I give her no choice but to get up.

"To the casino." Wrapping her hand around the crook of my elbow, we walk out of the restaurant and onto the sidewalk.

She throws her head back and groans to the stars.

"Regret agreeing to this yet?" I mock.

"I regretted it as soon as we left the library."

My laugh is the only sound exchanged between us on our walk to The Underground.

Heathen's Hell was my first solo venture within my company, the business I backed on my own. But The Underground is my legacy. For a lot more than people know.

I don't only deal in money and contracts, but secrets.

Secrets are my favorite thing to take.

Unfortunately, we're not going to the casino for fun. Reeve's text was about one of our members refusing to pay off his debt before leaving. Now I have to go handle the problem.

It's not our fault that he's a shitty player at cards.

My original plan was to take Sayer home after dinner, but

why not fucking kill two birds with one stone and bring her along.

Then her old classmates and parent's friends who are there can see her. And they'll talk. They always talk.

Which is what I want. The more people who see us together, the more of a chance it has to get back to Harlow. Wherever the fuck she is.

It's seven blocks from the restaurant to The Underground and Sayer's steps slow the closer we get. I take her through the back entrance, leading her to the gambling hall. She doesn't need to see anything else in the manor.

She's a curious little kitten and I don't need to be answering any more of her hundred and one questions tonight.

I hear the noise in the gambling room before we walk into it. The conversation, the chips clinking together, the music.

Right before we enter, Sayer squeezes my hand.

I look down at her.

She's nibbling on her bottom lip, worry in her eyes.

"What?" I snap. More irritated with myself than her. She shouldn't look as tempting as she does while worrying at her lip.

Fuck.

So innocent. So perfect.

I have this need to tarnish her shine.

"What?" I repeat.

Sayer doesn't say anything, just continues to stare at me.

I don't have time for this.

After I drop Sayer off, I have to go down to Kelly's, a bar on the opposite end of the city, to talk to a certain Irishman on an arrangement he hasn't made good on.

I'm not a patient man.

I turn away when she tugs back on my hand still in hers.

"You have three seconds to start talking, Sayer." I whirl around to face her.

"I don't think I should go in there."

A displeased sound rumbles in my throat. "And why's that?"

"It's—" she breaks off, wringing her hands. Nervous. She's nervous.

She's scared to go in there. I see the worry lining her deep gray eyes. Maybe there's a fourth thing that hasn't changed about Sayer Brooks. She doesn't want to be the center of attention.

Closing the space between us, I tilt her chin up to face me. My thumb traces her bottom lip. Those gray eyes fluttering as she parts them. For me.

This is what I mean. She'd let me take from her before she even realizes what's happening. I could easily replace my thumb with my lips and she'd lean into that just like she's leaning into me now.

My free hand fists at my side. "It's a little too late for that, Sayer."

"I know," she whispers. "I just thought I'd be honest."

Because that's what she wants between us.

Honesty.

No bullshit.

So different from her sister, who didn't care if I lied or cheated or took from her as long as she was with me in the end.

The Brooks sisters have always been opposites, even in their outward appearances. It's always fascinated me. Sayer's the blond to Harlow's brunette, the gray eyes to other's blue.

Back when I was a teenager I often questioned if my family was still alive, would I have been like Harlow? The outcast?

Or would I be as groomed as Sayer? Back when I was desperate to know where the fuck I belonged.

Now, I don't really give a shit. They're gone and I'm still here.

Callous, but true when I've been around longer than I had them.

Mourning people I don't remember doesn't seem like a viable use of my time.

Pushing my dead family to the wayside, I focus on Sayer.

On how different from her sister she is.

Differences I want to discover.

If Sayer's a curious kitten, I'm a lion on the prowl—stalking their prey.

"Let's go." I pull her in step with me as we walk into the gambling hall, not giving her a choice in the matter.

Once people see us tonight it'll spread like brushfire, one I fully intend to stroke.

I spy Reeve with two of our bouncers sitting in a booth on the opposite end of the room. I make a beeline for them, ignoring the whispers that follow me as I do.

At this point, the whispers are nothing but static noise.

Glancing to my side, Sayer walks with her chin pointed down and her blonde hair fanning across her face. She's trying to hide.

My teeth grind and I'm not entirely sure why. All I know is that I don't like her acting like this. Like she's meant to be invisible.

I let go of her hand when we make it to the table. Reeve gives me a look as I guide Sayer into the booth, my hand on the small of her back. I slide in after her.

Our patron sits directly in front of me, Dr. Rochester, plastic surgeon to the socialites. I don't focus on him. Not yet. Instead my attention is on my friend.

"You lose your shirt?" I stare at Reeve who's wearing nothing but a pinstriped blazer and a few corded necklaces over his bare chest, which is covered in splatters of paint and—I squint to double check, and yep—bite marks.

"Ruined, actually." He sighs, adjusting the top hat on his head. "Such a shame really. One of my favorite shirts destroyed over a lackluster fucking."

Mr. Rochester shifts in his seat while Sayer coughs beside me.

I grin.

Reeve winks, running his hand down his chest. "See anything you like?"

I roll my eyes. "Yes, Reeve. After all this time, here and now, is when I am finally succumbing to my desire for you." My voice in monotone.

He chuckles, turning to Sayer. "What about you, Baby Brooks?"

Sayer doesn't say anything as she stares, wide eyes and blushing cheeks.

"Enough," I growl.

Reeve stares at me for a beat too long before nodding.

Sayer scoots closer to me so her thigh is pressed against mine.

I focus on Dr. Rochester. "So. Charlie. I hear there's a problem with you not paying what you owe."

The man in question shakes his head before I'm even finished. "I don't owe anything. As I was telling your friend—"

Reeve coughs. "*Business partner.*"

Dr. Rochester cuts Reeve a dry look. "*Business partner,*" he amends, "that I don't owe—"

"Charlie." My elbows press into the table. "Do you take me for an idiot?"

His eyes widen. "What? Of course not—"

"Of course you don't." I nod, leaning forward. "So why are you trying to play me the fool?"

"I'm not." If possible his eyes go wider.

"Oh, but you are." My voice drops. "You owe us a quarter of a million dollars, Charlie. And that's not including the late fees."

Reeve leans in, mock whispering, "You don't want to see what we do to people who don't pay their late fees."

Rochester blanches as Reeve sits back, chuckling.

"Tell you what, Charlie," I draw the good doc's attention back to me. "You pay us in full tonight, and we won't add the late charges. But if you don't." I pull out my phone, scrolling through my camera roll. "Remember that video of your daughter you don't want getting out?" The one we purposely help hide for him when he found what his daughter did in Cabo during her spring break.

I find what I'm looking for and flip my phone around for him to see just as the sound kicks on to noises no father wants to hear from his daughter.

If possible, his pale skin goes even paler as a man's voice orders, "Suck it harder, baby" on the video.

"For every day you don't pay us, I'll email it to a few reporters I know around the city." I turn the video off.

Sayer's already tense body stiffens further and I can feel her horrified gaze on me. I'm not doing anything she already doesn't know.

I'm a cruel bastard.

I see the doc's throat constrict as he swallows. Leaning back in the booth, I know I've made my point abundantly clear.

"I'll pay tonight," he rasps.

I nod, knuckles knocking on the table as I get out of the booth. "Knew you'd see reason, Charlie."

I extend my hand to Sayer, who doesn't take it. She angles her body away from me as she marches in the direction of the exit.

Reeve nods, silently telling me he can handle the rest.

"Gentlemen." I dip my chin toward the table before setting off after Sayer.

It takes me less than three strides to catch up. My hand is reaching for her elbow when she whirls around. "Don't touch me."

Her voice is loud enough to earn a few looks from a few curious patrons. Ignoring her request, my fingers curl around her elbow and I pull her out of the room.

Wisely, she doesn't fight me.

"You don't get to tell me what to do," I growl when we're alone.

She yanks her elbow out of my grip, fire in her features. "I'll do whatever I like, Noah."

The way she says my name, always with a little frustration behind it, makes my dick twitch. So does her defiant tendency.

More and more I'm liking the new Sayer Brooks.

She can push back all she wants, I'll still be on top in the end.

"Not out there you don't." My tone is harsher than I intend. I don't change it. "Hate me in private, Sayer, but when we're out there, you better act like you're head over fucking heels for me."

Her lips flatten.

"You agreed to this," I remind her. "You signed that contract."

She glares at the reminder.

"Let's go." I turn her in the direction of the exit.

"Where are we going?"

"I'm taking you home. You're done for the night."

She sags in relief.

My driver Jenkins is waiting for us outside The Underground and as we're approaching the vehicle, he gets out. I shake his hand before getting in the driver seat and he walks around to open the door for Sayer.

Once she's inside and the door is closed, I pull away from the curb.

"What about him?" Sayer looks out the window.

"He was just dropping off the car. He'll be fine."

Jenkins is the driver I never use. My friends do, just not me.

I turn up the radio to cut out any conversation on the ride to Sayer's.

Not that it's needed, she's too busy nibbling on her fingernail while looking out the window, lost in thought.

We pull up outside Sayer's building and before the car is even in park, she's out the door.

"Fucking hell." Parking, I open my own door and start after her.

"Sayer," I say as she reaches the stairs to her building.

She stops and slowly turns around. "What?"

Closing the distance, I invade her personal space. "I'm picking you up tomorrow night at nine-thirty." Eyeing her outfit, I add, "So dress nice."

Her glare would make a lesser man bend.

I simply smirk as I walk away.

This is going to be fun.

seven

Sayer

I'M PUTTING IN AN EARRING WHEN A DEMANDING KNOCK beats against my front door. My phone confirms the time. Nine-thirty exactly.

Noah Kincaid is nothing if not punctual.

Too bad for him, I don't move from where I'm standing in my small foyer, staring at myself in the mirror. I need a minute to collect my thoughts.

It won't kill him to wait until 9:31. In fact, it'll be good for him. Patience is a virtue he never bothered to learn. Let this serve as a reminder that I'm not a little toy to push around.

I look ready. Makeup, done. Hair, done. Outfit, done. I look the part, I'm just not sure I can act it. My face thankfully doesn't portray the tangled mess I feel on the inside.

It's not butterflies, they're too delicate for this. Warring in my stomach are Atlas moths who are battling for dominance, stirring up waves of anxious energy.

It's been so long since I've been on a date—which this *isn't*—that I feel like my young teenage self about to go out with her crush for the first time. Not that I have a crush on Noah.

I don't.

Not anymore.

Not now.

I just have a healthy appreciation for the male form. *His* male form, especially.

The nerves mostly stem from the unknown. I don't know what to expect and I loathe not knowing. I like to have an idea on what I'm walking into but with Noah…he constantly keeps me on my toes. Tonight is as murky as the sky on a cloudy night.

The knock comes again, more impatient.

Still, I don't move. Let him stew out there.

My mind is too busy swimming with questions.

What's going to happen tonight?

How do I act?

Will he hold my hand?

Try to kiss me?

Will I have to be by his side the entire night?

The banging on the door happens again. Faster. Louder. Angrier.

Stealing a breath, I stare at my reflection. "Showtime," I whisper, moving toward the door. *To Noah.*

When I get there, I can feel the waves of anger rolling off him even with it still shut. It makes me happier than it probably should.

Not used to waiting, Mr. Kincaid?

With a smile, I open the door and lean against the frame. "You knocked?"

"I told you to be ready at nine-thirty."

"And I was." I swish my hips, making the skirt of my dress move between us.

He doesn't bother to glance at it. "It's nine thirty-three."

My smile grows. "I know."

Noah's glare can only be described as chilling, far from amused by my antics.

"Let's go," he growls, reaching for me.

"Wait!" I jump out of his reach, watching his eyes narrow as I do.

"Why?"

"I need to grab my purse."

Noah stares at me like I'm beyond dense. With a heavy sigh, he snaps, "Then go get it. *Quickly.*"

Touchy, touchy. Whatever he has planned tonight cannot be that time sensitive.

I resist the urge to flip him off before I disappear from the doorway and into my bedroom. His nasty attitude should be a warning to not poke him. *Should* being the keyword.

I don't know why Noah makes me want to be bolder, to get under his skin like he does mine. The more he orders me around, the more I want to rebel.

Which is why after the clutch is in my hands, I stay in my room for a little longer than necessary.

Pan's asleep on my bed and his engine-like purr sparks to light as I lean down to scratch his chin. My sweet child. His purring gets louder when he opens his green eyes. At first, I think it's because he's looking into the love of his life's face—aka me—but then a throat clears behind me

"Oh my God!" I jump in the air, arms wild as I spin around to find Noah glaring in my doorway.

"This is what was so important? You wanted to pet your damn cat?"

The look I give him is nowhere close to the level of animosity he's capable of, but I stare him down anyway. "He needs love."

Pan nudges my hand and I take that as his agreement. I look to Noah like, *see!*

"He's a cat," he states as if I didn't already know my pet's species. "They love themselves enough. They don't need your reassurance."

Pan meows and uncurls. He's still purring as he jumps off the bed.

"Clearly, someone has never had a pet before."

I watch as Pan saunters over to Noah, who eyes him with distaste.

"I hate animals," he states plainly.

My mouth drops with his admission. "That explains so much…"

He smirks, but it immediately gets wiped away as Pan rubs against his legs. If possible his engine-sounding purr gets louder as he leaves white fur against Noah's black slacks.

I swear my cat is smirking as he does it.

"Do something," he snaps.

"What do you want me to do?" I ask, trying not to laugh.

"Get him away from me."

"You're a man. Pick him up yourself." I cross my arms. "I didn't take you for someone who was afraid of a little pussy."

He makes a noise in the back of his throat, but before he can make a grab for my cat, I walk over and scoop Pan up. I would never subject my cat to Noah's wrath.

Only someone as cold and callous as Noah could hate animals. He's allergic to joy. And pets bring endless amounts of that. His poor black heart.

"Don't pity me now, Baby Brooks."

"You're confused." I drop Pan on the bed, and thankfully he stays there, curling back into a ball. "This face isn't one of pity. It's of disdain. I disdain you."

The smirk only grows. "You sure you're a grad student? That's not good English."

Gah!

This man. So infuriating.

"If you're done insulting me." I walk closer to him, hoping he'll move to let me pass.

He doesn't, standing at full height and blocking my doorway. "I'm not."

"Excuse me?" I raise a brow, my clutch heavy in hand. I wonder how well it would go over if I smacked him in the chest for the level of douchery he's brought into my bedroom.

"I'm not done evaluating you."

"This isn't a doctor's office, Noah—"

He cuts me off, head tilted to the side in mock-surprise. "Really, I had no idea."

"I don't have to go with you, you know."

"Actually, you do." His hands slide into his pant pockets. "We have a contract, remember?"

"A contract that won't stand in court." I wrote it in pink ink, for goodness sake!

"Until Harlow's back, you're in this with me, Brooks. You need to get used to it."

"I think I asked to be treated like an equal."

"And I am. Treating you equally to how I treat everyone else." Before I can bite a hole in my tongue or try to choke him with his tie—I swear I'm not usually a violent person, Noah Kincaid just seems to bring it out in me—he adds, "Now let's take a look at what you're wearing."

"I'm not changing." I cross my arms over my chest, feeling his appraisal.

"You are if I don't like your outfit."

"Hi, this is 2019, welcome to the twenty-first century. I'm not changing my outfit if you don't like it."

For the third time tonight he smirks, but this one is different than the others. Darker, the beast coming out to play. "Let's get one thing straight, Sayer. You're here to help me get your sister to come back. And how we're going to do that is appeal to her jealousy. Which is going to be obtained by us. What we do. How we act with each other. What we *wear*." His eyes scan my body for the second time. My skin feels warm as his eyes drink me in.

"I could be wearing a nun's habit and she'd try to eviscerate me."

Noah's expression doesn't change, but I like to think he's laughing on the inside, appreciating my humor, knowing it's true.

No matter what I do, what I wear, as long as I'm with Noah and my sister sees it, she will freak out.

We both know this. Noah doesn't need to police my outfits, he's just doing it to show his dominance. Which is completely unnecessary. His alpha attitude can be felt from across the room.

"We both know my outfit is fine," I say when his stare becomes too much for me, feeling it sink beneath my clothes. It's too much, feels too intimate even though he hasn't made a move to touch me. "Can we just go?"

His nod is sharp as he reaches for my wrist. I stare at it as he pulls me out of my room. Strong and masculine, he holds me in an almost delicate touch. He walks through my apartment like he owns it and I let him, too focused on the feel of his skin on mine. It feels right, having his hand on my body.

"Will you tell me where we're going?" I don't appreciate being kept in the dark. A point I made clear last night. Living with my parents and sister, I tended to be the last one to know everything.

"To a party."

He doesn't say anymore, but I can fill in the blanks to what he leaves out.

We're not going to a social gathering, but a social battle. Where people wear their clothes like armor and brandish their words like knives.

Of course Noah was going to pick that as our first official night out as—

"What are we?" I ask when we're in the lobby of my building.

"Well, to me you're a barely tolerable—"

I cut him off before his words can hit their intended target. It seems Noah sharpened his swords earlier than necessary. "I *meant*" —giving him a pointed look— "what are we going to tell people there?"

"Nothing."

"Nothing?" I echo.

He nods, his thumb tracing circles along my skin. The soft, methodic strokes are a contrast to how tight his body is wound. He's always on the offense, waiting for a fight.

"The less we say, the more they'll speculate. The more they'll talk," he elaborates, seeing the confusion on my face.

It comes as a shock to no one that I've never done anything like this before. I'm not sure of the protocol.

Noah's fingers find a home under my chin, tilting it up until our eyes lock. "Can you do this?"

I huff, pulling my chin away. "Of course." I hope my voice is more confident than how I feel. "Can you?"

He smiles, a soft, knowing smile, and pulls us into the cold winter night. As he escorts me to his idling car, I can't get his smile out of my mind. It reminds me of when we were younger, and he'd come to search me out. Secrets. It's a smile full of secrets that I'm desperate to learn.

As he drives us to our destination, I study his profile. Strong. Angular. Greco-Roman. A sinful man shrouded in secrets. But despite his appearance, it's what's underneath that pulls at me the most.

What he's keeping locked away.

…I wonder if I can find the key to unlock them.

Arms slip around my waist from behind. I go stiff as they pull me against their hard body before I force myself to relax. Noah. It's almost scary how instantaneous it is for me to recognize his touch.

"Relax," he whispers in my ear. I guess I didn't unwind as much as I thought. But it's hard. Agreeing to this.

If I felt uncomfortable and out of place at The Underground, it's ten times worse being here. People keep staring, their whispers are a constant white noise in my ears.

"I thought you said it didn't matter how I acted," I hiss under my breath.

Evidently, he lied.

"It does when it feels like I'm holding a corpse. You're too tense."

"Hey, there's an idea." I lean my head back onto his chest. "Maybe you don't need me after all. Harlow would be super jealous if you were suddenly into necrophilia."

He chuckles, spinning me around so fast the room blurs. His forehead rests on mine. "Not happening. I like my women warm and breathing."

"How else do you like your women?" I can't stop myself from asking, curiosity hooks me by her claws.

Noah hums, heat pooling in his eyes, his voice husky as he says, "I have a particular liking for blondes." He wraps a finger around my hair and tugs it. "And eyes like molten gun metal."

Me.

"Noah—" Swallowing, my hands go to his chest to create some healthy distance between us.

I can't let his words get to me. If I do, I'll let him in and if

I let him in, I'll be the one getting hurt in the end. But it's like pushing against a wall. He doesn't move. At least, not his feet.

His hands skim over my hips and around the curve of my ass. A gasp leaves me as he squeezes, pulling our bodies closer together. If he's trying to make me relax, he's doing it wrong. I'm wound tight, my chest beating wild.

Close. We're so close.

"I changed my mind," he whispers, his lips hover inches from mine.

"About what?" I breathe, too focused on his body against mine. His hard to my soft. The dark of his suit to the white of my dress.

We're opposites who shouldn't fit, but with our bodies this close it feels like we're a perfect match. Puzzle pieces made to go together.

"About how we act tonight." The stubble of his beard scratches my cheek as he moves to whisper in my ear. "I want you like this. Next to me. My hands on you. The entire time."

"But the contract," I protest weakly as his other hand moves behind my back, locking me to his chiseled chest. The flimsy excuse to protect me and my soft heart.

"Fuck the…" Noah's voice trails off as his hands tighten.

"You don't get to hog her the entire night, Kincaid," a voice says from behind me.

Thea le Veck.

I know without turning around. She sounds the same as she did when we were lab partners in tenth grade.

Noah cuts her a sharp look as I turn around. Unlike most people who'd buckle under the weight of Noah's stare, Thea ignores him, smiling at me. It's a warmer greeting than I expected. I haven't talked to her since prep school.

She hasn't changed appearance-wise, either. Her dark brown

skin is flawless and her hair still wild and big with voluminous tight curls that bounce when she moves.

I find myself smiling back, it growing wider when Noah makes a sound behind me.

He's not thrilled.

"What're you doing here, Thea?" he asks.

"Please, as if I wouldn't be here." She rolls her eyes before focusing back on me. "So. Sayer. Welcome home."

My smile falters a little.

Home. I wouldn't call this place home.

He can't see my face, but it's like Noah knows my mood has shifted. I feel his fingers brush against my lower back.

"Thanks."

"I can't tell you how happy our boy here is now that you're back. Well, I wouldn't exactly say happy since I doubt he lets him feel such a joyous emotion, but he's definitely less grumpy now."

Noah glares. "Seriously, Thea? Go away. We're in the middle of something."

She shakes her head. "Can't do that, Noah." Turning her body slightly, she points across the room to a man with reddish-brown hair and ink on his knuckles. "He wants to talk to you."

Noah's hand drops from my back and my body becomes cold as he moves away, angling his body semi in front of mine.

"You brought him here?" Noah's furious question is directed at Thea.

Thea, like with his glare, doesn't back down. She simply raises a sculpted brow. "Want to use your inside voice?"

"Want to tell me why you brought Seamus Kelly here?" he shoots back, not using a friendly tone.

"Who's Seamus?" I can't help but ask. He doesn't look the friendliest as he stares over here with a nasty scowl.

"No one," Noah answers the same time Thea says, "He's complicated."

Well then. It looks like the Complicated No One is walking this way.

Noah curses, glancing at me.

Thea's arm wraps around my shoulders, pulling me close. "Don't worry. I'll keep her company."

"That's what I'm worried about," he mumbles, looking at me. Another curse escapes. "Wait here," he tells me before meeting Seamus halfway.

With bent heads and low voices, they look tense in conversation before walking out of the room. Some mingling people watch them disappear before shooting looks at Thea and me.

I try to ignore them as I ask, "What's that about?"

"He's been giving Noah a hard time about some business they did recently. It's not a big deal." Thea simply shrugs, but her words are calculated. As if carefully picking them one by one before stringing them into a sentence.

Noah's anger at seeing Seamus didn't feel like a small deal, but if I press more, it's not going to result in anything. So I accept her answer for what it is and try to think of something to fill the lapse of conversation between us only to get distracted by my name in a nearby group.

"What's she doing here with him?" a woman asks in a failed whisper. Her bird-like gaze darts to me.

My lungs tighten while my ears strain to hear more.

"I don't know, but it doesn't surprise me," her friend answers, matching tone. "Don't you remember what people were saying when she mysterious moved away after graduation?"

What did people say? I watch the first woman with a whispering deficiency shake her head.

"It was because she was—"

I never get to know what she says next. Thea pulls me away from them. "C'mon, let's get you a drink."

eight

Sayer

ONE DRINK TURNS TO TWO AND TWO TURNS TO THREE. By the time I'm on my fourth—or is it fifth?—glass of champagne, Noah comes back, looking more agitated than when he left. I giggle as the crowd parts for him. So obedient, everyone is afraid to get in his way. To stand up to him.

Noah doesn't pay attention to them, they're peasants beneath him, as his eyes roam over the faces—looking for someone. Looking for *me*.

A cheap thrill caresses me with the knowledge.

He doesn't see me right away, I'm hiding behind a fake plant, the fake fronds tickle my exposed skin, but the spot gives me the perfect advantage to watch him undetected.

Like me, Noah doesn't fit in this world anymore, but unlike me, he's sitting on his throne at the top while I'm still trying to find my place somewhere near the bottom.

I take a sip of champagne, transfixed by him. His movements. Powerful like a panther, he prowls through the crowd. So proud in his steps, so sure. So angry. He walks like a king, an invisible crown upon his mussed hair.

Even from here, I spy the tension that rests in the corner of his eyes. Whatever business he had with Seamus, it didn't go well.

Hmm, interesting.

I don't even have that effect on him and it makes me wonder what happened to make his shoulders that taut, his frown so prominent. It creases more when he still doesn't see me.

Stopping in the middle of the room, he looks around. And I giggle at the lost look that takes over his face. It's small, so small no one else probably notices it, but I do. I see it. Like he somehow missed me.

Oh, how invisible I've become that all it takes is some well-placed shadows and a fake plant to hide me from even the most keen observer.

Something heavy settles in my stomach. Am I that lackluster? That insignificant? I start to move from behind my hiding spot, no longer enjoying being invisible, not from him, not from the man who has always been able to find me. I don't get more than a step before I stop.

A man I don't recognize takes a sip from his glass as he steps in front of Noah, and that must be a magical sip with the gift of bravery because the man so boldly reaches out to touch Noah's arm. He turns with a sneer and the bold man shrinks back.

Whatever Noah says it's too low for me to hear, but the man looks like he's about to make a mess in his sharp pants. He then starts to back up, steps hurried under the scrutiny of Noah's cool eyes.

He keeps walking backward, apologizing profusely for interrupting Noah, for not thinking before touching him, for thinking he was worth Noah's time at all.

What did Noah say to him?

The man's not paying attention to where he's going and my eyes widen, watching almost in slow motion as he runs into the tray of a passing by wait staff. They both tumble to the floor while the tray goes flying in the air, the drinks balancing along with it.

When the tray lands, it's without the drinks. The glasses go off in all directions, shattering on the hard floor. The contents go everywhere as well. On people, on furniture, on the ground.

It's eerily quiet. No one dares to move, except for another server who comes along and slips on the mess. Their tray clatters to the floor while these drinks get thrown on a person.

Noah.

He's soaked, the shirt drenched and sticking to his skin. His unruly hair flattened.

No one moves.

I'm not sure anyone even breathes.

The room hangs in a deafening silence. And I can't help it, can't stop it even if I wanted to. I laugh. Full on belly laughter that pulls at the muscles in my stomach, tears welling in my eyes.

Noah jerks in my direction, eyeing me with his hard, assessing eyes. Except, they're not that hard. Not right now. I see them melt when they latch onto me.

Soaking wet and smelling of alcohol, he's fighting a smile. One directed at me.

I smile back. Uninhibited and free, a feeling I don't think Noah allows himself to have. Even now he's battling with himself, I can see it when we lock eyes. But I feel something else. This magnetic pull pulses between us.

Forgetting everyone else, he takes a step closer.

In a mood to play, I take one backward.

He raises a brow with another step.

Gonna come get me, Kincaid? My eyes dance.

You bet your ass, BB. His seem to say back.

My smile grows with each step I take, with each step he takes.

Our connection is broken with the same man from before rushes toward Noah, profusely apologizing. *Again.*

This time I don't bother listening. I'm about to turn away to find something stronger than champagne when I see Noah shove the man out of his way and into a nearby couple.

Noah's eyes are on me, warning me not to take another step.

I take one teeny, tiny step and he closes the distance between us in what feels like a nanosecond. A giggle escapes as his hand curves along my waist.

"You smell." I'm still giggling.

Noah's facial expression doesn't change, but I see something softer in his eyes. "And you're drunk. How much did you drink? I wasn't gone for that long."

I hold up three fingers, or maybe I hold up four. Either way, it's a lie because I tell him, "Five."

"Five what?" he whispers, his hand moves up and down my body.

My body electrifies under his touch and Noah has to repeat the question. I blink. "Five glasses of champagne."

A smirk curves his chiseled face. "Lightweight."

Oh, I totally am, but it's not polite of him to point that out. "Ruuude." I smack his arm and if the unimpressed look he just gave me is any indication it doesn't intimidate him.

"Where's Thea?" I hear what he doesn't ask, *Why wasn't she watching you?*

Because I can take care of myself. I shrug, "I don't know. She got pulled away by like drink three and then a woman insulted my shoes after she stepped on them so then I started drinking without her just to keep myself sane. I don't like these people."

Noah doesn't tell me that I am one of these people. He knows I'm not. Not anymore.

He squeezes my waist. "Want to get out of here?"

I do, but I'm not ready to go home. Not yet. "Have we done enough?"

"Right now, I don't really care," he says as a flash goes off and we pull apart, seeing a man with a camera pointed at us.

"There," he whispers. "We'll be the biggest picture in the gossip column tomorrow."

"Who was that man?" I ask when he walks away.

"A reporter for the newspaper."

"So everyone will know about it."

"Don't sound so broken up about it. You're the one that wanted to do more tonight."

"I know," I whisper. "I just don't like attention on me."

When he doesn't answer, but I can feel Noah's stare, I chance a glance up to find him studying me.

"What?" I ask when his stare becomes too much.

"You're nothing like Harlow."

At first, I bristle at her name. He says it with disdain, and another quality I don't want to touch on. A quality I'm not a fan of.

And I don't like that I don't like it. A vicious circle.

But I don't want to be compared to my sister. Not by anyone, but especially Noah. He's the one person that knows her best. I was always compared to her growing up, held to a standard of how I shouldn't be.

At a young age, I was pitted against my sister and it ultimately destroyed us to where we're siblings in blood and nothing more. There's no heart between us.

How could there be when I was meant to be her replacement?

"Is that a good or bad thing?" I whisper.

"Good," he admits after a beat. Shocking me again with his honesty. "You seem surprised," he adds in a low octave.

"You seem to keep doing that to me."

A pause.

Then, in the same voice, he says, "I'm not all that you've heard, Sayer."

Behind the frames of his glasses, those glacial blues nail me where I stand.

"No," I agree. "I think you're more, Noah Kincaid. More than a story could ever hold."

The air is thick around us, humid with tension as he stares down at me with an unreadable expression.

So intense I take a step back.

He follows, erasing the distance between us. Not saying a word, his hand reaches my face.

I pull back, away from his touch. "This goes against the contract."

It feels feeble, protesting the contract when my body is pulled tight in anticipation and the words taste forced on my tongue, knowing the lie even if I deny it.

The clause of him not touching me is for self-preservation.

Noah's fingers graze the tops of my cheeks and I wonder if he can hear the beating in my chest, the unsteady rhythm of my heart.

I wonder if his heart beats at all. Or if there's just a black hole where it collapsed.

Noah's fingers dance toward my hair, pulling on a strand… holding up a green, shiny leaf. A piece from the fake plant.

I groan, my head hitting the wall behind me.

Noah smirks, rubbing the leaf between his fingers. "What were you doing hiding in that plant?"

"Waiting for you. To watch you like you always watch me."

"Like what you saw?"

"No." Another lie.

He knows it too, but for once, he doesn't call me on it.

We stare at each other for a beat more before Noah entwines his fingers with mine and we start to walk toward the elevator. As we pass by the serving station, I pull away from Noah and run toward the unsupervised counter.

"What're you doing?" he barks at me, but I don't answer as I lean across it and wrap my fingers around an unopened bottle of amber gold. I don't know what I'm doing except that there's a flurry of excitement taking root in my chest as I race toward the now opened elevator with Noah close on my heels.

A few people eye us, maybe because my wild laughter escapes as the elevator doors close behind us.

"What was that?" he asked, looking wild. He's eyeing me in confusion while his hair is starting to dry, some strands stick to his forehead while others stand in various directions. My fingers itch to sink into it, but I tighten them around the bottle instead.

Maybe it's the alcohol or maybe it's the feelings Noah has stirred inside me or maybe it's the simple fact I keep denying, that I've missed Noah more than I should, but whatever it is, I answer honestly.

"I want to keep the night going. I don't want it to be over yet." Instead of hitting the ground floor button, I hit the farthest one from it.

And up we go.

"Why did we come here?" He watches as I tilt my head back to look at the stars.

We're standing on the roof of the building.

I didn't want to say goodbye to you. I take a sip of the bourbon I stole from downstairs to keep from saying that. It's the alcohol talking anyway.

On top of the champagne, I've started to make a small dent in the stolen alcohol. I know I'm pushing myself past what

I can handle, but there's not a care left inside me. All my reservations, all my worries, for right now, are gone.

I'm twirling in tight circles, careful—*so careful*—to not get close to the edge. I'm fine if I stay in the center of the roof. As long as I don't see how far my fall down is, I'm fine.

Still spinning, I tilt the bottle back, but before the rich liquid can reach me, it's ripped from my grip.

"Hey!" I shout even though Noah is standing inches away. "Give me that!"

He doesn't. Instead, he quirks a brow as he places the bottle to *his* lips and takes a healthy swallow. Noah doesn't wince like I did with the first sip, he probably likes the burn.

Before I can make a grab for the bottle, Noah throws it over my head and I watch, open-mouthed, as it shatters against the wall.

My gaze is fixed on it for several beats, watching the glorious high-priced liquor slowly drip down.

That was mine. I was having fun. Why did my fun just shatter?

"What is wrong with you?" I whirl around and shove Noah's chest. He barely budges.

"You're drunk," he states plainly.

"I was enjoying that!" I push him again and get the same result as before. Noah is an unmoving statue of hard muscle. With my hands on his chest, my fingers curl into fists around the fabric of his coat.

"And now you're not." He doesn't make a move to touch me, but I feel him nonetheless.

He's always been this mystery. An orphaned boy who wants for little and yet is so angry, who walks the street of this city in the middle of the night. Noah Kincaid puts on a show for the world to see, but he forgets that he once showed me the broken boy that lies underneath.

I want to find the door that leads to the library of his mind and explore all the shelves he has to offer.

"What are you doing, Sayer?"

"Trying to crack your secrets," I admit with my liquor-loosened tongue.

"That so?" He huffs a laugh. "How's it working for you?"

My hands move down his chest until the tips of my fingers brush against the waistband of his pants. Apparently bourbon makes me brazen. I look up at him, our mouths almost touching. His eyes unblinking. "Can't seem to crack the code." I smirk. "Yet."

I push off his body, twirling away only for my ankles to catch on each other and I go tumbling down. If it wasn't for Noah's wild reflexes I would've fallen face first into a sea of broken glass.

His arms are wrapped around me, keeping me suspended mid-fall, his breath brushes against the back of my neck. I don't breathe as he pulls us away from the glass shards.

Even still Noah doesn't pull away. Instead his hands graze down to my hips, holding them tight like anchors, keeping me steady.

"Sayer…" he rasps my name, face close to mine.

I part my lips. He doesn't move any closer. This seems to be a trend with us, even when I pull away, I just snap back into Noah's orbit. Maybe that's why I think he's so dangerous. Not because the power he holds over the town, but for the power he holds over me.

A car alarm goes off somewhere down below, the hold he has over me broken.

I pull away like his body is breathing fire. He makes me feel vulnerable and I've worked very hard to be anything but in the last six years.

Noah's brows pinch in question.

"Stop doing that," I snap.

"Doing what?"

"*Touching* me." Curse alcohol gods for making my tongue so loose.

Noah enjoys it if his smirk is any indication.

A noise vibrates in the back of my throat. "Stop smirking."

His smirk grows.

My fingers curl at my sides. I want to slap it off but that would require getting close to him and that's not going to happen.

No more falling under his snare trap.

"Is it bothering you?"

"Your face bothers me in general." I'm a twenty-four-year-old reduced to playground tactics.

He laughs, unbothered and amused as he watches me shift from foot to foot trying to find warmth in this freezing cold.

I study him. My favorite piece of art to observe.

Aside from how laughter makes his features look less pissed, I notice how much tension has seeped out of his muscles since we've been up here. His rendezvous with the tattooed redhead forgotten.

Until I ruin it. "Who's Seamus?"

In a snap, his shoulders pull taut. "No one you need to concern your pretty little head with."

My fists clench tighter at his condescending tone. He's using it to distract me, so I go off on him instead of focusing on what he's not saying. It's not going to work. Not this time. I focus on the unspoken words.

"Does he have anything to do with my sister?"

"No." Sharp. Cold.

"Then why was he here?"

"It doesn't pertain to our situation, so you don't have to worry about it." His hands slip into his pant pockets.

But I am. "You were pissed when you came back."

"I'm pissed all the time."

I tilt my head. "Why?"

"Why what? Why am I pissed?" He steps toward me. "Why does anyone feel anything? Basic human emotion, Sayer."

"Is this your way of telling me you feel things? That you actually have a heart and aren't some robot?"

More distance is erased between us. I refuse to back up, choosing to hold my ground. Noah doesn't get to intimidate me.

"Yes, Sayer, that's exactly what I'm telling you." Behind his glasses, his eyes darken. "I'm feeling a lot right now, for example."

My throat constricts, it's hard to swallow. I want to ask him what he's feeling, but I'm not ready to open that can of worms. "Then why did Seamus make you so angry?"

He lets out a frustrated sigh. "Why do you want to know?"

"Because I want to know you!" I yell. "Because if I'm stuck with you for however long we're together, I want to know the man and not the shadow."

Silence settles between us.

I don't think he's going to answer, so I turn around and start to walk to the door, the buzz from my drinks has thoroughly worn off at this point and I'm freezing. I have it cracked open when his voice stops me.

"He's a lowlife bartender with ties to the Irish mob. He owes me money. A lot of money and he came tonight to try and get me to lower his debt."

I let go of the door and turn around. The Irish mob. Another quirk to Haven Harbor. "What does he owe you money for?"

"It doesn't matter." His tone says otherwise.

I don't call him out on it. He's talking to me. Noah is

opening up and revealing some of his secrets and it's doing things to me. I don't want it to stop. "What did he try and bargain with?"

"Says Harlow came to see him the night she skipped town."

Something strange takes over my heart. Half-elation, half-dread. "Do you believe him?"

"I believe he'd drop to his knees and suck my cock if he thinks it'd get rid of all the money he owes me. So no, I don't believe he has anything important about your sister leaving."

I nod, ignoring the weird satisfaction that washes over me.

I must not do a very good job, Noah calls me out on it. "Does this bother you?"

"You mean helping you find my sister?" He nods. I sigh. "Would you care if it did?"

Noah doesn't answer, his face unreadable.

No, he wouldn't care. Not if it got in the way of getting what he wants. It shouldn't be hard to forget I'm the pawn, but maybe I was hoping that after spending a night with me, Noah would see me as something different. Something more.

The crushing disappointment that I'm solely a pawn weighs heavy. Why does it even matter? I want to shake myself. It shouldn't matter what I am because no matter what I feel when it's just the two of us, it's never going to happen. I'm a piece on Noah's chessboard and nothing more.

Without a word, I turn around and head for the door hearing Noah's quiet steps behind me.

It's not until we're in the elevator, going down that the silence breaks between us.

"Did you find them?"

I look up at him. "Find what?"

"My secrets?"

Not even close.

nine

Sawyer

AFTER THAT NIGHT, NOAH AND I FALL INTO A ROUTINE. Night after night, it's a whirlwind of going out. We go to the casino, Heathen's Hell, charity parties, or sometimes, like last night, we do something simple and have dinner at a nice restaurant.

And it seems to be working.

People are talking. Pictures have been taken, articles have been written for Page Nine, the gossip column in the Haven Harbor.

My parents have called, leaving messages I haven't returned. I don't know what to say. They hate Noah and his friends with a blinding passion. Brin texts me screenshots every morning of my face next to Noah's along with a cryptic code of exclamation marks and emojis. Even a few people in my classes have asked me what Noah's really like. That's what everyone wants to know about.

Noah. Noah this, Noah that.

No one has asked about me. And I'm exhausted, the kind of exhaustion that stretches down to my bones. Between the late nights with Noah and early mornings with grad school, I'm lucky if I get an hour or two of sleep before the clock resets and it's time to start all over.

I'd forgotten how taxing it is to constantly be on guard around these people. Where each word out of my mouth has to be picked with calculated care. It's a mind game I'm not versed to play anymore and it's starting to take its toll.

After almost falling asleep not once, not twice, but *three* times in class today, I texted Noah to count me out of tonight, even though he's made it clear that I'm his every night until Harlow comes back. But right now I'm so tired I don't give a single damn.

Tonight isn't for him, it's for me. One full of recharging with face masks, wine, and kitty cuddles. A little self-care if you will.

By the time I get home from campus, I haven't heard back from Noah so with a victory smile I take an hour and a half nap before diving into my course work that has fallen to the wayside.

I work until I get comfortably ahead of the syllabus and then I crack open the first of many wine bottles of the night.

After about two glasses in, I'm hanging upside down on my couch, reading a historical romance while the news plays in the background.

Typically, I try to avoid the news as much as possible. It's too upsetting and depressing and spikes my anger like no other, but there's nothing else on right now, so I left it on a local station.

I'm turning the page when something the newscaster says catches my attention. "And today marks the ten year anniversary of when the Haven Harbor National Museum of Art was robbed by the Baron just two days after the Metropolitan Museum of Art robbery, which we know was also done by the Baron because of the burning cigar left behind at both scenes. It was his calling card." Scrambling, my body flips over to right-side up, my eyes glued to the TV. "Officials say they fear they will never find the stolen pieces."

The Baron.

A notorious thief who is more like a myth since stories of him being around has stretched all the way back to the 1930s, which would make him older than even my granddad, who died at eighty-four.

He's a ghost haunting the town and one of my personal obsessions. When I was in undergrad, I went as far as to write a final thesis on him for one of my art history classes. I've always wondered if we'll ever know his true name.

Three sharp and fast raps on my front door pull me from my thoughts. I don't need to see who's on the other side to know. I recognize that knock by now.

Pan, who's been asleep on the cushion next to me, picks up his head and hisses at the door.

I pet his head. *Good kitty.*

I still haven't moved when my phone vibrates with a message.

Noah: Open the door, Sayer.

My fingers itch to text back a no, but I know that will just cause more problems for me so begrudgingly, I force myself to the door. I don't open it, though.

"Go away!" I shout through it instead.

"Not happening, Brooks." I can practically feel his arms crossing in stubbornness.

Standing on my tip-toes, I look at him through the peephole.

On the other side, he's more dressed down than I've seen him. Noah's wearing hunter green joggers, a black shirt, his leather jacket, and yes, his fit arms crossed tightly over his chest. My chest squeezes tight at the sight of him.

And he's staring directly into the peephole, his blue eyes like lasers, honing on me.

"I'm not going out with you," I say through the door. "I sent you a text."

"Open the door." He ignores what I said.

"No."

"Open the door, Sayer or I'm going to force it open."

I double-check the locks.

"Doesn't matter if it's locked," he adds. "I can get in regardless."

I believe him. Something as insignificant as a lock wouldn't keep Noah from getting what he wants.

With a sigh, I open the door.

"Fancy seeing you here." I force a smile.

Noah takes in my penguin onesie. He doesn't look amused. "You going to invite me in?"

I don't want to, but I also don't want my nosey neighbors eavesdropping.

The door opens wider and Noah walks in, brushing by me as he heads into the living room.

Shutting the door, I rest my head against the cool metal.

Did I really think I could text him and have him listen? That's the gauge for the level of tired I am, evidently. It makes me delusional.

When I walk into the living room, I find Noah in a stare down with my cat.

"What're you doing?"

"He's staring at me." Noah doesn't take his eyes off Pan.

"He's a cat, Noah," I tell him, remembering he doesn't like animals. "He's not going to eat you."

Noah snorts like that idea is ridiculous, but he doesn't take his eyes off Pan. His baby-blues are full of distrust.

A laugh slips out. I can't help it. Here's a man who makes businessmen pee their pants in a stare down with my house cat.

Finally, after what feels like hours, Pan grows bored and curls back up on the couch.

Noah turns toward me, his face blank. "You said you weren't coming out tonight."

I nod.

"I don't remember telling you that you could have a night off."

My brows shoot up as irritation spikes my blood. "You're not my keeper, Noah."

"I am until we catch your sister."

Pompous, controlling, arrogant asshat. I stalk toward him with heat in my eyes. Noah watches with a curious expression.

"Listen," I hiss, stabbing my finger into his chest. "I agreed to help you, but that doesn't mean I'm your puppet you get to order around."

I expect him to argue, to fight me but my anger fades to surprise as his hand wraps around my wrist, pulling me close until we're chest to chest.

My heart beats against its cage, fighting to be freed from its shackles. I'm trapped against a body I shouldn't want, but tilt toward anyway.

"Then what are you, Sayer?" he whispers, head dipped low.

"Your prisoner," I whisper back. Caught in a trap of my own making.

Rubbing his jaw, Noah regards me in silence before looking behind me at the TV. They're still talking about the Baron and something unreadable passes over Noah's face.

He's quiet from a moment until he says, "I want to show you something."

I don't know what it is, the softness in his otherwise hard voice, the fact that I've been home all night and have found myself actually bored and kind of restless, or the fact that he's here now and I don't want to watch him leave unless I'm right beside him, that has me nodding.

After a quick change out of the penguin onesie, I slip on my coat and follow Noah into the hallway and God knows where else.

Noah's takes me to the Art District downtown, to Artwell Alley. A section of the city that's dedicated to local artists who come and paint whatever they desire in a long alleyway between two buildings.

I used to come here all the time when I was feeling lost. The place that was my point zero. Where I felt centered. Some people do yoga and meditation to feel realigned, some turn to religion to guide their purpose. I came here.

Art was my center. My therapy. My religion.

Full of expression, love and pain, darkness and light, paintings are a reflection of the hearts around us, tales left to interpretation, forever feeling and forever changing. It's how I found a purpose when I didn't know who I was meant to be.

Noah doesn't care about the art before us, stomping by them without a second glance while I trail behind at a slower pace, remembering. Remembering what it was like to get lost in a painting. The canvas was my church and the brush was my prayer. I'd spend hours at my church, feeding my creativity.

Until the day I found out my granddad was sick. I was in an art studio, working on a painting that is now in the back of my closet when he called. That was the last day I picked up a paintbrush.

Noah, noticing my snail pace, backtracks to where I am. Instead of forcing me to pick up speed, he simply walks beside me.

I look away from the art on the walls to take him in instead.

With the shadows hugging his sharp bone structure, he

looks like a fallen angel in search of his reckoning with his hair in a mess and eyes aged in knowledge. More knowledge than a twenty-eight-year-old should probably have.

He's irresistible in his appeal, the way the corner of his mouth is stretched a little higher than the other as he stares down at me. "Like what you see?"

Yes. I quickly turn back around. Returning to my safety net of beautiful things. The art.

And, surprisingly, he lets me. Whatever he wants to show me can wait.

From a goblin wearing a crown to a rotting sun. An outline of a lotus flower that holds drawings of various styles to script that reads *he who roams the night walks hand in hand with the Devil.*

The line strikes a chord.

Only my devil likes suits and wears black-framed glasses. *Speaking of…*

I don't feel him beside me anymore. The heat that usually accompanies him is absent, my coat no longer feels adequate to keep me warm by itself.

I pull it closer around me. It's too quiet. The kind of quiet that comes with being alone.

I spin around with an anxious heart, thinking he's walked farther down. He's not.

Noah is no longer in the alley with me.

Not anymore.

"Noah?" I call out, spinning around again only to stare at a painting on the opposite wall. A bleeding medieval cross with a broken crown hanging from the top.

I start to walk back to the street, thinking maybe he's out there when an arm goes around my waist.

I scream as a hand covers my mouth and pulls me into darkness.

A loud *bang* pierces the air. The sound of a door slamming shut.

My pulse spikes, breathing tight, but instead of letting myself panic I snap into fight mode. Kicking behind me, I connect with a shin. The hold around me becomes tighter and my struggling becomes more manic.

I bite down on the hand, hard. My captor doesn't even flinch.

Instead, my hair is pushed aside, and cold words are whispered into the shell of my ear. "Careful, Baby Brooks. Pain turns me on."

My heart feels weighted in my chest and my face hot despite feeling frozen moments ago.

Noah.

Now, after hearing his voice, I feel like an idiot. Of course, it's Noah. My skin feels tight under his touch, recognizing him faster than my brain did. I panicked, blocking out all logic. For a moment I slump against his solid frame, only to pull away.

Spinning around, I push against his chest. "Don't do that! You scared me!"

My heart still pounds with no sign of settling down anytime soon.

Noah's chuckle is as dark as this unlit room. "But I enjoy it."

"And I enjoy cheesecake, but you don't see me…"

I trail off as the lights flicker on and I gasp as the room becomes illuminated.

We're in an art gallery.

I turn to face Noah, only to find him watching me. "Why are we here?"

Without waiting for an answer, I look away from Noah to see more of the *here*.

So many paintings line the walls. A few are lined with an

assortment of more modern paintings, but they're few and far in-between.

The real *pièce de résistance* are the paintings that wear their age with pride.

My fingers reach out to touch the golden ornate frame, stopping myself when I'm only a hairsbreadth away.

An unsettling feeling overcomes me.

This belongs in a museum.

Noah steps close behind me.

"Where did you get these?" I breathe.

"These were donated for a local show by members of this fine city. Reeve's hosting an event." A pause. "You're invited, by the way."

Answering becomes hard when I feel Noah's fingers curl around my shoulders.

"Why are you so quiet, Sayer?" His hands skim down my arms to link our fingers, pulling our joined hands behind my back. "Do I make you nervous?"

"Yes." My voice is soft, honest.

He smiles against my ear. "Do I scare you?"

"No," I answer without thinking. Still the truth.

Noah doesn't scare me. He intimidates me, but he doesn't scare me. Not like he should.

If anything, I'm scared by how much he intrigues me. I'm scared how he's the one person I should keep my barriers up for and yet they always shudder, threatening to fall when he's around.

Noah spins us around to face a portrait of two lovers draped in a red cloth with a blackish backdrop. "I think you're a liar." I feel his teeth graze my ear. "I think I do scare you," he rasps. I shiver as my core tightens. "Just not in the way you want to admit. I think you're scared of how I make you feel, craving it all the same."

My heart is erratic, hammering against my chest.

He's so close, his words are soft against my skin, edged with truths he knows I won't admit.

"You feel like you shouldn't want me." He lets my hands go only to grab my hips, pulling me closer to his body. "Like you should bury those desires deep down because they're not what you've been told to feel when it comes to me.

"Why?" His hands caress my hips in almost lazy movements stringing my body tight. "Is it because of your sister? Because you feel like honoring some unspoken code about sister's ex?"

I don't answer, not sure I can.

"We were never together. Not really. So your sweet, innocent heart doesn't have to have that stain on it." The bombshell he drops falls to the wayside as he presses against me and I feel his strained bulge against my backside and his hands continue their movements, creeping lower and lower with each pass.

"This painting," he whispers. "Was donated by your parents. It's called, *Secrets after Midnight.*"

My heart's beating like a lead hammer as Noah's hands still. I bite my lip to keep my protest quiet.

"Look at the way he holds her." His lips graze my neck.

Jumping, I do. Drinking the image in.

The man holds the back of her neck in a grip with so much passion as if he's afraid she'll disappear at any moment, while the woman's head is thrown back in ecstasy, leaning into his possessive touch. Though he's the one that holds her, it's clear in the frame that she's the one in control.

His passion would be nothing without her.

"What do you think their secrets are, Sayer?" His hands slip under my coat, slowly stripping it off.

"Do you think one of them was married?" My coat drops to the floor with a soft thud. "And that's why they met at night?

Why they're cloaked in red?" His fingers trace down my spine, flirting with the zipper of my dress. "Are they the sinners of their time?"

"Why are you asking me this?" I whisper to the painting.

"Because I want to see you let go, to see what you'd be if you give into the sins you are trying to fight." He kisses my neck, hard and quick. So quick I want it back. "Sin with me, Sayer."

My shallow breathing is the only answer I can muster. I lean into him though, and Noah holds me tight. "If I reach under your skirt, I'd feel how wet you'd be, wouldn't I, Sayer?"

The lights go out, bathing us in darkness once more.

I tremble under his fingers as they brush along my thigh, wishing he'd move them over, to add some friction to the need building between my legs.

Just when I think Noah's going to do something, his hands leave my thighs.

Nooo. Put them back. Put them back. Put them back.

"What do you feel?"

"What?" My mind is too hazy to focus on anything other than where I want his hands.

"What do you feel?" he asks again.

"Like I want you to touch me," I dare to say aloud.

"Where?" he questions, drawing his fingers in lazy strokes on my arm. "Here?"

I shake my head. No, not there. "Lower."

He moves his hand to my waist. "How about here?"

Again, I shake my head, whispering the same command as before. *Lower.*

Noah's hands finally reach the place I wish he had started at, tracing my entrance through my panties, making a satisfied noise when he feels how soaked the lace fabric is. "What about now?"

I nod, unable to think of anything other than his touch. A disappointed noise slips out when he withdraws his fingers instead.

"What about the contract?" There's no missing the mocking quality of his voice.

I might wake up regretting this, but for now…it feels right. "Screw the contract—"

With a growl he spins me around, mouth attacking mine as he grips my thighs. Picking me up, he pushes me against the painting. The frame digs into my spine and I don't care. Not when Noah's mouth captures mine.

A man like Noah doesn't kiss. He claims.

And claim me he does.

Never the gentleman, his lips are demanding and tongue greedy as he makes himself felt across every inch of my body.

I've never been kissed this way where I'm robbed of my senses and replacing it with sensation. Nothing exists outside of this, outside of Noah as his tongue meets mine, as his teeth nip my bottom lip. He's the poison in my veins. Destroying me with every touch.

And I crave every moment of it.

Commanding and rough, he pushes up the skirt of my dress. A rumbling in his throat as his finger pushes my panties aside, teasing my entrance.

"So wet," he growls with approval. "You're practically dripping."

He pushes his finger in and I gasp, grabbing onto his shoulder as my walls clench around him as he fills me down to his knuckle.

It's not enough. I want more.

"Move, Noah," I order, or at least try to, it comes out in a desperate plea. My nails dig into his shoulder and I feel his hardness pulse against my thigh.

He really does enjoy pain… And not just my own.

"You're at my mercy, Sayer." He withdraws his finger. "I could leave you like this, starved for my touch, for the release you want me to take. I could drop you and walk away."

No. He's not allowed.

Tightening my legs around him, I refuse to let that happen. Noah's been a fixture in my head for too many days. Years, if I'm really being honest.

I want this. I want him.

He flicks my clit, and my back arches, sending heat up my spine. "How much do you want me, Sayer?"

His thumb brushes my clit again, and a noise I've never known escapes my throat. He's playing me like an instrument, tuning me to the sweetest sound.

"Enough for me to hate myself a little," I moan. Loathing mixing with lust, a delightfully lethal combination.

That's it.

That's all Noah needs to hear as he moves inside me with angry thrust after angry thrust, adding another finger in.

"Oh—oh God." My head lulls back, hitting the painting as Noah stretches me, filling me.

His grunts are in tune with his thrusts. "So tight. So fucking tight," he growls, his fingers pumping inside me.

I move against his hand, biting my lip to conceal how much he's torturing me. Passion churns in my lower stomach, heating more and more. It threatens to boil to the surface.

We're unable to see much with it nearly pitch black, only a thin veil of light from outside seeps in, but Noah's still able to find my mouth, pulling, sucking at my bottom lip like it's a piece of candy. "You don't hide from me. Let me hear you."

I don't. I keep my moans to myself, satisfaction building alongside them—until Noah makes it impossible to stay silent.

His angry thrusts turn starved; a man who knows what he

wants. And he wants me to come undone. He drops me to my feet as he gets down on his knees.

I'm panting as he pushes my skirt up, his head disappearing under it.

His lips press a kiss through the lace of my panties, the humming he makes in satisfaction fill my ears, pulling at my core. "Oh God."

"God's not here, baby," he says, husky and still on his knees. His hands skate up the back of my thighs, grabbing my ass and hauling me to his mouth. "Just me."

He pushes my panties to my side, replacing the job his fingers started with his tongue.

I almost buckle at the first swipe, his tongue gracing my entrance, teeth grazing my clit. He's not shy about tasting me, quickening his pace to devour me.

I did this.

I'm the reason for the sounds he makes in the back of his throat.

I'm the reason his tongue is moving like I'm his last meal as he builds me up for my fall.

Unable to stay silent, unable to keep any thoughts, I rise and rise, screaming his name as I hit my climax, coming harder than I have with any lover.

Dimly, I'm aware of him crawling out from between my legs and his forearms cage me in on either side of my head.

I'm still feeling the aftershocks wrack my muscles as he swirls his fingers around my lips.

They're still wet…

"Taste what I did to you," he whispers and I'm too sated to put up a fight. Not that I want to.

Right now, I'd agree to anything from him.

My tongue darts out, tasting myself. It tastes like I want to do this again.

Noah's thumb brushes my cheek. My eyes flutter. "Oh, we're going to have a lot of—"

A ding interrupts.

Noah looks down at his watch and I hear him sigh. It sounds pissed. "We have to go."

Taking out his phone, he turns on the flashlight. Noah swipes my jacket off the floor and holds it out to me.

He doesn't offer any more information as I slip it on.

"What about you?" My throat feels raw from my screaming.

He shakes his head, but the flashlight catches his face, highlighting the hunger that still resides there.

I'm sure mine mirrors him.

Not looking happy, Noah leads me through the maze of walls, out of the gallery and back into the alley.

I don't ask any more questions, not really sure I'm able to form words yet. My brain is too rattled from what just happened.

Noah Kincaid just finger fucked me against a priceless painting. There was something daring and dirty about doing what we did in the complete dark.

I move to take a step when Noah grabs me and lifts me up by my thighs like he did inside and walks until my back is pressed to the alley's wall.

With a quick glance, I see he's lined me up so I'm dead center on the bloody cross.

Is this my crucifixion? Dying, only to rise anew?

"I thought you had to go," I whisper, wondering if the words can be heard over my thundering pulse.

"Not before I do this." He leans in close.

For a moment I think he's going to kiss me again.

C'mon, lungs. Breathe. Don't fail me now.

I can't pass out, not when I'm about to have the second best kiss of my life. The first being the one inside the gallery.

My eyes even close in preparation.

I closed my eyes for a kiss that was never going to come.

Opening my eyes, Noah holds something in his hand.

Between two fingers sits the contract. The contract I never took out of my bag…

"Give that back!" I lean forward to make the grab, but he stops me. By using his hips. He's still so hard.

"Uh-uh." Noah shakes his head, stuffing it into his back pocket. "It needs to be amended now."

I could argue, but I'd rather keep feeling like this.

Tomorrow, tomorrow I'll be angry at myself for breaking the one rule I told myself was the only one I couldn't. Only I didn't just break it, I obliterated it.

He drops me to my feet. I lean against the wall as he shoves the contract into his pocket.

"This changes things." He wraps a piece of my hair around his finger. "I own you now."

My spine goes ramrod straight. "You don't own me, Noah." Voice as cold as the night.

He smiles. "You sure about that?" He pulls at my hair. "Not five minutes ago you were screaming my name, begging for me."

"That doesn't mean you get to put a collar around my neck and tell me what to do."

His eyes flash and I realize what I said. He's probably picturing me with a collar in bed, spread out before him…

"Let me rephrase. I own your moans, your sweet lips, and your tight little pussy. As long as I'm here, no other man is going to touch you."

Noah's watch dings again and he glances at it before

returning his attention to me. "Run along now, Sayer. Jenkins will meet you by my car to take you home."

Part of me wants to demand he take me home. But I don't utter a word.

He's already dismissed me with those parting words, slipping his phone out of his jacket. Fingers scrolling over the screen.

I turn away with, *Night,* dead on my lips.

He's already walking away.

And he doesn't look back.

Not once.

He's long gone as I get in the car with the feeling of someone's eyes attached to me, making the hair stand on the base of my neck.

But when I look over my shoulder, no one's there.

Ten

Sayer

MY NIGHT OFF FROM NOAH COMES THE NEXT NIGHT. I'm walking across campus when I get a text telling me something important came up and we won't be going out tonight.

Annoyed, I clutched my phone as I fought the urge to throw it at a tree.

Of course. When I want a night off for physical exhaustion, Noah says no. But now when it's on his terms, it's okay.

I'm tired of it always being on his terms.

Pan greets me at the door as I walk into my apartment, returning home from one of the worst days of my life. And for once it has nothing to do with Noah.

Oh no.

My day was doomed from the start.

It started when my alarm didn't wake me up and I slept through my first class, which according to one of the girls I befriended was a big mistake. There was a surprise test.

So, I failed it by not being there.

Then, when I finally got to school, I didn't realize I was wearing two different boots until Brin pointed it out as we were leaving lunch.

Each foot had a shoe different in color and style. One was over the knee while the other came to my mid-calf. I don't know how it happened, how I got all the way to campus without noticing, but yeah, I did that.

And because the fates wouldn't leave me to missing a test and wearing two different shoes, I also spilled my ice coffee in my last class. Liquid went all over me and my notebook and the floor and the people on either side of me.

The professors had to stop the lecture to see why the guy next to me jumped up cursing. Class was put on pause while I rushed to clean it, using my cardigan to soak up most of it.

Never have I been so mortified.

With my apartment door firmly shut behind me, hiding me from the god-awfulness that has been today, I strip off my coat and sweaters before dropping my keys in the bowl.

Pan weaves between my legs, purring as I bend down to scratch under his chin. But he darts away when I try to pick him up.

Shaking my head, I take off my mismatched boots and slip out of my shirt, leaving me in only my skirt, tights, and see-through lace bra.

Wanting to get the day off me, I can't get out of my clothes fast enough.

I head into the kitchen to brew some tea—no more coffee for me today—unrolling my tights when I get there. These clothes are bad juju.

As I'm placing the kettle on the burner, I notice the clock on the stove blinks with the wrong time. Did we lose power today?

But the power is on, confirmed by the lit entryway light. I flip the switch in the kitchen, and it comes on too.

I frown, checking over my shoulder to see if the clock by the sink is blinking too, but it's not.

Shrugging it off as nothing more than a power glitch, I reset the time on the stove.

As I wait for the kettle to whistle, I twist my hair into a bun and my thoughts, naturally, run wild with Noah.

He's the drug and I'm the addict. Not caring about how bad he might be for me, I want him anyway.

I've fought so hard to stay away, to keep myself at a distance, knowing that one little taste could wreck me.

And it did.

Now I want more.

Ever since I was fourteen and he crashed into my life, he's called to me, my curiosity. A giant question mark I want to find the answer to. Who is Noah behind the distant persona he shows the world?

At school, no one could tell him no. In life, he didn't ask for permission before taking.

His world has no limit, a fact he likes to test all the time.

I envied Noah for the freedom he had.

It's been ten years and I'm still trying to find that kind of freedom.

After the kettle whistles and I've made my tea, I head into my bedroom to put on something comfy.

Pan follows close behind.

I'll never live with the kind of freedom Noah does, because I believe in rules, but that doesn't mean I can't find reckless abandon in another way.

A naked way.

Naked with Noah.

If he can ignite me with a single look, and unravel me with his fingers, imagine what he can do with his entire body.

I must sound crazy, like I've lost my mind—but have I?

Maybe I found it instead.

Noah's alpha to the asshole level, but unlike the guys from prep school that my parents deemed worthy of dating and the frat boys in college, he hasn't tried to make me do anything I haven't wanted.

The girl I want to be isn't afraid or ashamed of what she wants. And I want Noah.

Around me, on top of me, exploring and fucking me.

I want it all.

Getting cozy in my penguin onesie, I'm about to crawl into bed when Pan meows, head butting my thigh.

Hungry.

"All right, all right," I say after he does the same to my chin. "C'mon, tubs, let's go."

He practically trips me going to the kitchen.

I'm placing the bowl of food down when I spy something on my bookshelf.

A vase of flowers grab my attention.

Flowers that weren't there when I left this morning…

An intense ring pierces my ears and my stomach hollows out. I can't tear my gaze from the bookshelf across the room.

The bowl falls from my grip, crashing to the floor.

I barely hear it.

Black roses sit in front of the picture of me and Pan. Attached to the flowers is a red envelope with my name lettered across.

With shaky hands and unsteady feet, I move across the room until my fingers brush against the envelope.

I hiss, a thorn pricking my finger in the process. Drops of blood drip onto the envelope, which feels heavier than it should in my hand.

Part of me wants to believe it's from Noah, but my gut knows it's not.

My breath is uneven as I exam the sealed envelope.

Slowly, I open it.

A letter falls out.

And so do dozens of pictures.

They all scatter at my feet.

Bending down with a pounding heart, I pick one up. Dropping it immediately.

I can feel my pulse in my neck as I unfold the letter and read it.

Sayer, Sayer, Darling Sayer.

Why do you keep doing this?

You know he won't take care of you. Not like the way you want. They won't protect you. They're only after her. Once they get her, you'll be kicked to the curb.

He's using you. It disgusts me how blindly you let him embrace you. Let him touch you.

I thought you were different.

Keep going down this road, Darling Sayer, and you'll force my hand to step in before I'm ready.

But let it be known, I'm coming for you.

X

A sharp pain pierces my chest as my knees give out and I slide to the floor.

I can't breathe.

I can't breathe.

Who? Who's coming for me?

Why did they take these pictures that are scattered around me?

Pictures of me.

Pictures of Noah.

Pictures of me and Noah.

Some are from our first nights out together while others are from two nights ago, of us in Artwell Alley.

Of us *inside* the art gallery.

Numbly, I trace the edges of the photo that captures

Noah's fingers inside me. This one is grainier than the others, like it was taken from a distorted lens.

Or…

Oh God.

There was a window in the gallery. A small one, high up.

I keep flipping through the photos, unable to stop, wondering why, feeling like I'm going to throw up.

Why me?

Because of my sister? Because of Noah?

Both?

Questions assault me and I have no way of knowing the answer, only a small truth.

Right now it doesn't matter who took them. What matters is whoever did got into my apartment while I was gone.

My apartment feels tainted now.

Scrambling to my feet, I have to get out of here. I can't stay. I need to leave.

Now.

Grabbing my coat and my cat, I run out the door to hail a cab to Noah's club. It's closer than his casino.

I don't even know where he lives.

I suck in a pained breath, my ribs tight.

The club. I can go to Heathen's Hell.

I don't even know if he's going to be there, but I don't know where else to go. I have nowhere else to go.

My breathing doesn't return to normal until my apartment is long out of sight, and even then, my chest remains tight.

He's not here.

At least, according to the bartender I asked.

And I'm not saying he's lying, I just think he thought I was deranged.

I feel deranged.

I mean, I'm standing in a packed club wearing a penguin onesie and have a cat clutched to my chest after finding a stack of pictures and a cryptic letter in my apartment. If my eyes aren't a little crazy, I'd be concerned for my state of mind.

And now that I know Noah's not here, I don't know what I should do. Lost with where I could go.

Not back to my apartment, that's for sure. My skin still crawls with the knowledge of a stranger taking photos of me, following me around. *Going inside* my apartment.

I can't go home. I don't feel safe there.

I could've gone to Brin's, but I don't want this near her. Don't want to worry her.

The only other place I could think of is my parents' house. They're still in Europe so it wouldn't be too bad, except I hate it there. It's cold, detached. More like a museum. A house instead of a home.

But I can't stay on the floor. People keep bumping into and jostling me. Making me want to scream.

It's too much.

All too much.

This. Here. Now.

I feel myself shutting down like I did when my granddad passed, slipping deep inside myself where emotions are hard to reach. They get stowed away to deal with later.

Right now, I need a plan.

And I need one fast.

Pan hates our new setting, his claws cut into my skin like little hooks.

"I know, baby," I whisper into his fur. He doesn't relax.

"Lady." The bartender who told me Noah wasn't here,

comes back over. Leaning across the bar he snaps, "You can't stay here with that thing." He points an angry finger at Pan.

I glare, not caring for his tone. But I don't have the energy to argue. I don't even have the energy to stand. So I nod, veering away from the bar and go in search of new refuge.

I move about two steps when the bartender with salt and pepper hair appears. "Sayer."

I feel myself looking at him, but I'm not really seeing him. Not really focusing on anything.

"It's me, Hotch." Is that what his name is? "What're you doing here? Are you okay?"

"Looking for Noah," I feel myself say, not feeling my lips move.

"He's not here."

"I know."

Pan squirms in my arms. The music has gotten louder, the crowd rowdier. Hotch watches me retreat even more into myself and his eyes narrow when I jump at the feel of his fingers brushing my arm. "C'mon," he says gently. "I know where you can wait."

He leads me off the floor and down a hallway until we get to a dark wooden door. Slowly, he opens it and motions for me to go in.

Stepping into the room, I turn on the light and am greeted with the inner sanctum of Noah Kincaid.

I hear the door start to close and I whirl around. "Wait, this is Noah's office."

Hotch nods his head. "You can wait in here until you're feeling better."

"Isn't Noah going to care that I'm in here?"

"Do you care?" He raises a brow.

"No. Not really."

He nods. "You're safe here, Sayer."

I startle, not knowing if he realizes how much his words actually mean to me but by the look I catch on his face as he clicks the door shut, I'd say he does. I could cry. But I don't. Instead, I take in Noah's office.

His office is actually how I pictured it. Dark cherry hardwood floors that match the bookshelf walls, a high chandelier hangs from the ceiling.

In the middle of the room sits a large, wooden desk with carvings etched into the paneling of it.

Pan cries and I set him down on it.

He must feel as tired as I do because he collapses as soon as my hands leave him. His eyes closing.

Not sure if my eyes will ever want to close again, I take everything in.

Dominant. Intimidating.

Noah's office has an air of authority mixed with smoke.

It's quiet in here. Too quiet. And as it turns out the quiet is worse than the noise on the floor.

I take a seat in Noah's chair. My fingers anxiously tapping on the wood.

I don't know where else to go. Coming here felt right, but I had been banking on Noah actually being here. I know he said he had to take care of something, but I had hoped it would be over by now. I mean, it's quickly approaching ten o'clock.

I could text him to see where he is, but something holds me back. Like I don't want to admit I need his help.

Biting my lip, I take in how impersonal this office feels. He spends half his time here and yet, it looks like a showroom set up.

I spin around in the chair, wondering if there's anything in here that would give me a little insight as to who the real Noah Kincaid is.

But before I can so much as open one door, I hear the sound of voices in the hall.

They're muffled, but I'm able to make out deep timbre of Noah's voice and a small, softer voice of a woman.

I know Hotch said I could wait in here, but I don't want to have to explain to Noah what happened with another person present.

My limbs lock up as I quickly and quietly, run to shut the light off. With my phone light, I make my way back to the desk, grabbing Pan just as the door starts to open.

Swiftly, I dart under the desk, thanking the stars that it's so large. There's enough space under here for me to hide comfortably.

My cat's paw hits my chin. Meeting his annoyed eyes, I press a kiss to the top of his head. *Please don't make any noise, Pan.*

Normally, he's a quiet cat, communicating in passive-aggressive glares, but with the way today is going Pan could choose now to use his voice.

I'm frozen as footsteps come closer to where I hide, going as far as to hold my breath every few seconds.

Becoming as still and quiet as I can.

My granddad used to say that Harlow and I had opposite talents. While hers were on the flamboyant side, according to him, mine were more reserved. I made the perfect fly on the wall.

"Wasn't expecting you, Bridget." Noah's voice is a shot of whiskey, fire warming my cold, numb body.

My eyes close only to snap back open.

Right above me, the desk creaks from someone putting weight on it. My eyes widen. Noah must be leaning against the front. He sounds right on top of me.

"Sorry, there was a change of plans," a woman with an

accent says. It's not quite British but somewhere in that region if I were to guess. "Seamus was getting a little antsy."

I glare at nothing, not liking that her voice gets closer with each word.

Jealousy is a fickle bitch whose claws I don't appreciate digging into me at the sound of the other woman's voice, only for the claws to turn on me for feeling like this in the first place.

"I don't do surprises." It shouldn't please me as much as it does that Noah sounds pissed off. "And you can go tell Seamus that this isn't a bank, I don't do loans or payments. He either gives me the money in full or every day he doesn't, I tack on another five grand."

Never has he taken that kind of tone with me.

A piece of me swells with triumph. Ha.

Never have I felt so petty as I smile in satisfaction.

"Noah—"

"Bridget," he shoots back. "I owe you shit until Seamus pays me back, so get the fuck out of my office."

It's quiet in the room, but even from under the desk I can feel the tension.

Noah's probably wearing his neutral face. It makes people more uncomfortable. Completely unreadable.

After a few tense moments of silence, I hear a soft sigh and one set of feet walking toward the door. Before the door shuts, Bridget says, "He's not going to like you dismissing me."

"And I don't like that he thinks he can dick me around. He wants a meeting? He can come to me himself."

Quietly, the door shuts.

Leaving me alone with Noah.

eleven

Sayer

SEVEN STEPS.

That's all it takes for his long strides to go from the door to his desk.

Each step feels like a nail being hammered into my chest.

It's one thing to come into Noah's office when I didn't think he was here, to find some kind of solace and security after finding out what I thought had been stripped away, but it's another for Noah finding me uninvited here.

It can't possibly end well. He doesn't sound like he's in the best of moods right now.

The chair pulls out, his legs filling my vision.

Scuttling back, I plaster myself as much as I can into a single corner of the desk. I mean, it's huge down here, more spacious than I'd imagine a desk to be, but I don't know the radius of Noah's sitting stance, how far his thighs will spread out.

He could easily spread eagle and knock into me.

Something shifts above me causing my eyes to go up on reflex. By the time I realize I'm not physically capable of seeing through the wood, it's too late.

A hand grabs my ankle.

A scream escapes my throat.

And Pan escapes my hold, running past Noah's crouching body.

His glasses are dipped low on his nose, letting me see how pissed he really is.

"Jesus Christ." He rubs his, undoubtedly ringing, ear. The underside of the desk is like a megaphone, amplifying my scream. Glaring, he adds, "What the fuck, Sayer."

I didn't mean too, it kind of just slipped out. Excuse me for being a little on edge tonight.

"You scared me." Not moving from my spot.

"What the hell are you doing here." It's not phrased as a question. "And why is your cat running around my office?"

"Your club was overwhelming. Pan didn't like it."

"What the fuck is he doing here in the first place?"

"Looking for you. But you weren't here."

"So you leave. You don't come to my office." He rubs the bridge of his nose.

"Hotch told me I could wait here."

A sound of annoyance rumbles from the back of his throat until he sees the expression on my face. He sighs. "C'mon. Get out from under there."

He stands.

I don't move.

"Sayer. It's best not to test me right now."

Sensing he's right, I heed his words and crawl out from the desk as dignified as I can. But before I can stand up, Noah's hand goes to my shoulder. Stopping me.

He gives me a cruel smile. Enjoying this, me on my hands and knees before him.

I wait for Noah to step aside so there's enough room for me, but like the gentleman he's not, he doesn't so much as twitch a brow.

Noah's stiff as a statue as I stand.

We're so close my breasts graze the buttons of his shirt.

And with every breath, our chests brush together. It sends fireworks across my skin, shooting off in all directions.

His lips give a small twitch on his otherwise hard face as he takes in my attire. "Got all dressed up for me, I see."

"Don't shame my pajamas." I cross my arms over the penguin's chest.

Again, his lips fight to form a smile. "I would never," he teases.

Wait.

Teases?

I can deal with a snarky Noah. Even a surly Noah. But a teasing Noah?

That's a level I have yet to unlock. I don't know what to do. It takes me several minutes to form any kind of response. "Sure you wouldn't."

Oh my God, that's the best my short-circuited, slightly traumatized brain could come up with?

Someone please put me out of my misery.

Noah chuckles, acknowledging how lame it was. "You can do better than that."

"I really can," I admit. "You just threw me off."

"How?" He sounds genuinely intrigued.

"You teased me. Usually you just insult me."

"No, I don't."

I raise a brow. "You really do live in a different world."

"Excuse me?" He matches my brow rising with one of his own.

"I said," raising my voice, "you really do live in a different world. You've insulted me so many times since we fell into this little bargain." I pause. "You know what. I shouldn't have even come here."

Why did I think coming to see him would make this day better?

I try to move. He sidesteps with me.

With narrow eyes, I try again. Only to get the same results.

"Let me by, Noah."

"Why did you come here?

"Forget it. I changed my mind." Looking down at my toes, I mumble, "I keep wanting you to be someone you're not."

It's quiet, save for Pan's purring as he explores Noah's office, and I have no doubt Noah heard me.

"Who do you want me to be?"

"I don't know," I whisper.

He stares at me and for a moment that cold, chiseled mask he usually has in place slips away and I see something move across his features. Until I blink and it's gone as he reaches for the zipper of my onesie.

Playing with it, he pulls it farther down until the peaks of my breasts are exposed.

His eyes heat when he sees I'm not wearing a bra.

I try to pull away, but his hands glide down my sides to my thighs.

He lifts me up, igniting my body. Fire he feeds as he places me on the desk, settling between my legs.

Noah wraps a lock of hair around his finger as he asks, "Now. Tell me why you were hiding under my desk."

When I don't answer right away, he tugs on the strand with enough force that my lips part. "I came looking for you. As I've said. Now I wish I hadn't."

His lips thin. "And you decided to wait under my desk?"

"It's quite comfortable."

He doesn't laugh.

"Who was that?" I ask, hoping to distract.

Noah's brow raises, seeing through me, but he plays along anyway. "A friend."

"It didn't sound very friendly."

"And how should it sound?" he asks, running a finger down my cheek.

"I don't know." I push past the lump in my throat. "Perhaps, *friendly*?"

"Mhm," he hums. His finger traces the pulse in my neck. "Perhaps."

I start to nod as his finger wanders lower. Oxygen leaves my lungs as he leans in close. Lips skimming my jaw.

My fingers curl around the lip of the desk.

"Perhaps, you'd rather I greet her like this." He pulls at the neckline of my onesie as his lips move along my jaw. "Maybe make her comfortable like this."

"I'd prefer you didn't," I whisper.

His lips stop moving. "And why's that?"

Not waiting for my answer, he hoists my legs around his hips, pressing me close.

I feel him in every iota.

"Maybe," his lips hover over mine. "I should greet her in a way I've wanted to since she first walked in my club after six long years away..."

My eyes skip to his. *What?*

All coherent thoughts leave as his head angles toward mine only to have him freeze above me. His gaze locked on my chest.

Naturally.

Huffing in annoyance, I snap my fingers. "I'm up here."

Noah doesn't respond.

"Noah." I move to touch his face when, like a viper, his hand catches my wrist.

"You're bleeding."

"What?"

"You're. Bleeding."

His free hand traces the small flecks of dried blood on my collarbone.

I yank my hand from him, disentangling my legs from his waist as well. "I'm fine."

Noah hasn't stopped tracing the blood. I can feel him holding back. "Why are you bleeding, Sayer?"

I shake my head, silently begging him not to make me answer. I'm unsure I could find the right words.

"Sayer." He cups my cheek.

Something flops to the floor and we pull apart to see Pan has knocked over my purse, the contents spilled on the floor.

Noah breaks away to pick it up and I'm quick to follow, rushing forward to gather everything before he can see…

The envelope.

His fingers wrap around it and without being told, he tears it open.

The photos fall out first, fanning across the desk. Touching me.

I recoil away from it as Noah, with slow, deliberate movements picks up the letter, reading it.

As his eyes move, his hands tighten around the paper. Wrinkling the edges.

I'm helpless as I watch his eyes go from the letter to the pictures.

The letter. The pictures. The pictures, the letter.

His face remains blank while he takes it all in.

The only sign he's feeling any emotion at all is by the cracking of his neck and the widening of his stance.

It's not until he's shredding the paper, making it snow flecks of paper onto the floor that he shows how pissed off he is.

Chest heaving, he asks, "Did they leave anything else?"

"Flowers," I whisper.

"Did they have anything in them?"

"N-no." I didn't even think to. They're just flowers. What could be hidden in them? "I ran out of my apartment as soon as I read it. Coming here."

Noah gives a short nod, not elaborating.

Pan meows, pawing at Noah's leg.

"That's why I brought Pan. I couldn't leave him there."

Noah nods again, barely hearing me.

"What would they hide in it?" I ask softly. My first thought goes to a bomb.

"A recording device. A camera."

"A bomb?"

He shrugs. "Sure."

"That doesn't make me feel any better." I wrap my arms around my waist.

"It's not supposed to."

I grimace at him. "Gee. Thanks."

"I didn't say it to comfort you, Sayer." He moves toward me. I look up at him feeling lost. I feel tired and lightheaded and I just want someone to hug me.

Screw it!

I throw my arms around Noah's neck, thinking he'd immediately push me away, only to be thankfully surprised when his arms wrap around my waist and I'm being held tight.

"You're safe."

My body deflates, not knowing I needed to hear those words come from Noah to relax. Knowing it's true.

Noah rubs my back in reassuring circles. I think he's waiting for me to lose it and cry and if that's true, he's going to be massively disappointed. I haven't cried in a very long time.

I didn't even cry at my granddad's funeral. I'm not crying now.

"What're we going to do, Noah?"

"I don't know." He sounds angry about it. "But I'm going to keep you safe."

"How? Will you get better security at my apartment or… what? Why are you looking me like that?"

"Sayer." By the way he says my name, I know I'm not going to like what's coming next. "You're not fucking going back to that apartment."

Twelve

WORDS CAN BE DEADLIER THAN ANY WEAPON AND more often than not, my favorite to wield. I love to watch them fly toward their target, curious on how the recipient will react.

I physically see when they hit Sayer.

Her eyes narrow, lips purse tight "Excuse me?" She's not happy.

My lips twitch.

It's cute how she thinks it's intimidating. She looks like a disgruntled penguin thanks to that ridiculous *thing* she's wearing. Twenty-four but dressed like she's ten.

Did I really think she was the best option to lure out her sister?

Maybe she wasn't the best choice, any girl would've done, truthfully, but I *wanted* Sayer.

And now someone has her scared and frazzled. Her normally pale skin has faded to alabaster. Her hands give a slight shake while her eyes have gone dull. I can't stand it.

Someone has stolen her luster, her shine. Those pictures burn in my mind but it's the letter. The letter that pushed me over the edge. Admittedly, I shouldn't have shredded it. If I were thinking rationally, I'd save it for Thea to run it through her computers to see if she could match the handwriting.

But that's what Sayer does to me, stealing all rationale.

"Noah," she snaps when I don't answer her question. "What do you mean?"

"You're moving in with me." Thought that was obvious when I said she wasn't going back to her apartment. Peering at her more closely, I ask, "Did you hit your head today?"

"No," she glowers.

"Huh." I shrug. "You're just slow on the uptake today it seems."

She calls me a colorful name under her breath that has me grinning. I love that I bring out this side of her. The one that curses and fights. It feels like I'm unraveling her piece by piece. And I'm captivated to see who's left when I'm done.

"No," she repeats, arms crossed.

"No, what?" I pluck a white hair from my suit, glaring at her cat who's busy licking his asshole. *Creature from hell.*

"I'm not moving in with you." Her voice shakes and I don't think it's from fear. "No, absolutely not."

My grin grows. "This is non-negotiable, Baby Brooks. You *are* moving in."

Sayer shakes her head. Her mouth opening in what I'm sure is another protest, but I tune her out as I take out my phone and send off a quick text. Complain and fight all she wants, it *is* happening.

This isn't the first time this lamely named X person has tried to contact Sayer. A couple nights ago when I was picking her up to go to a charity auction, there was a note that was slid halfway under her front door. I snatched it up and read what was inside, not caring that it could've been something personal.

It was personal, all right, but in a way that was much like the letter Sayer got tonight. Personal in a way that would rattle her. And just like tonight, I got rid of the letter. Both times I wasn't thinking and instead listened to the fiery rage inside me instead of logic, disposing of it while texting Thea, the tech wiz extraordinaire to get me video surveillance of Sayer's apartment.

This is what Sayer does to me. Rattles me into listening to my emotions instead of my head.

Emotions make for the weak.

"Noah!" Sayer snaps, frustration bleeding in her tone. "Are you even listening to me?"

"No." I slip my phone back into my coat pocket before looking at her. Her gray eyes melt with heated silver, showing how frustrated she is. She used to be so prim and proper, never without a strand of hair out of place and seeing her now with strands sticking this way and that gives me a deep satisfaction knowing I can make her unravel.

She makes a noise in the back of her throat that I think is supposed to be a growl but sounds more like a clogged esophagus.

She's fallen so far since I last saw her, but I'm more drawn to her than ever. Captivated even. My eyes can't stop drinking her in when we're together, always discovering something new.

Take the first time I saw her. I noticed all the major changes, how she had changed from a shy teenager to a confident woman. I soaked up the obvious changes, but every run-in that's followed has been the small, minute details synching my attention.

Today it's the little crease that forms between her brows as she glares at me. I like it. Like that her face moves, unlike the Botox injected Barbies of this town.

"Noah!" She's three seconds away from stomping her foot. The crease deepens.

"Yes?"

"You're doing it again."

"Doing what?"

"Not listening to me." She tries to keep the hurt out, but I hear it. Sayer's spent most of her life with her voice not being heard.

"I feel like you're not the one listening here. I don't even know why we're having a discussion when there's nothing to discuss." My phone vibrates and I'm reaching for it when Sayer stops me.

"I swear to God Noah if you reach for that phone, I will yank it from your hand."

I'd like to see her try, but my hand falls to my side. "You came here for help, right?" I don't wait for an answer. "Well, this is the only way I can protect you properly."

"You can't just hire a security team or something?"

"Would that make you more comfortable? Having strangers following you around, living in an apartment you no longer feel safe in?"

She swallows before biting at her nail. She won't answer, not when she knows I'm right.

"You should be thanking me."

"For what?" she asks around her nail but when I don't answer she pulls it away. "You're joking."

She eyes me, waiting for a punch line.

I don't give her one.

Walking to my desk, I unbutton my suit jacket before sitting down. Once comfortable, I level Sayer with a serious look. "For offering you my place. No one is hardly allowed over, let alone live there."

One time my cousin was visiting, and I made him get a hotel. When I hook up with women, it's either in this club, a storage closet or I go back to her place.

My space is for me. No one else.

So Sayer should feel honored that I'm being this generous.

At least, that's what I keep telling myself to distract from the unfamiliar pang in my chest at the idea of Sayer being in danger.

Sayer stands in the middle of my office, wringing her hands in front of her. The sight alone stirs up that discomfort of wanting to take care of her. To comfort her. To distract her.

To hold her in my arms again.

Getting up, I walk around my desk to meet her.

"Are you scared to live with me, Sayer?" I tilt my head toward hers. "You are, aren't you?"

She doesn't answer, too busy worrying at her bottom lip.

With my thumb I pull it from her teeth, tracing it slowly, watching as her eyes start to close only to snap back open.

Her head jerks back. Remembering herself, this place, and me. "Why do you want me to?"

"I don't appreciate someone messing with you." Her eyes narrow. "And if you move in, well…" I shrug. "It can only help my plan."

One stone, two birds.

She slips from my hold, crossing her arms. A barrier to keep me at a distance.

I frown.

"Do you think this was from Harlow?" Walking to my desk, her hand scoops up shredded flakes of the letter, letting them fall through her fingers to the floor.

My jaw clenches at the mess, but I force myself to ignore it. "It's not her handwriting."

"She could've had someone else write it."

I raise a brow at the conviction in her voice. "Do you want it to be your sister?"

"I'd rather it be her than someone I don't know."

Understanding, I nod. It's easier to prepare when you know your enemy.

But in this case, it's not Harlow.

I'd bet The Underground on it.

"It could be anyone," I tell her. "A person at your school, someone I've done business with. Or a stranger you glanced at when at the grocery store. It could be anyone," I repeat. "Except Harlow."

Something in her face changes. It's small, but I still see it.

She draws me in like an open book sitting on a table, walking by I can't help but take a peek, getting drawn in by the language of words written.

Lyrical, powerful, even beautiful. Sayer's a book I want to explore more of. To have the pages memorized beneath my hands.

Before I can ask what's working in that dangerous mind of hers, my door opens, and Reeve and Gabe walk in.

"You rang?" Reeve's eyeing Sayer in a way that if it was anyone else—including Gabe—I'd throw their face into the wall, but Reeve isn't a threat. Not to me when it comes to Sayer.

"Ms. Brooks here needs an escort to my place. She'll also need some of her things relocated there for the time being."

"Noah…" she starts.

I turn to face her, giving her my full attention. "I don't know why you're fighting this, Sayer, we both know who's going to win."

I like that she fights me.

In fact, I crave it.

It's refreshing, being challenged. It doesn't happen often anymore. The times where I can verbally spare with a person is few and far between these days except when Sayer's around. Always keeping me on my toes, always has—since she was a teenager.

But that doesn't mean she's going to win.

"What about my cat?"

I look to the creature in question as it tries to crawl into the bottom shelf of the bar cart I have in the corner of my office.

"Not coming." My tone is firm. "There's only one pussy moving in and it's not covered in hair."

Her cheeks redden at my reminder of last night. I wonder if her thoughts jumped to when I got down on my knees before her and became very familiar with the sounds she makes as I unraveled her.

Sounds I wouldn't mind hearing again.

Low chuckles rumble behind her and with a look of panic, she looks at Reeve and Gabe, forgetting they were in the room.

"Reeve can take it," I tell her, watching his smile curl higher.

"I'd love to." He stares at Sayer, who's shaking her head furiously. He walks across the room and scoops the thing up.

"No, absolutely not." She shakes her head.

"Non-negotiable. I don't like animals, remember?"

"You don't like me either," she reminds me.

Oh, that's where she's wrong. There's a lot that comes to mind when I think of Sayer Brooks and not liking her isn't one of them.

I ignore her, focusing on my men. "Take her back to my place."

The look Sayer gives me is full of defiance as she crosses her arms over her chest, rooting herself in her spot. "You can speak like I'm in the damn room."

Keep fighting me, Sayer, I'm going to love watching you break.

"Fine." I give her my hard stare. "Take Sayer here back to my place."

Reeve snickers as they move to flank either side of her and she steps away from them. Toward me.

The rest of the distance between us erases with my steps.

"Do you even want to go back there? To your apartment where a creep with a hard-on for taking pictures of you can get in? To the place where you desperately ran away from?"

She shivers, not denying it. I see the moment she lets go of the fight inside her, letting the exhaustion of the day take over instead. Her tense shoulders deflate and the worry lining her face shifts to fatigue.

I reach up to cup her cheek, touch the fallen strands of her hair, I don't know—I never get to find out. Without another word she turns and leaves my office, Gabe and Reeve right behind her.

She goes quietly and willingly but the look in her eye as she does?

A kiss of retribution will be waiting for me when I get home.

No more than twenty minutes later I'm closing out of my computer. Shit hasn't gotten done since Sayer left my office.

Ten minutes ago I got a text from Gabe that said they made it to my place and she was in a mood. Reeve apparently wouldn't stop taunting her about taking her cat.

They're gone now and Sayer's alone in my place.

I slip out the back entrance, down a cramped, narrow alley, the same time my phone rings.

"What?" I bark in answer.

"Why did I just hear that you moved Sayer into your apartment?" Thea sounds concerned on the other line and I'd bet five grand it isn't for me.

"Because I moved Sayer into my apartment."

"Noah…"

"Don't want to hear it, Thea."

"Well tough shit."

Oh, she sounds angry. Keeping the phone pressed to my ear, I unlock my sports car and slip in.

"What do you think you're doing?"

"Killing two birds with one stone. Someone's after her, Thea."

She's quiet, already aware of this. I've had her pull up surveillance around Sayer's building. I had hoped that was what she was calling about. Not to give a heavy, judgmental sigh in my ear instead.

"You're going to break the poor girl."

"That's the plan."

Another deep sigh.

Thea doesn't get it though.

I don't want to break Sayer as a person. I want to break her in another way. It involves her naked and withering beneath me. I want to break her down sexually, stripping her bare.

"I like her, Noah. I've always liked her. She's not like Harlow. You can't play the same games you do with her. She's too sweet for that."

The more Thea lectures me, the more my teeth grind. By the time I'm able to push out words they're a rumble in my chest. "I know."

Thea's quiet on the other end, no doubt able to feel my anger from across town. "Just—just be careful with her."

My hand tightens around the steering wheel and I rev the engine around a slow ass fucker, the tires tattooing the asphalt as I weave through traffic. "I'll treat her how I fucking want, Thea."

Click.

I end the call and toss the phone in the passenger seat with a growl. I don't take kindly to others telling me how I should act. Never have. But when it comes from a person who knows me as well as Thea does, who has seen me at my absolute lowest and isn't afraid to call me out on any bullshit, it sets me off even more.

If I wasn't a stubborn ass, I'd probably admit it's because they're right. But I am, so I won't. Sayer is mine to deal with and no one else gets a say in shit.

I've waited for years to have her. I'm not letting her go now.

"You bastard!"

I'm barely out of the elevator that leads into the foyer of my penthouse when a plate crashes into the wall next to me.

I fix my glare on the five-seven angry blonde standing a few feet in front of me with one of my expensive as shit bottles of wine dangling from her dainty fingers and one of my plates in her other.

Murder blazes in her eyes.

"Honey, I'm home." My voice deadpan.

"You bastard," she shouts again, winding up the plate. I lunge forward and grab her wrist before she lets it go.

"So you say." I keep my voice low, lethal in deliverance, and she shivers against me, the heat in her eyes shifting to another kind. "But what, pray tell, did I do this time?"

"Where are all my clothes?"

"In your room."

"No." She grits her teeth. "They are not."

My lips curl up. "All the pieces that matter are."

She moves to whack me, but I'm still holding her wrist captive, so she just leans closer into me. I can smell the wine on her skin. Drunk. Sayer's drunk. An angry one at that.

Why does that appeal to me so much?

"It's the middle of winter, Noah, and all that's there are gowns and dresses that barely cover my butt!"

"I know."

Her face pinches and a soft thud connects with my shin.

My lips curl even higher. "That was cute, Baby Brooks."

Her lips snarl and it looks like she's constipated. "It was supposed to hurt."

I stare at her, she stares at me. The anger in her slate-gray eyes shift into a different fire, one that burns brighter. Hotter. They dart to my lips as she bites hers.

Fuck, she's destroying me, even without her touch.

She doesn't want to want me. And I shouldn't want to touch her as much as I do.

But damn if I do. Especially when I see how much she wants me, but she's letting her fear get in the way.

Fear of wanting this. She was bred for perfection and I'm the farthest thing from it.

Maybe that's why I can't stop myself. She's the light to my dark, the angel to my devil. I want to take what makes her pristine and ruin it, to have her revel in sin with me.

Letting go of her wrist, I grab her ass and haul her closer. I don't know what it is about her that makes me want to eliminate all the distance between us. She's a siren who calls to me.

A gasp leaves her as my hand continues to glide down her body.

She makes me want things that I don't want for more than a night, and never from the same woman, but she makes me want to keep coming back for more. And I hate it. But I chase it all the same.

My hands coast down her body, committing every inch to memory, a map for me to explore later.

Her eyes flutter closed and her fingers dig into my shirt, my chest. A smile slowly curves onto my face as my hand goes lower and lower until I feel what I'm after. And I don't hesitate to take.

Sayer's gasp is sweet music for my ears as I yank the wine bottle from her hand. Her eyes snap open to glare at me. I bring the bottle to my lips with a smirk.

"Let's play a game," I say.

"Wh—what?" she stutters.

"A. Game," I speak slowly.

She eyes me suspiciously as I take another pull from the expensive ass bottle of wine I hadn't planned on opening yet. "What kind of game?"

Without answering, I walk through my open floor plan until I'm in the living room. Quiet footsteps let me know Sayer's following. I knew she would. Her curiosity is like a ball of yarn, toy with it a little and the whole thing will unravel.

I watch her approach from the comfort of my couch. She stands on the other side of my glass coffee table, hands on her hips.

"What kind of game?" she repeats.

I put the bottle on the table between us. "A game I intend to win."

She quirks a brow. Arms crossed and waiting for elaboration.

"Ever played Never Have I Ever?" I brace my elbows on my knees.

Sayer's brow stretches higher in surprise. "Yeah. In college. Aren't you a little old for that though?"

I smirk. "We're not playing it. But it's something similar. I don't know you anymore, Sayer, and I don't like letting strangers into my home." I see a dozen questions in her eyes, none of them louder than *did you ever know me?* Something growls in my chest with a resounding *yes*. "So, we're going to play Answer or Drink. I'm going to ask you a question and you'll have to—"

"Answer or Drink," she finishes, ignoring the narrowed look I give her for interrupting.

I expect her to ask more questions, like why I want to do this, what's the point, or any other trivial shit she could throw my way, but once again, Sayer surprises me by nodding her head. "Okay, let's play."

My mouth opens, the first question on my tongue when Sayer decides to interrupt, again. "But only if I get to ask some questions of my own."

How did I ever think she'd make this easy for me?

I lean back on the couch. "By all means, then, ladies first."

"Where are the rest of my clothes, Noah? How long am I to stay here?"

"Uh-uh." I wave my finger in the air. "That's two questions."

"So pick one and answer it."

"My, my, someone is feisty tonight." I eye the bottle of wine. "How much did you drink before I came home?"

She crosses her arms over her chest. "Is that your question? Because if it is, you're cheating."

Oh, if she only knew how much of life I did cheat…

With my eyes locked on hers, I lean over to grab the wine and take a healthy sip. Her eyes harden.

"Your clothes are in hiding. My turn." I put the bottle back down. "Why'd you come home?"

She startles, not expecting that question. Her eyes go wide, and she looks away briefly.

I can't help but wonder if anyone has asked her that since she got here. Has no one else questioned how she was gone for six years and then randomly decided to transfer to Haven Harbor University in her last semester?

Pregnant silence pulls between us to the point where I

don't think she's going to answer and I'm about to nudge the bottle in her direction when she whispers in a choked up voice, "My granddad."

I freeze, my steady heart misses a beat. Broken. She sounds so broken that even the blackness inside me aches for her. She won't meet my gaze and I know if she did her eyes would be shiny with unshed tears.

Her granddad was her best friend, the only person related to Sayer to love her the way family was intended to.

"My granddad is the reason I came back," she says it again, more to herself than me.

I shift against the couch until my knees practically touch the coffee table, compelled with the desire to comfort her but my hands hang uselessly at my sides. If I was ever made for comfort, it was taken from me in the plane crash that took my family.

I have no right to comfort Sayer. Not about this.

But the way she stares at me when her eyes finally lift from the floor makes me wish I was a different man. A better man.

"It's stupid, isn't it?" she asks. "To move back for someone who is no longer here."

I shake my head. If I don't know how to comfort with my arms, I sure as shit don't know how to with my words but for reasons that only accompany me when it comes to Sayer, I want to try.

"It's not stupid," I tell her. My voice has as much emotion as a robot. I clear my throat to try again when my phone goes off. I almost ignore it, but it could be Thea with an update on who left the note in Sayer's apartment.

The text is from Thea, but it's not about the note.

Got a hit on Harlow. Want the coordinates?

thirteen

Sawyer

If Haven Harbor is my prison, Noah's penthouse apartment is the cell that keeps me contained with its floor to ceiling windows that open up to the skyline of the city, showing me all that I don't feel a part of.

Beautiful and distant. Matching the man I'm now living with but haven't seen since my first night here.

That was three days ago.

Three days.

Three days where he got a text that had him storming out of his apartment, leaving me alone to stew in my loneliness and anger.

And oh, I'm a firework waiting to go off. Especially when I know he's been home. Home and avoiding me.

His beautiful black and gray chessboard with the white and red pieces says as much. It sits on his industrial glass coffee table and remained untouched the night I was moved in, but by the next morning, when I came down the sleek, metal floating staircase, I noticed that a red pawn had been moved.

I stared at it for what felt like hours, knowing exactly what it was. An invitation. One I readily accepted. Now I'm locked in a chess game that's moving at a snail pace, not that I mind the speed. It's been years since I played the game, so my rusty talent is thankful I'm able to ease back into it.

Rusty or not, I've never lost a game of chess and I'm not about to let Noah beat me.

This game means more than winning though. As much as it pains me to admit it.

It's been my only line of communication with him since he decided to go ghost on me. I don't get that man.

First, he all but forces me into moving in with him, then he hides all my clothes except for the most impractical, illogical pieces in my closet, *then* he drags me into playing a game where he wanted me to spill my secrets only to leave me angry and buzzed and wanting to break another one of his plates when his sculpted, suit wearing back disappeared inside the elevator.

The house felt quiet, with a stillness that only came with being alone, but Noah's presence is a ghost I feel every moment I'm here. It's in his décor, which is dark and cold. Metals and blacks that make it feel as welcoming as a cave. Even the floor to ceiling windows aren't enough to make this place feel bright enough.

The ground is black tile under gray rugs, a black marble mantle sits above an electric fireplace that is bordered by smooth gray stone. Blacks, grays, and whites with splashes of reds thrown in here and there, Noah's home is sleek and industrial with a touch of gothic flare and fits him so properly.

I couldn't imagine him living somewhere with plants and bright colors. Everything has a place, or it did until I moved in.

It's only been three days, but I've made sure to leave as much of my stuff in Noah's space as I can. Textbooks on the counter, shoes and coats by the elevator. Used wine glasses on the coffee table. Whatever I could, whatever I had here, was left out to annoy Noah, the clean freak that he is.

I even left a bra on the couch last night.

Call it spiteful, call it whatever, I had thought that if I

dirtied up his quarters, sprinkling traces of me throughout, he'd remember that you know, I live here now.

No such luck.

Though this morning I did find my bra in the middle of the chessboard, carefully placed on it to not disturb our game, and nothing else.

I saw red when I spotted it, and not just because that was the color the bra was, but because he's purposely ignoring me and I don't know why.

Actually, I do, and it twists my stomach to admit it. This is just for show, an act, and I'm only needed when it's my part to play.

Nothing is real, except these feelings budding inside me say differently. I've grown so used to seeing Noah every day that an attachment I didn't allow has formed and now a hollow is carved in my chest with him being gone.

I miss him. I miss his brooding face, his piercing eyes. I miss his presence and the constant hum in my blood when he's around.

And that's what's making me angry. How fucking dare he.

He moves me into his *penthouse* and makes me feel these things for him after years of convincing myself my childhood crush would stay in the past and then just leave. Poof. Without a word. Which is why I didn't stop at leaving my things around his place to get his attention.

Oh no, I blew up that boy's phone as well.

The first day of him being gone I waited until it was around nine at night to send him a text message. He never replied. He also never replied to the slew I sent after either.

Not that I expected him to respond to the last one, which I so eloquently typed: FUCK YOU KINCAID!

But seriously, fuck him.

I was a prisoner in his home without my cat.

And I'm sick of it.

Is Noah even looking for who broke into my apartment? Is he doing anything to help me?

I wouldn't know because *he isn't here!*

So here I sit on his supple leather couch with my laptop on a throw pillow. My frustration is evident with every word I type for this paper. My fingers ache from how hard they're smashing each key. I don't even know what I'm actually typing, it's hard to focus on that when my mind keeps wandering elsewhere.

He uproots my life only to be a ghost that walks his own home.

It's quiet save for the keyboard clicking away when the elevator to the penthouse opens.

Is today the day I'm finally graced with his royal assness?

A strange sense settles over me. My fingers slow, unable to focus on anything aside from my straining ears, desperate to hear the sound of Noah's aggressive steps.

The man always moves like he's pissed at the world, out to rectify vendettas.

But I don't hear those piercing, lethal steps. I try to ignore the swell of disappointment at the sound of lighter, bouncing steps—definitely not Noah—as I twist around to see who's arrived.

Thea le Veck.

She walks like she owns the place, smiling when she sees me. Her wild hair bouncing with each step.

"Sayer!" She draws closer to me.

"Hi, Thea."

She plops down on the couch next to me, stretching her legs out on the coffee table and crosses her ankles. "How are you liking your stay at the Kincaid Hotel?"

I fight a smile, the first time my facial muscles have

worked like that in days. "Their customer service could use some work."

She laughs. "Yeah, Noah can be as welcoming as a prickly cactus."

I stare at her, wondering why she's here. I haven't seen her since that party where I stole a bottle of scotch. That was two weeks ago and now she's acting like we're the best of friends. "Don't take this the wrong way, Thea, but what're you doing here?"

If Thea's offended by my question, she doesn't show it. Uncrossing her ankles, she twists to face me. "I came to check on you."

"Why?" *To see if I'm going to run away?*

"Because I had a feeling you were bored out of your mind."

I eye her skeptically. It's not that I don't trust Thea, it's that I don't know her well enough to understand her motives.

"I'm right, aren't I?" Thea grins when I don't respond.

"I haven't had time to be bored." And it's true, I haven't. Having Noah not around has been good on my schoolwork, which was starting to fall to the wayside from all the nights I had been spending with him.

Thea's grin shifts into a frown. "That sounds boring in itself."

"I'm actually working on a paper." I reach for my laptop. "So if you don't mind—"

"Actually, I do." She takes the laptop from me before I can even process she moved. I stare as she puts it on the coffee table, next to the chessboard. "Let's have a party."

I blink. Surely, I heard her wrong. "Excuse me?"

"A party. Let's have one." She gets up from the couch.

I'm almost afraid to ask, "Where?"

"Here, silly." She stares down at me with her hands on her hips.

I remain sitting.

The idea doesn't thrill me as much as it does her. "Yeah, no thank you."

"C'mon, Sayer!" She pulls me off the couch. "It'll be fun!"

"For who?"

"You?"

Yeah, not likely. "Parties aren't my thing."

"Parties are everyone's thing," she argues.

"Not if you don't like human interaction."

Thea shakes her head. "You're an odd one, Sayer Brooks."

I've been called a lot of things in my life—timid, mute, goodie goodie—but never odd. The word rolls over in my head.

Odd. Different. Unique.

I don't hate it.

Walking away from Thea, I head for the kitchen. She follows close behind, perching herself on the counter, watching silently as I sift through Noah's wine collection, the one I've been making an impressive dent in.

The man has quite the extensive selection. And someone might as well appreciate it.

"You don't want a glass?" Thea watches with her dark brown eyes as I bring the open bottle to my lips after uncorking it.

"Nope." I pop the P for dramatic flair. There's a chance I already drank a bottle before she showed up, before starting my paper. "And I won't have you judge me for it."

She holds up her palms. "No judgment here. Just curiosity. Didn't your mother teach you class?"

I can't help but laugh. "Oh yes, she did. She'd have a heart attack if she could see me now." I jump on the counter opposite of her, extending the bottle. "Do you want some?" Because drinking alone isn't fun and kind of sad. I'm tired of being sad. I'm tired of a lot of things.

Thea shakes her head. Pulling out a pink, rhinestone flask. "I prefer the hard stuff." She cheers me before taking a sip.

"How are you really doing here?" she asks, lowering it to her lap.

Again, maybe it's the wine or the lack of human interaction lately, but I find myself spilling probably more than I should to her. But even with the threat of her running back to tell Noah my words verbatim, it doesn't stop me from being honest.

"I hate this. I hate him," I say softly, looking down at my bottle. I hate that he has me at war with my feelings.

"Has he been cruel?"

I shake my head. "He hasn't been around to be cruel."

She's quiet, gathering her thoughts. "Do you want him to be?"

"Do I want him to be what?" I look at her. "Cruel?"

"Around."

I shrug. "Not particularly."

Wow, that lie doesn't even sound believable to me.

And one Thea sees through with no problem. "Bullshit."

I shrug again, not bothering to argue. "It's not like I can do anything to make him come back here."

"You'd be surprised what Noah would do for you."

"What's that supposed to mean?"

"Nothing." She takes a hit from her flask, her eyes wide like she's said too much. But before I can demand an answer, Thea changes the subject. Kind of. "So you want Noah around more and I know exactly how to drag his brooding ass here."

"Let me guess." I eye her warily, "With a party?"

She nods. "With a party."

I look around Noah's apartment, at my things scattered

about. Clearly that hasn't been working, but with a party… Noah wouldn't stay away for that. It's two of his least favorite things combined. People in his apartment and cluttered disarray.

Thea sees the answer in my face before I can say it.

Before I even make it down the stairs, I hear it. The music. The people. I feel the excitement pulsing in the air.

When Thea sent me up to my room to change into more "party appropriate" attire, apparently my lounge wear didn't make the cut, she said she could get a party going in under thirty minutes.

She wasn't lying.

With five minutes to spare, this place is packed with people.

From my vantage point on the second-story, I take in the zoo that is downstairs.

It feels like I'm back in Heathen's Hell with the sea of bodies greeting me.

This isn't your typical house party. It's a party for the haves, not the haves not. Where debauchery is in full swing, and scandal isn't expected but encouraged.

Walking down the stairs, I take in the chaos.

Scantily clad women wearing only lingerie dance on the furniture, bottles of champagne and wine in hand. They dance with assuredness and confidence even when they're in nothing but see-through lace.

Thea's one of them. Her matching white bra and panties pop against her dark skin.

In the kitchen, on the counter, she's stripped down to her underwear and is grinding against another half-naked girl, moving seductively down her body, while other guys and girls are ensnared at the sight.

And that's only in the kitchen.

When I see what's happening in the living room, I want to divert my eyes and not look away at the same time.

Reeve Morgan lounges on the leather couch with a paint canvas in his lap, pieces of his black hair falling along his forehead. His pale fingers are stained with paint.

He brings the brush to his mouth as he surveys the line of naked men before him. They're all different heights and sizes and races.

All beautiful as they pose in various positions before Reeve, who shoots appreciative gazes that linger every time he glances up from his creation.

I'm watching with rapt fascination as Reeve tells the man in the middle to lower his hand. The man does with a smirk, his thumb tracing the base of his cock.

Reeve bites down on his lip and shifts on the couch.

My cheeks heat.

I look away. *Who knew the inner circle was such a fan of so much nudity.*

Nobody else gawks like me, not fazed by these displays in the least.

They're mingling, going about their party business as if strip teases and Greco-Roman art practices are everyday occurrences. Perhaps for them, they are.

I've been to a lot of parties. Prep school, college, and house parties, but never have I been to one like this.

I don't know what to do. Where to look. I feel like a fly on the wall, a voyeur watching.

The party is made even more seductive with the vibe of Noah's decor. The fireplace is on and the lights dimmed low.

Since I was forced here, it's reminded me of a cave carved

for a wicked creature, but now it feels like a sinful lair of sweet release.

Searching the room to see if anything else can scandalize me, like a full on orgy, I spot Gabriel Ruiz in a corner, under the stairs sans orgy. Instead he has a beaten leather book in hand.

Who can read with all this going on?

But that's Gabe for you. Always with the serious, pensive looks on his expertly sculpted face.

Aside from Thea, the only other person from their circle I shared a class with was Gabe. We were in pottery together his senior year. He would always make these beautiful vases that he said could be found in his mother's hometown in Spain.

Harlow used to call him the pussy of the group, but my sister doesn't always know what she's talking about.

It's the silent types you have to watch out for.

His eyes flick up, staring at me. Those deep brown eyes of his pierce into me. My pulse spikes, feeling like I got caught doing something I shouldn't.

Unsure what to do—turn away and leave him to read? — Gabe decides for me when he closes his book and stands up. Walking toward me.

Nope. No, I do not want that.

I'm still angry with him (and *Reeve*) for following Noah's orders like puppets, bringing me here and catnapping my sweet Pan.

I cut him a dry, hard stare but quickly turn away only to find myself face to face with the last person I thought I'd ever see here.

"Dickie?" my voice is incredulous.

He seems just as surprised as me. "Sayer?"

Richard aka "Dickie" aka "the Dick" Abernathy, my parents' dream of a guy for me back in prep school, stands before me, wearing nothing but a pair of shiny gold underwear. And not boxer style, but tight, compression hot shorts.

A smear of white powder decorates under his nose. Dark eyes dilated. High.

Yeah, he's a catch I'm glad I released.

"What're you doing here?" I ask in disbelief. "And is this some kind of nudist party I didn't know about?"

"It's a game," he says in lieu of the second question.

I want to roll my eyes. Of *course* it's a game. But I don't bother to ask what kind requires you to lose your pants. I don't want to know.

"What're you doing here, Dickie?" I ask again.

He clears his throat, running a hand through his blonde locks. "It's just Richard now, actually."

"Richard," I repeat. It feels weird to say after spending my entire adolescence calling him Dickie. "I prefer Richard a lot more."

He chuckles. "You and me both."

His eyes widen as they look behind me and I don't need to look as to know the why.

Gabe is closing in fast.

Time to move.

I grab his hand and pull Dickie-now-Richard into the crowd of people, away from Gabe.

Dickie comes along easily, grinning when he shouldn't be. He tries to put his hand on my butt, and I have to bat him off. We're not off to do anything illicit. Dickie is only my means to escape.

Once we're across the room and a quick glance to see if Gabe is following us and confirming that he hasn't, Dickie has served his purpose.

But when I try to drop his hand, he squeezes back, not letting go. "You look good, Say."

His husky voice brings chills to my skin as I blink, his thumb tracing invisible circles on the back of my hand.

He's never called me Say before. Few people have ever called me that, actually. It's always Sayer or Baby Brooks. And if I remember correctly, Dickie was one of the people who always called me Baby Brooks.

My skin crawls, feeling trapped.

I really don't want his hand holding mine.

"Thank you," I force out.

"I haven't seen you in forever," he goes on, oblivious to my growing discomfort.

I didn't talk to him because I missed him. Seeing him here was a surprise, that's all. Now the surprise has worn off and it's time for me to go.

Except *he still won't give me my hand back!*

Instead he shifts closer to me, causing me to back up into the wall. His breath is on my neck, stale alcohol and too much cologne invade my senses, making my head pulse. "You've grown up."

"Six years will do that to you." My hands settle on his chest, attempting to push him away without any luck.

He takes it as invitation to lean in closer.

"Hmm." He drops his voice, nuzzling my throat as bile rises in it. "Guess so."

I don't like this. I don't like this at all. Panic tightens in wild vines around my lungs.

"Dickie, let me go." I try pushing again, but he presses more of his body onto me.

He doesn't listen, instead his hands move up my sides, just below my bra. Not touching my breasts…not yet.

Air is tight in my lungs as I struggle in his hold, wanting him to let me go. I need him to let me go.

His hands creep higher and my eyes sting. I'm about to

jam my knee in the Abernathy jewels when he pins his body to mine.

"We have some catching up to do, don't you—" He cuts himself off with a shout before the wall behind me vibrates, his solid form slamming into it, chest first.

My eyes blink, slowly processing what's unfolded in front of me.

A seething Noah stands before me, his hand locked in a vise grip around Dick's neck, keeping his body pinned to the wall. "I believe the lady asked you to let her go."

fourteen

Sayer

EVERYTHING STOPS. THE TALKING, THE MUSIC.

My lungs.

At least, that's how it feels as Noah slams Dickie into the wall again, who's eyes practically bulge from his skull in terror.

My heart leaps with it and leaps again when I catch sight of Noah's face.

He looks like a ravaged animal who just escaped their cage, ready to strike as he squeezes Dick's neck to the point of him making a strained, choking sound.

Dickie starts to bang uncontrollably on the wall. The punches speak like a code.

Bang. Help. *Bang.* Me.

No one comes to his rescue.

"What?" Noah laughs, the sound darker than I've ever heard. It brings goosebumps to my skin. "Want me to let go?"

Dickie can't nod, but his eyes widen, pleading.

I'm paralyzed, unable to do anything but listen as blood pounds in my ears at the scene before me.

It's madness. It's chaos. Noah looks ready to kill. And all around the crowd is living for it. They stop and stare, fixated at Noah, who draws Dick's head back, and loosens his fingers around Dickie's throat.

Dickie deflates as he gulps oxygen greedily.

But it's too soon.

As Dickie exhales, leaning against the wall in a false security, Noah rams his face into the drywall, smashing his nose. Blood smears on the paint. A Jackson Pollock of the bloody variety.

"We don't disrespect women in my home." Noah's voice is cold, barely in control. I've never seen him like this.

So ravaged, hungry for punishment. But he still looks put together, the same Noah. His tie is straight, no hair out of place. Even his glasses sit perfectly straight on his nose.

Physically, Noah moves with precision and purpose, a man on autopilot. His face is no different than his usual exterior aside from the hard set of his jaw, it clenches in anger.

He's the eye of the storm, calm as he causes chaos.

"I didn't do anything!" Dickie wails, the words muffled by his lips being squished against the wall, fighting to get free.

"And I didn't do this." Noah rams his fist into Dick's kidneys, who wails in agony.

A hand touches my arm and I jump. Thea stands next to me, her focus on me while Reeve and Gabe have their eyes trained on Noah. The two don't look as concerned as they do entertained.

"Do something!" I shout at them, waving my hand at the wailing going on behind me. I get ignored.

My stomach twists as I hear another grunt from Dickie, fists beating flesh.

"Thea," I plead, looking into her warm, brown eyes. Only to be met with disappointment.

Thea shakes her head. "I can't, Sayer."

"Why?" Glancing behind me, I see that Dickie's face is becoming more unrecognizable with each hit. His lip is busted, and his nose is crooked, blood flowing like a waterfall from it. Sucking in a breath, I look back at Thea, my eyes now begging.

But Thea is strong, shaking her head. "Noah needs to get this out."

I stare at her, hoping my ears deceive me and that what she said wasn't just crazy. "He's going to kill Dickie!

Thea rolls her eyes like I'm being dramatic, but I know I'm not. Not as I turn around and watch as Dickie falls to the floor, crawling backward like a drunk crab to escape Noah's slow, leisurely pursuit.

He's going to kill him. There's a menacing glint in those depthless blues as he prowls toward Dickie, the smile that brings chills to my skin grows as Dick's back collides with the wall.

It's a promise. It's a threat. It's a kiss of death.

I glance at Noah's friends, but they still don't seem concerned. Reeve and Gabe wear almost matching grins to Noah. Thea is the only one who seems to have a slightly somber expression, but there's something calculated in her dark brown eyes.

I can't let Noah do this. I'm watching with piercing horror as he closes in on Dickie, one of his hands wraps around Dick's neck, slamming his head into the wall. The only sound in the penthouse is the crack the contact makes. Sharp and thunderous.

I suck in a tight breath. I don't like this. I don't like the look on Noah's face. I could give a shit about Dickie, I'm barely paying attention to him. My entire focus is on Noah.

The stone coldness, it's a stranger on the face of a man I'm just beginning to get to know again. I know he has a temper, I know I was already putting him in a mood by having this party, but I never intended for this to happen.

Not that it's my fault Dickie doesn't understand the word *no.* I don't feel responsible for his actions in the slightest.

I just don't want to be a character witness to a murder.

Noah lands a punch to Dickie's nose, blood splattering on the wall. My entire body recoils. I'm not a fan of violence. With each blow Noah lands, the more sick I feel. I can't keep watching this. I refuse.

Without a second thought, my feet take off and I'm catapulting myself onto Noah's back, locking around him like a spider monkey as he's gearing up for another punch. The second my skin touches his, his entire body locks up. Dickie stares at us with wild and dazed bruising eyes.

"Sayer," I feel Noah say more than hear, his chest moving under my palms. "Get off me." He's coiled so tight, tense with a need to fight.

"Can't do that," I tell him with all sincerity. "I have this fear of blood and you're splattering it around the apartment."

Noah's silent, his body still geared in his fighting stance while his hand is still wrapped tightly around Dickie's neck, but his attention is on me. Listening.

Pressing my chest against his back, I bring my lips to the shell of his ear. "Noah," I whisper softly, "Please stop."

Dropping his hold on Dickie, who collapses to the ground in a boneless heap, I feel Noah's body shift against mine and I squeeze him tight.

"Enough, Noah," I whisper in his ear, hoping I can soothe this raging storm. "I'm okay. I'm here. With you."

That seems to reach him.

Noah grabs my ankles that are locked around his waist, and he squeezes them. Not painfully, not gently. Reassuringly.

"Get him out of here," Noah orders, voice rough. "Before I do what I really want to."

Reeve and Gabe appear, flanking either side of Dickie and drag his limp body to the elevator where they unceremoniously throw him in.

As soon as the doors to the elevator closes, the music

turns back on and the people disperse. Almost like the past five minutes never happened and they're back to on their journeys of not remembering tomorrow.

I try to shimmy down Noah's back, but he locks his hands around my legs.

"Noah." I tap his shoulder. "I'm ready to get down now."

"Too damn bad."

"Seriously, Noah. Put me down." I try to wiggle, only for friction to grow between my legs, feeling his muscled body against mine. Suddenly, I don't mind being wrapped around him.

Until he opens his mouth.

"Hey, Sayer? Stop talking."

Rude. Always so rude.

Normally, I wouldn't, especially not when he barks it at me like an order, but there's something in his tone that makes me heed his advice. So, my lips are sealed…for now.

Noah might fight with his fists, but I use my words, and I have a whole lot to say for him abandoning me in his cold, dark home all without a simple text explaining *why*.

Fused to his back, Noah walks across the apartment to a little door tucked beside his kitchen.

It leads into the laundry room, which quietly shuts behind us, cutting off the light and encasing us in darkness.

But before the door can shut completely, as Noah pulls me off his body and sets me on the washer, the metal cool against my thighs, I get a look at his face.

Wild eyes and a stone jaw, he's still wired from the fight. And with Dickie gone, Noah's changed his focus, shifting to another target.

Me.

And I welcome it with two words. Bring. It.

He wants a fight. He's going to get one.

I sharpened my claws just for the occasion. After all, this is why I agreed to the party.

I'd rather fight with Noah than have him ignore me. At least when we fight, I know he sees me.

How messed up is that?

"What were you thinking?" he growls in my ear, the timbre as rough as tree bark. It grates against my skin, raising my defenses.

"Excuse me?" I force out, unsure what he's implying. "I wasn't doing anything. *Dickie* was—"

"Not that." Noah cuts me off, pulling my knees apart and settles between my thighs. Bringing us closer.

"I don't pay attention to you, so you decide to throw a party?" He speaks in a hushed tone that's like a caress on my skin. "Think I'd come running back for the little girl wanting attention?"

Each question feels like a dart hitting the board, each sting more bitter than the last.

"You invite that little fuck here in an attempt to make me jealous?"

My eyes narrow in a glare he can't see. I hate how he can always read me, knowing my motives even when I'm unsure of them myself.

"It worked, didn't it?" I challenge. "You're here and you're jealous."

"I'm here, all right." He chuckles. "Gabe sent me a picture of all the fun I was missing. But I wouldn't hold my breath on the jealous part."

"Right. Because I beat up people all the time just for the hell of it." I don't mean to, but my voice gets louder the longer I speak.

We might be trapped in darkness, making his face hidden,

but that doesn't change how tense the air is around us, crackling in vexation.

"He was in the way," is all he says, tone neutral.

"You had him up against a wall!" I point out.

"He was in the way to get to you."

He doesn't say it in the way that speaks of butterflies swelling in my stomach, but more like a tornado ready to destroy me from the inside out.

Being in the dark, everything feels heightened. More intense than when we were in the closet at Heathen's Hell, even more so than at the art gallery. Each had some, if little light.

Not like here. Where I only have my touch to guide me. Where I can only feel.

And he feels so strong, so sure between my legs I can't focus on anything else as he shifts closer, eating the little distance between us.

My breath catches when I feel a stiffness brush against my thigh. His palm cups my cheek, finding my bottom lip. He traces it. "Why'd you do it?"

"Do what?" Lost in the feel of his touch, the fight inside me morphing to something else.

"Have this party?"

"Because I wanted you to notice me."

Maybe it's the room, the lack of light that makes things feel more alive, or maybe it's the wine I drank earlier that has me opening up in a piece of raw honesty, though by now the alcohol has left my system.

So maybe I'm tired of playing games and even though I started one to get him here, I want Noah to know what's been eating me.

"I notice you," his voice rough.

"Then why have you been avoiding me?"

"You're a weakness."

"I'm not weak." Indignation fills me. So does hurt. "Sure I'm not the most physically active or fit but—"

His mouth covers mine, promptly shutting me up. "You're not weak, Sayer." His nose traces my jaw, my lips parting as I'm robbed of air. "But you make *me* weak." His nose leads him on a path to my ear where his teeth graze the lobe, pulling at it. "In the eyes of the world, you're my weakness."

His words pierce my chest, but not as much as the emotion behind them do. Raw and real, honesty bleeds through them. An arrow piercing my chest, a bullseye to my heart.

I reach up, grabbing the ends of his hair. "Show me," I dare, pulling him back to my lips.

But before we can touch, something crashes outside the door, sounding like it shattered into unfixable pieces.

With a sound of frustration, Noah pulls away and storms out of the room. Leaving me flushed on a dryer.

"Everyone out!" he roars, moving to the speakers and shutting off the music.

I trail after him, not leaving the doorway of the laundry room as people make a mad rush to leave the apartment, wanting to get away from Noah's wrath.

"Except you three." He points to Thea, Reeve, and Gabe. "Don't fucking move."

Thea and Gabe stop walking.

Reeve wraps an arm around Gabe's shoulders smiling. "We're in trouble," he mock-whispers into Gabe's ear.

Gabe doesn't react.

It takes three trips and Noah packing the elevator past the capacity limit to get all the party guests out, but when they are, Noah takes inventory of his littered apartment.

He toes an empty champagne bottle, that sharp jaw jumping as he kicks it to Gabe, who stops it like a soccer ball.

Noah walks to the couch and thumbs the paint that's dotted the cushion. His thumb comes back with red paint.

He cuts Reeve a nasty look. "You're paying for this."

Reeve shrugs, uncaring.

When he finds a bra hanging from a lamp, he picks it up with two fingers. His eyes flick to me, down my chest.

I glare as I cross my arms over my chest. *Yeah, I'm stilling wearing one, perv.*

The bra falls to the floor.

"Clean this shit up," he barks at the four of us, stomping across the room to the elevator.

"Where are you going?" I call out, displeasure rising. He's leaving? *Again?*

"Out."

Out. I don't like that word. "Stay," I counter, moving toward him, but he shakes his head, the doors starting to close.

And he doesn't stop them.

I glare, leaning into the anger that's pumping my veins instead of the little crack in my chest that stings with the knowledge he just left me. Again.

Once he's gone and it's the four of us, I expect them to leave as well, leaving me to clean up a mess I didn't help create, and I'm not proven wrong.

Gabe's phone dings with a text. Without looking up from the screen, he says, "Let's go."

Thea and Reeve fall into step as Gabe walks to the elevator.

"Uh, no." I step in front of them. "You're not leaving me here to take care of this by myself." The three share a look and some kind of silent communication happens before me.

"No," Gabe says sternly while looking down at Thea, who's doing a weird dance.

"Oh yes," she nods.

"This won't end well, Thea," Gabe warns.

"Which is exactly why you should let her do it, G," Reeve interjects. "Keep our boy on his toes."

"What are you three talking about?" I ask the three of them, feeling out of the loop.

Gabe sighs, the sound defeated, as he motions for Thea to explain.

Slowly, she looks at me and grins. "Do you want to see where Noah went?

fifteen

Sayer

They won't tell me where we're going, but Thea did give me a set of rules in the elevator ride down for when we get to our destination.

Rule one: Stick close to her side.

Rule two: Do not engage in conversation of any sort.

Rule three: Do not look at anyone for longer than three seconds.

When I asked where the heck we were going, she added a fourth rule: No questions.

I still asked questions even though they all went unanswered.

Why did I need to listen to these rules? Why were they being so secretive about our destination? What am I letting them lead me into? Why is Reeve smiling like he ate the canary? Seriously, out of all three of them, he was looking like he was on the best high of his life, ecstatic for what's to come.

Even some of Thea's excitement had been replaced with anxious energy by the time we slide into the backseat of the waiting car Jensen had pulled around to the front of the building.

It only took about two minutes of being squished between Thea and Reeve to piece together where we're headed.

The wharf.

Confusion fills me. There's nothing there but warehouses and loading docks. Why would Noah go here?

The city is full of so many secrets and buildings pretending to be something they're not, we could be going to a whorehouse masquerading as boat storage and I wouldn't be surprised. Lead drops in the pit of my stomach with that thought, images of Noah with someone else…it's not a picture I want to see live.

Our tires crunch on a loose gravel path as Jenkins brings the SUV to a crawl until we're parked in front of a rusted out industrial warehouse. I stare at it. Noah's here? Not to stereotype his rich ass, but this looks like the farthest place his Italian loafers would ever touch.

But I'm the only one that seems to think so. In unison, Thea, Gabe, and Reeve open their respective doors and climb out.

When I don't move, Reeve reaches in and yanks me out. My feet stumble and I slam into his chest.

His arms snake around my shoulders, keeping me pinned to him. "If you wanted me to hold you, all you had to do was ask, Baby Brooks." His lips graze my neck before I pull away. Gabe slaps him upside the head.

"Knock it off," Gabe grumbles, the sound close to a roaring storm.

"Why? Are you jealous?" Grinning, he saunters closer to Gabe. "Do you want your big body wrapped up in these arms, Ruiz?"

Gabe's face doesn't change, but his eyes crinkle in the corners in amusement. He pushes Reeve away, who laughs and sends Gabe a wink.

"Children," Thea chides with a smile.

How are they all smiling? It's freezing out tonight, made even colder by the frigid ocean breeze. Ice daggers pierce past my coat, stabbing my skin. "What're we doing here?"

"For the show." Reeve's smile stretches and it does nothing to comfort me.

"Show?" My voice is small, drowned out by the sharp wind.

Thea links her arm with mine, giving me a reassuring squeeze. "Don't worry, you're safe with us."

Safe. I haven't felt safe since finding out someone was in my apartment. The word feels lost inside me, the meaning clear but the action missing. I don't know if I'll ever feel safe again. No matter who's around.

But I squeeze Thea's arm back as we move toward the rusted door, and as we walk, I take in our surroundings. Or lack thereof. This place is abandoned, save for our car, aside from our footsteps and the shrieking wind, it's as quiet as a cemetery tonight.

My heart beats in tune with Gabe's fist as it bangs against the door.

A little slat on the door opens, revealing only a pair of eyes. "Password."

Seriously? I feel my eyes widen. I want to make a joke about us being five, but I bite my tongue. Something tells me the password isn't going to be 'fart for brains' or something of equal juncture.

And sure enough, Gabe shucks off his jacket and rolls up his shirt sleeve, flashing them a tattoo on his forearm. It's small, about the size of a half-dollar.

I don't have to be next to Gabe to know what it is.

A black dragon mid-flight with webbed wings.

Of course I recognize it.

My sister has the same one. Noah has one. They all do. Tattoos they got in high school. At the time I thought they were living up to their reckless reputations, getting matching tattoos for the hell of it. I never attached any other meaning behind them.

Until now.

But what exactly?

The slat closes and the heavy door opens with a groan, revealing nothing but darkness.

Gabe goes in first with Reeve close behind, but neither Thea and I move, our arms still locked together.

"Thea," I start, wanting to know what the tattoo means but she squeezes my arm.

In a soft whisper, she says, "Remember what I told you."

I barely have time to nod before she pulls me through the door which shuts immediately behind us and causes me to jump.

"It's okay," Thea reassures me before pulling me farther into the space. My steps are unsure by not being able to see right in front of me. It's so dark. So quiet. Even are steps are light, barely making a noise.

I feel so off center, not hearing or seeing anything, until a soft crescendo starts to build, hitting my ears and building with our strides.

Voices. People.

Cheering. People are cheering.

What they're cheering, I can't decipher, but the noise soon becomes deafening as we get the first taste of light. A warm glow halos above an open door.

We walk through it and into a hell pit.

Literally.

My jaw drops, eyes widening.

It's hotter than an inferno, and not just because there are people crowded in the room, packed like sardines. Wild flames dance on the wall in torches.

No one seems to care about the fires, though, not when their attention is focused on the center of the room. Where a metal cage sits.

A ring for fighting.

And in the center, on opposite sides, are two men. Waiting. One bounces with anxious energy, headphones in his ears, while the other stands there. So still. My eyes hone in on him. Bare-chested and broad-shouldered, his knuckles taped tight.

A perfectly sculpted back with muscles chiseled by an artist.

He's turned away from us, but I know who it is.

Noah.

Tense and ready to fight.

I can't take my eyes off him, not even to watch where I'm going. All I know is that Thea is leading me closer to the cage while Gabe and Reeve shove people out of our way.

A loud *bang* washes over the room, shaking the building.

Everything goes quiet as a girl with heels and a gold silk robe steps forward with a black cue card. A red number one is painted on it.

She walks it around the ring, her steps methodical as a few whistle or catcall toward her.

Asshats.

While the room seems to be focusing on the card girl, I look farther into the ring. Meeting the burning stare of my blue-eyed devil.

With his mouth pressed in a tense line and his eyes sharp and deadly, Noah looks every bit as frightening that he's been rumored to be.

Back at his apartment, I realize, he was holding himself back. Controlled in all aspects including his anger.

Except for now, where the man can step aside and let the control go.

The opponents bump knuckles as a bang rings around the room.

And so round one begins.

Noah's opponent makes the first move, fist to the face. Which Noah narrowly avoids, shifting backward before lunging forward with a punch of his own.

When Noah's knuckles hit flesh, the crowd goes wild, screaming and jumping. Knocking their elbows and various limbs into me.

"If I leave here with bruises," I hiss into Thea's ear. "I'm never hanging out with you again."

"Yeah, okay." She laughs.

"Who's Noah fighting?"

"I think his name is Thomas." She shrugs beside me. "People are always volunteering to go up against him."

People *volunteer* to get their face pounded?

"What is this place?" I turn back to the ring as Thomas gets up.

He staggers a step before he faces Noah, his face bloody with bruises already swelling his cheeks.

Who would volunteer to get their face beat in? Archaic simpletons. Masochists. The fragile masculine ego.

People who want to feel anything instead of always being numb.

"The Ring," Thea answers. Both our focuses are on Thomas as he nails a jab to Noah's side. I flinch at the sound of flesh hitting flesh, of Noah's grunt that shouldn't be heard over the deafening crowd but one I feel anyway.

"Noah comes here when he needs to work off aggression," she adds, but I barely hear her. My entire focus is on what's unfolding inside the ring.

On Noah.

He comes here when he needs to work off aggression. Me. I'm the aggression that's thrown him in there tonight.

And he's a force to reckon with. Moving with agile reflexes, he's more calculated than his opponent, who's throwing punches into the wind and hoping they hit. Noah's are more purposeful. He knows when to advance and when to wane. While one moves like a rabbit on caffeine, the other conserves energy, building toward greater impact.

Thomas juts out a fist and hits Noah in the face.

I flinch at the sound and grow tense with Noah's retaliation.

He fires back with enough force for Thomas's head to snap back.

Thomas roars, not backing down. Landing two hits before Noah serves one back.

It's vicious and bloody and dirty.

I hate it. I hate every second of being here. Of seeing Noah getting hit.

With every punch that lands somewhere on Noah, I recoil, stomach churning.

The cheers are ear-splitting when Noah lands a hit that has Thomas knocked to the ground. It spurs the crowd, making them get rowdier. They surge forward—propelling me into the fence.

A cry of pain escapes as my cheek gets embedded with the rough metal. I hear Thea shout my name, but I can't call back, the air gets sucked out of me with the masses piling against me.

Noah's head snaps to the sound, spotting me. I want to yell at him to pay attention to the fight, but I can't. An elbow digs into my kidney making me cry out again. My eyes water.

The crowd's focused on Noah while Noah's focused on me. He starts toward me and my eyes bulge.

Is he crazy?

Focus on the fight! I want to shout.

Thomas, using Noah's distraction to his advantage, charges.

Turn around! I try to scream, getting a taste of rusted metal instead.

Noah doesn't. He keeps walking toward me and with a sucker's move, Thomas tackles Noah to the ground, hitting his head.

The sound cracks like thunder around the room, taking my breath with it.

He doesn't move.

Noah doesn't move.

The room is still loud, people still screaming, but to me— it's silent.

Silent as I stare at the broad, flattened form that is Noah.

He hasn't so much as twitched.

No.

No.

No.

Get up.

Get up, I silently beg.

Any second, any second, he's going to pick his head up.

Except, seconds turn to minutes and Noah still hasn't moved.

Come on, Noah. Get up.

My gaze is locked on his still form, a weird sense of emotions overcoming me. I need Noah to be okay. He has to be okay. If Noah's not okay, I feel I won't be okay.

And I don't know how to process that last thought.

The "ref" starts toward Noah, no doubt to call the round when Noah's hand shoots out and grabs the ref's ankle.

I gasp.

Slowly, Noah's body moves, a swelling overtakes my chest as he shifts his face and meets my worried eyes.

Blood streaked face, he grins at me, still looking a little dazed, before twisting around in a roar.

Thomas is too busy doing a victory dance for the crowd to notice Noah, but he sure as heck notices him when his body gets tackled to the ground by a two-hundred-pound seething Kincaid.

Noah straddles the other man's body, punching once, twice. That's it. That's all it takes.

Playtime is over, Noah's had enough.

Now it's Thomas's turn to not move. The sight of him sprawled out on the bloody, sweaty ground does nothing but bring dark satisfaction to me.

Noah climbs off him, snarling, "It's over."

He stalks out of the ring, much to the chagrin of the audience who groan and shout for him to get his ass back in there.

Noah doesn't listen.

He hops over the fence next to me and pulls us away from the hoarding masses.

"Move!" he roars, shaking the building as much as the banging had.

People instantly part, his red sea moving with his command, and he pulls me through the crowd, into a door Reeve opens for us.

This man and his doors to hidden places.

We're in a poorly lit hallway when he lets go of my arm, only to get in my face.

"What in the *hell* are you doing here?" he yells, even though we're mere inches apart.

I cross my arms. "Thea invited me."

"Did she tell you where you'd be going?"

I shake my head.

"And you decided what? To tag along on an adventure?" His hands pin themselves to the wall on either side of my head.

His anger grates against my skin. This man. I swear one

minute he has me worried about him and in the next he has me wanting to rip his head off.

"You mean instead of staying locked in your penthouse with no form of entertainment, slowly going bored to the point of insanity?" I push at his sweaty chest. "Sorry, that's not how I wanted to spend my night!"

"You aren't supposed to be here."

"And where do you want me, Noah? I feel like if it were up to you, I wouldn't be allowed to leave your penthouse."

"It's for your safety," he growls. "Isn't that what I'm here for?"

"To *protect me!*" My voice rises. "Not to keep me as your prisoner."

"I never said you weren't allowed to leave. Come and go as you please." He crowds me. "You're not my prisoner, Sayer."

"Then what am I? Why am I staying at your apartment if you're never there?"

"Why'd you throw that party tonight?" he counters, avoiding my question.

"Thea threw it."

"You didn't stop it."

"No." I agreed to it.

"Why?"

I look him in the eye. "Because I wanted to see you."

"Here I am."

"Here you are," I echo in a whisper.

We're close, chest to heaving chest, our anger festering into something more. Something that tightens my chest, steals my breath and robs me of sense. I start to lean into him and him into me when a throat clears.

Reality washes over me as Noah pulls away with a curse. "*What.*"

Gabe stands behind Noah with his hands in his pockets. "We got a problem."

Noah doesn't move.

"It's Seamus," Gabe continues. "He's outside asking for you."

Noah swears under his breath, reaching around to grab my hand. We walk down the hall to where Reeve and Thea are standing, waiting for us.

Thea's lips twitching is the only reaction from any of them. Their focus is somewhere else. On some*one* else.

"Seamus from Mrs. Montgomery's party?" I ask, remembering his tattooed knuckles.

They ignore me. I huff, feeling Noah's hand squeeze mine.

"What does he want?" Noah asks, and of course they answer him.

I glare at nothing in particular.

Thea worries her hands. "We don't know. He's just asking for you."

Noah looks down at me. "After I deal with him, we're going home."

Knowing now is not the time to be difficult, I nod.

"When we go out there, get in the car and don't open the door."

Again, I nod.

Reeve hands Noah his glasses, a thermal black shirt and coat, which he quickly changes into.

Once he's clothed, he grabs my hand again and we go outside where the wintery air bites into my cheeks.

We only get a short distance before Noah stops, letting go of my hand. A man in a charcoal coat and beanie leans against Noah's car, running his finger along a knife's blade.

Seamus.

"You rang?" Noah has a posture of leisure but his jaw ticks.

"We have business to discuss." Seamus looks at everyone, including me, and it looks like he lingers on Thea for the longest.

She flips him off.

He only grins.

Noah ignores the interaction. "The only thing I have to discuss is the money you owe us before I start charging you interest up your skinny ass."

"I'm here to change the agreement."

Noah coughs a laugh.

"Oh, I think you'll like this."

Noah waits.

"A fight. You. Me. A week from now."

"What's in it for me? Aside from kicking your ass." Noah's indifference doesn't change, but he's intrigued. I can tell by the subtle way his stance changes, the widening of his legs, the crossing of his chest.

"Information."

"Like you have anything we'd want," Thea says, hands on her hips.

Seamus spares her the briefest of glances before turning back to Noah. "So you don't want to know who's after that hot piece of ass behind you? Or where you can find her sister?"

sixteen

Sayer

WHEN WE GET BACK AT NOAH'S, WE VENTURE OFF in two different directions.

He heads for the bar, grabbing the first bottle within reach, while I go into the little bathroom near the kitchen, ransacking the cabinets for supplies. Thankfully, Noah keeps his first aid kit stocked.

Quickly, I grab hydrogen peroxide, cotton balls, and whatever else I can carry before leaving the bathroom to find Noah sprawled out on the couch, the bottle of whiskey dangling between his fingers.

The apartment isn't as messy as I remember it. Most of the damage is confined to the kitchen and surrounding areas. The couch and the space surrounding it, including the coffee table, where Reeve was painting is surprisingly the cleanest. Those naked models were good for more than one thing it seems.

As I walk toward Noah, he lazily watches my approach.

He looks relaxed, dazed out in bliss, but I know he's anything but.

Our car ride home from the harbor was in tense silence. Noah didn't speak as he escorted me to his car leaving his friends and Jenkins with Seamus. He didn't make a sound as he drove through the city.

I watched him the entire way. How the cuts on his face bled, at the stretched, cracked skin on his knuckles. He didn't show he was in pain, but my poor, weak and caring heart wanted to tend to him nonetheless.

His eyes continue to follow me as I sit across from him on his coffee table, conscious of our ongoing chess game, not wanting to knock it over.

He doesn't ask me what I'm doing as I methodically soak a cotton ball in peroxide and bring it to his face. He doesn't wince as it touches his cut, instead he keeps his chaotic eyes on me.

But the stillness is a façade. Being this close, I can feel the energy buzzing through his veins.

Ignoring the hum that's always present when we're this close together, I go about tending to his wounds, putting bloody cotton ball after bloody cotton ball on the table next to me.

We don't talk. But we don't need to.

My skin is warm under his stare. I try not to focus on that as I soak another cotton ball, but it's impossible. The magnetic pull that is Noah Kincaid is getting to me. Like a lasso around my body, he makes me want to lean in closer and closer until there's no space left between us.

I try not to look directly at him as I bring the cotton to the cut by his mouth. My hand rests on his cheek and I pretend not to notice how he tilts his head into my palm. I pretend I don't feel my chest beating to the point of pain.

I pretend to be wholly unaffected.

Until I look up.

And lock on his lips.

His lips that smirk when I'm unable to look away. It's been too long since I've felt them move against mine. So long since I've felt the commanding touch of his.

Needing to distract myself, I ask the question that's been on my mind since we left the wharf. "Why'd you do it?"

He doesn't ask what I'm talking about. He knows.

Why'd he agree to the fight with Seamus? I mean, I know why. He wants to fight in exchange for information—secrets—his favorite bets to place. What I want to know is the *who*.

Was it for me or was it for my sister. I almost don't want Noah to answer, for fear of the latter.

But it's that damn Achilles heel of mine, my budding inquisitiveness.

Noah takes a swig of whiskey, swirling the amber liquid between us while his lips glisten with unclaimed alcohol. I want to drink it from them. "Why do you think?"

"If I was fine with assumptions, I wouldn't have asked." I level him a stare. "I want you to tell me."

"Demanding little thing tonight, aren't you?"

"Will you tell me?" I roll a cotton ball between my fingers.

"There's nothing to tell." He shrugs. "We had a deal."

"Bullshit," I call, despite the seed of disappointment taking root inside me.

Noah's brow raises. "Oh, is it?"

"It is," I whisper. "I think you did it for something more. Something else."

"And why's that?" He's still jazzed from the fight, but his movements are controlled, almost painfully, as he again takes a pull from the bottle. I didn't see how much was in it when he picked it up, but it's almost empty now.

"Because I don't think you believe he knows where my sister is. And I think you're desperate enough to find out who's after me."

He shifts on the couch, scooting closer so our knees are interlocked. He moves a hand up my thigh as he leans in close. "I can't have anyone hurt you." I suck in a breath as he wraps a piece of my hair around his finger. "And if Seamus has the answers, I'm going to get them."

"Why?" I'm desperate to know. "Why are you doing this all for me?"

He leans in even closer, close enough for me to smell the whiskey on his tongue. "Don't take me to be your hero."

Slowly, Noah leans back and drains the rest of the whiskey before placing the empty bottle on the table next to my thigh. His cool fingers brush against me in the process bringing a weight to my chest and a pulse between my legs. A simple touch. He can do so much to my body with a single touch.

I take the cotton ball still in my hand and focus on my task. Cleaning his wounds. I'm about to dab it on the split skin above his eye when Noah's hand shoots up, grabbing my wrist before I can make contact with his skin.

"Why are you doing this?" he asks, huskily. The sound washes over me. "Taking care of me."

I bite my lip. "I don't like seeing you like this."

He still holds my wrist, keeping it suspended between us. "If it makes you feel better, I don't feel it."

It doesn't. "Do you feel anything?"

He raises his split brow. "Is that really the question you want to ask, Sayer?"

Maybe it's the way he says my name, a dare waiting, or maybe it's because this has been on my mind since the night Noah came back into my life, but I feel the seal on my lips break, wanting to know the answers to questions I've been too afraid to ask.

"Do you hate me like you hate my sister?"

A pause. But his thumb moves in slow circles on my wrist. "No."

I hold my breath, waiting for more. *Needing* more.

"No, I don't hate you, Sayer." I feel him press against me. "I hate how you make me feel."

Ba-bump. Ba-ba-bump.

"How do I make you feel?" I ask, quietly.

"Crazy. Alive." Noah's grip tightens on my wrist. "Like the light has finally returned to my dark life. Like I need to protect you when all I want is to destroy you myself."

"So do it." My voice is breathless.

With a growl and a tug on my wrist, Noah pulls me into his lap. "You make me insane."

"Ditto," I breathe right before our lips slam together, hungry for what's been building between us since the night at the art gallery. Since the first night at Heathen's Hell…maybe it's been building for even longer. Maybe since I was fourteen and he searched me out in my childhood home.

We've kissed before but never has it felt like this.

An all-consuming, soul rendering kiss. It courses through my body, down to my core, all the way to my toes. His fingers lace through my hair, holding me firm, like he's trying to keep me from going anywhere.

Trust me, I want to whisper as his tongue finds mine, *I'm not going anywhere.*

But since I don't have control over my words, I'll tell him with my actions.

Clinging to him, I dig my nails into his shoulders, greedily taking all that he gives me.

And he gives me his all.

The kiss is primal and possessive. Our tongues dance until Noah pulls my hair, pulling my head back. His mouth trails kisses down my neck to my collarbone. They're not the gentle kind of kisses, but the kind that feel like branding. Marking me as his. I want to mark him back.

Skating my hands down his chest, I pull at the hem of his sweater. "I want this off."

His gruff chuckle vibrates against my throat, stretching

down to my core and I shift, wanting more friction. But Noah's hands go to my hips, keeping me still.

"Noah." I fight to move, but his grip is firm.

Giving me a smile that feeds the fervor growing in me, especially when one of his hands trails down my hip, fingers dancing along my thigh as they finger the hem of my dress. "And I want this off."

Desire feeds his stare as he looks into my eyes.

"Then take it off," I whisper, and the room turns into a blur as Noah stands up with my legs around his waist and a rumble in his throat.

Walking around to the end of the couch, he sets me down, pressing my thighs into the arm of it. In a quick, swift motion Noah pulls the dress over my head and sinks down to his knees, ripping my tights in two.

And with it goes the last remaining calm in my chest.

He finds my tattoo, the little rose outline I got last year. His eyes dance as he leans in to trace the pattern with his tongue. Leaving a trail of passion in his wake.

"*Noah.*" My hand stretches out, gripping his hair and pulling him even closer. But even that doesn't feel like enough.

My skin is scorched as his hands grip the back of my legs and his mouth presses to my aching center.

"Hmm." The sound vibrates against me, making my body purr. "I've barely touched you and already you're so wet for me."

I clench around him, his words are husky and rough and I whimper as he pulls away. I want him back, finishing the job he started.

Only to whimper again, more tormented than before, from the feel of his tongue licking me. Tasting me. *Ruining* me.

His moan of satisfaction thunders from his throat. "So

wet," he hums, his tongue darts out licking between my folds, circling my clit. My hips buck. "I could play with you all night."

I'd be a puddle by the end of it.

Already my legs quake, my breathing erratic. If Noah drags this out for hours, I don't know if I'd actually survive it.

He's already robbing me of thoughts as he goes back to pleasuring me. My body arches against the couch when his teeth graze my clit, hips pressing more into his face. Aroused by not only the feelings he's stirring up in me, but by the fact that I've brought Noah to his knees not once, but twice now.

It fills me with a power, a high I've never felt before.

Noah puts all the adrenaline in his veins into torturing me, taking my body higher and higher; building me up for a crash that doesn't come.

He pulls away and my head snaps up, glaring at his devious face as he pushes himself up. His chest brushes mine as he stands. In a touch almost too gentle to be felt, he cups my cheek, crashing his mouth to mine.

The feel of his sweater is too coarse against my chest. Reaching down, I grab the hem and pull it up, over his shoulders. Noah unfuses our mouths to let me finish, stripping him free of the layer between us.

Once it's tossed somewhere across his apartment, his arms lock around me, pulling us together. Mouth back on mine.

I feel lightheaded, drunk on his touch. His lips a sin I never want to atone for.

Pushing him away long enough to catch the breath he's robbing me of, I see the feral look in his eyes, wondering if a twin expression is in mine.

"You have freckles," I marvel breathlessly, my fingers reach out to trace the dark spots that dust across his shoulders, traveling to his back. Brown and tan paint splotches splattered along his skin.

Almost memorized, I trace them with my fingers and then with my mouth. Wanting to taste them. To taste *him.*

Pressing kisses on his shoulders and down his chest. Soon the freckles fade away but I'm still traveling a path with no guide.

Noah's chest moves steadily beneath my touch, his fists clenched at his sides until I'm on my knees, eye level to his belt, his straining hard-on salutes me as my fingers work quickly to undo the buckle.

"Sayer," he growls as I dare to press my mouth to his hard tip with only the fabric between us. "Don't start what you can't finish."

He thinks I won't. I see the mischief, the disbelief as I stare up at him.

"I don't plan on it." I smirk.

I start to pull his hardness from his pants when my hands get slapped away. Before I have time to process why, I'm being hauled to my feet. The room spins and my back is pressed to Noah's chest.

But only for a moment before he bends me over the couch. My forearms catch my fall before Noah blankets my body with his.

"I'm going to make you scream my name, Sayer. Scream it because it's going to be the only thought in your head while I'm fucking you senseless."

My throat closes up, heavy with excitement, with nerves, with need. A chariot of horses race in my chest, their steps gaining speed when I hear the unmistakable sound of foil ripping.

And he slides in with one powerful thrust.

I gasp, he fills me to the hilt and it's almost too much.

I feel full. Close to breaking as Noah slams into me, making my body sing.

Blood and death have marred his hands, but when they touch me, they breathe life into my body, awakening senses that had long since gone quiet.

He's the bad, the wolf I shouldn't want, but it's hard to remember that when he makes me feel so good.

More than good.

Extraordinary.

He works me over, reducing me to only noises and incoherent words.

"Noah."

His name is like a prayer to be heard from the stars. A prayer that turns to a chant as he licks and sucks and bites in tune with his thrusts, taking me to heights no man has achieved before.

It's not until I'm sweating and shaking, *it's too much, it's too much*, that he stops, leaving me suspended.

I whimper, trying to clench my thighs together to soothe the ache he caused and left.

"Noah," I beg, my voice hoarse and trembling. Desperate.

He doesn't say anything, but I feel his fingers on my spine, pushing me until I'm arching like a bow, an arrow cocked back ready to be pulled.

I almost fall against the cushion, but Noah's other arm snakes around my chest and grips my neck. Noah moves at a controlled, torturous pace.

"I can't," I moan as he starts to pick up speed, giving himself over to the demand. The need.

He sticks two fingers in my mouth, his stubble brushing my cheek. "You *can*. Now suck."

I do, taking his fingers in my mouth and am rewarded with another thrust. And another.

"That's it, Sayer," he burns into my skin.

Thrust. "You'll take everything I give you, Sayer."

Thrust. "You'll beg for more."

Thrust. Grunt. Thrust. "But this is mine." His hand goes to my clit, rubbing the swollen bud and making me jolt. A tiny noise escaping. "You're mine."

He flicks my clit and that's enough to send me over the edge, screaming his name. Noah's hips pick up speed, more aggressive and wild before he quickly follows me in release.

My arms give out and I collapse into the couch, forehead resting on the cushions as I try to find my breathing.

I'm a limp, sweaty mess when I feel Noah's hands reach for me. With one arm around my back, he dips low for his other to go to the bend in my knees, picking me up.

I'm cradled to his chest, barely able to keep my eyes open as he walks across the room to the stairs. I twist into his body, breathing him in. He smells like he always does, leather and amber and mahogany, mixed with more. Sex and me.

My eyes close before we make it halfway up the stairs, but I don't care. I fall asleep feeling Noah's lips on mine once more…even if it's only part of my dreams.

seventeen

Noah

"Fuck," I mumble, tripping over something solid as I get off the elevator. Glaring at the culprit, I see Sayer's school bag. What the fuck does she have in there? Bricks? Lead? Water bottles?

Eyeing it with distaste, I shove the bag against the wall before walking farther into my home.

Looking for the blonde that has me going up the damn wall.

I've spent *hours*, countless, painstakingly useless hours looking for the person who sent her that letter. As I have every day since she showed it to me. But today was different.

Last night, long after she went to sleep, a text was sent to her phone from an unsaved number.

I had some things to take care of after I put her in bed, knowing she was out by the time I laid her out on the mattress and maybe that's why I felt compelled to give her the sweet kiss that I did, but when I came back downstairs to grab my phone, I heard hers go off.

Not caring it was going against her privacy, I checked it. I had to.

And I almost threw her phone across the room when I saw what was on it.

A picture zoomed in on Sayer and me, naked with her bent over the couch. A face of pure ecstasy.

Accompanied by it was a message.

Or rather, messages.

Sluts must run in the family.

Hope you enjoy your sister's seconds.

It's only a matter of time before he grows tired of you and I get my hands on you.

X

Forgetting the work I was going to do, I strolled to the window. The appearance of calm was just that, an appearance. I wanted to smash the phone, shatter the windows. And keep Sayer locked away.

I won't do that though.

Sayer's a bird that will never go back in a cage.

The number the texts were sent from was a burner phone, completely useless.

But the picture had to be taken from one of the neighboring buildings. I took inventory. Assessed what floor could have potential to see into my place with a camera zoom. I made a list.

A list that got me fucking nowhere today.

The only lead I got was from one room. It was abandoned. It was actually in the perfect position to spy into my downstairs. But there was no trace, no clues. Gabe and I went there finding nothing. We even dusted for prints and got nothing. Thea looked on the security and ATM cameras and struck out as well.

Sayer doesn't know about the messages. I deleted it and blocked the number right after sending everything to Thea.

And Sayer isn't going to know.

I made a promise to keep her safe. And I've taken it more seriously than I ever intended to.

I mean, she's living with me for fuck's sake. All of her stuff is scattered around like it's her place. No wonder her family's cleaning service was over every single day.

Sayer Brooks is kind of a slob.

And her hair.

Her goddamn hair.

It's everywhere.

It's like living with a mangy cat, shedding and shedding. How is she not bald yet? How much hair can one person have?

It grates against my skin, my OCD. She has no sense of order. Perfectly content to leave her shit laying around. She might not have wanted to live with me, but she has had no problem getting comfortable.

Maybe it's because for the first few days she was here, I wasn't around…

Speaking of leads that went nowhere. The lead Thea sent me about Harlow also went nowhere.

I used to be good at finding people, finding things, but now I'm starting to question myself.

I blame Sayer for it.

She's soaked into my skin, embedded in my veins.

I find her sitting on one of the stools at my kitchen bar. A leg pulled tight to her chest, her chin rests on her knee as she fiddles away on her laptop, headphones in her ears. I see the white buds sticking out between pieces of her haphazardly thrown up hair.

She doesn't hear my approach, but I can hear the angsty screams of her music as I close in behind her.

When I first heard her listening to this music at the library, I'm not shy to admit I was shocked. Sayer has always shocked me. Not in big, obvious gestures but in the little finite details that make Sayer, Sayer.

Like how she drinks iced coffee even when it's freezing outside. Or how her lips almost always rest in a small smile.

Peeking over her shoulder, I see what has her rapt attention. Paintings.

A notebook sits next to her, scribbled with various colors of ink.

Homework.

That's another thing that's spewed all over my penthouse.

Her textbooks, notebooks. With her hair stuck between the pages of both.

And she still doesn't realize I'm here.

With a smirk, I lean forward. My breath hitting the back of her neck as I take out one of the buds. The minute my fingers brush against her skin, Sayer screams.

Twisting around, she smacks my arm.

Her eyes widen when she sees that it's me. But only for less than a second before they turn into a glare.

"Asshole!" She hits me again. "You don't sneak up on people!"

"I didn't sneak up." I hold up her headphone. "You would've heard me if you weren't causing damage to your eardrums."

Her glare narrows. "Do I tell you how to listen to your music? No. So don't question mine." She tries to grab the bud from me, but I close my palm around it. Keeping it from her. "Noah. Give it back."

"What if I want to listen too? I could love this song."

"Do you love this song?"

I do, actually. But I don't admit that. Our shared music tastes are just one of the surprises.

Instead, I give her the smirk that I know gets her riled up. Only this time…it doesn't.

She turns away from me, returning back to her computer screen. "I made dinner earlier. There's a plate for you in the fridge."

An uncomfortable pang fills the hollow of my chest. Something in her voice reaches past my cold exterior, grabbing me around the lungs. She cooked me dinner?

When was the last time someone cooked for me? Took care of me? Did something for me without expecting anything in return?

Never.

Dumbfounded, I stare at her backside.

Not since Sayer.

She's a breath of fresh air in my toxic world. The nice to my not, the warm to my cold. She makes me feel things I wish she wouldn't which is why I shove my foot into my mouth. "Going domestic on me now?"

She bristles, slowly turning around to face me again. "Excuse me?"

"I mean, we had sex one time last night and now you're making me dinner. What do you think this is?" They shouldn't, but each word tastes like ash on my tongue.

I see the words branded into her eyes. *Asshole.*

The look is a punch I can't block and almost knocks me over. I hate that I put that sad, hurt look in her eyes but I don't know how to stop it. I don't know how to be a sweet man.

But for her, I'm willing to try.

"It's called being nice, Noah. It wasn't meant to be taken as anything but that. You know what…" She gives me a look of hatred as she slides off the stool, shouldering past me on her way through the kitchen.

Her steps are angry, purposeful, as she stomps to the refrigerator, yanking open the door and snatching a plate with plastic wrap around it.

I lean against the bar with my arms crossed, watching her huff and puff and drop the plate, literally *dropping it,* onto my black marble countertop, not caring if the ceramic dish shattered on impact.

Sayer tears off the plastic wrap, ripping it into stretched out shreds. Some pieces fall to the floor and I rub my jaw. And she throws the plate into the microwave too fast for me to see what she actually made.

She looks at me with fierce eyes. "I changed my mind."

"About what?"

"This isn't for you, you ungrateful ass."

After thirty seconds of nuking she takes it out. It's some kind of noodle dish that she starts stabbing with a fork and shoving it into her mouth.

Forkful after forkful, noodles go into her mouth until she's not giving herself time to swallow, making her cheeks jut out like an overstuffed chipmunk.

"You're going to choke," I warn.

She does nothing but give me a cold stare over her full cheeks. Until she gets a peculiar look in her eyes and throws her fork to the floor. She runs to the sink, spitting it all out.

I rub my jaw.

After rinsing her mouth out with water, she turns around and leans against the sink.

"You've never been more attractive," I deadpan.

She isn't amused. "At least you can finally admit I'm attractive."

"Don't do that."

"Do what?" She tilts her head.

"Fish for compliments." I push away from the bar and walk toward her, swiping a bottle of alcohol off the nearby counter as I go.

An eyebrow goes up. "Pardon me for never knowing where I stand with you."

"And me saying you're attractive does?"

"Yeah." She shrugs. "At least you're not repulsed by me."

"I had my dick inside you last night. Don't know if I would call that repulsed." I stop in front of her, holding out the bottle of tequila.

"What's that for?" she asks, not moving to take it.

"To wash your mouth out." The bottle hangs between us.

"Why?"

"I don't want the taste of noodles in my mouth when I kiss you."

"You're going to kiss me?" She doesn't sound as excited as I thought.

"I'm fucking trying to."

She takes the bottle, *finally*, but sets it on the counter. "No, thanks. I'm good." She smiles up at me, not making a move to get away.

I cross my arms. "You're good?"

"Yep." She nods, a little too much. "Last night was enough to sate my curiosity."

"That so?" I don't believe her. Especially when her eyes follow my hand as it goes to my tie, loosening it.

"Ye—yeah." She clears her throat. "Totally good now. Thanks so much for those orgasms."

I chuckle, loving how her cheeks grow red as I start to undo the buttons at the collar of my shirt.

She grabs the bottle and takes a swig, wincing at the stinging taste.

Her eyes dip to my lips. But it's too late. I changed my mind.

"I'm not going to kiss you," I tell her when I shuck my shirt off, reaching around her to put it on the counter.

"I don't want you to." Her eyes dip to take in my bare chest. She swallows.

Yes, she does, she can't stop drinking me in. She's just hurt from my comment about last night changing nothing.

And it doesn't. Not my objective, not what she's here for. The only difference is now I want more. More of her bent forward, me on top of her. I want to push her body to limits no other man can take her.

She's created this appetite inside me, one only she can curb.

And I know I've stirred up the same in her.

I rub my hand down my abs, thumb brushing right above my pants. Sayer follows my movements.

"Well," I say, withdrawing my hand from my body. "Have a good night, Sayer."

Before I can turn away, she pushes away from the bar and puts her lips to mine.

I don't move, waiting for her to take charge.

Almost hesitantly, shyly, she moves her lips against mine. Sweetly at first, but quickly turning sensual. Her hands twist into my hair, her breasts push into my chest as she steps closer into my body. She tastes like tequila and desire.

"Sometimes I really hate you," she says into my lips. "You make me go crazy."

"Welcome to my fucking world." I pick her up by the back of her thighs, holding her as tightly to my chest as physically possible. "My beautiful, sweet siren," I mumble into her skin before fusing my mouth back to hers.

The kiss isn't gentle. It's rough and hungry and full of clashing teeth and a power struggle. Not between us physically, but between her heart and my mind.

She's tempted me like no one else before. Not because of her looks, even though I do find her stunning. A beautiful girl with a soft heart has never done it for me, but there's an innocence to her that I have long since lost. It draws me in, how unassuming she is. How much she's changed from her teenage years but is still inherently Sayer Brooks.

I want to explore her more.

Not just her body.

But her mind.

Just not her heart.

I have no business being in there. No business to go poking around in there. She deserves better than me. But even with that knowledge, I'm not going to stop myself from having her while I can, for however long she lets me.

With her secure in my grip, I walk her up the stairs, kissing her as I do.

It's not until we reach the top that she pulls away, squirming in my arms. I'm walking us past my bedroom door when she pulls at the end of my hair, wanting me to stop.

"Let's go in there," she breathes with impatient need.

"No," I tell her, continuing farther until we reach her room.

We're not going in my room. She can't go in there. It's the only space in the house, aside from my office, that's still just mine.

I lead us into her room, tossing her on the bed, and undoing my belt. "Let's see if we can top last night."

In a foggy haze, I reach out looking for the warmth I crave only to get empty coldness instead. Popping an eye open, I notice the space in bed next to me is how it is every night.

Empty.

Except I didn't go to sleep that way, and this isn't my bed.

Leaning up on my elbow, I reach for my glasses on the table beside me and take note of the room. Clothes and shoes are thrown around haphazardly. That's all I need to know where I am. Forget the basic, oatmeal colored walls or the nondescript furniture.

I'm in my guest room.

The one Sayer has been staying in.

I hadn't planned on sleeping here after we had sex. I hadn't planned on sleeping at all, just like I hadn't for the past week, but somehow after our last round, I collapsed on top of her and started lazily tracing circles on her soft and sated body.

I told myself I'd stay there for a few minutes, to catch my breath before I went back to searching for her sister and X but somehow a few minutes turned into more and Sayer left me to go to the bathroom, but I still didn't leave.

For the first time in twenty-eight years, I stayed.

Sayer was surprised as well when she came back out and saw me, raising an eyebrow as she walked back to her bed.

I didn't say anything as she crawled on the mattress, reaching for the covers, I didn't have an excuse when I grabbed her hand and pulled her into me.

"Noah…" she says, her hands finding a home on my chest.

I didn't want to talk. I didn't want to search for the reason why I was still here. All I knew is that I didn't want to leave and having her in my arms awoke something in me I didn't want to explore.

The last thing I remember was falling asleep to the sounds of Sayer's rhythmic breathing and the smell of honey and almond and *her*.

But Sayer isn't in here now.

Where is she?

After a quick glance to see if she's in the bathroom only for the door to be open and the light to be off, I jump out of bed.

I've learned to rely on my gut. Instead of letting emotions control me, I let my gut do the steering, but right now it's silent and that's what has my pulse kicking up.

Something's wrong.

I tear out of her room and through the second floor, only to not find her.

She's fine. She's fine. I try to rationalize with myself. My home is secure. Security is top of the line. No one can get in without me knowing…No one can leave either.

Not that I think Sayer would leave at this point. If she hadn't after me ditching her the first few nights, then she wouldn't now. I know her and I know she feels safer here than she would back at her apartment.

Then where the hell is she?

My feet pound like thunder down the stairs, I'm about to whip out my phone when I skid to a stop.

Sayer's standing at the window, overlooking the city's sky-line. The shirt I was wearing earlier swimming around her thighs.

"It's your move," she says, not turning around, but I see her twirling one of my chess pieces in the reflection.

I don't care about the game right now. I want to pull her away from the window. "What're you doing here?"

"I couldn't sleep." She sounds exhausted though.

Timid, like approaching a spooked animal, I approach her. I don't speak until my chest brushes her back. "Why?"

She seems so small right now. I can almost physically see her shrinking into herself as she says, "I'm scared."

Sayer turns around and looks at me with wide, shaken eyes.

My chest seizes. "About what?"

Maybe it's the late night hour or the fact that she's always pulled at parts I've kept hidden from everyone including myself, but I want to wrap her in my arms and never let her go.

"About everything!" she explains. "So much is happening around me and I don't know anything. I'm in the dark and I hate it, Noah. The reason why I left here was because I hated all the secrets my family kept from me. I ran from the toxic town only to find my way back after almost a year of feeling lost, but I don't feel found. If anything, I feel more lost than before. I just want to know what's going to happen. Who's after me. And what you're going to do when you find my sister."

I stare at her, dumbfounded and lost for words. She's asking me questions I don't have the answers to.

I'm not one to believe in divinity, but even I don't know what the future holds, every day brings a challenge and for me, another threat, but you can't stop it from coming, you can only be ready to face it.

And if I knew who was after her, I wouldn't be spending my nights sleeplessly trying to find them. As for her sister…her punishment has yet to be determined.

We're still standing in front of the window and I'm all too aware of voyeur assholes with a photo-taking complex. I pull her away and into the kitchen, far enough away that if anyone is watching us this early morning, they won't be able to see us from the shadows.

With my hands on Sayer's waist, I pick her up and set her on the counter as I settle between her legs. My fingers brush against hers as we both rest them on her thighs. "I came back to feel at home because the only place I've ever felt at home was my granddad's, but I don't have that anymore."

There's still a dazed look in her face, even as I move my palms up and down her bare skin. The last time she was like this was the night she found the note in her apartment. And I remember wishing I knew how to comfort her in the way she needed. I didn't think I could then and I'm not sure I can now, but the other night, when she threw the party, I recognized something in her that has always lived inside me.

Sayer Brooks is lonely.

And I have an idea on how to make her feel a little less.

"Go get dressed. We're taking a little trip."

eighteen

THE FAMILIAR HIGH RISE BRINGS A WAVE OF MEMORIES to the forefront of my mind, assaulting me one by one. So many hours, days, months, and years I spent here. A place I haven't visited in a year, but one I know better than all the apps on my phone.

Noah parks the car and I turn toward him. "What are we doing here?"

"You said you only felt at home at your grandpa's." He rubs the back of his neck, tugs at the beanie on his head, not exactly meeting my eyes.

"So you brought me to his apartment?" My eyes are wide as they rove over the familiar architecture. Just the sight fills me to the brim. Elation, hope. Only for them to quickly vanish. Replaced with images I can no longer touch.

My memories are ghosts stalking the halls.

As I open the door and step onto the cold sidewalk, my nostrils flare at the intoxicating smell of pastries wafting from the bakery a few buildings down.

I walk toward the building and run my hand along the brick, over the burn marks Harlow made when she threw a flaming newspaper at me. It's not a noticeable mark unless you know what to look for. And there it is. Faded charring over reddish brown bricks.

I feel Noah watching me as I take in how my life has

changed while the building hasn't. I've been broken and empty while the building remains strong and constant.

I guess some things just withstand time better.

Twisting around, I look at the man responsible for bringing me here. "Want to go to the roof?" There's something I want to see. To check if it's still there.

Without waiting for his response, I walk to the side of the building and reach for the fire escape. My fingers wrap around the iron bars and I pull myself up with a soft huff of breath.

As I climb the short distance, I hear the old metal creak behind me, knowing he followed. A small smile touches my lips.

When we get to the roof, I see string lights stretching across the sky above us. The small bodega owned by Helga, this woman a few years younger than my granddad who loves to garden, is still here which fills me with hope.

"Why'd we come up here?" Noah sounds annoyed and I find him glaring at the freshly ripped hole in his jacket.

"You didn't have to follow."

"You invited me."

"And since when do you listen to me?"

"I brought you here, didn't I?"

Touché.

"It's weird," he says.

"What is?"

"Being back."

My granddad has lived in the same apartment complex since I was born. I almost forgot that Noah has probably spent as much time here as I did back when he was a teenager. Sometimes I'd find him here without my sister. It was weird, but that was my granddad. Always picking up strays, always charming the pants off everyone he meets. Granddad was the kind of man who sat at a coffee shop for an hour and left being best friends with the owner.

"I know," I tell him, but already the cavity in my chest feels a little more full. "I haven't been here since he died and my parents made me clean out his apartment."

A look I can't decipher passes over Noah's face, but before I can ask about it, he steps closer. "He was a good man."

A stinging pricks my eyes. I blink it away. "The best."

Silence forms between us but it's not awkward. It's a silence that's content in the memory of someone who touched us both.

"You weren't at his funeral," I tell him. None of them were. But then again, even Harlow didn't show up.

"I was there."

"You were?" I look at him, surprised. "I never saw you."

"That's because your parents kicked me out before I could make it through the doors of the church." His jaw ticks. A year later and he's still angry.

Hell. I'm angry. My parents have always lived to be in control. "They had no right."

Noah chuckles, dark and pissed. "They think the world is at their mercy, Sayer. In their minds, they had every right." He shrugs, the movement stiff. "But I'm not here to talk about your fucking parents. We're here for you."

We're here for you.

Flutters attack my stomach. I don't know what's brought on this side of Noah, but it reminds me of the man I knew back in prep school when it was just him and I and we found each other at the lake on my parents' property. Where we talked about nothing and everything, back when I thought he hung the moon and I dreamed of a life in the stars.

The past few weeks of being in his presence, I thought that version was gone for good. He's still intense, he still wears his cold expressions, but there's a softness present in those cool blue eyes of his.

It's just as overwhelming as his intimidating stares.

"I love this view," I blurt, tearing my gaze away from his, ignoring the prickling of my skin under his stare. It's always present, always annoying.

I never want it to stop.

From the corner of my eye, I see Noah rotate to look out at the city as well. It's different from his, where the skyline is all tall buildings and shiny metals.

This is part of the city that, like my granddad's building, remains untouched by time. On the opposite side of Haven Harbor, away from the buildings with Kincaid stamped all over it is a neighborhood that feels like you're transported back to the 1930s when the town was formed.

Where kids ride their bikes between alleys, along the sidewalks. A paperboy throws newspapers onto stoups. Everyone knows everyone, everyone looks out for everyone.

I think that's why I always loved coming up here. The view brought me comfort, wrapped me in a hug while I felt nothing but coldness on the inside.

God, I sound pathetic. And I feel the pensive gaze of Noah, watching my profile diligently. Trying to get into my head. But that's the last place I want him to be right now.

He doesn't need to hear how starved for love I am on the inside. I barely admit it to myself. Who wants to say they have no one? Because that's what I have. No one.

Sure, I have Brin and other friends, but they're busy with their own lives. I don't have any family. Not any that care, anyway.

I suck in a sharp breath, the move pierces the hollow in my chest.

It's a truth I've long since avoided admitting.

I have no one.

"Sayer."

I look up, caught in the snare of Noah's face. He's watching me with a blank expression, eyes searching.

He stands so close if I twitch my fingers they'd brush his wrist and I'm still so alone. A puzzle missing pieces.

Noah reaches out, fingers grasp my chin. "You're shivering."

"A-a-am I?" I hear myself ask, teeth rattling with the wind.

"Yes," he growls like he's personally offended. He rips the beanie off his head and puts it on mine, pulling it down until it touches my eyebrows.

God. Why'd he have to do that, now his hair has the perfect tousled look going on. I love how that's the only part of himself he ever allows to be wild.

We're still so close, my breath mingling with his, and he smells so nice. Feels so warm.

He starts to lean into me, and I lean into him. His hands slide along my cold cheeks when I pull back.

That's not why I came up here.

I spin away before I do something stupid and try to kiss him on the rooftop, under the twinkling lights and fading stars and rising sun.

Instead, I move toward Helga's bodega, walking down memory lane in the process.

Yes. It's still here.

My granddad's record player. I gave it to Helga after he passed.

"I would come here when I'd fight with my parents. Granddad would come and pick me up whenever I called him." I glance over my shoulder and find him collapsing onto a deck chair. "He was always there when I needed someone. He'd never ask me any questions, either. Just showed up and took me back to his place. I'd come up here and just listen to music." Dropping to my knees, I pull out a box, flip through to my favorite vinyl and pop it on the record player.

I wonder if Helga comes up and still uses it, or if any other of Granddad's friends do, it's still in great condition.

The music filters out and fills the roof deck.

I sway to the beat, feeling more grounded than I have in a long time.

This. Being here. This is what I've been searching for. This is like coming home.

And it's because of Noah. Because he decided to bring me here. When I woke up to his body wrapped around mine, I almost didn't want to get up. I didn't want to let go of the feeling of him, but even with that feeling, I felt like I was drowning with no one around to see.

But I forgot. No matter how much of an ass he is, Noah sees all.

Like right now.

When I turn around to face him, he's wearing the same expression he does when he's buried deep inside me. Hungry. Desperate for more. Shifting in his seat, his hungry gaze taking their fill as I walk toward him—slowly.

"Sayer," he growls, low and warning. Yet he doesn't protest as I run my hands up his legs, tracing the edge of his waistline. "This isn't why I brought you here."

This isn't why I came here, but here we are.

His legs spread out and his knuckles grip the armrest on the chair.

"I don't care." I straddle his lap. Arms wrapped around his neck. "Thank you for this."

He nods, his signature broody expression in place, but he hauls me closer and nips playfully at my chin. I almost jerk back. What is happening? Who is this man? So different from the guarded one I know.

He's like a new, illustrious creature and I don't want to scare him off.

So instead I bring my lips to his and kiss him, showing my thanks in a way words can never achieve. For this. For taking me home.

We make out as the sun starts to rise, painting the sky in vibrant hues, but something just as colorful is happening inside me.

I'm falling harder for Noah Kincaid than I ever thought possible and I'm scared I'm not going to survive the heartbreak to follow.

Yesterday changed something. Within me, with Noah. Going back to my granddad's unlocked secrets I've kept away, truths I've hidden from myself.

I've always been afraid to live. I grew up sheltered, locked in a gilded cage of wealth. The only thing I ever learned how to do was be alone. Even when I left at eighteen, I merely escaped a prison to find myself in another, only this time the chains holding me back were mine.

And my only reason for it was that I didn't know *how* to live.

I had no idea what I was doing at eighteen, had never taken care of myself.

Distractions, I lived within distractions so I couldn't acknowledge just how lost, how lonely, how completely miserable I was.

Painting, creating, was my escape but for the past year, I haven't even had that.

It wasn't until Noah came back into my life that I wanted to learn.

Learn how to let go, be free from all shackles, from all the weight of the past, and *live*.

Noah has opened my eyes to many things since I've been with him, casinos and caged fights. He's piqued my curiosity and teased my wanting desire.

He brought me to the one place that's always been my home and since returning back from that rooftop palace I've realized what's been holding me back all these years.

I'm scared.

Scared to walk outside all the crafted lines.

Scared to be anything like my wild sister.

Scared to be a disappointment when that's all I've ever been to myself.

And I'm tired of it.

Noah has shown me that letting go can be more than scary. It can be bold. Thrilling.

It can be electrifying.

Noah is electrifying. Setting me ablaze with a single stare, a passing touch. Part of the reason I agreed to help Noah in the first place was because he made me feel the very thing I've been searching for.

And yesterday, I saw a different side of him.

The urgency of his steps as he rushed down the stairs, I saw that he always tries to keep tucked away.

His humanity. The part that makes him soft, the caring side that looked at me with wild eyes and held me in his arms as the sun kissed the morning sky.

Something changed between us during those early morning hours.

And I'm not quite sure I can put a name on it. Not sure that I want to.

Because the second I do it has the chance to get ruined.

I'm too interested in where it'll take me. What other secrets I can uncover from him and what else he can draw out of me.

I'm walking across campus when a familiar figure catches my eye, a sense of déjà vu washing over me.

With what feels like a lifetime ago, the same man was in that same spot, wearing the same exact charcoal pea coat, waiting for me.

Slowly, I approach him. "What're you doing here?"

"Do I need a reason to visit the person I'm dating?" He pushes off the pole.

Oh, right. We're in public. Time to put on my thespian mask.

"When it comes to you?" I force a playful smile on my face. "Always."

He puts an arm around my shoulders and pulls me close. And despite myself, I melt into him. I tell myself it's because I want to steal his body heat and not because when I woke I was craving this very thing.

Noah. His arms around me.

"I thought we could go out to eat," Noah says, walking us down the sidewalk. I feel the eyes of some people watching us as we go and it's the only thing that makes me want to pull away. I don't want this to be a spectacle. I don't want to be a prop on display.

But I stay tucked under Noah's arm. For the extra warmth.

And because I'm hungry.

As if on cue my stomach rumbles.

Noah chuckles in response.

"Where are we going?" I ask when we reach his car, the sleek black sports car that's still idling in a no park zone. "Not worried about someone stealing your car?"

He gives me a look from over the hood before popping his door open, disappearing from view.

Right, of course. No one would dare take his car. How silly of me to ask.

I open the passenger door and slide in, thankful for seat warmers.

It's not until we're pulling out of the parking lot and onto the main road that Noah answers my first question. "I was thinking Thai."

My favorite.

When I don't respond, Noah spares me a quick glance, only to smirk at the surprised expression on my face.

"I like it."

"Like what?" I study his profile. Strong and profound, I'll never get over how he's like a flesh and bone statue.

"Surprising you." That smirk grows, pulling at his cheek and crinkling the corner of his eye.

"I'm sure I'm not the only one."

"I like surprising *you,* Sayer." He shoots me another quick glance. "The way your lips part and how a crease appears between your eyebrows. It reminds me of the face you make when I'm inside you."

I feel my cheeks twinge in color, shifting in my seat. Knowing he studies me as much as I study him has my stomach doing flips.

A quip is set on my tongue when a chime from Noah's phone stops me as a sharp curse brushes his lips at the sound.

"What?" he growls in answer, the device held in a tight grip against his ear.

I strain to hear what's being said on the other line, but Noah is the only person who has his volume turned deathly low. It doesn't help that he's only answering in nonverbal sounds.

A grunt here, a growl there. Slamming on his brakes so fast that the seatbelt digs into my throat.

It's only when the call is over and he's throwing his phone up on the dash that he speaks again. Low and pissed. "I'm taking you home."

"What? Why?!" I should be embarrassed by how panicked I sound over it. For allowing him to see a weakness. "What about food?"

I don't really care about the food. I care about what that phone call was about. What flipped his mood so fast.

"There's been a change of plans."

When he doesn't elaborate further, I poke his arm. Hard. "Which is…?"

"An alert from one of your sister's old hangouts."

"What kind of alert?"

"The kind we set up to know if or when she visits them."

Suddenly it feels like my heart is locked in my throat, beating fiercely. This is my chance to uncover more secrets, to see more of his world.

To live.

"I'm going with you, Noah."

He spares me a sharp look. "No, you're not."

He wasn't budging on this, but I refused to go back to that apartment. It was stagnant without him and I refused to play house cat while he was off gallivanting the city. He was taking me with him. Even if I have to force my way.

And there's only one way I'm going to do that.

It's time I start thinking like Noah, like I'm the smartest guy in the room. I might not have the strength of an ox like Gabe or the muscles behind blurring fists like Noah, but I have my mind. And my granddad always used to say the mind was the sharpest weapon in a person's arsenal.

And my mind? I'm going to wield it like a whip.

"Yes, I am," I counter, a smug smile fighting for entrance on my face. "Because by the time you turn around and take me back to your place it could be too late. And you're not going to risk that chance. Not when Harlow could be within your grasp."

His hands tighten around the leather laced steering wheel.

That smile wins, tugging at my lips as I stare at his profile, clenched in agitation. *He knows I'm right.*

Everyone has a weakness, my granddad used to say. And Noah's is my sister. I can see the war raging in his mind as he weighs the pros and cons of bringing me along. And I see the moment he makes the decision. His grip tightens one last time before he exhales the tension out and his posture deflates with it.

I'm not fooled by it, he's a viper between the blades. Relaxed, yet waiting to strike.

"Fine," he grits out like it pains him to say it. And it just might. Noah just relinquished some control. Control that I now possess. "But you're sticking close to me. One step out of line and I'm tying and locking you up."

"Kinky." I turn away to gaze out the window.

"Sayer." His growl brings chills to my skin. "I'm not kidding."

I twist back around, staring at his profile. "Neither am I."

He glares at the road from behind his glasses, frustration packed behind it.

A small smile touches my face as I look back out the window, at the passing city. I might not have all the answers when it comes to Noah Kincaid, about what's going on with my sister, but I'm about to get a little taste.

nineteen

Sayer

As Noah pulls up in front of the building, this is the last place I'd ever expect to find my sister, further cementing the fact that we are related in blood only and strangers in everything else.

Noah doesn't look shocked as he turns the engine off. His features are set in determination, humming with pent up aggression, as his fingers find my chin and tilts my face to his. "Remember what I said."

I jerk out of his grip and push open my door. I don't look back at him as I say, "I remember."

Stick close to him like peanut butter on bread, got it. No complaints from me.

I feel more than see him round his car and stop at my side as I stare up the grand steps to the old, behemoth building. "My sister really frequented the library?" I can't keep the disbelief from my tone.

It feels so outside the realm of possibilities, but then again, before a couple weeks ago, I never thought I'd be in the position that I am. Living with Noah Kincaid. *Sleeping* with Noah Kincaid.

Still, Harlow wasn't much of a reader.

I look up at Noah for answers, already to find him watching me. "She frequented what's beneath it."

My skin tingles. "Beneath it?" I echo.

Noah nods, reaching for my hand. "I'll show you."

As we walk up the steps, I lace our fingers together, expecting him to pull away only for a smile to grow when he doesn't.

We walk through the library, between the stacks of well-worn books, all the way to the back of the building where a funny smell lingers, like mayo mixed with a warm egg sandwich.

My nose scrunches in disgust the farther back we go. "If you're leading me to some kind of torture dungeon, I'd like to know—"

"If I was planning on locking you away it wouldn't be anywhere near the smell of rancid food."

"Then where are we going?"

"Haven't you heard you're supposed to not talk in a library?" He shoots me an annoyed glance.

"Aren't you the one that believes rules are supposed to be broken?" I ask as we go down a brightly lit hallway where the bathrooms are along with a door marked for authorized personnel only.

He stops walking and I have to push my hands out to keep from running into his back. "Not the rules set up to keep you safe."

"Thought I wasn't in any danger if I stuck with you."

A frown creases his face. "Baby Brooks, you've never been less safe than when you're alone with me."

Maybe that should scare me, maybe I shouldn't welcome the little thrill that shoots through me. Maybe I should do this, maybe I should do that. Maybe I should stop caring about what falls under should and shouldn't and just give myself over to them instead.

Pushing up on my toes, I bring our mouths centimeters apart. "I don't believe you."

A rumble takes root in his chest and his arms shoot out to grab me only for them to grasp air instead.

I slip out of reach, my back pressed against the *do not enter* door.

It swings open beneath me. I start to stumble backward until Noah's hands shoot out to stabilize me. "Always a klutz," he murmurs, almost too low for me to hear. There's amusement behind it.

I brush his hands away. "I like to keep things interesting."

"That you do."

"Liar," I laugh. "I'm dreadfully boring."

He looks at me like I've sprouted three heads. "You're a lot of things, Sayer Brooks, but boring is a word I'd never associate with you."

His words touch me more than I can say. Words I'm not going to say as I push at his chest to get him to move out of the way. But of course, he doesn't budge against my might.

We're still standing in the entryway to a set of stairs that lead down to the basement or something. No doubt to a lair of gross spiders.

"Noah, move. Aren't we supposed to be looking for my sister?"

As I talk, I notice that the beginning of a smirk forming on his smug face and my ears pick up the faint sounds of music playing.

My brows pinch in confusion until I remember what he said on the sidewalk.

She frequented what's beneath it.

His smugness only grows as he takes my elbow. "Down we go, Miss Brooks."

"Down where?" I question as I take the first step. Noah's standing just behind me, following me.

"Go find out."

Letting me lead.

A sense of power, control takes hold of me as I turn on the flashlight from my phone—because there is no way I'm walking down there without some sort of light. I'd break my neck and my ankle and bruise my butt if I tried. Noah moves silently behind me. Not complaining as I take the stairs one slow step at a time.

There's a fire in my pulse, a drum in my chest as the music gets louder. Excitement. I can hear saxophones, a piano. And is…is that at trumpet?

With the help of my flashlight, I see a door at the bottom of the stairs.

Where does it go and the soulful music lead?

I try to find out when I reach the base of them, but there is no doorknob. I try to push against it. Nothing.

Behind me, Noah chuckles as his arm reaches over my shoulder and does a quick, three knuckle knock against it.

The door swings open.

"I loosened it for you," I grumble.

Noah chuckles in my ear as his hand finds the small of my back and urges me forward.

My mouth drops open as I do.

"This lurks beneath a library?" *This* is the place my sister regularly visited? "A jazz bar?"

Noah doesn't say anything, just pushes me farther inside. I stumble into the lounge, eyes wide and soaking up everything.

Lit up in an inferno of red, there is a little stage where a singer in a beaded shift dress croons into a microphone, where a trio of saxophones sing, and piano keys dance.

People sit enraptured at the tables near the stage, on the couches along the fabric walls.

"Took you long enough," a familiar voice says from a

couch close to the entrance. "I didn't know we could bring friends."

Reeve watches us with amusement as a clean-cut man in a white button-down and suspenders plays with the corded necklaces that sit on Reeve's chest.

"Looks like you found a friend yourself." I cross my arms over my chest as if that'll protect me from the glare he sends my way.

"Ah." Reeve pats his friend's head before pushing away and sliding off the couch. He moves with the grace of a cat. "He was just a means to pass the time since my boy here," he waves a hand in Noah's direction, "was uncharacteristically late. At least I now know why."

Speaking of cats…

"How's Pan?" I miss my little fluff ball so much. I've asked Noah to let him come back and he's still firm on the 'no animal in my house' rule, but he lets Reeve still come over soooo it's not the strongest argument.

"Didn't you get the picture I sent you?" He tilts his head to the side in question.

Reeve sends me pictures of him almost daily, going so far as to making Pan pose with different props. The one he sent this morning had Pan wearing a top hat, bow tie, and a suit jacket with coattails. He looked adorable in his outfit and murderous expression.

Noah mimics my stance of arms crossed as he draws the conversation away from my cat. "Where's Gabe?"

"The handsome Gabriel couldn't make it tonight, unfortunately." Reeve frowns. "We had a fight."

"About what?" I take it the two men hardly ever fight from the way Noah's watching Reeve.

"Oh, just something trivial. Nothing of relevance." He

waves Noah's concern away. "Not like your reasoning for bringing *her*."

He says it as if I'm not standing right in front of him. "Uh, hello. Hi. I'm right here. And he brought me here because I asked him to."

Reeve squints at me. "I don't remember you talking back as much."

"I feel like it's a recent development," Noah chimes in. "Apparently I bring it out of her."

Again with the talking like I'm not in hearing distance! "As thrilling as this talk of my sass is, aren't we here for a different reason?"

"Yes, we are, Baby Brooks." Reeve rotates his entire body to face me. I don't like the look on his face, like he wants to put me in my place. One far, far away from him. "Why don't you make yourself useful and tell us why your sister would come here."

He knows I don't have the answer to that, I see that as his lips curl into a cruel smile. I didn't know my sister came here at all. I'd sooner place her at an axe throwing competition than at a soothing and decadent place like this.

Reeve's smile grows the longer I'm quiet and I force myself to dig into my memory. Searching for any clues. And the only connection to this place I can make is hearing her sing in the shower.

Sure, let's go with that. Why not? "She came to sing?"

Once I say it, I wish to swallow the words up immediately. *She came to sing?* Really, Sayer? I see the same question on Noah's face. Reeve doesn't even pretend to be polite as he laughs, a deep belly laugh, at my answer.

"No!" He grabs his stomach like it's pinching him from all his amusement. "She came here for him."

He points to a man behind the bar, with dark skin and bright eyes, which are trained on us even as he pours a drink.

"How the hell was I supposed to know that?" I glare at Reeve.

"You weren't. Which means you shouldn't be here. Luckily we're close enough to the door. Go wait outside while us big kids play."

His condescending tone grates against my skin.

"I'm staying," I say the same time Noah growls, "She's staying."

Reeve snarls but doesn't further comment. It doesn't take a genius to know which one he actually listened to, but I'm going to pretend it was me.

"Why would she come see the bartender?" I ask Noah since Reeve is already stalking over to him. We're following at a more relaxed pace.

"He's a dealer. And they were sleeping together."

"Is he going to tell us anything?"

"He's the one that tipped us off."

Reeve, the perpetual flirt, is already leaning across the bar tracing the rolled up sleeve of the bartender's shirt by the time we arrive. "Miss me, Rand?"

"Still straight, Reeve." His eyes flick from Reeve to Noah, to me, where they stay.

"Everyone is a little gay." His fingers dance up Rand's.

Rand pushes him away. "Who'd you bring with you, Kincaid? I don't recognize your friend."

"Then I guess you're not reading the paper."

My face has been plastered next to his every time we go out. I like that Rand doesn't already know who I am. In a city where recognition is everything, it's nice to live with a little anonymity. Where I can be Sayer Brooks the person instead of Sayer Brooks the name.

Rand's lip curls. "I'm not one for elitist lies."

"Sure don't mind sleeping with them, though," Noah drawls.

Tension weaves between the four of us.

"I'm Sayer." I step toward the bar with my hand stretched out. Always one for manners even when trying to diffuse the thick tautness around all three men.

Rand stares at my hand before gripping it with his own. "You're the sister."

"I prefer Sayer, actually." We're still shaking hands and Noah clears his throat. I feel his hand at my elbow, pulling it out of Rand's.

Rand shoots him a look while I can barely contain my smile. *Is Mr. Kincaid a little jealous of Rand holding my tiny hand?*

"Enough niceties," Noah growls, glaring at Rand. *Why, yes, I do say he is.* "Why'd you contact us? Did Harlow reach out to you?"

He nods, reaching into his back pocket. He slides a piece of paper across the bar and Reeve snatches it up. I careen my neck to read what it says, but the ass has it tilted just enough for me not to see.

Looking unhappy, he passes it to Noah. "You're a little late on inviting me to your lover's rendezvous."

"And you're a lot late letting us know about it," Noah snarls, his eyes looking up from the paper.

Noah hands me the paper, but I don't need to read it to know what it says. Rand met up with my sister. Rand saw my sister. My sister is near. Or at least, she was. And we're too late.

I look at Noah to see his face cold, jaw hard and his eyes blazing with a thousand fires as he stares down Rand. "Why contact us at all, then, Rand?" He leans across the bar and pulls the other man in close by the back of his neck. "Wanted to rub it in my face?"

Despite the rage on Noah's face and the grip on his neck, Rand smiles. Cool and indifferent. "She wanted me to give you a message."

Noah lets go of Rand and pushes him away.

Rand stumbles a few steps and his keen eyes latch onto me. I glare at him. His stare makes me uncomfortable, holding secrets I can't touch, but I'm not going to look away. I won't cower under this stranger's scrutiny. He's heard stories about me from my sister. He expects me to shake and crumble. I've always been the scared little rabbit in the eyes of my sister.

But this rabbit has learned to grow a pair of horns and satisfaction fills me as I see the surprise on his face when I raise my middle finger and flip him off.

"Yo." Reeve snaps his fingers in Rand's face. "The message, fuck boy."

Annoyed, Rand looks to Noah. He smiles. "She's going to win."

Noah slams the door at the top of the stairs. It rattles on its hinges, giving away just how angry he is. I give him a wide birth as we walk back down the hall, Reeve decided to go find the new friend he made, leaving me alone with Noah and his temper. It pulses off him like a radiator.

When we were younger, he used to scare me like this. When he'd storm the hall of our prep school with his lacrosse stick in hand and blood on his knuckles. Now, the man has control over the anger the boy did not. He internalizes it.

I can practically see the wheels churning behind his eyes. He's thinking, plotting.

As a man who always needs to be the smartest person

in the room, needs to be several steps ahead of all his opponents, he's internalizing too much. Overthinking to the point of flaws.

And he's not going to pull himself out of it alone.

As we're walking out of the hall and through the library, I grab his arm and pull him between the stacks. His eyes blaze bright and nostrils flare as I grab his face. Forcing him to look at me.

"Calm down," I order. My voice is calm, soothing.

It doesn't work. Noah's not even focused on my face. He's not focused on anything except his thoughts.

"Noah," I try again, but he doesn't react. Doesn't blink.

He's shaking under my palms. Vibrating with anger. My sister was here. Under his nose and he didn't know. None of us did.

Not knowing what else to do, I do the one thing that seems to always work in the movies.

I kiss him. Up on my toes, lips pressed to firm lips.

Nothing. No reaction.

It's like having my lips against a brick wall, rough and cold. Unresponsive.

Looks like the movies have this wrong—

Noah makes a noise in the back of his throat, caught somewhere between a moan and a growl, that vibrates against my lips. From my lips down to my toes, that's where I feel it. Everywhere.

And he's kissing me back. Taking the helm and pushing me against the shelves. Pinning me there with his hands, his hips. His lips.

All that aggression, frustration is put into his kiss. Bruising his lips against mine. His fingers bite into my waist, pulling me closer.

Closer and closer until there's no space between us.

More, I want to moan, but there's no space for words. No wasted breath, not when Noah's too busy stealing mine with the way he holds me. The way he's devouring me.

More, more, more. I pull at his hair, his neck. The more I touch him, the harder I kiss him back, the more he melts under my touch. That anger thawing into something else. Something more.

Calming. Savoring.

His lips move down my neck, finding the sweet hollow spot that has me gasping under his match.

He's the fire and I'm the kindling. He feeds me, burning me from the inside out and making me forget where we are or how we got here or what happens next.

I'm not focused on anything except—

He pushes me back hard enough for the shelf to wobble. I pull away with wide, dazed eyes.

The library. We're in the public library.

Noah's forehead goes to mine. "God, Sayer. What're you doing to me?"

Husky and like sandpaper, his voice has my heart pounding.

"Why don't you tell me?" I challenge in a whisper. Surprised I can even get that much out as I stare at his lips and resist the urge to bring them back to mine, wishing they traveled to other places as well.

"You're a siren sent to tempt me."

"And do I tempt you?"

I lean in close only for him to pull back. Heat simmering in his gaze.

"More than I anticipated."

An elevator closing isn't as satisfying as the sound of a slamming door. How I long for the sharp, angry sound of a good door slam right now.

"*NOAH!*" I yell, stomping into the apartment.

I get no answer.

But I know he's here.

He wasn't at the club. He wasn't at the casino.

When I called Thea to ask where her asshat of a friend was after he took it upon himself to ruin my day, she told me he went home to work.

He never works from home.

Which lets me know he orchestrated this on purpose.

"*NOAH! YOU STUPID PRICK!*" I stomp toward the steps, taking them two at a time until I reach his office.

The door crashes into the wall as I throw it open.

There he is. Sitting at his desk. Waiting for me.

"You yelled?" His hands are folded behind his head.

"What. Did. You. Do?" Each word is spat through gritted teeth.

"What's wrong, BB?" he asks, grinning.

"You towed my car!"

He smirks in answer.

My fists clench tighter "You made me miss my lunch with Brin!"

He keeps his smirk. "You're welcome."

Momentarily, my anger washes away, replaced with confusion as I stare at him and his smugness. "Excuse me?"

"You. Are. Welcome." He punctuates each period harder than the last.

"Noah, if you don't stop being vague-mystery guy I am going to—"

"There was suspicious activity around your car while you were in class. Thea went to go check it out and noticed something strapped underneath it."

Air leaves my chest.

He stands from his desk, walking toward me.

"Wh—what?" I whisper, unable to process much of what he said, only that it's left me cold. Numb. So numb, I barely feel his thumb brushing my cheekbone.

Jerking away from his touch, I demand an explanation.

"Will a video do?" he responds.

He has a video?

I nod, making a hand motion for him to hand it over. He doesn't, instead, he holds the phone in front of me.

I press the play button.

In black and white images, a person with a hood pulled over their head glances around the parking lot before dropping to the ground and crawls under my car.

The video feed doesn't show what happens underneath, but after a few minutes, they crawl out and walk away.

Oh my God.

"We thought it was a bomb," he says, returning his phone to his pocket. "Turns out he only cut the brakes."

My eyes widen. "*Only?*"

"Compared to an explosive, yes."

So many thoughts float in my head. Wrapping my arms

around my waist, I look to find his face blank. "Did you catch him?"

He shakes his head. "We're working on it."

I nod, but it does nothing to reassure me. Why me? What did I do to bring this on? According to Noah, nothing. But cutting my brakes doesn't feel like nothing.

"They're not going to touch you," he growls, protectiveness creeping in.

"But if they do?" I can't help but worry.

"They won't," he vows. A promise as strong as a contract, as the mountain ridges.

"Noah—"

"When are you going to realize that you're mine?" He pulls on my hair, voice husky. "That no one is going to touch you."

"Around the same time you realize I'm not a pet to be owned."

He grabs my wrist, twisting and pinning it behind my back, pulling me close. "I think it's about time you learned something, Baby Brooks."

"And what's that?" Defiant. Always a joy. Challenging him.

I like the taste of defiance on my tongue, full of empowerment and steel.

It tastes freeing.

By the way Noah's eyes dance, I think he enjoys it as much as I do.

"I don't want to own you." Noah's fingers drift under my chin, directing my gaze to meet his wicked eyes. Eyes of a man who knows what he wants and won't stop until he gets it. "I want to see the world from your point of view. I want to taste you and fuck you until I have every inch of your skin committed to memory."

I shiver, face heating with his words.

Since the morning he took me to my granddad's old apartment, things have been different. Noah hasn't been as cold, almost playful. And he's been around. Every morning, I might wake up alone, but all I have to do is travel downstairs to find him seated at the bar.

We still play our chess game, with one move a day. It's slow going, but it's one of my favorite parts of the day.

"Be careful with those words, Noah, or you might have me catching feelings." I smirk while a small voice inside me hisses, *too late.*

I try my best to ignore it.

"That'd be the stupidest thing you could do."

I ignore the sting his words bring. He's right, but that doesn't mean I'm going to listen. Logic and the heart don't always go hand in hand. If it did, I would've never stepped foot back in this town.

Originally, I came in here to ream his ass out but now, this close to him, wrapped in the intoxication that is Noah Kincaid, I've decided I want something else.

I run a hand down his tie, feeling his gaze as I wrap it around my hand. Once, twice, pulling him close until there's no space between us.

Stretching on my tiptoes, I lean in until our lips are a hairsbreadth away. "How much do you want me, Noah?"

He doesn't answer save for his fists clenching at his sides. His sharp intake of breath.

He doesn't need to.

Not when I have my answer in the form of his hard-on brushing against my stomach. Steel encased in a custom suit, just waiting to be let free.

I loosen my grip on his tie, smoothing it on his chest as I sink to the ground.

"Sayer." His voice is gruff, fist clenching my hair.

My eyes dance as I look at his dick still straining against his zipper.

It's a struggle to keep from licking my bottom lip.

"Perfect," he murmurs. "You look so perfect on your knees with those flushed cheeks and plump swollen lips, just waiting for my cock."

My thighs clench as lava churns deep in my core.

His thumb traces my bottom lip while heat and desire simmer in his eyes. "Do you want to suck me off?"

"No," I tell him as my eyes betray me by drifting toward his erection. My fingers itch to let him free.

"I think you do." Each word is more strained than the last. He's struggling, edging on losing control.

Smiling, I peer up at him from under my lashes. "I think you're the one that wants to get me off."

"Damn right I do." His nostrils flare.

I return my attention back to his cock. "What do I get if I do?"

Noah doesn't speak for a long time, or at least it seems that way as I feel the carpet fibers bite into my knees.

Finally, he says, "You don't know what you're asking for, Baby Brooks." There's the grin I loathe to love. "But you're about to find out."

Before I can articulate a response, he has me by my armpits, hoisting me up, setting me on the edge of his desk.

I barely get my hands wrapped around the lip of the desk before he's pushing at the hem of my dress and splitting my legs apart.

Fitting himself between them, he wraps a hand gently around my neck, thumb brushing my pulse when a throat clears from behind Noah.

I jump while he freezes.

His hand doesn't leave my throat as he shifts his head to

peer over his shoulder. I stretch my neck like a giraffe to see past his frame.

Gabe stands in the doorway, his thick arms are crossed loosely over his chest, amused as he stares at us. "Don't stop on my account."

Noah's hand disappears from my neck, and as he turns around, his arms reach behind him to knock my knees together.

"What are you doing here?" he growls.

Gabe raises a brow. "How quickly he forgets." Pushing off from the doorframe, he walks farther into the room.

"Gabriel."

Gabe grins. "I'm here to escort you to the fight."

"Fight?" Noah echoes my thoughts.

What fight?

Gabe's brow goes higher as he clicks his teeth. "I'm disappointed in you, Noah. Never have you lost your mind over the taste of pussy before."

"Gabriel," Noah growls again, the sound deep in his chest. Warning.

Gabe grins. "Fine, I'll fill your sex-clouded minds. The fight with Seamus is tonight. You still want those answers, right?"

Crap! I forgot that was tonight. And by the way Noah looks when I peer around his shoulder, so did he.

Noah nods.

Slowly, I slide off the desk. My body brushing against Noah's backside.

"C'mon, boss," Gabe calls, a dark smile on his face. "Let's go have some fun."

"Give me a second," Noah tells him before turning to me. "Thea's going to come get you and take you there. I need you to stick close to her and listen in case anything gets out of hand."

I lift a brow. "Plan on things getting out of hand?"

He gives me a cold, serious look. "You never know at these kinds of things. So for both our sakes, stick close to Thea. Please."

It's the please that gets me. It sounds foreign on his tongue and I hear the worry behind it. It's what has me nodding, promising I'll stay with Thea.

Some relief finds its way onto his face and he kisses me so hard and fast, I barely feel it before he's following Gabe out the door.

I don't know what's going to happen tonight, but hopefully we're one step closer to the madness ending.

A heavy feeling presses down on my chest...the sooner this is over the sooner I'll have to say goodbye to Noah.

Thea comes to collect me exactly ten minutes after Noah left.

"What're you doing?" Thea asks when she finds me still in Noah's office.

"Staring."

She shakes her head at me and grabs my arm, pulling me out of the room. "We have to go."

"Why am I even going?" I ask, hearing the pounding flesh from a couple of nights ago in my ears.

I don't think I could handle watching Noah get hit again. The last time was bad enough. Him sprawled out on the ground is still fresh in my mind.

"Noah needs you there."

Hearing the words Noah and need in the same sentence do things to me I can't describe.

I let Thea lead us downstairs, to the car where Jenkins is waiting.

"Why does Noah have a driver if he never uses him?"

"He's more for everyone else than Noah." Jenkins glances at us from the rearview mirror.

"Why?" A light bulb goes off. "Because his parents?"

Thea nods. "He has to be in control. He doesn't trust anyone else."

I'm quiet for the rest of the ride.

Thankfully, it feels quicker than the last time we came here.

Once we're out of the car, Thea walks ahead to the building's door. After she bangs on it, a slate opens to reveal a set of eyes.

No words are traded as Thea pushes up the layers of her clothes to reveal her marked arm.

The slate closes and the door opens.

We're in.

Before we reach the door that leads to the ring, Thea grabs my arm and slows our steps. "The same rules apply as last time, Sayer."

I nod. My promise to Noah nags me.

"I'm going to add one more."

I wait for her to elaborate.

"If anything happens, you run and hide like hell. Wait for me or one of the guys to find you."

Her tone is grave and swallowing becomes difficult as I take in the matching expression on her face.

"What's going to happen?"

"I don't know. Just promise me."

I nod again, in promise.

She smiles, but it doesn't touch her eyes. "Ready?"

I don't get to answer before we walk into chaos.

The pits of hell are even more crowded than the last time. The air is more potent. Everyone buzzing with anticipation.

Thea, without the assistance of Gabe and Reeve this time, elbows our way through the crowd until we're up on the chained link fence.

The ring is empty.

"Where are they?"

"This fight is a little different," Thea tells me as if she heard my thoughts. "Noah and Seamus are going to be making an entrance."

As Thea's explaining, the lights go off in the ring and a hush falls around the crowded room.

Everyone antsy with what's to come.

Two mega lights flip on, each illuminating the entrances to the ring, Spotlights that capture our opponents.

"In one corner," Thea whispers for only me to hear. "Weighing in at two hundred and ten barrels of whiskey we have Seamus Kelly."

The crowd goes wild, screaming and booing. Someone even throws a shoe. Seamus remains unfazed, a cool look of indifference on his face, the robe he wears falling to the ground when entering the ring, showing his stalk of fiery red hair.

"And in the other corner," she continues. "Weighing two hundred twenty pounds of bad attitude is Noah Kincaid."

Noah steps out and the screams are deafening. But he remains wholly unaffected as he makes his way down the small walkway, dropping his robe as he goes. He doesn't stop until he's in the center of the ring, his sole focus on Seamus.

Reeve, dressed in a black and white striped blazer with no shirt, who is the ref, makes the two opponents step forward. I watch his lips move but can't make out the words.

He steps away as Seamus springs forward. Squaring a fist in Noah's jaw.

I cringe, my stomach twisting, feeling the hit as if it was my own.

But Noah doesn't waste any time with his retaliation. He attacks Seamus with a vigor I've never seen from him, punches with a vigor that shouldn't belong to any man.

He hits and hits and hits, landing on Seamus's ribcage, his shoulder, his gut and everywhere in between, leaving welts the size of fists in his wake.

Next to me, I feel Thea cringe with every hit Noah lands. I stare at her.

When she sees my questioning gaze, she looks away with a hardened face. "Kick his ass, Noah!" she screams.

The fight is dirty and gritty, neither man holding anything back. A couple of minutes in and already sweat sheens their bodies.

"When does the fight end?" I shout in Thea's ear. The crowd rowdier than the other night.

"When one of them can't stand up anymore."

Vicious. Archaic. People really enjoy this? I don't understand it, not when my gut tightens and churns.

My throat closes when Seamus gets out of the hold Noah had him in, slamming an elbow on Noah's back. He stumbles before righting himself.

Unable to stomach anymore, I look around at the crowd. Hoping that will distract me when I see a figure who catches my attention.

Not because I recognize them or because they stick out in a crowd. I notice them because they shouldn't.

Dark pants, baggy jacket, and low hood pulled over their head.

Noah and his friends wear similar attire all the time.

It shouldn't matter to me, it shouldn't be worthy of garnering my attention.

But it does.

And as if they feel my stare, they shift toward me. A sea of people separate us, but I know they're looking right at me.

Invisible spiders crawl down my back, making me shiver.

Slowly, everything else fades away. And not the kind of fading when it comes to Noah, where it's just him and I in the room even when surrounded by people.

No, this is different, where everything disappears in stages.

First the noise goes, then the people, then it's only the stagnant air and the feeling of knowing something's going to happen, but you don't know what.

Until I do.

They reach behind their back and suddenly a gun is in their hand, held above their head as one, two, three shots fire in the air.

All hell breaks loose with it.

People scream and shove, turning into frantic mayhem as it takes Noah and Seamus a minute to catch on that the sound wasn't encouragement or cheering.

It was a threat.

A threat that's staring at me. Barrel aimed at me. Chamber loaded for me.

I'm immobilized, railed to the ground in fear.

Some people have a fight or flight instinct in the face of death.

I have a scared opossum reaction where I freeze up.

I can't move. Not even when my head is screaming at my legs to *go, go, go.*

The only movement I'm able to do is looking at Noah when he calls my name.

I see my truth in his face.

The pain in the knowledge that he won't be able to reach me in time.

It's so pure, so full of things he's never said that my heart cracks knowing I'll never see that raw emotion on his face again.

I don't know where Thea went, or where everyone aside from Noah is, as another shot rings out. Masses are pushing and shoving, screaming and crying to reach an exit when everything happens so fast.

I wait for a blow that doesn't come.

Instead, I get tackled to the ground. Hard.

My elbows and chin collide with the floor, unprepared. A loud popping pierces the air.

My body tenses and not just because there's a man of hard, solid muscle sprawled out on top of me.

It's enough to shake me from my possum chamber.

I buck my hips, shouting, "Get off—"

He smothers my mouth with his hand. I feel his lips press into my ear as he angrily whispers, "Shut the fuck up."

Gabe.

I relax into the sound of his voice.

The popping goes off again, this time longer and even louder than before and my body goes tense again. It sounds closer.

My body starts to shake.

Gabe squeezes my shoulders, shaking his head against my temple. "You're going to be fine." His whisper barely audible.

Gabe shifts behind me and I peek to see him reach behind, pulling out a sleek gun of his own. He leans up a little and starts firing back.

I feel something zip by me. A bullet.

And then another one.

More fly.

Until suddenly…

They stop.

Gabe rolls off me as footsteps race toward us.

"Gabe," I whisper, not getting an answer in return. Gabe gets to his feet, the gun rests casually between his fingers at his side as if he was holding a cell phone.

The footsteps get louder. Until they stop.

Reeve and Thea stop just short of where Gabe is standing above me. Both holding guns.

"The shooter ran off," Thea pants.

"What happened? Where's Noah?" Looking around I don't see him anywhere. Dread settles in my stomach while my words seem to light a fire under Reeve's skin.

"What happened?" Reeve growls, glaring at me as I get to my feet. "What happened was that some fucker decided to open fire on you and Gabe saved your life instead of going after the fucker."

His words are accusing. As if he thinks I called up the people with the guns and asked them to shoot at me. Nothing like a little target practice to get the blood flowing.

I hug my elbows as I glare back. "Don't act like this was my fault. I didn't ask to be dragged here."

"You're fucking bad luck, Brooks. Throwing all the shits and balances off. I'll blame you however I damn well please."

Thea tries to put a hand on his chest, to calm him, but he growls at her, smacking her hand away.

"He's drunk," she explains.

"So you let him handle a gun?" I balk.

She rolls her eyes. "He's not that drunk."

"I'm not drunk at all, idiot," Reeve growls at her. "My hatred for Sayer trumps my compassion for something that's her fault to begin with."

"Reeve!" Thea snaps. "Leave her the fuck alone. She didn't plan this!"

"Why should I leave her alone?" He steps in her space,

tilting his head. "Because you finally like a girl Noah's fucking? Not my problem you don't have friends outside of us."

Noah. His name causes a siege in my chest. He's still not with us.

Thea's eyes widen in hurt that she blinks away as I look around the now abandoned warehouse. "Where's Noah?" I ask again.

"Here."

Twisting around to the sound of his voice, low and decadent, his face is fierce as he stalks toward us. Toward me. Even with the distance separating us I feel his eyes on my body, assessing it. Drinking me in.

Thea and Reeve continue to argue, but I don't hear them.

I'm too busy being entranced by Noah's powerful strides. And I don't think. I run. Eating the distance between us with my steps until there is none and I'm jumping on him. My arms around his neck and legs twisted around his waist.

He catches me easily, not stumbling back in step. He's solid beneath me, not moving. I'm not even sure I feel him breathing.

I don't know what just came over me, but it was like an outside force controlling my body. And now I'm wrapped around him, holding tight while his hands are still at his sides.

Too grateful that he's okay to care at first he's not hugging me back. The feel of him is enough—a lie I try to convince myself of until I can't.

He's still not hugging me.

While he's as still as an unmoving tree, my thoughts run at the pace of a sharp winter's breeze.

Why isn't he hugging me?

Should I not be hugging him?

I want to let go, but my body isn't listening. I feel like it never listens when Noah is around.

And then slowly, almost unperceivable, his arms start to move.

They wrap around the base of my back, locking around me like bands of iron.

His head tilts, resting on top of mine. I don't know what to do now for a whole new reason.

Noah's touching me in a way he never has before. It's not tender—a word like that could never be used for a man like Noah. He holds me as a necessity, like he needs to and can't let go.

And I need him.

"They're gone," he growls, frustration bleeding from his tone.

"Gone?" Thea asks.

"Just fucking disappeared. I need you to get on the city cameras."

The events of tonight have crashed down on me like rubble from a tumbling mountain and I hold him a little tighter. His hold adjusts as well, matching my strength with his own.

Nothing else outside of us exists, not when I'm in his arms. Not when I never want them to leave now that I have them. And especially not as he whispers, "I got you, Sayer. It's okay."

His hand comes up to cup my neck and his thumb brushes my pulse. "It's okay."

At first, I'm confused, why is he saying that?

But then I feel something small and wet roll down my cheek, down my chest and realize why.

I'm crying.

I'm crying and didn't even know it.

How numb have I really become?

Pulling away, just enough to be able to look into his restless face—a combination of fierce fighter still on the offensive and budding concern for me—I start to say something when Thea screams for us.

In a blur, Noah drops me from his chest and is shoving me behind him as he reaches for his gun…I balk, not even knowing he was holding one.

That killing machine was pressed against my back. He held me with such a need, such urgency, I didn't even realize…

Not even being offended by Noah shoving me behind him, he is the one with the gun after all, I simply stretch on my toes and peer over his shoulder.

And see why Thea yelled.

It's Gabe.

Gabe who's been quiet this whole time.

Gabe who's swaying with a nonexistent breeze.

Gabe who presses a hand to his side.

Gabe whose body just seems to crumble. Falling at the knees to the ground.

Reeve lets loose a string of curses, pushing his gun into Thea's hand, and lunges to catch his friend before he hits the floor.

Gently, a word I never thought I'd think in terms of Reeve Morgan, he lowers Gabe to the ground, talking to him in a voice too low for me to hear.

I shoot a look at Thea, who mouths, *Are you okay?*

I'm a mess. And have been for weeks now…longer if I'm being honest.

Reeve clears his throat and I'm shocked at what I see.

Gone is the look of playful indifference and in place is an expression I never thought I'd see on Reeve Morgan.

Fear.

"Gabe's been shot."

twenty-one

Sayer

FINGERS WRAP AROUND THE BACK OF MY NECK, AN ARM secure at my waist. Sweaty forehead to sweaty forehead. I don't know whose embrace I'm in, only that their hips grind into mine and my pulse beats in tune with the song.

Multicolored laser lights zip between us. The weight of his body is enough for me to ignore what will be awaiting me when I venture home.

The wrath of my keeper.

This morning he told me not to leave the apartment. As he has told me for the past few days. Ever since Gabe was shot.

Not that I care what Noah says right now.

I haven't cared about anything the past few days.

Not him.

Not my sister.

Not this fake dating thing we've put on.

Not the feelings that have taken root inside me.

Nothing. I don't give a single shit about anything.

Gabe might've been the one that got shot but as the hours ticked on that night, the more locked up I became. To the point where even Noah couldn't provoke a response out of me.

I don't even know why I'm like this, other than the fact that I can't shake the knowledge of a gun being pointed at me.

They were after me.

And someone got hurt because of it.

Gabe's fine, sleeping the days away in Noah's other guest room.

The night he was shot, everyone moved at a frantic pace to get him back to Noah's where a doctor on their retainer met us. She was able to stabilize him and remove the bullet, but she was concerned about him getting sick or an infection, so he's been the latest addition to the Kincaid Hotel.

He's fine. The bullet missed all major arteries.

But having him at Noah's place has just been too much. A reminder that these people who have been trying to help me are getting hurt.

And maybe I shouldn't care, but I do because I can't not. That's just who I am.

So when Thea texted me, wanting to go out tonight, I couldn't respond YES fast enough. Normally, clubs are the last place I want to be but tonight is different.

I need one night.

One night to get away from Noah and everything. Where I can be free and numb and just dance.

A faceless person in a sea of strangers.

And that's what I'm doing at Harlots, the rival club to Heathen's Hell. When Thea asked where I wanted to go, I said anywhere but Heathen's Hell.

So, Harlots, we came.

And I'm having a *blast*.

I've danced with Thea for half the night. We've drunk and danced and laughed, but she got pulled away by some stranger two songs ago and before I could follow, I had a stranger of my own wanting to dance.

So I did, letting them help forget what a tailspin my life has taken in the recent weeks and enjoying tonight as if it might be my last.

And it very well could be.

No doubt Noah knows I left.

He didn't *really* think I was going to listen, right?

If he didn't know I left as soon as I got in the elevator, he found out when I slipped the shadows he assigned to me. That's right, I get put on house arrest and receive two bodyguards.

How lucky am I?

As soon as I lost the guards, they probably alerted Noah to what I'm doing. Oh well. I'll deal with that when the time comes.

My guy's hands snake lower, down my sides and over my hips. He pulls me closer as I feel his lips graze the side of my neck.

I wish I could make myself lean into him, but I can't.

His touch is wrong.

Nice and welcomed, but so wrong. Subtle, not demanding.

Leading but not wielding.

He doesn't hold me like he can't help himself, drawing himself to me like a magnet.

His touch doesn't hold power.

His touch isn't Noah's.

And that's the root of the problem.

I crave the touch of a man who sends me spiraling with a single glare and ignites me with a passing touch.

I don't have that man right now, though, so I search for those feelings in the one I have, leaning into him—pushing aside who I want for what I have.

But no matter how hard I pretend, the hands on me still feel amiss.

I close my eyes, pressing into him harder, wishing they felt right, when he pulls away.

Before I can turn around, hands slide around my waist. Different hands. *Familiar* hands.

I stop dancing. Chest heavy.

My former dance partner now stands in front of me, brushing off his pants. He shoots a glare over my shoulder, hands balled into fists before his eyes widen at the person behind me.

"This is why you disobeyed my request? To dance?" His voice is thick, his laugh cruel. "Then let's dance." His hips roll once, twice—embers crackle within me.

I try to pull away from Noah in frustration, but his hold on me is tight, keeping me locked to his body.

"Let me go."

His head dips low as he answers simply, "No."

I begin to struggle, but his grip doesn't relent, only tightens. I spent time dancing with the other guy wishing his touch was like Noah's, but now that I have Noah's arms around me I want them gone.

It's a vicious cycle.

"I told you to stay at home, Sayer," he rumbles at the low octave, rich bourbon on ice.

Too bad all I feel is the ice. "Just because you said it doesn't mean I'm going to listen."

His fingers sting my skin. "Does it?" He sounds amused.

With his head dipped low, I feel his scruff scratch the shell of my ear.

He missed his shave today.

"It's not going to work." If I had control over my arms, I'd cross them.

"What is?"

"You trying to intimidate me."

"Is that what I'm doing right now?" he asks, his hips

move at a sensual pace. "Here I thought I was trying to get a pretty girl to dance with me."

Pretty girl.

My heart leaps, the first reaction I've felt in days.

I twist in his arms. Chest to chest.

Looking into his eyes, I find myself shocked at what stares back.

With a face carved like his, it's always going to be hard, but there's something in his expression that has me sucking in a breath. A look that robs me of thought.

An openness that he's never shown me before. Cupping my cheeks, he brings our foreheads together. Our noses touch.

"I want you to come back to me, Sayer." His hands move from my cheeks to the back of my neck. "I don't like you like this. So close but so far out of reach."

It's the realist he's ever been with me. "Noah—"

His mouth crashes against mine, shutting me up and stealing my words. Cradling the back of my head, he devours me like I'm his last meal. I cling to him, opening for more. My nails bite his flesh.

He's not kind or soft. He's possessive and in control.

And it awakens pieces that have wilted within me.

His touch is sin. His kiss poison. And I'm too busy drowning in him to care about a cure.

Breaking the kiss, but not going far, Noah's thumb caresses my pulse. "I can't believe you're making me do this in fucking Harlots."

We're still close enough so my lips brush his as I say, "I'm not making you do anything. I just wanted to dance."

"By dance, you mean grinding your ass on some other guy's dick to get my attention."

"Let's get something clear, Noah." I push against his chest, wanting out of his grip. He doesn't twitch. "I didn't do anything to get your attention. Didn't even know you were here! So, go deflate that big ego of yours and take a step back. Not everything is about you."

He tilts his head.

"Maybe," I continue, unable to not tempt the tiger. "I wanted to dance with him. For his hands to be on me instead of yours. Maybe he makes me feel things that you don't."

My words are bitter.

A taste Noah doesn't care for.

"You wanted to dance with him. You wanted him to touch this." He runs his hands down my body.

I step out of his grip and his eyes flash. "Wanted him to touch *my body*?" I correct. "Yeah."

Never mind the fact that I wanted the touch to be yours.

"I don't share." Slowly, he curls his fists.

"There's nothing to share when I'm not yours, Noah!"

The air turns to ice as Noah's eyes flash and his jaw ticks when he hears my words. It was the wrong thing to say, I knew that the moment I said them but I couldn't stop myself. A kernel of me wanted it. Wanted to say the words and inflict some kind of reaction.

To prove me a liar.

He's not a man of words, they're his weapon and he only knows how to inflict pain with them.

He's a man of touch, his hands speaking a language that's foreign to his tongue.

And my words…they struck a chord.

"Wrong thing to say," he growls, grabbing my arms and hauling me to his chest. "You think I do this for anyone? Let someone come into my home and leave their clothes, books, fucking strands of hair everywhere and making a mess in the order I've created."

My breathing turns labored and not because of all the dancing I've done.

"I didn't need you to get Harlow back," he continues. "I didn't need all the chaos you created when you came back into my life. But have I complained once about helping you? No. Why? Because I *wanted* you. I want you."

His admission shocks me, robs me of speech.

Staring at him, my eyes frantically look for the lie. His tell. But he's steady as ever. Of course, he's calm in the wake of his words. Why not? He's melting the ice in me.

And he's not done.

"You're mine because you fucking own me, Sayer Brooks. And I'm pissed as hell that you're making me say this in fucking Harlots."

I blink, suddenly remembering where we are. Not alone, but in a club. Standing still while madness moves around us.

And it's too much.

It doesn't feel real.

Maybe it would if we weren't in public. If it was just him and I, but I can't trust anything that leaves his mouth when we're in public.

None of this is real.

His touch can lie as much as his words.

And I don't believe his hold now.

I tear away from Noah.

He tries to grab me, but I dart away, spinning into the crowd.

Pushing and shoving my way through, I hear Noah shout behind me, but I don't stop and soon I have the exit in view.

"Sayer." Noah grabs my arm, stopping me from escaping.

"Let me go, Noah." I keep facing forward until he doesn't give me a choice, turning me around.

"Sayer—" Someone knocks into him and the hold on me

loosens. Not wasting a second, I pull free and all but run to the exit.

However, I get stopped again when a very tall man steps in my path. I slam into his chest and his arms shoot out to steady me. Not letting me go.

Blinking up at him, it takes me a minute to process who it is.

Seamus grins down at me. "Going so soon?"

He's bigger than I remember, bulkier where the leather of his jacket strains against his shoulders. More bruised too. I'm close enough to realize that his face isn't just covered in bruises and his hands aren't only home to tattoos, but also freckles. Small, light freckles.

Noah's freckles are better.

I start to back up, but he follows me like a snake charmer, weaving his body to the music while making my exit impossible.

My back hits the table's edge and the charmer's arms go on either side, a cage of ripped muscle and soft leather and smoky cloves.

"How rude of me. You and I haven't been properly introduced." He leans down. "I'm Seamus."

When I don't say anything, he tsks. "This is where you say who you are."

"You already know who I am." My jaw aches from how hard I'm clenching it.

"Indeed, I do. But what I don't know is: what does he want from you?" His voice sends a shiver down my body. And not from the sensual sound of the octave or the timbre that shakes his Adam's apple against my shoulder. "What makes you so special?"

"What does who want from me?" I play coy. It's not hard to guess who he means, though.

"Aw, don't play dumb, blondie." He sounds disappointed. "That's such a stereotype."

He leans even closer. "Let me be more—"

A fist skims my face as it protrudes from behind me—slamming into Seamus's nose.

"Mother*fucker*," he roars as he stumbles back.

A cold hand grabs my shoulder, pulling me back.

Noah.

The face of a seething man stares down at me for a moment, his eyes swirling with hatred.

"Go back home, Sayer," he whispers. He doesn't wait to see if I listen before turning his back on me and gave his full attention to Seamus.

I stay where I am even as the neon EXIT sign beckons from across the floor.

"She's not a part of this, Seamus."

"How I beg to differ." Seamus leers at where I still stand over Noah's shoulder. His attention wracks over my body.

When Noah looks over his shoulder to find me still here, his eyes narrow.

Seamus mumbles something low. Too low for me to hear, but by the slits that once were Noah's eyes, I'm guessing it's not good.

Noah swings around and decks Seamus again. With a hook packed with enough force that I cringe at the sound of it connecting to his jaw, Seamus falls to the ground while cradling his face.

It's like fight night all over again, except Noah appears more unhinged.

Noah steps forward, but a body slips between and makes a grab for him. *Gabe.*

Reeve, Thea, and Gabe circle around us. Gabe, who was

bedridden for most of the day, has his arms wrapped around Noah, restraining him. Barely.

Seamus stumbles to his feet, spitting blood. "She a better lay than Harlow? Maybe I'll have a go of her when you're done."

Noah yells and lunges. Gabe grits his teeth, trying to keep his grip.

My cheeks flame as I feel Thea touch my shoulder. I twist around in time to watch her school her face, concealing the emotions she doesn't want anyone else to see. But I do. And I frown.

Thea doesn't see. She's stuck on Seamus.

Seamus continues his taunting, "What do you say, Brooks? Want another round of your sister's sloppy seconds?"

I recoil. My sister…and *Seamus*?

"Leave her out of this, Seamus," Noah growls, lunging for him again. Gabe's skin looks clammy as he struggles to hold him, with beads of sweat lining his forehead.

Reeve, who's been standing next to a stunned Thea, steps between them. He pushes Noah into Gabe, keeping him back.

"Go home, Sayer," Gabe sneers over his shoulder, adjusting his hold on Noah, arms wrapped around his neck and sternum. "We got this."

Noah grunts, struggling to get free.

I catch Thea's eyes and know that this is long from being over. Noah's just getting started, especially when Seamus rasps, "Don't you want to know where Harlow is?"

It's like a flip switches Noah's focus. He stops struggling against his friends. "You don't know where she is."

"Are you willing to bet on that?" Seamus's eyes flick to me.

Noah's not. He never got answers from the other night.

And it's not just because of me.

It's about my sister. It's about revenge. Justice.

My time here is done.

So I turn around before Noah can answer. I don't need to stick around to hear it. I don't have to.

He's going to say yes.

Because Harlow will always win. Even when she's not here.

Without a backward glance, I leave Harlots and hail a taxi to drive me off into the foggy night.

I knew his words on the dance floor were an act.

twenty-two

Sayer

I STARE AT THE CHESSBOARD, AT THE PIECES THAT HAVEN'T moved for days. They're waiting, like me, for when the next move will be made.

Noah hasn't been home in two days. Haven't seen him since I left Harlots.

He called a couple hours after I got home that night, saying Seamus came through with a lead on where Harlow was. Since then, radio silence.

For the past two days, I've been nothing but a bundle of questions.

Where is he? Is he okay? Why hasn't he contacted me?

Is it because he hasn't found Harlow? Is it because he *has*?

There's a hurricane of swirling emotions inside me. Worry from his silence, anxiety over him and Harlow together again, but the biggest one of all? Fury. Slow burning embers roasting over charcoal.

He left.

Said all those things to me at Harlots, sent my heart aflutter and pulse into a tizzy and then *left*.

Sure, he sent a measly text, but that doesn't even count. I'm not counting it. He wants to go off without keeping me updated? Fine.

While the Devil's away, this siren will play.

I march into the elevator, hitting the button for the lobby. I'm not going to stay locked in this tower awaiting his return.

No longer does his penthouse feel like my prison and I no longer a prisoner. I'm comfortable in a place that started out as my cell. I never thought that'd happen, but it did. I like it here.

No, I more than like.

I *love* Noah's apartment.

I love the windows downstairs that display the skyline of this messed up town.

I love the open floor plan.

And even with the dark decor, I've started to find a comfort in it.

But most of all, I enjoy the man who lives here.

But without him here it's too quiet. Too still.

Too empty without Noah's arrogant ass to help fill it.

I don't know where I'm going as I ride the elevator down, all I know is that I'm bored and hungry and will not waste my life away in Noah's glass and marble castle.

And if he happens to return while I'm out?

Well…

He can come find me.

It's not until I'm stepping into the lobby that I see the gruff, sullen faces of my two bodyguards. Silent One and Silent Two as I like to call them since they've refused to say anything, even their names.

They stare at me with dead eyes and crossed arms.

"Hiya boys." I give them a wide smile, walking toward them like their presence doesn't annoy me.

I know why I have them, why they're necessary. But that doesn't mean I have to like it. They make me feel helpless. Like I can't protect myself.

Maybe if I hadn't frozen at the sight of the gun, I'd feel different.

Sure, I'm not the strongest and I refuse to touch or carry a gun, but I know the signs of danger. I know basic moves in case I'm attacked. I took classes in college.

And I dare anyone in my position who's never had a gun pointed at them do something different. Because I bet they wouldn't. Saying and doing are two different actions when actually put in the position to show it.

I don't need two intimidating shadows as a reminder. Not when I'm just going down the block to get some food.

"Right, so." I grip the strap of my bag. "I'm going to get some sushi. And you two are going to stay here."

Neither of them blinks, neither react at all. It's like I haven't spoken. They're not going to listen to me. I think they're still a little angry with me ditching them the night I went to Harlots.

I'm locked in an epic stare down with them and I'm pretty sure neither of these men even know what the word *blink* is, when someone joins us in the lobby, bringing in a blast of cold air.

"Hi, hi!" a sing-song voice calls, ultimately making me lose as I look up to find Thea, a cheerful smile plastered on her face only for it to slip when she sees three angry faces greeting her. "What's going on here?"

"I'm going out for dinner." I glance at the goons. "*Alone.*"
Silent Two's nostrils flare.

"Well, that's a coincidence." Thea glides closer to us. "I was just going to see if you wanted to hang out."

Yes! I want to shout. Thank God for Thea, who doesn't care about following orders from Noah.

"What did you have in mind?" I turn toward her, giving the goons my back.

Her smile is slow. "Something incredibly dangerous and maybe life-threatening."

I feel the silent twins tense behind me.

Thea's smile blooms in full as she says, "Shopping."

"I don't know." I give a smile of my own. "Some of the stores can be pretty small and jammed tight. I don't know if these two" —I hook a finger over my shoulder— "could go in with us. What with their muscular builds and imposing attitudes I don't know if they'd fit."

"Hmm." Thea taps her chin, playing along. "No, no I don't think they would." She looks at them over my shoulder. "Boys, you'll have to stay here."

They don't answer, but I don't take that to mean they're agreeing. In fact, as I take a step toward Thea and the door so do they.

Bastards. I twist around to glare while Thea tsks at them. "Now, boys. I believe we just said you weren't invited." She walks over, linking her arm with mine, and sequentially opens her coat to reveal her gun. "I don't think anything is going to happen," she continues. "But if something were? I guarantee I'm a better shot than either of you."

Mic drop.

And with that, we turn around and walk out of the lobby. A smile on both of our faces.

"What did you want to get, anyway?" I ask Thea when we're safely in the waiting car Jensen had idling in front of the building.

"I was thinking of getting some more decorations for Noah's. It's too gothic for my tastes. I'm thinking pinks. Lots and lots of pink. What do you think?"

I'm thinking Noah Kincaid shouldn't have let me alone.

Three hours, countless stores, and copious amounts of laughter later, Thea and I find ourselves at my favorite sushi bar.

Across the table, Thea giggles. "I can't get Jenkins's face out of my head."

I laugh, picturing it myself. How shocked he was to see

how many bags we were able to get in the few hours we were out.

My arms still feel the weight of them.

"I needed this tonight." Thea plays with a pair of chopsticks.

"I did too."

I don't remember the last time I laughed so hard or smiled so much. Thea is an easy person to get along with. She has this carefree personality that is warm and welcoming. Take tonight, she didn't need to come check on me, but she did because she wanted to see how I was doing.

And while out shopping we saw a homeless man on the street and she pulled me into the nearest coffee shop ordering the largest hot chocolate they had and a dozen assorted baked goods.

She gave them to the man with a wide smile.

A big heart and caring soul.

She's such a stark contrast to the guys she hangs out with but equally badass.

"Seriously, Sayer." She looks me dead in the face. "This is the most normal thing I've done in years."

"Shopping?"

She shakes her head with a sad smile. "Hanging out with a friend."

I set my chopsticks on the table, confused. "Aren't you friends with Noah and the guys?"

"Yeah, but not a lot of girl friends. Most of the girls that are in The Underground stay away from me, thinking we can't be friends because I'm in the 'inner circle.'" She uses air quotes around *inner circle*.

"What does that even mean? Inner circle?"

"Just that I'm close with the guys." She rolls her eyes. "An original founder if you will since I have a share in the building.

The four of us built The Underground from nothing." She speaks with such pride on her face.

"You're proud of what you've built?"

"We all are," she tells me. "We've all come from money, but we don't depend on our parents. We've made our own way."

I bite my lip. I know she's not talking about me, but it's still a reminder that even though I know what it's like to earn a dollar, I'm relying on the money my granddad left me.

"Shit." Thea stares at me. "I didn't mean—"

"I know," I reassure her.

"Seriously, Sayer—"

"I know, Thea," I repeat, cutting her off. Not wanting to talk about this anymore I change the subject to something that's been in the back of my mind this entire night. "Have you heard from Noah?"

She takes a long, slow sip from her drink. *Yes, yes she has.*

I try not to let my fists curl, those embers roaring into flames. He can reach out to Thea but not me?

She sees the question on my face. "He needed my help, Sayer," she explains. "It wasn't a social call."

And his call to me would be. In my lap, my fists tighten. When she doesn't offer any more information, I try a different tactic. All a girl is trying to do is get a little information. "Why didn't you go with him?"

"Yeah, not my kind of field trip." Thea snorts. "I'm more of an indoor person."

"They're somewhere outdoors?" I try to keep my voice relaxed.

It doesn't work. I'm too starved to know *anything.*

Thea gives me a look that says *nice try.* "Outside for me is anything not my office. I'm kind of a desk-body. It's like a homebody, but I basically live at my desk with my fingers glued to my keyboards."

It dawns on me I don't really know what Thea does. I know she works with Noah. So do Gabe and Reeve, but I've never paid close enough attention to know all their titles and roles. "What exactly do you do for Kincaid Enterprises?"

Her lips curl in a grin. "I do too much, but mostly it's a lot of IT stuff."

"And what do you do at The Underground?"

"The same." She smiles, but it's full of secrets. Secrets I'm not going to get out of her.

"Can I ask you something?" I trace my finger over the condensation of the glass.

"What have you been doing this entire time?" she asks playfully, but when I don't offer any humor in return, she sobers up.

"What am I supposed to do when this is over?"

"Then you get to go back to your apartment with your cat and return to life as usual."

She says it like it's nothing, but I hear the sadness in her voice.

It's the same sadness that has found its way into my chest.

Going back to that life after all I've seen…is that really what I want?

I ignore the sadness in her voice as I'm hit with a realization.

What I was living before wasn't a life. Existing without *living*.

When I left at eighteen, I had nothing to stand on. I got a clean start. No family name was going to carry me, I had to carve my own path.

I threw myself into school, into the art I once painted, but when I lost my granddad I slipped. Fell into a hole I'm climbing to get out of.

Who am I outside school and textbooks?

I'm still the girl that left at eighteen, looking for her place in the world.

I don't want that.

I don't want that at all.

My throat closes at the mere thought.

Not when I think I'm close to finding what I came home looking for.

I stand up from the table so abruptly Thea flinches at the sound of my chair screeching against the tile.

"Sayer?" she calls. "Where are you going?"

"Bathroom," I call as our waiter walks past me with the food.

Heading down the hall that has the bathrooms, I march past to the last door and push it open. The cold air welcomes me as I step into the night.

I just need a little air, I tell myself. *I just need to collect my thoughts and the restaurant was too loud.*

Except, a little air turns into me slowly walking down the street and foot traffic weaving around my slow, lost steps.

But no matter how far my feet carry me, I can't escape Thea's words.

I know she didn't mean them in the way they hit me, but it doesn't stop the sting any less.

I don't want that life anymore. The one I've spent six years convincing myself was right for me.

All because I got a little taste.

All because of Noah.

Noah, the infuriating asshole who just leaves without a goodbye.

Noah, the man who unravels me like no one else.

Noah, who's found a home in the one place I never expected him to be.

My heart.

Frustrated, I kick a littered soda can in my path and it rolls into the street, a car swerving to not hit it. The driver honks and flips me off.

Without thinking, I do it back.

It's too dark for them to see, but it feels good all the same.

I keep walking until I reach the pier, the cool sea air tangling my hair, tickling my skin.

Maybe if the breeze grows strong enough like a bird, I can fly away.

My elbows rest on the wooden rail and I stare at the ocean, onyx black and furious—deafening waves crash below.

I don't know how long I stand out here before another person joins me.

"Give me like three minutes, Thea." I sigh.

"Sayer."

I freeze while my body ignites at the voice.

It's deeper than Thea's.

Intoxicating and lethal.

Noah.

Slowly, my head turns, taking him in.

Standing next to me, mirroring my stance, our elbows almost touch on the rail. He stares at me with his usual unreadable expression, but those intense blue eyes hook me nonetheless.

A battle rages behind them when he looks at me, fighting what's churning in his head.

"You're home." My tone is neutral.

"Miss me?" He grins, but his eyes remain the same, an internal battle.

His words fuel me with anger as I narrow my gaze at him, veins humming in irritation. All the missing I've felt for him shriveled away with his sentence.

"No." I look back to the dark ocean, dismissing him. "To be honest, I forgot you were gone."

"That so?"

My sharp nod is the only answer he gets out of me. He's back in the city. And he didn't tell me.

Did he even leave the city?

Everything in me is ignited as he slides closer, arms caging me in, pressing me up against the wood.

Invading my personal space, he leans in so his scratchy stubble grazes my cheek. "Liar."

It's a whisper. It's an accusation.

Pulling away, I give him a fiery stare. He doesn't get to act all casual and sensual. "Someone's ego is hungry tonight."

Noah doesn't heed the warning in my tone. He shifts closer, his body curving around mine. "Admit it, Sayer. You missed me."

His lips press down on the curve of my neck, they feel like venom.

"No." My teeth grind together as my hands go to Noah's chest, giving him a shove with each word. "I." *Shove.* "Didn't."

He barely moves, barely shifts his weight.

I shove again.

Leather gloves cover my bare, cold fingers, keeping them on his chest. "For someone who didn't miss me, you are protesting quite vocally."

"That's because I'm pissed!" I shout, the sound echoing around us. In a lower voice, I add, "I'm pissed that you left to go after my sister and haven't told me anything." *You left me.*

His eyes soften while his words are still sharp. "I don't report to you."

"We're partners in this," I remind him. "You don't get to keep me in the dark."

"I will if I need to, Sayer. If it means keeping you safe, then you bet your ass I will," he tells me. "If I could, I'd lock you in my home until this is all over."

My already narrowed gaze hardens like steel. "I dare you."

"You really want to make that bet?" He steps closer.

A disgusted noise escapes my throat as I push him away. "You don't…"

My voice trails off as his face shifts, catching the light from the lamppost.

"What happened?" I whispered, taking in his bruised face, the swelling around his eye.

With a tentative hand, I reach up to touch it only for him to grab it with his, pulling it to our sides. "You're shivering."

He tries to pull me toward him, but I'm not having it. I step away from his touch. "Did you find her?"

He freezes, eyes narrowing.

"If I did, we wouldn't be here right now."

It feels like a punch in my throat, in my gut. Of course we wouldn't be here. Because I'm nothing more than a means to an end.

Seeing my reaction, his jaw hardens, hands flexing at his sides, but he doesn't try to reach for me again. He doesn't say anything.

Good. I'd probably knee him in the groin if he did.

Words don't begin to cover how I feel right now, crashing into the deep abyss of the sea with nothing to rescue me.

"C'mon, let's go home." He starts to walk away, expecting me to follow, which I do. If only because I've lost feeling in my fingers and I refuse to lose any of them because I was too stubborn and too naive to let Noah worm his way into a place he had no business being in the first place.

twenty-three

Sawyer

TONIGHT I'M ON A DATE WITH A DEVIL.

A devil with black-framed glasses and a tailored suit to be exact.

I've tried to ignore the little stab in my chest, tried to ignore it all day. Tried to ignore it for a couple days. Ever since he came back empty from his manhunt of my sister.

Apparently, the lead Noah was given was a cold one, taking him and Reeve all the way to Maine for nothing.

Now he's in a frantic search to find her. And I've become background noise, competing with the newest houseguest of Hotel Kincaid—the ghost of my sister.

"Are you going to be like this the whole time?" he grumbles as we pull up to the valet outside of Reeve's art gallery. The same art gallery where Noah finger banged me against the painting.

Turning my head, I blink once, twice, taking in the frustration on his face.

I haven't said a word to him all day, not when he handed me a box that held the dress I'm wearing now. Not when he took my hand in his, leading me to the couch to gift me a pair of shoes.

Or re-gift since they were the shoes he stole from me the first night at Heathen's Hell.

I didn't say anything as he slipped them on. Fastening the

strap around my ankle, where his hand lingered for the briefest of touches before I stood up.

"Depends," I answer, hand going to the door. Already wanting this night to be over. I'm tired of pretending.

"On?"

"Are you going to keep ignoring me or go back to acknowledging my existence?" I open the door and get out before he can respond.

He follows suit, handing the keys to the valet before walking over, grabbing my elbow and pulling me to his side. "I don't think I need to remind you of tonight's objective."

I grind my teeth before remembering we're in a place people can see us. Plastering on the fakest smile I can muster, I stare into his soulless eyes. "Of course not, darling."

His eyes narrow at my endearment.

I know my role perfectly at this point.

Together, arm in arm, we walk into the room, gaining attention within seconds.

In the eyes of society, I'm the darling daughter of a prominent family and he's the orphan who owns half their properties.

I'm their equal while Noah's their superior.

"You have to at least act like you like me, Sayer." He pulls me close, but I'm stiff against his side.

After several tense breaths, I force myself to relax.

"It feels weird. Being here," I admit as Noah grabs two flutes of champagne from a passing tray.

He stiffens before handing me one. "Why?"

Not for the reasons it should.

"It reminds me of Winter Formal." I down half the glass of bubbly at the thought. With the lights on and all the people here, I feel like I'm about to make my debut all over again. We had it in the city's museum. Art was everywhere like it is now. It was the only part I enjoyed about that night.

He chuckles. "Only with a better escort this time."

My head whips to his. "You remember who my escort was?"

"Mark Tulaen."

Wide-eyed, I stare at him. That was over eight years ago. "H—how…" I flounder, searching for sentences that have left me.

"I remember everything about you." He says it so casually, so flippantly before he takes a sip of champagne. I stare at him with my mouth open in a little O.

He remembers…

I stare up at him, into his eyes and almost suck in a breath at what's staring back. Open and honest, I see the truth swimming in the depths of his arctic blues. My heart trips over itself as all my annoyance and anger at him for the past couple days fades away.

Noah hasn't forgotten me, and he wasn't lying to me at Harlots.

He wants me.

He's protected me.

He's made me feel safe and has helped me feel more whole. He took me to my granddad's when I was too afraid to go by myself.

He's always seen me when I've only ever felt invisible.

Noah leans in, wrapping his fingers around my chin. "Close your mouth, Sayer. It isn't proper."

"Neither is this." I lean on my toes and brush my lips against his neck. I breathe in his scent of clean minty soap, leather, and rich spices.

I pull back to say something, but the words leave my lips, leave my mind as Noah's mouth crashes on mine. He kisses me like we aren't in public, touches me like we're the only two in the room.

He drowns out the worries, the whispers, and I lean into him. Lean into the freedom he's given me and kiss him like I always wanted to as a lovesick teenager.

I get lost in his lips. My fingers find themselves woven into his hair.

This really isn't proper. And I really don't give a damn. Especially as his tongue greets mine.

But all too soon he's pulling away. "Not yet. Soon, but not yet," he whispers. Heat simmers behind his glasses. "Stay here, I'm going to get us some more drinks."

It looks like the last thing he wants, but I understand. We're here to coax out my sister and if we were to disappear, it'd defeat the purpose of us being here tonight.

Soon, I echo, watching as Noah walks to the bar, leaving me alone.

Alone with the whispers and stares and speculation. My arms wrap around my middle—a shield from the gossip.

Trying to ignore them, I focus on what makes me happy. Art.

I catch myself staring at the painting Noah showed me, the one about the lovers. He had said it was donated by my parents and while I might have been distracted at the time, what with his roaming hands and whispered words, now with him a healthy distance away from me, I can attest to never seeing that painting before.

Not even in my granddad's collection, which we inherited most of with his passing.

Noah said they were donated, but he must've been confused by which painting was donated by my parents because the lovers one isn't it.

Or is it?

I go through my memory trying to remember all the paintings they have in their collection and which ones they kept after my granddad's passing, but between both my parents and granddad, so many paintings came and went through their houses while I was growing up it sometimes felt we were a temporary holding facility.

Mom was always redecorating, and Granddad always had paintings waiting for his clients to pick up.

The more I study the painting, the more I don't know if my parents donated it.

Why is it bothering me so much?

"What's that look on your face for?" Noah's arm winds around my shoulders.

I don't get the chance to say anything before his grip tightens around my shoulder. Holding me in place. His jaw's clenched and body ramrod straight.

What…

Following his gaze, I see why.

My parents have returned from their European vacation, walking into the event with an air of superiority.

And they're staring straight at me.

When I was younger, my father used to get this look on his face. One that didn't quite convey anger, nor did it scream disappointment. Somehow he had perfected a look that fell in between. I called it his lawyer face since it resembled the expression he usually wore when he was in his office or in court.

My father is a handsome man who has been treated kind with age. Salt and pepper hair and soft worry lines that crease between his eyes from all the frowning he's done over the years.

He's one of the only adults in this town that hasn't gotten some kind of injection to make them disappear. He doesn't seem to mind them. I don't either. They make him look more refined in a way.

Not tonight, though.

The deep scowling makes those worry lines more prominent, angry and harsh.

Together, with my mother's hand resting in the crook of his elbow, they walk as a unit toward Noah and I. My hand squeezes Noah's forearm warning him to let go.

Naturally, he doesn't.

Bastard. I glare at him.

He winks back.

"Noah," I plea under my breath. "Let go. You're only going to make this worse. *Please.*"

Surprisingly, he does. His arm drops from my shoulders, but he doesn't leave my side as he whispers back, "Don't ask me to walk away because I won't. I'm not leaving you alone with them."

My chest warms with his declaration, but it quickly sours with where it came from. Noah remembers what I was like around my parents as a teenager. A coward, a shell. I let them control me, to make me who they wanted to be.

But not anymore. No longer will I allow them to have power over me.

"Mom, Dad!" I force a smile that hurts my cheeks as they stand in front of us. Entrapping us in a small, intimate circle of animosity.

My parents hardly acknowledge me. How could they? They're too busy staring at Noah with enough hatred to melt a couple of icebergs.

I've never fully grasped why my parents hate him. Even before he and Harlow started dating, they had despised the Kincaid name. At first, I thought it was because Noah's parents owned a majority of the city, places that now belong to Noah.

The one time I asked my mom about it, she brushed some hair out of my face while telling me people like Noah didn't deserve to inherit the money he did, not when he didn't have parents around to teach him how to act appropriately.

It was cold and harsh. How could she hate a boy that lost his parents?

But the more Noah came around in prep school, the more I got to see them interact. My parents' loathing of Noah wasn't just rooted in his inheritance and lack of propriety. It stemmed deeper than that. Almost like it came from a place of fear.

Fear of what?

I watch the three of them, feeling out of place, out of the loop. None of them so much as look my way and I can't help but feel like there's a conversation going on here, one I am not privy too.

I clear my throat, nudging Noah's side with my elbow and he blinks, whatever was transpiring between the three of them is now over.

Noah's hand finds a home on my lower back. "Want to introduce me to your folks?"

"They know who you are," I hiss under my breath for only him to hear.

He looks highly amused at the situation.

So glad he's having fun.

"What are you doing here, Sayer? With *him?*" My mother doesn't sound amused.

"I didn't know you two were back," I say, sidestepping her question.

"Yes, well," my mother draws out. "If you answered your phone when we called you, you would've."

I don't answer, not when she just called me out on exactly what I've been doing. Ignoring their calls.

Both parents look to me in silent question, waiting for an

explanation on my date. An explanation they've been wanting since they left for Europe.

A few of their friends, like Mrs. Fletcher and Mrs. Rochester, glance over, whispering to each other.

Noah's hand presses into my back.

"Mom, Dad," I force cheer into my tone. "You know Noah. We've been kind of dating."

My mother's upper lip snarls and father's scowl deepens further, if that's even possible, while Noah turns to me slowly as his fingers dig tighter into my back, letting me know he's here. He's ready to step in if I need him. To fight the backlash for me.

"Sayer Brooks." My name is a verbal lashing on my mother's tongue.

I don't have a middle name and it's time like these that I'm glad I don't. Two names sound bad enough. I don't want to imagine what kind of wounds she could inflict with a third.

My father stands beside her, not saying anything. He doesn't have to. Not when his twisted lips and throbbing vein above his eyebrow say it all.

If we weren't in a crowded room full of their friends and journalists, they would ream me out and possibly strangle me. I'm with the one person who, in their eyes, helped tarnish our family name.

I don't have time to pay attention to my father, though. Or my mother.

Not when Noah is rigid at my side.

Noah stands quiet, not moving. I don't even know if he's breathing.

He glances down at me and I feel sweat gathering along my hairline as a shiver crawls up my spine.

Something's wrong.

Before any more words can be shared, the lights go out

and people scream in panic. Names get shouted and people start to rush in an unseen panic. Bodies knock into me. Noah's hand falls away and I feel his body heat leave mine.

I hear him call my name. At least, I think I do.

Just as I begin to move, to answer him, unfamiliar hands wrap around my waist and my mouth and I'm pulled back into a solid chest of a tall, tall man.

A man who's not Noah.

I struggle, kick and bite, trying to get free but they hold me to the point of tears stinging my eyes and I can do nothing as something goes over my head and tightens around my neck, the pressure making it hard to breathe, let alone scream.

With my voice stolen, I feel something sharp pierce my skin. Everything goes dark behind my eyes as I'm carried away into the unknown.

Twenty-four

Sayer

I DON'T KNOW HOW LONG I'M KNOCKED OUT FOR BEFORE I wake up against a leafless tree, dead from the winter. My face is frozen and limbs rigid as I struggle to stand up.

Dazed, I look around.

Where am I?

Slowly, the memories of the art gallery come to me. Of stranger's hands grabbing me. A prickling sensation in my neck.

I lift a hand, touching the spot. A little knot now resides there.

What happened?

I see nothing but trees. Barren, hibernating trees. Dark with only the faintest stars for light.

Am I in a field?

I take a few hesitant steps only to stop dead.

It's not a field. It's a cemetery.

Rows and rows and rows of headstones greet me.

My body is frozen and not only from the cold.

Spinning around, I look for an exit. Iron gates are a beacon in the distance. I start toward them.

With every step, another question forms: how did I get here? Who grabbed me?

Why am I here?

Somehow finding the courage, I take a step and then another toward the exit only for a body to step into my path.

A black hood pulled low over their head steps in front of my path. I freeze, memories of another night with a stranger wearing a black hoodie come rushing back to me.

Is this the same guy?

Holy crap I've forgotten how to breathe. My chest is tight, lungs not working. Time slows down as they walk toward me with a cat-like grace, lazy and unhurried. His hood falls revealing a full-faced mask. Set in a shiny plastic smile, a voice asks, "Ready to play?"

No. I run instead. Laughter trails after me.

I'm close to the exit when I no longer hear the laughter. No longer hear anything but my footsteps breaking leaves that have dried and fallen to the ground.

Arms wrap around my waist, pulling me back just as I'm about to reach the destination.

A hand wraps around my throat. The hold tighter than I've ever felt, enough to know my skin is turning a suffocating shade. I can't breathe. I don't move. Even my heart feels frozen in my chest, already failing. Giving up. Accepting fate.

Too bad for them, I'm not. I kick my legs in a wild manner, striking their legs. We buckle but are quickly righted.

"That was very naughty of you, Sayer." My name rolls like a purr from his throat in a voice I don't recognize. His fingers dig into my pulse. Where it should be. I've gone numb. "I think I have to teach you a lesson."

He swings me around to face the graves before shoving me down on the ground.

Dirt, sticks, and horror dig into my knees and outstretched palms.

Air. Air. Air. I need air. And it's not coming in fast enough.

A boot presses into my lower back, pushing me farther to the ground.

I try to fight, but can't.

He pushes down harder until I'm flat on my stomach. Once I'm pressed close to the ground, he removes his boot only to stand on either side of my hips.

Fingers tightly wrap around my hair and tug, twisting my head to the side. Seeing him crouched above me. "You can't escape me, pet. You will not win and in the end, you will only cause more harm to yourself. Is that what you want, Sayer? To hurt yourself?"

I try to shake my head, to answer, and his grip tightens around my hair. Fisting more and limiting all movement.

"Such fear in your eyes," he marvels. I squirm, getting filthier and filthier as my clothes rub along the sodded lawn. "I wonder how far that fear can go."

He lets go of my hair and stands up. Quickly, before his mind changes or he makes his next move, I twist around, scrambling away from him. My palms and soles carry me backward until I collide into something, no longer able to move.

My body nails into something strong, something hard. Something rough and carved.

Peeking around, I see a headstone.

I jump up, choking on rising bile.

Hands clap. "Fascinating. How much do you fear death?"

I shake my head. Doesn't everyone fear death?

"Stop moving," he orders, no longer sounding like the delighted sociopath and more hardened. Like a creature from Hell itself.

"Now, *run.*"

I look back to the entrance. A cloaked figure now stands in front of it. Arms crossed.

He steps in my line of sight and shakes his head. "You're not leaving this cemetery tonight, Sayer. Now. *Run!* Let us chase you."

I have a choice.

Do as he says and think of a plan or eat more dirt with him physically assaulting me. He's already established he can overpower me so if I pick option A, at least it gives me time to think of a way to escape this hell I've woken up to.

So I run. Run as fast as my shaking, beat up legs can carry me, once again weaving between headstones and silently apologizing to every grave I run on, for disturbing their peace and to take their revenge on the fiend chasing me.

Except.

He's not.

Stealing a glance over my shoulder, no one is behind me. He's nowhere in sight.

I stop. Turning in this direction, then that. *Where is he?*

"Did I say you could stop?" Amplified by hidden speakers, his voice roars around me. Stuttering my already erratic heartbeat. I feel the muscles straining. Feel my lungs seizing. Trying to fight as my legs take off once again, farther into the cemetery, where the dates of the deceased go further and further back in time.

I'm glancing over my shoulder to see if anyone is behind me when I run into an ancient and elaborate grave marker. The force of the blow causes me to fall backward, eyes stinging with tears.

Crunk. Crunk.

I look to my left, where leaves crunch under pressured weight and see several feet away, a hooded body. Standing. Shadows cast over his face, making it impossible to see his features. It's not a man though. This build is smaller, more petite.

A woman.

Pushing up, I run in the opposite direction only to skid to a stop. Another person steps into my path. Cornered. I'm surrounded on all sides, each one of them moving closer and closer to me.

I'm trapped. They caught me.

The man who grabbed me tsks down at me, sucking air from behind his teeth. As if he's disappointed in me. "I had higher hopes for you. Thought you'd last longer."

They all shift to line up before me, stepping closer and closer. Forcing me to walk back. My feet stumble but I right myself. Huffing a breath as I do, one that quickly plummets as the ground below me turns to air.

No.

I fall with a scream, going down and landing on something soft. A box. My hands wrap around either side as I fight for the breath that got knocked out of me on the landing.

As my breathing catches up to me, I realize a few things. The first is that I'm flat on my back. The three people who were chasing me have doubled. Six people stand above me.

And the last thing is that I'm not in a box. I'm in a coffin.

With six hooded figures standing above me, sinking lower and lower in the ground.

The descent is slow, and I can't even scream. Not when my body is being taken over by a new kind of fear. One that's pure terror. One that locks my muscles.

A hand goes to the casket's lid and flicks it with enough force to close. "Sleep tight, darling Sayer."

I don't move. Can't. My eyes won't even blink as I struggle. It's like my body is locked in a cage from within, fingernails clawing at the lock to free me. To free my limbs, my mouth.

Thunk

Thunk

Thunk

The cage unlocks enough for my eyes to search for the sound. To feel the vibrations from above.

Thunk

Thunk

Thunk.

Something coarse and grainy falls to my fingers. Dirt.

With desperate clawing, the cage fully opens, and my hands stretch out to the tufted lid. Scratching at the plush linen.

"*Nonononononononononono,*" escapes my lips as I desperately try to stop what's happening from the outside. To break out and stop them from throwing dirt on me. Because if there's one thing I hate more than heights, it's the thought of being trapped in confined spaces. Of being buried alive.

Exhaustion soon takes over, laced with the feeling of my blood flow slowing down, frighteningly so. All I can think of as my hands start to lower is, "*You're not leaving this cemetery tonight, Sayer.*"

twenty-five

Sayer

PANIC KEEPS ME AWAKE, BUT I MIGHT AS WELL BE asleep. No matter how much my head screams to move, I'm frozen in place, weighed down.

It's more than hot under here, wondering how much oxygen I can really get with every breath. It's like being a kid again when Harlow would throw a blanket over me.

Suffocating.

I'm suffocating.

How long has it been since I've been in here? Too long it feels and not long at all.

How much time do I have left? Mere minutes or is it seconds until I can't breathe any longer? When all the oxygen is gone.

Nothing is visible, not even the limp hand I raise before my face.

Utter darkness is my only companion.

My eyes feel heavy, weighted sandbags that push and push farther down until I can't fight to keep my lids open any longer.

Slowly they close—

Close

Close

Until I'm sinking farther down a spiral that has no exit.

twenty-six

Noah

THE SCENES FROM THE ART GALLERY PLAY OUT WITH each step I take. The lights going off, the panic, bodies bumping into one and other.

Sayer's hand slipping from mine…

When the lights flickered back on, restoring a calm tranquility to the crowd—like it never happened.

Except that it did, and with the lights back on I noticed Sayer wasn't by my side…

My boots crunch on the brittle grass, running to the cemetery gates and the three huddled figures waiting for me outside it. The weather tonight is brutal, wind dipped in icicles try to pierce past my coat, but the chill in the air can't make me feel any stiffer, any more numb, than I already do.

This shouldn't have happened.

We shouldn't be here right now.

Sayer and I should be back at my home, me peeling off her underwear with my teeth, our naked bodies sweaty and tangled in her sheets.

Instead I'm running toward a goddamn cemetery.

A single stream of thought goes through my head the closer I get to the gates.

A face and a name. Gray eyes and blonde hair. Sayer. Sayer. Sayer.

Her smiling, her laughing, her scolding and yelling at me.

I can't stop the moments, of all the hours we spent together and how—

Not going there. I refuse to go there.

It's quiet out. Not even a bird flutters in the sky. No owls hoot. The sound of branches rattle in the wind, it's gone. I see them moving, but I hear no sound.

My ears ring of static. Static and the gentle, muffled sound of my hurried, angry steps.

I'm not running fast enough. We're going to run out of time.

In the home of death is a life. A life I'm going to do any-fucking-thing to save.

I close in on my friends, hearing them gossip in leisure. My veins simmer in fury.

Why are they fucking standing here? We're not on a picnic. We're on a rescue mission. I'm about to shout for them to get their lazy asses in gear when I hear Reeve's smug voice.

"What if she's dead?" Facing my direction, catching my approaching form, he smiles.

Bastard.

My fists clench. Not close enough to do what I want to with them.

"Don't *smile* about that." Thea smacks his stomach, not hard enough for my liking. He's not on the ground whimpering in agonizing pain.

"It's totally possible," he continues. "You said you tracked her in the ground. That means no air. Which means—"

I come to a stop in front of him. So close I step on his toes, the steel in my boots crunching on his bones. His knees buckle but other than that, he doesn't show any reaction. Reeve could be bleeding, on the horizon of death and still be laughing.

I level him with a glare. "She's not dead." It's a vow. A

resolution. I don't believe in much I can't control, but I have to believe this.

Reeve doesn't cower. He doesn't show remorse as his lips stretch farther apart. *Enjoying* the situation while I struggle to keep reign on my composure.

"We don't have time for this." Shouldering past their huddle, I march to the gates, kicking them open. Somewhere. Sayer's somewhere in here.

"I'm just saying." Reeve follows behind, *still* running his mouth. "How convenient would that be? She's already in a grave. Funerals are expensive *and* it would draw out Harlow, no doubt. It's a win-fucking-win if you ask—"

"Hey, Reeve?" I growl. "Shut the fuck up." *Before I shove your face into the decaying ground.*

He raises his hands, palms up. "Touchy, touchy."

I'm not touchy, I'm a bomb about to go off. I can feel it. The suppressed wrath being held down by only my worry for Sayer.

It's strange.

This feeling of caring. Deeper than what I possess for the three people in front of me. Richer and more poignant than how I care for even myself. It's been so long since another person's wellbeing has affected my own, it goes past someone taking her. The thirst for revenge doesn't touch the need to protect her. As if I didn't already know she had a firm grip on my balls.

I'm scouring what's in front of me, looking for clues.

"Ah, cemeteries, don't you just love them?" Reeve slides his hands into his jacket pockets.

"No," we all answer in unison, Reeve looks disappointed.

"We split up," I tell them, voice controlled while I feel anything but inside.

Both Gabe and Thea stare back, grave-faced, nodding.

Reeve nods as well, but that smug smile is going to get punched off his face if he doesn't stop.

I've been good. Controlled since I couldn't find Sayer after the lights came back on at the art gallery.

Thea, who was checking on security at the same time the power went out, found me immediately. All she said was, "She's gone."

Two words. Two minuscule words that seized me by the throat, constricted my lungs. An unfamiliar feeling of help-lessness settled over me with realization, I let her go.

In the chaos, she slipped through my fingers.

Reliving it now, I bark at them to get moving and the four of us break off into a separate section of the huge cemetery. But even doing this, I fear it's not enough.

I'm not one to feel fear. Or guilt.

But I feel them now.

Fear over Sayer's wellbeing, her safety. Over *her.*

Guilt for letting this happen. I should've held onto her for dear life the second the lights went out.

Both emotions taste bitter, stinging with the knowledge of failure.

I've spent my life, *prided* myself, on not letting anyone in. Not letting them get past the shields I've long since put up, but I wasn't counting on Sayer Brooks to be as formidable as she is.

A siren I can't ignore the call of. And I've *tried.*

Tried to put some boundaries between us, like not sleep-ing in my room. Physical shields to back my internal ones.

She looks at me like I'm made of steel, but if she'd ask I'd bend like aluminum.

She draws me in, captivating not only my time and atten-tion but all my thoughts, even when they shouldn't.

What started out as an attempt to satisfy a craving, a way

to pass the time on my path of revenge, has turned into something I couldn't anticipate.

Evolved into something that makes me uncomfortable.

Sayer Brooks has become important to me.

Ground crunches beneath my shoes as I walk between the headstones, observing, looking for signs. The sound fragile, disrupting the serenity only found in a graveyard.

This is Sayer's nightmare—as well as mine.

Her being in a cramped, dark space. Dying.

Me not being able to keep her safe.

She's not dying, I growl at myself. *I'm getting her back.*

When I asked Thea who took Sayer, she said she didn't know, they wore a hood over a mask. Mask or not, they're only safe for as long as it takes me to find them.

Because I will.

And when I do, I'm going to rip their limbs apart.

But my need to find Sayer outweighs my hunger for vengeance. At least, until she's safe in my arms.

Not that she's even safe there, evidently.

My fists tighten at my sides.

Little reactions. That's all I've been giving to the tornado wreaking havoc inside me.

Emotions cloud judgment and right now, I need as clear as head as possible.

There's no time for mistakes.

The unseen clock is already ticking down.

Around me, nothing looks suspicious or out of place. Just old and worn and weathered with time. Nothing like a freshly dug grave.

"Anything?" I snap into the coms unit in my ear, it's been silent for too long. My tone is the only sign to my slipping composure.

"Nothing on the west side," Gabe says through his.

"Nothing on the south side." Thea on hers.

Damn it.

That only leaves the one person who joked about her being dead went, his line remains quiet.

"Reeve. Sound off." Restless, my hands flex.

It's quiet, save for a crackle. I've already started heading in Reeve's direction. "You guys need to get over here. Now." A pause. "We have a problem."

My feet start running before he's finished, weaving between the headstones. In my ear, Gabe asks what's wrong.

I pump my arms harder, propelling me faster.

By the time I reach Reeve, he's standing on a freshly covered grave, leaning against a shovel that's sticking out of the ground. A joint sits between his lips. "Took you long enough."

Ignoring him, I elbow him away from the shovel. He laughs as I pick it up, starting to dig. And dig. Until the metal clangs. Hitting a casket.

Fuck. Fuck. Fuck.

Reeve perks up at the sound when Gabe and Thea show up. Gabe, who is struggling to catch his breath while Thea nibbles anxiously on her thumb.

"Out of shape?" Reeve teases him, but I tune out Gabe's response.

My digging becoming more erratic. Desperate as I'm trying to get it free enough to open the lid.

Finally, with sweat building inside my coat, I do just that.

Reeve and Gabe step forward to help open it.

And as they do, I feel Thea close behind me.

"She has to be okay, right?" Thea whispers and in this moment, I'm reminded how big of a heart this woman has. She's as conniving as the rest of us, but she truly doesn't like to see horrible things happen to good people. Only the deserving.

And out of all of us, Sayer is the purest.

I squeeze Thea's shoulder as Gabe and Reeve work on un-latching the coffin.

It takes longer than I like, but we finally get the coffin open and in it, with her eyes closed, is Sayer.

She looks calm, peaceful as her pale skin looks even more bleached, stealing my breath and robbing my heart of beats.

She's still. She's too fucking still.

I don't take another step closer. Can't. Seeing here in the coffin brings up shit I've long since pushed away, never to re-surface. My friends know it as well.

My parents. My mentor. The people I let in, the people I love, always end up in caskets.

Gabe is the one to move, jumping down to scoop her up. Carefully, he passes her to me and I cradle Sayer in my arms. She feels so small and fragile—like hand-blown glass.

Her chest is barely moving.

Thea hovers close by, taking off her coat and passing it to me.

"You wore two coats?" I ask.

"I thought she might need one."

I stare at Thea when a small moan hits my ears. Looking down at Sayer, bundled in my arms, her lashes flutter against her cheekbones, trying to open.

I move us away from the group, only for Thea to follow. Reeve and Gabe stay behind, Gabe reprimanding Reeve about his insensitivity.

"Sayer." My voice is low, but tone is harsh. It's always harsh. Any softness I had had been pounded out of me years ago. I wish I could make it gentler. "Open your eyes."

Her eyes flicker and my breath fogs between us, waiting.

I feel Thea peek around me before she begins pacing.

"Thea," I snap, and she freezes. "Go back to the others."

"But—"

"*GO.*"

I wait until Thea's back with guys before I sweep some hair out of Sayer's face, my hand resting against her throat. With my thumb tracing her jaw, I wait for the beat of her pulse to meet my palm.

"Open your eyes, Sayer."

Nothing.

"C'mon, Sayer. Come back to me. I need you to come back to me."

Thump.

It's faint—but it's there.

Thump. Thump thump.

With every beat, it grows stronger against my palm.

And it's as I'm celebrating that little victory, those hypnotic gray eyes open and meet mine.

She blinks once, twice, two more times. Like she doesn't trust that it's me. "Noah?"

"Sayer."

"Noah!" she cries, throwing her arms around my neck. Her cold lips brush against my skin as she buries in close.

My hand cradles the back of her head and for a moment we just stand like that, locked in this embrace, before I feel something cold and damp hit my skin.

Tears.

She's crying.

Big, thick droplets roll down my skin, soaking into my clothes as she trembles. My arms constrict tighter, as if trying to reassure her she's safe. Safe with me.

Having Sayer cry into me stirs an uncomfortable lump in my chest.

I don't like this.

I didn't ask to feel these things.

They need to stop.

But instead of untangling her limbs from my neck, I weave my fingers into her hair, keeping her close.

And she cries, each tear heavier than the last…until they're not. They drop lighter and lighter before they stop falling altogether.

When they stop, she pulls away, no longer needing me. A pillar strong enough to stand on her own.

But I'm not strong enough to be without the feel of her, which is why my hand reaches for her waist as she stumbles with unsure footing, to keep her steady.

"What happened?" I ask, quietly. Hopefully gently.

She blinks, eyes puffy and face red, cheeks stained with tear tracks.

"I don't know," she whispers and my ears strain to hear, she's talking so soft. "Someone grabbed me when the lights went out and stabbed my neck with something."

Her hand goes to her neck as she talks, but I push her hand away, feeling the little knot left behind. It's small and almost circular, tense under her skin.

I breathe through my nose, careful to not hurt her as I cradle her neck.

"I don't remember anything after until I woke up here," she continues, voice shaking. "I didn't know what was happening at first, but then…then I saw these people. They were wearing masks and hoods and they were fast. So fast. They chased me." Her eyes are wild. "They chased me, Noah, and I fell. Fell into that grave and—" She sways, and I stumble to bear her weight. I'm about to tell her she can lean on me when I notice her eyes are closing and her breathing is evening out.

I've never seen her so defeated, not even when Harlow would tear into her as a fragile teenager. So exhausted.

"It's okay. You can sleep." My voice is the gentlest I've ever heard it. I kiss the top of her head. "I got you. I got you. You're safe."

She nods into my chest. And I bend down to cradle her to it. Making sure the coat is covering her.

"Noah," Reeve calls, drawing my gaze away from Sayer's sleeping face. "Look."

Following where he's pointing, he directs me to a head-stone. Above the grave we just got Sayer out from is a message in dripping red paint.

Here lies Darling Sayer.

Darling Sayer.

Her letter was addressed the same way.

Son of a bitch.

"What do you want us to do?" Gabe asks, seeing the fury on my face.

My grip tightens around Sayer. "Find them."

It's time their fun ends.

twenty-seven

Sayer

MY EYES OPEN TO THE SOUND OF YELLING. FIGHTING. It's loud, words traded like weapons dipped in malice. My sleep-addled brain is struggling to keep up.

The arguing doesn't even matter.

Not to me. Not when cool, crisp air is going into my lungs, each breath tasting of winter and salvation.

No longer am I shrouded in darkness but bathed in artificial light that has me squinting. Arms are coiled tightly around me, keeping my body tethered to a warm chest.

A chest vibrating with anger.

"Noah," I croak, the words hoarse as they slide past my throat.

The fighting stops as the arms tighten around me, almost to the point of pain. "I got you," he whispers for only me to hear.

"Leave," he orders the person who is not me, the one he was arguing with.

In a herculean effort, I lift my head from Noah's chest to see Gabe cast me a grim face look before he walks out of the room.

A room I don't recognize.

Noah's fingers run through my hair as I take my fill of the space. Of the dark walls and red curtains that greet me across the room. Of the vintage brass gothic-style chandelier set to dim hanging above us.

Dark and dangerous and mysterious.

Just like the man tangling his fingers in my hair.

My body stills, knowledge soaking into my skin.

We're in Noah's bedroom.

We're in Noah's bedroom.

A forbidden escape I never imagined I'd get access to.

Pushing away from Noah even more, my fingers slip, losing traction on silk, charcoal sheets. Cool air kisses my arms, my chest, but I ignore it.

Too transfixed that I'm finally here.

I've lived here for weeks, though on some days it's felt like months, but have never stepped foot in the inner sanctum of Noah Kincaid. And it fits him perfectly. From the dark colors to the steel and copper furnishings. Windows like the ones downstairs that open up to the city.

His city.

I can easily see him waking up and taking in the city that bends to his will, his authority.

A king watching over his kingdom.

Noah's hands move up my neck, his fingers lacing through my hair to cradle my head and creating a shiver down my spine. His touch gentle, revenant almost, as he turns my head to meet his gaze.

My breath skips with what he shows me in his penetrating blue eyes. His normally guarded and closed off expression is cracked, open for me to see. A look I never thought I'd see on Noah's face.

Scared—no, *terrified*. Backed by relief.

I'm okay, I want to say, but words can't find their way to my lips. He has me trapped within his gaze that it takes me a moment to realize that we're both shirtless, me even braless.

He pulls me close, skin to skin.

I slip my palms between us, going to his chest. "What happened? Where are my clothes?"

Noah's hands skim down my arms to my wrists, where he laces his fingers between mine.

My brows furrow at them. We've held hands before, quite a few times. Especially when we've been in the public eye, but he's almost scaring me more than anything that happened.

Who is he and where is the broody, stone of a Noah I know?

"Your body temperature was low when we got you back home and heat is best transferred between naked bodies." He doesn't say it cocky or teasing, simply straight to the fact. And that's when I know it was bad.

"How was I?"

"You woke up when we first got you out of the coffin and you were able to tell us what happened, but your voice was low, hoarse, with lips tinged blue." His thumb rubs along my hand.

In the silence of the room, images of what happened come flooding back to me. Being grabbed and chased and buried alive.

It almost doesn't feel real, but the throbbing in my feet and the aching muscles and the taste of dirt in my mouth are all there.

Panic climbs my throat, setting over my mind as I hear the footsteps behind me, my screams. Reliving the terror that consumed me.

I had always thought a strong person was based on the muscles packed beneath their skin, that I'd never be strong because I'm too lazy to lift weights more than ten pounds at the gym twice a year, but slowly, throughout my time with Noah I've realized that's a lie.

I am strong. I'm strong because I opened my eyes today,

because what I feel inside me isn't only fear but there's also anger and relief and gratefulness to have another day. I'm strong because I woke up today. Because I'm okay. Because I'm safe. And I will continue to fight to be okay.

My spine straightens, remembering something else from the cemetery.

"What is it?" Noah asks, squeezing my fingers.

"Darling Sayer," I whisper.

Noah's jaw clenches, giving a curt nod.

"The letter," I breathe.

Another tight nod.

The anger in my veins begins to boil. And I try to pull away from Noah, but he's fast, keeping me close.

"Noah," I protest. "Let go."

"No." His grip doesn't tighten, but it feels firmer anyway.

"Noah." I tug, but it's useless. He doesn't budge. My teeth grit in frustration.

"No." He glares, leaning in.

"Why am I here if you're just going to be difficult and not listen to me!" I yell, despite him centimeters away. Our lips almost touch.

"Because last night I felt helpless when I found you gone, and a cavity was carved into the base of my chest as I raced to the cemetery. I failed you."

Those three words. *I* and *failed* and *you*.

They do something to me.

There's still so much to talk about, so much left unsaid between us, but…it can wait.

Right now I don't want to think. I just want to feel.

My hand reaches out, going for his glasses. Noah's still as he watches me place them on the black bedside table next to us.

Turning back to him, I see how heavy he's breathing, as wholly affected by this as me.

My arms wrapped around him, not wanting to ever let go, as he buries his face into the side of my neck. He holds me as my heavy heart beats between us.

"You're safe," he murmurs into my throat. "You're safe," he repeats, almost as if he's trying to convince himself as much as me.

"You saved me," I say after a while when the room is silent except for our even breathing.

"I promised to protect you," he reminds me.

He did and that's what he's done, but as I stare at him, I know one person he can't protect me from.

Himself.

His hands skim down my body. "You're mine."

Noah lowers my body back on the mattress, covering mine with his. I focus on the way Noah's mouth moves against my throat and down my chest, between the valley of my breasts.

His touch breathes new life into me, and I give myself over to him, letting him coax and fill me, making me whole.

"Make me forget."

"Forget what?" He pulls one of my taut nipples between his teeth.

"Everything."

His wicked smile feels like a brand on my skin, skating down my body as he makes good on my request, making me forget everything outside this room.

Everything except him.

And his tongue and fingers, working me over.

Right now, there's nothing more I want.

Noah spreads my legs with his thighs, fitting himself between them. His touch feather light and wrong. Like I'm a fragile doll with too many cracks.

No.

I don't want soft.

I want him. How rough he always is.

He's never treated me like I'm a fragile doll before and I don't want him to start now.

"Touch me like you mean it." I lock my legs around his waist. "I'm not going to break, Noah."

I back my words with a challenge, a dare I know he won't be able to resist. And he doesn't disappoint as he pins my hands into my mattress. Restraining my touch.

"Is that right?"

My chin jerks, letting him see the heat in my eyes.

"Just remember," he warns as an immoral grin overtakes his face, and he's thrusting into me hard and fast enough for my vision to waver. "You asked for this."

He pulls all the way out only to ram back inside.

A sound I've never heard passes my lips.

He does it again.

Ooooh, God. Yes, yes. More, more.

He rolls his hips into mine, over and over again. Shaking the mattress, my breasts, my everything.

He has my hips pinned to the bed, keeping my withering body at his mercy while his mouth sucks at my neck, the peaks of my breasts.

Our hips move at a frantic, unrhythmic pace. Our lips crash together in the need for more.

We don't talk. Gone is the teasing. We're moving too fast, too hard. Only cries and pants and grunts leave our mouths, but Noah moves his body like a message. Words he can't get out to say.

Thrust.

I failed you.

Thrust.

I got you.

Thrust.

Forgive me.

Thrust. Thrust. Thrust.

I got you. I got you. I got you.

He's everywhere. Marking me, filling me, branding me.

But he's not the only one. My own nails dig into the back of his neck, pushing his mouth closer, harder into my skin. My own teeth find his freckled shoulders where I bite and lick.

It's hard and fast and delicious.

I asked him to make me forget, but I want to remember this.

The reverence in his eyes as he's inside me, never looking away from my face.

How he handles me, like I'm seconds from slipping through his fingers.

I asked him for hard, which he's giving me, but he's also given me something else. He makes me feel whole. Cherished.

In the wee hours of morning as the sun is inching across the horizon, I fall with the man who's stolen my heart and branded my soul.

Hours later I walk out of Noah's bathroom to find him sitting on the edge of the bed, his elbows digging into his thighs, talking on the phone.

He glances up to find me leaning against the doorframe, wearing one of his white dress shirts. My ankles are crossed. He smirks and motions for me to come closer.

With a small smile, I shake my head, content to stay like this. Watching him.

I get to see Noah Kincaid like this. Ruffled and unkempt.

His dark blonde hair is tousled from my fingers running through the thick strands, pulling at them. He's missing his shirt, not that I'm complaining, his chest is toned, and I can see the start of his freckles at the height of his shoulders. Even from here I can see the indents on his chest, on his neck, from where my teeth nipped at his skin.

I wish he hadn't put on those gray sweatpants earlier, but now, I'm not really complaining. There's something magical about a man in gray sweatpants. But on Noah? They're lethal.

God. I have it bad.

"Call me when you get something useful," he orders into the phone with authority before hanging up. In the same breath, he tosses the phone behind him, turning his full attention to me.

"Like what you see?" he asks, not missing any of my ogling.

"No, you're far too hideous."

He chuckles and my toes curl at the low sound. Sensual and knowing. "Bullshit."

Noah spreads his legs, patting the top of his thigh in invitation.

I hesitate. I want to, but I know if I do, he'll put his hands on me thus distracting me from all the questions swimming in my head. He's already distracted me thoroughly this morning by just being shirtless and rumpled.

So, I stay firmly planted where I am, hugging the doorframe between his bedroom and bathroom. "Why was Gabe here earlier?"

"To check on you."

"I doubt that." I remember the heated argument happening as I was waking up, though the words still escape me. "Why was he really here?"

"Why does it matter?" he counters.

With a glare, I push away from the doorframe. "Should I recount the last twenty-four hours to you?"

"Yes, I seem to have forgotten," he snarks back. "Please go on."

"Noah. Can't you be serious?"

"What do you want me to say, Sayer?"

"I want you to tell me how we're going to catch this bastard. It's the same person who sent me the letter and photos!"

Darling Sayer. The name makes my skin crawl.

"We?" He lifts a brow. "There is no *we* in this, Sayer." He stands up from the bed, meeting me in the middle of his bedroom. "There's you, then there's me. You're not getting near this."

"I'm already in this!" I shout. "Or have you been so focused on my sister that you forgot why I'm actually here?"

A look crosses his faces as his feet eat the distance between us. "You think I forgot?" That authoritative tone is back in his voice, but I'm not one to bend. "I still have dirt under my fingernails from the cemetery where I dug you out."

"I want to help..." My voice trails off, Noah's already shaking his head. Not budging. My fists clench and I resist the urge to do what I really want, which is punching Noah in the throat.

He's so stubborn!

But before I can carry out my crime, there's a knock on Noah's door.

It opens before Noah can give the okay, and Gabe's head is peeking in. "Got what you asked for."

Noah doesn't say anything, he doesn't look away from me as he raises two fingers waving him in.

As the door opens, my eyes widen. Gabe's not alone. In his hands is a small bundle of fur. "Pan!"

Breaking away from Noah, I run to Gabe and grab my cat from his hands.

The comfort of his purring is a balm to my ears, soothing the places my shower couldn't reach. I bury my face in his fur, never wanting to let him go again.

"I'd be careful next time you see Reeve," Gabe warns.

"Why?" I ask, picking my head up.

"He wasn't too happy I took your cat back. My boy has gotten quite attached to that flea infested fur ball."

"Pan doesn't have fleas!" I hold my cat closer, insulted on his behalf. Turning away from Gabe, I march to Noah's bed and place Pan on the mattress, inspecting him.

He looks the same, fluffy white fur and yellow-green eyes that still shine with judgments and sass, and it feels like he's gained a little weight.

He's perfect.

I turn to Noah. "Why did you ask for him?"

"For you," he replies, glaring at the feline as he walks across the mattress headed for the pillows. "I thought you might've missed him."

An unspoken thought lingers: *I thought you might need him.*

At a loss for what to say, Gabe saves me from saying anything. "Do you need anything else?"

Noah shakes his head. "Go meet up with Reeve, he'll fill you in."

"Yeah, Noah can't say anything with me in the room," I snark. "I'm not allowed to know anything. I'm just supposed to sit here and look pretty."

Gabe and Noah share a look before he leaves, shutting the door quietly behind him.

I look at Noah. He's back to glaring at my cat. "If you don't like animals, why—"

"Why am I allowing it now?" he fills in.

I nod.

"Because I wanted you to be happy."

My eyes widen. Before I can say anything, Noah's phone goes off. Moving to get it, he eyes Pan with indifference.

He reads what's on the screen, only to curse as he brings it to his ear.

My own ears strain to listen, but I can't hear anything.

Noah moves around the room on autopilot, getting dressed as he listens to whatever is being said on the other line. With another curse, he hangs up and shoves the phone into his pocket.

"I have to go," he tells me, synching his watch to his wrist. "There'll be two people in the lobby if you want to leave, but I think you might be wanting to stay in today." He casts a glance at Pan.

I freeze. The thought of being alone…No. I can't let what happen control me. I can be alone. I love being alone.

I must not look that convincing.

Noah walks over to me and cups my cheek. "I won't be gone long."

"Is this about who took me?"

He nods, starting to pull away.

I grab his wrist to stop him. "Can I just request one thing?"

"We both know you're going to anyway, so go on."

"Can you keep me updated? I need to know what's happening. For my own sanity."

It takes him several seconds until he nods, pulling away from me and walking out the door. Leaving me alone with my cat.

Turning to Pan, I scratch under his skin. "So, what've you been up to?"

twenty-eight

THE NEXT WEEK GOES BY IN A BLUR. IT'S THE KIND OF week that doesn't feel like any time has passed, but when you look at the calendar, you realize you're already on Friday when you thought it was either Tuesday or Wednesday.

It's also the kind of week, where everything feels different but changes subtly occur.

Changes like the calendar shifting from January to February. The weather from cold to frigid.

Changes like I'm no longer okay in the dark. Ever since the night in the cemetery I can't be in utter darkness. I start to sweat, my chest pinches, my breathing almost stops. I now need a nightlight when I sleep, so when I jolt awake in terror, I'm reminded that it's okay, I'm okay. I'm safe.

But the biggest change has been the dynamics between Noah and me. He's been around so much, to the point where it's become overbearing.

Everywhere I am, he is. Sometimes by my side and other times he lurks like a creeper in the shadows. Eyes following my every move.

After the cemetery, there was a moment where I thought Noah was going to try and chain me to his apartment, just to keep me from going out when he couldn't follow. We fought for hours about it until he finally relented and I let him tie me up in another, more fun way.

That night stole a sense of safety from me, solace in the dark, but I'll be damn if it steals my independence too.

Gone are Silent One and Silent Two. Noah and Thea have since replaced them after Noah reamed them out for their shitty protective skills. They were at the gallery the night I was taken.

While Noah and Thea play shadow, Reeve and Gabe have been trying to find who took me from the art gallery. There was a list of guests, so they've been going through it meticulously, interrogating each person.

So far they haven't had much luck.

With each passing day of them not finding the person, Noah grows more and more frustrated.

Every night, he storms into his office and locks himself inside the room for hours.

It's not until I'm getting ready for bed that he ventures out to pull me out of my bedroom and into his. Because that's where I sleep now. In Noah's room with his arms wrapped around me like a boa.

Never would I have pegged Noah to be a cuddler, but in the middle of the night I wake up to his chest pressed against my back, one arm wrapped around my waist while the other cups one of my boobs.

Although, I'm not sure Noah would call it cuddling. From the way he's wrapped around my body it feels like he's putting himself in front of me to ward off another attack.

My guard. My shield. My protector.

Sometimes I catch him watching me as if I'm going to vanish. I called him out on it one night, but in typical Noah fashion, he didn't answer me. Just smirked and pulled me to his chest, his lips finding mine. That night he kissed me like he needed reassurance.

One morning when Thea was walking with me to class, I told her about it, and she reminded me that he lost his parents when he was young and emotions work differently with Noah.

He was a broken, damaged boy who grew up to be a callous and merciless man. But underneath that hard shell exterior, I knew there was a man whose heart beat red.

A man who currently stands in the kitchen; bare-chested as he makes us breakfast.

"You're staring."

"You want me to stare," I remind him. If he didn't want me ogling him, he'd put on a shirt. I watch him as much as he watches me. It's hard not to when he's a magnet for my gaze.

We pull to each other, opposite ends of the same string.

He smirks into the pan as I make myself more comfortable on the kitchen stool.

Today has been canceled. Literally. More snow than predicted fell during the night with inches piling up on the streets and roads.

It's six a.m. and already half the city has lost power. Shut down for the day.

So this is how I'm choosing to spend it. Watching Noah make an elaborate feast for two. Eggs, pancakes, bacon, sausage, toast, and champagne, I can't stop myself from thinking he's trying to butter me up for a snow day sex fest.

And if that's the case, he's going to be sorely disappointed. I'm behind on schoolwork so today has to be my catch-up day. And I will not let him distract me.

He's the reason I'm behind to begin with.

I tear my gaze from Noah, opening my laptop to force myself to work.

As I'm typing away, my body shivers. Maybe I picked the wrong outfit to wear, a stolen button-down from Noah's floor, and socks. It's not cozy enough for a snow day. I need to be cozy.

About twenty minutes in and one assignment finished, I decide to check the weather radar before jumping into the next.

When I see what they're reporting, my eyes widen. God, that's so much snow predicted.

Why did I move back here again?

A throat clears, startling me.

Noah frowns as he jerks his chin to the two plates on the counter stacked with food.

Ah, we're back to his native tongue. Caveman.

Too bad for him, I chose French in school.

"Use your words, Noah." I grin, closing my laptop.

He glares at my teasing tone. "Food. Now."

Such a caveman. He slides me a plate while standing on the other side of the bar to eat his.

We're eating our food in companionable silence when the lights to the apartment go off. So do the surrounding lights from the buildings around us. I stiffen as they flicker off.

"Looks like the blackout is spreading." Noah doesn't bother to pick his head up from where it hovers above his plate. He's wolfing his food down while I've barely touched mine.

Noah wipes his mouth with a napkin, putting his empty dish in the sink. "You don't like it?" He frowns at my picked at plate.

"No, it's delicious," I reassure him, seeing some tension leave his shoulders. But I set my fork down, anyway. "I'm going to go change, though."

I need a second, or several, alone. It's not as bad as when I wake up in the middle of the night, not knowing my surroundings for a second, but it takes me a minute to ease the pain in my lungs. I need to get up. Do something. Change outfits. Something to feel in control again.

"Why do you want to do that?" He takes in my hard nipples that pierce through the shirt's fabric.

"Because this" —I trace the pert bud and his nostrils flare— "means I'm cold. They're not for you to stare at."

"What about suck on?" he prowls toward me.

I knew it! He wants a sexfest. I put my hands out to keep him at a distance. He walks right into my palms, not caring.

I scramble off the chair and dart away. "Oh no you don't, mister!" I run around the island. "There will be none of that until I get my schoolwork done."

Noah groans but concedes.

However, I don't trust him though as I skirt around him and to the stairs, expecting him to reach out and grab me. But he doesn't. Doesn't even make a sound until I reach the stairs.

That's when I hear him mumble, "It better not be that damn penguin onesie."

I stop mid-step, shooting him a look. "There's nothing wrong with my onesie."

"You're going to come back down in it, aren't you?"

"Maybe." I can't fight the grin on my face. "You're just going to have to be patient and find out."

"One day I'm going to burn that thing."

I gasp, leaning over the railing so he sees how serious I am when I say, "You will do no such thing, Noah Kincaid. If I ever find it missing, I will smother you in your sleep and call Thea to help me dispose of your body."

He raises a brow, not scared but impressed. "I don't know if I like you hanging out with Thea. She's putting murderous thoughts into your head."

"Oh no, Thea didn't do that," I correct him, continuing my climb up the stairs. "You did, Noah. A long time ago."

His laugh follows me up to the second floor and I find

myself grinning at the sound. Never did I think this would be us, that it would feel this effortless in our dynamics.

There's no pushing or pulling.

There's only Noah and me. Existing, laughing. Thriving together in a way that feels right. Natural and has always been.

What I felt for him back when I was in prep school is on another plane right now. Heightened to the point of him being my first thought of the day and my last at night.

I came back here because I was lost and hollow, but now I hardly remember what that feels like.

Now, I feel weightless and my laughs are more genuine, my shoulders less tense.

And it's in thanks to that man downstairs. He's opened my eyes and showed me what I've been missing. A world I didn't see before. He's shown me that it's okay to live outside the black and white, finding excitement in the shades of gray.

He's a match and I'm a firework, his spark igniting mine.

In my room, I sort through all the stuff on the floor, looking for my onesie. Because why would it be in the dresser or in the closet? That's too much work when the floor is readily available.

Oh, if my mother could see this now. She'd have my head.

And I know my messiness bothers Noah and his type A personality, but he takes the mess because it comes with me. Because he accepts me for how I am, not looking to change me.

Aha! Found it! Underneath a pile of schoolbooks.

I zip it on, flipping the hood up so I look like a cute and cuddly penguin. I was serious in my threat to Noah if he ever got rid of this. It's my favorite.

I'm headed toward the stairs when I noticed the door to Noah's office is cracked open. I pause outside of it, curiosity hooking me with her claws.

Do I go in or walk away?

The polite thing would be to walk away, but despite Noah's smothering and my insistent asking, he hasn't told me much on my sister's location or the person who buried me alive.

What if the answers are in there? I inch my toe forward. It hits the door, which opens wider.

Well, would you look at that.

I slip inside. I'll only be a minute. Two tops.

Unlike the rest of Noah's place, his office looks lived in. Littered with empty scotch glasses and sprinkled with little trinkets. Personal items.

And it's those items that steal my attention once I'm inside.

I walk to the shelves, looking at the little mementos he's collected. Mostly knives and bullet casings. There are old, rare, collectible books. First editions from some of the world's greatest authors. My mouth drops as my eyes run over the titles.

As I'm reading them, my eyes scan past a trinket that mingles with the books, only to dart right back.

Ice spikes my veins as I blink, hoping for an illusion. Hoping that my tired eyes are playing tricks on me.

It can't be.

With a shaky hand, I reach up to grab it. Feeling the embossed filigree and cool metal in my palm, I know I'm not imagining things.

This is real.

But how?

Dread rises with my heart rate as confusion clouds my thoughts. I rub my thumb over my granddad's pocket watch, the chain dangling between my fingers. He used it every day, kept on his person at all times. It was the only thing my granddad cherished as much as his grandkids, his art.

The pocket watch was his father's, and his father before that.

A family heirloom we couldn't find after he passed. My mother was in a tizzy. My father fuming, thinking that Granddad got rid of it just out of spite.

If they only knew who had it now.

But why does he have it? How did Noah get it?

The gold is polished while the scratches detailing its age are still there. And it's still ticking. I hold it up to my ear, listening to the rhythmic tick, tock, tick, tock and feeling the sound deep in my bones. It sounds like my granddad when I used to wrap my arms around him.

It sounds like home.

My hands shake as I click the watch open. Seeing the engraving that's always stuck with my granddad. *Family first* in Gaelic.

"Sayer," Noah calls from the doorway.

I didn't hear him come up.

I turn around, my fist closed tight around the face. He raises a brow when he sees I'm holding something.

"What do you have there?" he asks like he already knows.

Slowly, I open my fist, the object shaking in my palm. "What is this?"

Noah doesn't answer and his silence is almost worse.

"What is this, Noah? Why do you have my granddad's watch?"

Still, he remains silent.

"Answer me!" I scream, my voice cracking at the end.

"He gave it to me."

Everything stops. My breathing. The watch. The snow outside. It's silence save for the static in my head.

His words don't compute. Granddad wouldn't give it to Noah. He'd give it to me or Harlow. Or my dad. His family.

Not a friend of Harlow's. Definitely not a friend.

It doesn't make sense.

"Did you *steal* it?" Anger is behind my words.

Noah pursed his lips as he locks his jaw. "Want to know the story or are you just going to throw accusations my way?"

He thinks he's allowed to have attitude right now? I don't think so.

"I'm going to act however I want until I know why you have my granddad's watch!" My voice gets louder with every word until I'm yelling.

"I need you to think long and hard about this, Sayer. If you want to know, it's going to change everything."

"Stop. Just stop trying to scare me, Noah. I don't care what you think it's going to do to me. This is my grandfather's!" I shake my fist between us. The chain rattles. "I deserve to know."

His jaw ticks. "Fine. Come downstairs."

I shake my head. "No, tell me now."

"Sayer," he growls like it's going to intimidate me. Too bad for him I'm far past being intimidated.

"Tell me, Noah."

He walks over to me, moving to touch my cheek but I jerk away. His eyes flare.

"Get downstairs, Sayer."

"Why? Why can't you tell me up here?"

Instead of answering, Noah shakes his head and before I can demand answers, I'm being lifted into the air, thrown over his shoulder.

The watch falls from my hands.

He walks out of the office and down the stairs without paying mind to any of my protesting. I try to kick him, but his arms are locked so tight around my legs I'm immobilized.

He drops me down on the couch and I'm nothing short of fuming.

Anger that only grows as Noah walks over to his bar and pours a generous amount of scotch into a glass. Then pours another.

He walks back to me, handing me a glass.

I don't take it. I sink into the couch with my arms crossed, instead.

Without saying a word, he sits on his coffee table next to the chess set. I stare at the pieces. It's my move, has been for days, and I haven't figured out which one would be best. Noah's currently winning, collecting more of my pieces than me his. He already has all of my pawns.

He's always several steps ahead of me.

"Tell me," I whisper.

He takes his time sipping his scotch before talking. "You know we would always hang out at his place with Harlow."

Slowly, I nod.

"Well, over time, your grandfather started to become a mentor to me. To all of us."

A mentor? "My grandfather never did anything with real estate or property investments. He was an art consultant."

The look Noah gives me makes me feel small, naïve.

"Have you ever wondered about the Baron? About his identity?"

"Of course," I answer. Everyone has. "I wrote a paper about him for one of my classes in undergrad." The more I talk, the more heavy my lungs feel.

"Sayer." Noah reaches for my hands, anchoring me to him. "Your grandfather was the Baron."

"No," I whisper. Unable to wrap my head around what he's saying.

"Think about it, Sayer."

"No," I repeat, louder this time. "My granddad wasn't a thief. He was a good man."

"He was a great man," Noah agrees. "But he was a thief."

I don't want to believe this is true. That my sweet and caring and loving granddad was a hardened criminal but the more I turn the words over, the more I see the signs. The lessons he would always give me and my sister, to observe every room we entered, to find blind spots in cameras and how to pick locks.

Growing up, I thought they were little games. Things I didn't realize other kids weren't playing with their grandparents.

How hard my parents molded me into a society accepting girl, of how hard they tried to fit in with other members of the city's elite. How they didn't like me spending time with him.

I think back to all the traveling my granddad did, all the places he'd seen. All the paintings he had in his collection, of all the art he'd bring back from his travels.

The constant rotation of art moving through his home.

My home.

Oh *God.*

I chalked it up to his job. But even as I'm majoring in art conservation and want to be an art consultant, the things I've researched haven't always lined up with what he did.

The more I think about it, the more it makes sense. The more signs are there. My granddad was an art thief. He was the Baron. "I feel so stupid."

"No," Noah argues. "He didn't want you to know, Sayer."

"Then why did you?" I ask. "Did Harlow know? Did my parents?"

It takes him several seconds before he nods.

"So I was the only one kept in the dark?"

Again, he nods. This time slower.

I wrap my arms around myself, suddenly cold. But it's a

cold no blankets or layers can touch. It's formed on the inside, where the love of my granddad always kept me steady.

He was my best friend, but it turns out I barely knew him. I only knew the lies he fed me.

"You mentioned he was a mentor to you." I move my hands under my thighs. They tingle with nerves, the feeling of going numb without actually being numb.

"He taught us the tricks of the trade."

"You're art thieves?" My mouth parts. A firework goes off in my head. "Those paintings at the art gallery weren't donated, were they?"

"Some of them. Others were forgeries curtsey of Reeve."

I stare at him.

I don't know how to answer.

"We're a little bit of everything, Sayer. We steal, we con, we kill. There's nothing really we don't do. The casino? It's a front. The Underground started long before we ever bought that property. It started in prep school with just me, your sister, and the boys. Thea came in shortly after. The Baron was our mentor and we were his students. We'd go to school, but it wasn't until after that our actual lessons started."

Another sign I completely ignored, only seeing what I wanted to.

Harlow would always go over to our granddad's apartment after school and never let me come.

I don't know what to think anymore. The static I had back in Noah's office is even louder now. "My grandfather was a thief," I repeat.

"The best."

"He created The Underground."

Noah nods.

"And he left it all to you?"

Again, he nods.

I feel so stupid for saying this. So stupid for never knowing. It was all in my face this entire time and I never knew…

"Why? Why didn't he tell me?"

Noah shrugs, but it's almost hesitant. Noah doesn't hesitate.

"He didn't think you could handle this life."

He's right, I think. This bomb has left me in pieces.

I drain the rest of my drink, welcoming the burn. It helps me pretend I'm whole when all I feel is hollow.

The lights flicker back on, but I still feel like I'm in the dark.

Setting the glass down, I meet Noah's unwavering stare.

"I want to see it."

twenty-nine

Sayer

Noah takes me to the casino. The Underground. *I can't believe it. I can't freaking believe it.* It's been under my nose—er, rather—right above my head the whole time.

Silently—it's been quiet between us since we left the apartment—Noah takes out a key and unlocks the only door on the top floor.

I let him pull me inside the dark room, too afraid I'll run back down the stairs if he doesn't. Part of me believes that if I don't see what lays inside this room, it's not true. That my grandfather is still the man I've always thought him to be.

My granddad was a good man.

My granddad was a thief.

The best.

Noah lets go of my hand and walks farther into the room. I hear his steps, slow and methodic. Then there is silence. Silence and darkness.

And then—a click.

The lights flicker on.

"Oh my God," I breathe.

At first, I do nothing but stare.

Stare and not comprehend what's before me.

But it's not what I thought would grab my attention first.

An entire wall is made up of windows, very much like the ones at Noah's, looking down on the casino floor.

"How did I not notice this when I was here?" I spin around to see Noah's still by the light switch, blank-faced.

"This town is an illusion. You only see what we want you to see." He walks toward me. "We can see you, but you can't see us."

Chills caress my arms, my neck.

Breathe, Sayer, breathe.

My eyes stray from the window to take in more of the room.

It's a museum… if a museum housed stolen artwork.

Paintings are framed on the wall, some trapped in glass casings. Vases and busts sit on ornately carved podiums.

Little plaques are situated beneath each piece. Getting closer, I see that they state the day they were stolen and by who. Chills brush my skin as I run my finger along the closest:

The Baron, 1975.

I trace over each curve and line of every letter, running my nail along the numbers. It's here right in front of me, but it still doesn't feel tangible.

"Why are these all here?"

"It's a holding facility of sorts," Noah explains. "Where we keep the paintings we want to sell, display the ones we don't. It's like our own private museum."

My mind can't wrap around this. It's a fantasyland, a nightmare. I'm still sleeping. I have to be. There's no other reason.

But no, this is the real world where stories don't have happily ever afters. Grandpas aren't only cute little old men who wear newsboy caps and give you chocolate from their sweater pockets.

They're liars and cheats and sneaks.

"How did I not know?" I ask around the shattering of my heart.

"Because—"

I whirl around to face Noah, who I didn't notice had moved closer to me. He's right behind me. "I swear to God, Noah if you say it's because he didn't want me to know, I will fucking scream."

I don't need excuses. I need time to process this.

"Just—" I lower my voice, poorly hiding the frustration in it. "Just let me be. For ten minutes."

I need to get away. Not from this room, but from him.

As I walk farther into the room, past paintings that have my eyes bulging, Noah calls, "You run, and I chase you."

I turn around, walking backward. "I'm not running. I'm hiding." There's a difference.

He doesn't respond so I carry on. Some of these paintings have been missing for years. Decades, maybe even centuries for a few.

I wander until I find a little alcove. It's small, with only enough space for half of my body.

Bringing my knees to my chest, I rest my chin on my knees as my brain struggles to digest all this.

The stories of the town are true. A truth bomb that never should've gone off.

The Baron.

My grandfather.

God. I bang my forehead against my knees.

How many signs were there that I missed? How many times did I feel left out when he took Harlow on a "business" trip all over the world, even when I was the one that loved art and painting and had never been anywhere my parents didn't want me to go.

Countless.

Growing up, I wasn't allowed to travel like Brin, who could travel free of her parents.

Mine were the overbearing protective type, they would go out to do things while I was to stay home and focus on school.

Picking my head up, I see a painting that startles me. More than the rest. I *know* that painting. Intimately.

And underneath it sits the man I know intimately.

Noah watches me like he's waiting for me to break. "Your ten minutes are up."

My lips twitch in a sad smile. "Always so punctual." I sound so far away, eyes jumping above his head. "He made me paint that painting, you know. Over and over one weekend."

My granddad had just returned home after a week in Paris, looking ragged from travel when he came by my house to pick me up.

I was so excited to spend time with him just the two of us. It had been so long since we'd done that.

This was back when I was in seventh grade and seeing my granddad started to become a little more infrequent when I felt his time was given more to Harlow.

And boy, Harlow was so angry that night he picked me up. I can still recall how loud her feet stomped up the stairs when she found out she wasn't invited.

Meanwhile, I couldn't stop grinning the entire drive to his little apartment.

It wasn't until we were eating dinner that he broke away from the table to pull out a circular tube from his suitcase.

"I want you to paint this," he said. "Just for fun."

He didn't need to tell me twice. One of the reasons I loved coming over was because he would always have me paint his findings.

It was the best way to learn, he always said.

That particular painting was called *The Girl Lost in the Sunflowers.*

"It's yours," Noah tells me.

I barely hear him. "What?"

"This painting" —he points above his head— "is one you painted."

"What happened to the original?" I focus on that. If I focus on the fact that I basically did a forgery I'm afraid I'll go into cardiac arrest.

"He fenced it."

Fenced. So technical. I've heard it before on crime shows and movies. Basically, it means, my granddad got rid of it. Sold it on some kind of illegal market.

I suck in a breath. It's shaky. Like my hands as I rub my face.

"How are you doing?"

Such a simple question for such a loaded answer.

"Well. Let's see." I scoot out from the alcove, closer to him. "I just found out my granddad is a thief and was a crime lord—"

"He wasn't a crime lord."

I spike a brow. "Oh, I'm sorry. What would you call it then?" I lean over, squinting my eyes. "*What* is your role here? You said he left you this. What are you?"

"The mastermind."

Despite everything, I snort. He's so serious. "That doesn't sound cheesy at all."

He doesn't react. "We all have roles here, Sayer. That one happens to be mine."

Mastermind, I muse over. It's fitting. The ruthless and cunning businessman is in charge of all this. He's the one that gets shit done. And has the money and resources to keep it hidden.

Connections stuffed in his back pocket.

And isn't that how I always thought of him on the chessboard? The king. The *mastermind*.

"What about the others?"

"Thea's a hacker. The tech wiz." She told me she did IT work...

He pushes off the wall, scooting closer to me. "Reeve is the forger." Right, he did mention that some of the paintings at the art gallery were done by him. "And Gabe's our hitman."

I choke. "Excuse me? *Hitman?* Like he kills people for money?"

"He does it for The Underground," Noah states as if it is *no big deal*. "When we need him too, which isn't too often. Mostly he's the brute muscle."

Gabe. Out of everything that's been dropped on me today, learning Gabe is basically an assassin is up there with my granddad being a thief.

Gabe, who wrote poetry in the margins of his notebook in that class we shared back in prep school. Gabe, who reads leather bound books at parties.

The quietest ones are the most dangerous, I remind myself.

"What about my sister? What did she do?"

"She was the thief on jobs."

Now I'm confused. "Aren't you all thieves?"

It feels weird to say. Almost unreal. A fantasy that I never wanted to be in.

If Noah's frustrated by my question, he doesn't show it. He scoots even closer, grabbing my ankle, tethering us together.

"We are, but when we go out on jobs, we each have a role. A task to carry out that best suits our skills. And your sister would always be the one to do the actual stealing." He looks down at his hand around my ankle. "She was the best."

Bitter jealousy stabs at me when hearing the pride in

which he speaks on my sister's skills. I want to shake myself, that's nothing to be jealous about.

No more words are exchanged between us as we sit in the middle of the room, surrounded by stolen and counterfeit art.

Noah doesn't push, doesn't bother me to share my thoughts. He just sits with me as I process.

For so long, my entire life really, I've wanted to know what went on with my sister and her friends, was always curious if the rumors around town were true, but now I kind of wish I didn't.

It feels like a spoiler to a book, where the build-up is so intense, so consuming, you've been squirming in anticipation only for someone else to tell you what happens. Ruining the illusion to the point where you now don't want to see the end through.

That's how it feels as I look at Noah.

And it twists my stomach tighter than I've ever felt.

I feel numb as he pulls us up, as he tells me we're going to go home.

Trailing behind him, I feel like broken glass someone has poorly pieced back together. One wrong breath and I'll break.

"Tell me about him."

Noah picks his head up from his hands. He's sitting on the edge of the couch, a glass of golden liquid beside him.

Coming back to Haven Harbor was supposed to make me feel closer to my grandfather, but I'm further away than ever.

The man I knew was not the man he was.

Noah knows the man he was.

He's watching me now, assessing me. I cross my arms, staring at him blankly. Expectantly.

"What do you want to know?" he asks, carefully.

Everything. Nothing. I don't know.

The man I grew up with now feels like a stranger. I didn't know Jack Brooks like I thought I did. But Noah did.

Noah knows more about my granddad than I ever will.

I step closer to the couch, to him.

It's been hours since we got back, hours that have felt like days. Minutes that have passed like seconds.

Noah pats the cushion next to him.

Slowly, I lower myself next to him, pressing my back into the arm of the leather couch. Facing him. There are centimeters between us, space he can easily eat up, but he doesn't.

That doesn't stop his penetrating gaze from hooking mine. "Where do you want to start?"

"I don't know. I just want to understand the Jack Brooks you knew," I finally admit in a whisper. "I want to understand."

Noah studies my face. Worry creeps into his expression. At any other time, I would've melted at the sight of vulnerability peeking through, but right now all I wonder is if my face looks as drained, as empty as I feel.

"Your sister introduced us," he starts. "But Baron took me under his wing after the second time we met."

"Why?" Why did he take a liking to Noah?

The corner of Noah's lip twitches up. "I stole from him. I remember how I didn't even have a reason. I just saw his wallet in his jacket pocket and swiped it. There's this thrill with getting away with something, something that you're taught to be wrong. A high that no drug can touch. That's what I felt when I stole his wallet."

"What happened after?"

"He told me you can't con a con man and slowly, he started to introduce Harlow and me into this new world." He rolls his head with a heavy sigh. "I've always been bored of high society.

There was nothing exciting about it. Everything was too superficial for me. Baron gave me a place to find myself."

My eyebrow raises. "He taught you how to steal and through that you found yourself?"

Noah nods. "He gave me something to work toward. He gave me a challenge."

I nod, still feeling lost.

"He also asked me to protect you."

My eyes snap to his. "When?"

"The night he died."

A slice of pain slashes my heart, remembering holding his hand as he drew his last breath.

"He made me swear to keep you safe."

I'm a little insulted he didn't think I could protect myself, but I know my grandfather has always seen me as a butterfly in a field of wasps.

I can't stop myself from thinking is that why Noah agreed to protect me? Because of my grandfather? Somehow that makes the pain in my chest sting worse.

"It's not." Noah's voice is low.

"What's not?"

"I haven't upheaved my life for the past several weeks just because of my promise." He levels me a serious look. "I went a year ignoring it. But then you came back…you came back and I couldn't ignore you. Even if it wasn't for Baron or your sister leaving, I still would've found a way to you."

I still would've found a way to you.

My breathing feels heavy, each breath tighter than the last with Noah's admission.

I still would've found a way to you.

Almost hesitantly, a move so unsure for Noah, he places his hand on my knee. I stare at it, barbells pressing on my chest.

It's too much. So when my phone goes off, I welcome the reprieve. Only to wish I hadn't as my eyes skim over the text message.

Groaning, I toss my phone to the floor.

"What?" Noah asks.

"Hope you don't have any plans this weekend."

He quirks a brow, looking intrigued. He's not going to be looking like that after I tell him the news.

"Don't get too excited, big boy. We're going to my parents.'"

It's interesting watching someone's expression change as subtly as Noah's and know that little change has a bigger impact than he'll reveal. "Why?" One word. Clipped and cold.

"My mother has decided to throw me a birthday party."

And that might be more startling news than finding out my grandfather was a renowned art thief.

An art thief. Wow. The more I think about it, the more I say it, the more I come to terms with it. But that doesn't mean I still don't have questions. I have so many.

But I don't want to talk anymore.

With careful fingers I reach up to take Noah's glasses off, placing them on the coffee table.

This morning I woke up so happy. So content. But all of a sudden I feel like I did my first week back. Wandering with no destination.

Until Noah.

He gave me a destination that wasn't on any map. An off-road I don't mind getting lost on.

But right now, I feel stuck in a ditch. I don't want that. I want to be back on the drive.

Usually, he's the one that feels so far away. But now his secrets are out. Oh, I'm sure he has more, but right now I don't care about those. This time it's me, I'm the one with the wall up.

A disconnect has been created between us and I want it gone.

My hands go to his shoulders, climbing into his lap. Straddling him.

"What're you doing?" He's cautious, hands going to the back of my thighs.

"I don't want to talk anymore." My lips find his. Tasting him, needing him.

He lets me take the lead, letting me guide…until my tongue traces his lips, seeking entrance. With a groan, Noah flips me onto the couch, covering his body with mine.

Devouring me.

This kiss feels different. Feels free.

And I lose myself in it. Lose myself in him. Sitting up, I pull off my shirt, then Noah's.

Everything else is forgotten…at least for now.

thirty

Sawyer

TWENTY-FIVE.

A quarter of a century.

That's how long I've been alive as of today. Somehow I thought it would feel different. More revolutionary. Ground-breaking.

Unfortunately for me, that happened a few days prior. Which I'm still trying to come to grips with.

I've never cared about my birthday.

Growing up it was a spectacle for my mother to plan some elaborate party that would somehow focus more on her than me.

In fact, if it wasn't for the party she's throwing me, I would've had a pretty relaxing, if not a subtle day, with me staying in bed for most of it. Pan curled on one side and a box of chocolates Thea sent over on the other.

Noah spent the morning with me although it wasn't the kind of morning where we did a lot of talking. And after making me a breakfast of French toast and peach bellinis, he left. Saying he had some business he had to take care of.

I was left to wonder exactly what kind of work he was going to take care of.

Was it with his company or with his army? Legal or illicit?

Whatever it was, Noah made it back in time to escort me to my birthday party at my childhood home.

Which is where we are now.

"Remind me why we're here?" I ask Noah, who glares at everything. Personally offended with what he sees.

When my mom said she was throwing me a birthday party, I didn't expect her to roll out a gold carpet in my honor, but I'd be lying if I said I didn't expect *some* kind of decoration. Anything to show that it was a party for her daughter.

Instead, I get a wait staff in tuxes and people dressed to the nines while a string band plays in the foyer.

It doesn't feel like a birthday.

It feels like every other party my mother has thrown here. I don't even know if any of my friends are going to be here. So far, I've only seen my parents' friends. Some have even stopped to ask me where they were. Not an utterance of a happy birthday on their tongue.

And now I can't help but stare at the art that hangs on the walls, at the vases and china locked away in a curio cabinet, at the imported tile on the ground.

All the money your family has is dirty, Sayer. Blood money.

Maybe that's why I never liked having it. Not because I feel holier-than-thou, but because it never felt like mine to have.

"You're here for answers," Noah reminds me.

Right, I nod. My parents owe me answers to the questions that have been burning in my head for two days since I found out my granddad was a thief.

"You can do this, Sayer," Noah encourages, offering me his elbow, which I take. Nodding my head again though I don't believe it myself.

Since finding out, Noah's been different around me. More open. But not open enough for me to know where I stand. With him. With his life.

Where do I go when Harlow is caught and my stalker is dealt with?

"You okay?" Noah asks.

I look up at him, realizing I've stopped walking, too lost in my thoughts, and nod. "Yeah," I feel myself say, but not feeling my lips move in the process. "I just don't want to be here."

"We can leave after you talk to them." His thumb strokes my lower back. "I'm here."

But for how long?

I bite my tongue to keep from asking, instead I nod again, feeling like a bobblehead.

His words are meant to provide comfort, but they bring a hole to my chest instead. Those blue eyes that penetrate my soul stare at me, knowing something is off.

But he doesn't get a chance to call me out on it because someone wraps their arms around me from behind, shouting in my ear, "Happy birthday!"

I wince at the ringing in my ears, turning around to see Brin's wide, smiling face before she tackle hugs me. We fall back into Noah, whose hands go to my waist, laughing.

Over Brin's shoulder, Thea stands behind her, waving. I break away from Brin and Noah, to hug her. "What're you two doing here?"

There's a high chance my mother invited Brin since our parents are friends, but I know for a fact that she wouldn't have invited Thea.

It now makes sense why they never liked the circle Harlow ran around with. Because they all could expose them for the frauds they were.

Maybe I'm being a little harsh. My dad is a very successful lawyer so I'm sure not all our money is from crime, but there is no doubt in my mind that the people my parents call friends wouldn't turn their backs on them the second they found out.

"Noah invited us." Brin looks over my shoulder at a scowling Noah. Always with the hard faces.

"You did?" I look up at him.

"You don't have to sound so surprised." He rights his askew glasses.

Thea giggles. "He doesn't want you to know he did something nice."

"Why?" I ask Noah.

"It's your birthday, Sayer. I didn't want you to not have some friends of your own here." He shrugs like it's no big deal. It is a big deal though, and he knows that. Which is why he's watching me, trying to gage my reaction.

I give him a soft smile, mouthing a quick *thank you*.

"Isn't that adorable?" Brin smiles at him.

"Totally adorable," I agree, still watching him.

"I also invited Reeve and Gabe," Noah adds as if that takes away from the gesture we're praising him for.

"Speaking of…" Thea looks around. "Where are they?"

Noah shrugs, not particularly bothered.

"Sayer."

My name sounds like a whip lashing in the wind.

My friends stop talking as I turn around. "Mother."

She looks elegant in a form-fitting white dress, but her eyes are thrashing with rage, locking on Noah. Not wanting to create a scene, she briskly walks over to us. "I need to speak to you."

Thea and Noah share a look while Brin looks at me in alarm. Kathy Brooks does *not* sound happy.

I'm not intimidated. "What a coincidence, Mother. So do I."

"Your father is waiting for us in his office."

"Perfect," I say as she turns around, walking and smiling at her guests. The smile says nothing is wrong, but any person who knows anything about body language can see it's a lie.

Her shoulders are too far back, her spine uncomfortably

straight, and that smile…there has never been a more plastic, overstretched smile in this house.

I start to follow her with Noah close behind. My mom stops, hearing the extra set of feet following her. Quickly turning around, she looks to Noah. "You're not coming."

He stares at her, hands leisurely in his pockets. Unimpressed.

"This is a family affair."

"Then shouldn't he be included?" I keep my voice low. "After all, Granddad thought he was his family."

My mother is the Queen B of Botox, but even that can't keep the shock off her face. She turns to Noah. "You told her?"

He shrugs, continuing to give her nonverbal answers.

They're locked in a stare down that gains the interest of some nearby guests, wondering what's going on, when a man with thinning hair taps Noah on the shoulder.

At first, it looks like Noah isn't going to turn around and acknowledge the intruder, but he finally tears his gaze from my mother and whirls around to the man.

Noah simply raises a brow. There's so much discontentment in a single movement.

"Mr. Kincaid. I've been trying to get a meeting with you." This brave man doesn't cower as Noah's gaze turns darker as if to say *you really interrupted me for this*?

Yes, apparently, the man is.

If looks could burn people, Noah's would eviscerate him on the spot.

As the man drones on about some property he wants to acquire, my mother grabs my elbow and yanks me to her side. "Let's go."

Noah whips his head around, hearing her.

I shake my head, letting him know it's fine. I can handle

this on my own. I'm not fourteen anymore. My parents can't intimidate me into bending.

His eyes narrow, not agreeing with me.

As I let my mother pull me away, Noah tries to follow, but the man with thinning hair is *insistent*. He actually grabs Noah's arm to keep him in place.

I have to give credit where credit is due. The man is ballsy.

My mother leads us through the house to the end of the hallway where my father's office is.

She pushes me inside first.

My father sits behind his desk, a fat cigar in hand. Waiting.

I'm inhaling the rich, smoky aroma when the door clicks shut.

"Have a seat," my mother instructs, not really giving me a choice as she pushes me farther into the room, into one of the chairs before my father.

He regards me with quiet eyes and a closed off face.

"She knows." My mother walks to my father's side, resting a dainty hand on his shoulder.

The frown on his face deepens.

"You don't have to pretend I just found out you're spies or anything." I cross my legs, fighting calm. "I simply found out my grandfather stole art for a living and was one of the most notorious criminals never to be arrested. Pretty tame things."

"Sayer." My father's voice is very much like his cigars. Thick and smoky. My name is a scold, a reminder to watch my tone.

I ignore the warning. "I just want to know why. Why was I kept from knowing?"

They share a look and it's quiet in the room.

I want to shake them. I want the truth, not planned and strategic words. I'm tired of all these mind games.

"Stop stalling. Just tell me."

And after I know, I'm leaving.

Maybe I'll even try to salvage my birthday when I go.

"We made a deal with him. He got Harlow and we got you."

I look between them. "What does that mean?"

"It means." My father puts his burning cigar on the ashtray. "We got to raise you how we wanted to and we gave Harlow to your grandfather for what he wanted."

"You just gave Harlow to him?" That doesn't make any sense. "She lived with us."

"But he was in charge of her." My mother shrugs like she's talking about a car service, not her daughter. "Don't you remember how he would always come over whenever she got in trouble?"

Actually, I do. He even cut some of his "business" trips short because of some of Harlow's incidents.

"Then why did she live with us?" I push. If they didn't want my sister, why was she here? Why torture her with living with two people who didn't love her enough to raise her.

"For appearance purposes. Think of the scandal if she didn't live with us. Everyone would think we couldn't take care of our children."

"You couldn't."

My words drop like a bomb, creating a calm that's unsettling.

Until my mother speaks.

"Excuse me?" She speaks slowly, controlled. Holding herself back. She reminds me of when I told her I wanted to quit cheerleading. Frightening made even more so by the frozen muscles of her face.

"You couldn't," I repeat. "I wish you would've let Granddad have us both." Maybe then Harlow and I would've gotten along. Instead we were strangers living together, always at odds.

My mother walks away from my silent father, he'll let my mother handle this until the very end. When he'll deliver his closer. She walks until she's right in front of me, blocking Father from my view.

Bending at the waist, she makes us eye level. "You should be grateful. We gave you a beautiful life. Don't be ungrateful like your sister. When your father and I married, we didn't even want kids. We just had one because we thought we needed one." She speaks almost clinically. "Harlow, though, we knew right away she would be too much. Take too much time. So we tried again. And we got you. You were perfect. So impressionable."

That should hurt or at least, sting. But it doesn't. Because it makes sense. I always felt more like an accessory for them than a person.

"You had kids to climb the ranks," I summarize. "Do you really like this life so much?" Where you're more fake than real? Where money speaks louder than words?

Apparently they do.

"We had you to protect our assets."

I start to stand up, hearing enough, but my mom pushes me back down.

"You wanted someone to protect the money Granddad got from stealing." There's irony somewhere in this.

I scoot the chair back, far enough away to where my mother can't shove me back down and stand up. We're eye level now. "Were you never going to tell me the truth?"

She purses her lips together before shaking her head. No. No, they weren't. They were going to let me keep living a lie. All because of what?

"Why?"

"Because you were ours! I was always afraid to send you to your grandfather's, afraid one day he'd tell you and have both my girls. He always wanted to teach me, but my mother wouldn't let him. She didn't want me to have that life and I didn't want you to either. We did it to protect you, Sayer."

"No." I shake my head. "You did it for what you said, protecting your assets. It had nothing to do with me. If it did, you would've given me a choice."

They didn't give me the option.

Instead, they did what they always did.

Decided for me.

My free will is just that. My own. And I was never given the chance to choose it.

I think my time is done here. They're not going to apologize.

But that's okay.

I know now and they can't take that away from me.

I turn away going for the door.

"Where are you going?" my father asks.

"I'm leaving." And because I know it'll piss them off, I add, "With Noah."

"He's using you." My mother stares at me.

I know, a tiny voice says, but that's nothing new. I willingly agreed to that. We've used each other. "At least he's the one that told me the truth."

My hand wraps around the door handle, but before I leave, I look over my shoulder. "Why did you even throw me this party?"

"You're back home now, Sayer. It was expected."

I nod. Right. Of course.

Leaving the room, I don't look back.

And they don't stop me.

As I walk down the hall, I tell myself to go find Noah, but when I get back out to where everyone's mingling, I see him still talking to the man from earlier.

Noah looks ready to snap the other man's neck.

I should save him.

But I don't.

Instead, I decide to clear my head first.

So with my chin held high, I wander outside, grabbing the first coat I pass on the way, where the noise of the party doesn't reach.

I trail along the path I've had memorized since I was eight years old when I wanted to escape the frigid temperatures of my house. No matter the time of year, I always found the outside to be warmer than in there.

Past the pool, the basketball and tennis courts, through the thin line of trees is a little lake that's always helped clear my thoughts.

Thankfully my parents have lined the property with little lights in the ground.

Coming here was a mistake. And the disappointment I'm feeling right now is no one's fault but my own. Why did I think this would be any different than any other party my mother has thrown for me? They always end up with me feeling more battered than loved.

How different my life would've been if I knew from the beginning. Would I be like Reeve, a forger? Or like my sister, a thief? Or would I still be me, in grad school wanting to save art instead of steal it?

As weird as it might sound, I'm happy my sister has something she's good at.

After growing up and hearing my parents say Harlow would never amount to anything, it's nice to know that she proved them wrong. Even if it's with something illegal.

What my granddad made gave my sister a way to live her life. Gave Noah's life a purpose when he was lost and looking for his way. I remember hearing about his parents' plane crash.

How he went to go live with his aunt and uncle in New York. They sent him to boarding school with his cousin in England, not consoling a boy in his time of grief.

He was in England for three years before he came back. His uncle, supposedly, was able to get him access to part of his parents' trust early, making it so Noah was emancipated by the time he was sixteen.

What if my granddad was the one that saved him?

I'm lost in thought, pulling the borrowed coat tighter around me, when I hear voices build against the night.

"Gabriel! Get your ass back here!" It's Reeve. And he doesn't sound happy as I see Gabe briskly walk across the grass in the close distance.

Reeve stomps after him, his hands running through his hair.

Gabe doesn't stop, not until Reeve sets off in a jog and grabs his elbow, twisting him around. They stand so close, almost chest to chest. Though their tones are anything but hushed.

"What is your fucking problem?" Reeve's hands are tight on the lapels of Gabe's jacket. Refusing to let him go. "Why do you always run?"

Gabe shakes his head. "I can't keep doing this, Reeve. I can't."

From where I stand, I can see Reeve's throat constrict. Struggling. His stance screams that he's on the brink and he's trying not to break. "Why?"

One word. One question. And the sadness in his tone has my heart tripping over itself. It sounds so pained, asking around broken glass.

I've never thought of Reeve as an emotionally sound being. He finds humor in darkness.

Never did I know he could sound so vulnerable.

My frown pulls at my face as I watch them.

Gabe's eyes flick toward me for the briefest of moments and he grabs Reeve, pulling him back in the direction of the pool.

Reeve and Gabe?

Pushing them away, I continue the walk to my lake, leaning against the giant oak tree once I'm there.

But I'm not alone for long.

A branch snaps causing me to whip my head to the sound. My heart jumps until I see the culprit. Noah stands in the clearing, hands in his pockets. Watching me with worry.

"Couldn't even give me five minutes?" I ask, a small smile touching my face. Thankful that he's here. Aside from light, he's the only thing to chase my fears of the dark away.

"Please," he says, walking toward me. "I had to get away from Donald Rodgers before I strangled him. He wouldn't fucking shut up."

"It's not like you would've went away for murder. Everyone is in your pocket."

"Not everyone," he says, giving me a pointed look.

Is he talking about me?

I don't get a chance to ask.

He's close enough now for his hand to cup my cheek, tilting my face up to meet his eyes. His touch brings a burn to my skin. One that thaws me as I lean into it.

"Are you going to ask me how it went?" I ask when it's quiet for too long.

"No." His thumb strokes my cheekbone. "I can take a healthy guess, but you're out here, so that's enough for me to know not well. This is where you always went when you were overwhelmed back when you were a teenager."

I blink up at him in surprise. "You remembered."

He smirks, but it's sweeter than any he's given me in the

past. Less arrogant. "You're a hard person to forget, Sayer Brooks."

I suck in a breath, seeing the emotion behind his glasses, but I'm robbed from saying anything as Noah lowers his mouth to mine.

A kiss that never comes.

"Well, isn't this adorable."

We pull apart as someone else joins us.

My chest feels heavy as I see who it is.

Stepping out of the trees, with a twisted, nasty look on her face as she takes in me and Noah, is my elusive sister. "My invitation must've gotten lost in the mail."

thirty-one

Noah

HARLOW BROOKS.

The antithesis of Sayer.

Where Sayer is smiles, Harlow is snarls.

Where Sayer is timid, Harlow oozes confidence.

One who bleeds with her heart, the other who drips apathy with her soul.

Two siblings who couldn't be more different.

Wearing her usual all black ensemble, Harlow looks the same as she did when she stole my ledger, except there's an ugly look twisted on her face as she drinks in my embrace with her sister.

Untangling from Sayer, I have this urge to do two things. Two reactions pulling me in opposite directions.

To get my hands on Harlow like I've wanted to for weeks—*finally* she's here in front of me, only strides separate us. It wouldn't take much.

But it's the other part of me that's holding me back. The need, the promise, to protect Sayer.

I try to step practically in front of her. But in typical Sayer fashion, she has to be stubborn and fight me, stepping around my provided shield so we're standing shoulder to shoulder.

"Aw, don't let me interrupt. This is so sweet I might throw up." Harlow sneers at us.

"Where have you been, Harlow?" I try to keep my temper even as I probe her for questions. I fail.

"Oh, around." She turns her blue, almost indigo, eyes on me. "But I got tired of waiting for you to come get me, baby, so I decided to come find you."

Sayer bristles at *baby*.

I want to reach out, to reassure Sayer but I don't.

Can't.

Not when I have to keep my focus on Harlow.

"You kept running when I'd get close," I remind her. Every lead I followed was cold. She had been there but was always gone by the time I showed up.

"I was hurt," she pouts. "I wasn't ready to see you yet. You replaced me with *her*." Harlow casts a scalding glare at her sister. "Just like everyone else."

"Not Granddad," Sayer says quietly, but confidently. "He never replaced you with me."

"Look who's finally clued in." Harlow raises a brow, coming closer. "I bet you just hate knowing that. Knowing he chose me over you. You idolized that man and he was nothing more than me."

No. He was better than Harlow will ever be. "He loved Sayer," I remind her.

"But he loved you most of all, didn't he, Noah." She turns that hateful stare to me. "He left you everything."

"Is that why you stole my ledger?"

"It's supposed to be mine!" she snaps, shouting. "Everything of his was supposed to be mine! I was his family! Not you."

"That's not true and we both know it." She hasn't been able to get past this. Not since Baron gave me The Underground and all that inhabits it.

Harlow wasn't happy then. And she sure as hell isn't happy now. "Where's my ledger, Harlow?"

She could've taken anything else and I wouldn't have given a damn. But that's why she took it. It's the only thing I keep that could incriminate me. My friends. Sayer says I have everyone in my back pocket, but that's only in this city.

Everywhere else I'm fair game and depending on who Harlow showed that information to, it could send me away for a long time.

It's a record of all our illicit dealings, all the fencing we've done, all the paintings and art pieces we intend to fence. It's a record of our trades essentially.

And I'm going to need it back.

"In a place where only I can find it." She bats her eyes. "I needed to have some kind of bargaining chip with me."

"Some kind of bargaining chip," I repeat, rolling my eyes. "It's not going to make me give you The Underground."

What she wants goes hand in hand with the ledger. It does nothing for me to give her that. Not that I would. She could steal anything, and I still wouldn't give her The Underground.

Not when it's been entrusted to me.

"I'm not talking about that." There's a rogue look on Harlow's face. A smug smile. "I'm talking about her." She points to Sayer and before either of us can react, a bald man materializes from the trees behind us, seizing Sayer.

His arms constrict around her, hand covering her mouth as she lets out an ear-splitting, barren tree branch-shaking scream.

Lunging for them, my hand goes for the holster strapped along my back.

Sayer's wide, shaken eyes stare at me. Begging me to be smart, to not do anything rash or bold. There's another threat with us tonight. And I know she's right, know I should focus on Harlow, but I can't think of anything past this fucker touching her.

A clean, crisp click pierces the air.

"I wouldn't do that, Noah." Harlow points a gun at Sayer. "Sam can just as easily snap her neck before you so much as blink."

I freeze. My heart throbs in trepidation. Breathing shallowly.

There's no doubt in my mind that Harlow wouldn't shoot her sister, especially when she's never seen Sayer as anything more than her rival.

Tread carefully, Kincaid. No longer is it me or The Underground or the damn ledger I'm worried about.

It's *her.*

My siren.

Sayer.

"Harlow…" I try to coax her attention to me.

It doesn't work.

She keeps her gaze and the gun trained on Sayer. "*She's my leverage. Has been all along.*"

Sayer makes a muffled sound as she struggles to break free of Sam's hold while I feel like my brain has short-circuited.

She's my leverage. Has been all along.

Weights drop to the pit of my stomach.

"What's wrong, Noah?" Harlow taunts. "You look a little shell-shocked."

I glare at her. "What did you do."

It's not phrased as a question.

She clucks her tongue. "I'm disappointed. Aren't you supposed to be one step ahead of everything? The all-seeing master?"

My hands clench, but I don't say anything. She hasn't lowered the gun from Sayer. Now isn't the time to provoke her.

"Have I bested you?" She smirks. "You fell right into the trap."

Sayer continues to struggle, her aggravation muffled by the hand still covering her mouth. She stares at her sister with a look I've never seen grace her emotional gray eyes. Sayer is far past angry.

"Quiet her, Sam. I'm not done talking." Harlow taps her foot.

Sam tightens his hold and Sayer winces, but she doesn't give either of them the satisfaction of crying out in pain.

"Now where was I. Oh! Right. You're not as invincible as you think yourself to be, Noah. All I had to do was throw Sayer in your face and that's all it took for you to revert back to when we were dating. Always watching my sister. So *sick.*" She spits the last word.

My jaw clenches as events snap into place. "You went to her apartment because you knew I'd go after her to learn where you went."

"Ding-ding-ding, give the man a prize!" she shouts to the trees. "You became horribly predictable after that. I'm quite disappointed in you actually, Noah. I didn't think you'd become so wrapped around my sister like you did. I thought you were better than that. Oh well." She shrugs. "That just works better for me."

She was animated as she talked, relishing in the fact that she one-upped me, but now it's like someone has flipped a switch and she's back to being serious.

I'm physically shaking, restraining myself the best I can.

"Give me The Underground or I'll shoot your darling Sayer."

The color of Sayer's face washes away. Harlow's words ring in my ears. *Darling Sayer.*

More pieces click into place.

The pictures. The text. The headstone.

Harlow.

Sayer comes to the same conclusion, staring at her sister with a haunted, betrayed look.

And I'm a fucking idiot for not seeing it.

Sayer did. She called it from the beginning back in my office.

Fuck.

Harlow's been behind it all.

Not only for putting Sayer in my path, but also for all the attacking she's done on her sister.

She's been the puppeteer and we've been her toys on strings.

How did I not see this…

Because it's fucking Harlow. Impulsive, impatient Harlow. Who's laughing at the look on my face.

"You underestimated the wrong person this time, Noah." She smiles, a chaotic, invigorating smile. "Now. The Underground."

"You're not getting it." It's the wrong thing to say.

"Is that so?" She cocks her head to the side. "Sam."

Sam grins and it actually brings a chill to my skin, only for the cold to grow as he produces a knife and brings it to Sayer's throat. Her gray eyes look black, her pupils dilated with fright. The blade winks as he digs it into her skin. Sayer doesn't make a sound, she doesn't wince. The only indication that she feels anything is her eyes growing wider.

But I feel it. I feel it deep in my bones as if it was my neck the blade touched.

"Stop," I bark at Harlow and that manic smile of hers grows, but she holds up a hand to Sam and his movement stops.

Even from here I can see a thin, dark line on Sayer's perfect neck.

My blood boils. My fists clench. It's taking every muscle I have not to lose myself in the rage inside me.

And it's not like I can do anything. Harlow still has her gun pointed at Sayer.

Patience, I breathe icy air into my lungs. It does nothing to smother the flames rising inside me. I need to channel patience.

"Now. Let's try this again." She lowers her gun, holding it like an accessory at her side.

There's she is. The Harlow I've always known. Overconfident. Cocky. She thinks she's won.

That she's outmatched me.

Harlow continues, not seeing the gears churning in my head. "You're going to hand over The Underground and Sayer gets to walk away unscathed." She glances at her sister, cooing. "Ooh, well. Maybe a little scathed."

As discreetly as I can, I press the small button on the side of my watch, sending an alert to Gabe, Reeve, and Thea's matching watches, and hope like hell my friends get here in time. It's a little noise, nothing more than three beeps, but we all know what it means. If it works like she designed it to, I'll give Thea all the money she wants to design more of her little inventions.

A grunt at my side snags my attention and my neck snaps toward it.

Sayer digs her elbow into Sam's gut causing him to double over in pain, but his hold on her is still tight. She moves her leg, jamming her heel into his foot before she rams the base of her palm into this nose. He hollers in pain, only for it to be amplified when her fist is brought down on his dick.

The big, bad bald man crumples like a piece of paper.

Sayer kicks him there for good measure before stepping over his body.

Harlow shouts. Her gun fires.

I don't so much as blink before tackling Sayer to the ground. Covering her body with mine. No more harm will come to her tonight.

Ever—if I can help it.

"What the hell was that?" I hiss in her ear.

"That was the SING method," she says like it should be obvious.

It's not.

"The fuck is the sing method?"

"It's from a movie and" —she waves a hand at Sam's curled up body— "very effective."

My brow raises appreciatively. Full of surprises with my siren. "As long as you don't use that on me."

"No promises—"

Another shot rings out.

"Excuse me!" Harlow yells, unhinged. "As gross as this banter is, I have other matters of importance to get to and I'm really getting tired of all these distractions."

I pick my head up while my hand reaches for my gun. Tight in my grip, I pull it out of the holster and point it at Harlow. I fire. One shot, two shots.

Harlow retaliates and I throw my head down, shifting on top of Sayer to make sure she's still covered. The bullet just grazes my bicep and I grit my teeth as my muscles spasm and fire shoots up my arm. Fucking hell.

I glare at Harlow. *Bitch.*

"You're not going to win—" I cut Harlow off with a bullet to her thigh. She screams as another gun goes off. This time from behind and Harlow screams again, dropping her gun to clutch her shoulder.

Sayer pushes me off her the same time Reeve, Gabe, and Thea break out of the trees.

"Welcome home, bitch." Thea lowers her gun, glaring at Harlow, who yells and charges Thea.

They hit the ground with a hard thud.

Reeve and Gabe step forward to break them up when a guttural moan hits my ear and snares my attention.

Sam, who's been on the ground, starts to get up and his eyes are locked on Sayer, who's watching Thea wrestle her way on top of her sister and slam Harlow's head into the ground.

Oh no, he fucking doesn't.

Before he can fully stand, I tackle him to the ground. He doesn't even have time to react before my fists wail on his face.

I'll get my hands on Harlow when Thea's done. Right now is my time to get revenge on this bastard.

Each punch is for every second he had his hands on Sayer.

It's not until my knuckles are split and Sam's ugly mug is unrecognizable that a set of hands pull me off him. I swing around before realizing it's Gabe. "I got him."

I nod, knowing he does, but before I can so much as take a step away, another gunshot pierces the night.

I reach my gun and look for the threat when I see who pulled the trigger.

Sayer.

Sayer's holding Harlow's gun above her head.

Sayer who hates guns has steady hands as she lowers it.

"Enough," she barks with enough authority to make everyone stop and listen. Even Thea and Harlow momentarily pause. The latter looking at her sister like she's never heard this voice before. "It's my birthday and this is soooo not how I planned on spending it."

She waves the gun around and I want to tell her to stop, to be careful. As far as I know, she's never shot a gun before this in her entire life. The last thing we need is her shooting someone.

Not even Harlow. Her tender heart couldn't handle hurting her sister even given everything Harlow's put her through.

But that's what makes them different.

I'm edging my way toward her when Reeve gets there first and gently takes the gun from Sayer. He clicks the safety on.

"Thea, get off my sister."

Thea's still sitting on Harlow with her hands pinned to the dirt. She looks to me for permission when Sayer snaps her name again. This time harder, sharper. No room for arguments.

Slowly, Thea does. Yanking Harlow to her feet as well. She doesn't let go either. Both of them look a mess. Scratch marks and swelling on both their arms, faces, and fuck knows where else.

Sayer marches over to Harlow. Reeve looks at me like I know what she's about to do but I'm as stumped as he is.

What's she going to do?

Sayer is the furthest thing from a fighter.

What's she thinking?

Her face is carefully blank. She stops when she's toe-to-toe with her sister. Leaning in so they're almost touching noses, Sayer says, "You lose."

Harlow screeches, lunging for her sister, but Thea jerks her back. Keeping her restrained. That only makes her screech louder.

Sayer smiles, but it's not one that fits her face. It's too dark, too cruel. It mirrors my own. It's wiped away when she looks at me. "Can we go do something fun now?"

I nod, eyes assessing her. "Get them out of here," I tell my friends, not looking away from Sayer as I close the distance between us.

She comes willingly into my arms, melting into my side.

"You always had a flair for the dramatics, Har." Reeve shakes his head, reaching into his back pocket to produce a pair of handcuffs. "Never knew when to shut up."

"You're one to talk, rocket man." Harlow makes a sound in the back of her throat.

"I'm rubber and you're glue whatever you say…"

"Reeve," Gabe snaps from where he's snapping another pair of handcuffs on Sam. "Knock it off."

He glares. "Your wish is my command." There's a hardness I've never heard Reeve use with Gabe.

"Don't touch me with those!" Harlow struggles as Reeve tries to cuff her. "I don't know where they've been."

Undeterred and with the help of Thea, Reeve is able to slap them on. Tightening to the point of Harlow hissing in pain and her skin is discolored around them.

"Well, isn't it lucky then, you now have all this time to listen as I tell you."

Harlow snarls at him. Reeve blows her a kiss.

Behind me Gabe sighs, sounding as exasperated as I feel.

I look at Thea. "Looks like your gadget worked."

Thea grins. Soaking up the praise. "Got here just in time to save your ass."

"Easy now," I warn.

At another time I'll tell her she can create anything she wants. Right now we have other things to take care of.

"Where are we taking them?" Gabe asks, pushing a hobbling Sam forward.

"The Underground."

They all nod, knowing where to go from there.

And as I'm standing with Sayer at her parents' lake watching my friends lead her sister and Sam away, it almost doesn't feel possible.

For weeks I've been hunting Harlow and now that she's here her reckoning has finally come.

Tomorrow morning, as the sun rises, we deal with Harlow but tonight…tonight belongs to me and Sayer.

Once they're out of sight, I pull away from Sayer, holding her at arm's length. She's still staring at the path that her sister disappeared down.

"Sayer."

Painfully slow, she looks at me. I see the energy and adrenaline drain from her eyes.

"Are you okay?" My eyes hone in the mark left behind from the knife. Gently, I trace it.

"Take me home, Noah."

I hold out my hand waiting for her to take it. There's a tightness in my chest that only loosens when her small hand slips into mine.

Sayer wakes up before me the next morning and I find her standing under the shower, steam covering the mirrors, filling the room. When we got home last night, she stripped out of her clothes and crawled into bed. Both her cat and I stood in the doorway and watched her until he turned that feline gaze to me and meowed. Like he was telling me to fix it.

If I knew how, I would. But I didn't. Instead, I stripped out of my clothes and crawled into bed beside her, not even complaining as Pan followed. I hated that he slept on the bed. His white hair got all over my sheets, his kneading nails have destroyed the silk fabric. But how could I kick him off tonight as he fitted himself on Sayer's other side, snuggled in close? We both wanted the same thing.

For our siren to be okay.

And in the early hours of the morning, I plan to help her with that.

So I strip out of my sweats and I step into the shower where I have to bite back a curse. *Jesus Christ*, it feels like the flaming pits of hell are raining down upon her. Her pale, pale skin is scorched a molten red.

My hands reach out, tracing down her arms to lace over where her hands are folded over her stomach.

"I woke up wishing I never came back," she whispers.

I tighten my grip around her like she's about to slip through my fingers and melt down the drain.

I keep quiet. I don't agree with her. Coming back home was the best thing she could've done. For me. Selfish, I know, but I don't give a damn. Her life might've been easier when she was away, but it wasn't as full. And I'm cocky enough to think that she's seeing the world in a wider spectrum of colors now.

I know I am.

"Why do you say that?" I finally ask.

"Everything would've been easier. I would've just had school to focus on. No sister. No family secrets revealed. No weapons trying to harm me." She twists her neck to look up at me, and I notice there's still a faint knife mark on it. With one hand I reach up and trace it.

"But then I got to thinking." She turns in my arms, pressing her chest to mine. "If I never came back, I wouldn't have had this." Her hands move up my body, finding a home around my neck. "I wouldn't have had this time with you."

My eyes narrow at her words as her lips touch mine. It sounds like she's forming a goodbye. I don't like it. So when I kiss her back, I make sure my lips imprint against hers, that she feels them skate across her entire body as they travel down her neck, her chest, and knows there's more between us than this physical need.

I need her like I need the air in my lungs.

Like the sun needs the sky and the moon needs the stars.

She's the light to my dark.

Self-expression and words don't go hand and hand for me. The best way I can tell Sayer what I can't put in words is through my actions.

So I sink to my knees, scalding water beating down my back as I kiss down Sayer's stomach, down to her sex.

She trembles under my touch and her fingers pull at my hair. "Noah." She sounds broken and I want to be the bandage keeping her together. "We don't have time for this."

Technically she's right. We have to get to The Underground and deal with Harlow, but I've spent weeks letting Harlow pull me away from Sayer and I'm not about to let it happen again.

Harlow can wait.

Sayer can't.

There once was a time when I said I didn't want Sayer's heart but I'd give everything to steal it now.

"We have all the time. They can wait," I tell her as I massage her ass cheeks. "You can't."

She doesn't protest as I bring my lips toward her, tasting the sweetness that's her. God, I could have her for breakfast, lunch, and dinner never going hungry again.

Sayer sucks in a breath as my tongue reaches out to trace her clit, jolting under my hands.

I smile into her skin. So responsive to my touch.

Once I thought of Sayer Brooks as a weakness, a downfall I refused to let happen. Turns out I was wrong. She's a strength I never knew I was missing.

I wanted to go slow, to savor her, but a taste isn't enough. Slow isn't who I am. Who we are. With my hands tight on her ass, I haul her to my mouth, holding her there as I devour her.

Her hips rock against my face as she breathes my name, begs for more.

I tease her, play with her like the doll she is. So perfect and put together, I love watching her come undone like this, by my mouth, my hands. Her nails bite into my shoulders as my teeth graze her clit, her walls spasm around my tongue.

With a growl I push her against the shower wall, hauling one of her legs over my shoulder for better access at the sweet pussy she's given me.

"Noah, I'm close." Her nails dig deeper into my skin. Hard enough to draw blood and the thought alone has another growl slip through.

God, she's perfect as she gets lost in herself, in the sensation building inside her. She's glorious as she comes undone, my name whimpered in a strangled worship.

And it's here, on my knees before this beautiful woman, that I know.

Sayer Brooks is the siren that's ruined me.

thirty-two

TREPIDATION PUMPS IN MY VEINS. I'M STANDING WITH Reeve behind a one-way window, staring at Noah as he sits across from my sister at a metal table. Gabe stands behind her, his arms crossed over his chest and his face wiped clean of any emotion.

The only person missing is Thea and when I asked Reeve where she was, he told me not to worry about it.

We're in another room at The Underground, on a floor between their stolen gallery and the casino floor. Noah told me this is where they bring people who try and cheat at the card tables.

"This feels like an interrogation room in a police department," I mumble as I stare at my sister and my—well—Noah.

"Have a lot of experience in one of those?" Reeve asks from where he leans on the opposite side. He doesn't look at me, his gaze trained on the room before us as well.

"No, but I bet you have."

Reeve chuckles, but it's cold, devoid of any humor. "Sweets, you have no idea the kind of prisons I've been in, but I can promise you none of them have been like this."

I tear my eyes away from the glass. "What do you mean?"

"Never been arrested, but that doesn't mean everything has been all sunshine and rainbows."

I frown.

"You look good, baby." Harlow's voice snaps my attention back to the room. She can't see us through the glass from her side of the room, but she stares at the exact spot I'm standing and her lips pull into a smile.

"And you look like you're deranged." Noah sounds almost bored. The tautness in his shoulders says otherwise.

The chilling smile drops to a frown. "She's turned you against me. I always knew this would happen."

She.

Harlow means me.

We're all tense, waiting to see what happens now. This has been the entire point of everything, Noah and me, but now that it's here the pill is almost too big for me to swallow.

My sister is back.

My sister is the one who sent the letter, the pictures.

My sister was behind it all.

I know we never got along and there's no love lost between us, but I never knew the hatred she had for me was so strong. Ran so deep.

When Noah brought me into this room, he and I didn't exchange words. We didn't have to. He let me in by dropping the screen that's always present behind his eyes. He was gaging to see where I'm at, how I'm holding up.

He's been doing that all morning. Taking care of me.

After going down on me in the shower, he haphazardly dried us off before picking me up and carried me toward his bed. He tossed me down and made sure no thoughts occupied my head but him and us and the amazing heights he was bringing me to.

Noah ravished me to the point of the bed sheets popping off the mattress and made me question if I'd be walking funny after.

Harlow reaches across the table toward Noah. Gabe stops her, grabbing her wrist and pinning it to the table.

No touching.

My sister simply smiles up at Gabe's sullen face. Gabe does nothing but keep her arm flat on the table. She looks back to Noah. "So you have me. Congratulations. What're you going to do with me, now?"

"I've spent countless hours since you were gone imagining seeing you again." Noah shifts forward.

Harlow smiles, not listening to the malice in his tone, only his words.

"Would I wrap my hands around that dainty neck and shake you until I heard a snap?" I shiver at the darkness that's crept into his tone. "Would I tie you under the pier and let the tide decide your fate? *Hours,* Harlow. I've spent hours trying to decide what to do with you, but now that you're here I can't do any of those things. Care to guess why?"

I thought I knew all the sides of Noah Kincaid, but hearing his voice and the dark pleasure in which he speaks makes it clear that there are still some layers I've yet to peel back. And right now I'm seeing the mastermind, the ringleader of The Underground at work.

He should frighten me right now, the voice he's using is one of nightmares, but if anything, my body hums with seeing him in this position. In power.

Harlow and I were born with many differences, but it seems we have one thing in common.

Our reaction to Noah Kincaid.

She's staring at him the same way I do, like he's a mystery waiting to be solved, a magnet we want stuck to our side. "Because you don't have the ledger," she sings, pride clear in her words. She still has the upper hand.

The room goes quiet.

"As long as I have it," she continues. "You can't do anything."

"You so sure about that?" Noah's voice is soft, lethal and has Harlow straightening her spine.

"What did you—"

"You talk in your sleep, Harlow. I've never forgotten that. A person can have a full-blown conversation with you, and you won't even know it."

I don't need to see Noah's face to know he's starting to smirk as some color drains from Harlow's face.

"It was so easy for Thea to ask you in between snores where the ledger was and for you to tell her. I think she was even a little disappointed she couldn't have more fun coaxing it out of you."

I startle, hearing a knock from the other side of the glass. Gabe smiles as Noah tilts his head toward the door. "Don't you love when people are right on time?"

A crease appears between my sister's eyebrows as Gabe opens the door and Thea walks in. Noah turns his head to watch her and I see that devilish smirk firmly in place.

Thea struts in the room, fanning herself with a thick, worn leather book.

"That's the ledger?" I ask, tearing my gaze away from the room to look at Reeve, who doesn't bother to spare me a glance as he nods.

When I turn back to the scene unfolding before me, I see my sister unravel. See the confidence she's sat there with slip and be replaced with a nervous nibble to her lip. "No," she whispers, only to say it again a little louder.

Noah pushes away from the table to take the ledger from Thea. He runs a hand down the spine like it's a tender animal. As he walks back to my sister, he glances at where I stand from behind the glass and winks.

"Is it killing you?" I ask Reeve, seeing three of his friends. "To not be in there—"

I'm asking an empty room. Reeve just waltzed into the interrogation room. Leaving me all alone.

"Fuck this," I say and storm out, walking the short distance and bursting through the door. It clangs against the wall and every. Single. Head swings toward mine.

"Sayer," Noah growls, his face stone while his eyes rage a fire at seeing me here. Not that I can really fault him. Last time I was this close to my sister she had a man hold me at knifepoint. And he did tell me to stay put.

It's not my fault he hasn't learned I'm not going to listen.

"What's she doing here?" my sister hisses through her teeth. If disdain could kill, I'd be dead on the floor right now.

I give her a small wave.

She lunges at me.

And the room erupts into chaos.

Noah moves toward me the same time Thea pushes Harlow back into Gabe, whose arms lock around her in a vise grip. She struggles in it and almost kicks Thea in the chin with how high she's able to get her leg. Luckily, Thea's able to catch my sister's ankle and twist, making Harlow turn into Gabe's chest.

Reeve stands between us all, chuckling.

"What're you doing here?" Noah asks again. We're so close, standing toe to toe and I breathe in his scent. The familiar smell of amber and mahogany mixed with deep tobacco instantly making my muscles relax.

"Reeve left the room and I got lonely. All the fun was being had in here."

Noah watches me and I hope he doesn't call me out in the sarcasm I couldn't quite keep out of my words. I hope he knows that I have to be here like everyone else in the room, maybe even more so.

Harlow might've stolen and sent them on a wild goose chase, but for twenty-five years she's made my life literal hell. What other person can say that their sister buried them alive? That's taking sibling antics to a whole new level.

I have to be here because I can't keep hiding from Harlow. Not standing up to a bully isn't going to make them stop.

Seeing all this pass over my face, Noah gives me a sharp nod before turning back to my sister. He doesn't move away, choosing to stay close to me.

Harlow stares at us with an icy glare, still trapped in Gabe's hold.

"Now." Clearing his throat, Noah speaks like the last five minutes didn't transpire. "What were you saying about having the ledger?"

Harlow looks away from glaring at me to stare at the ledger, seeing that her bargaining chip is no more.

She's lost.

"What're you going to do to me, Noah?" But that doesn't stop her from using a flirtatious tone with Noah right in front of me.

My fists clench at my sides.

"Nothing."

Excuse me?

Everyone looks to him in shock.

He's not going to do anything? After all this time, seriously?

Before I can slap him upside the head, he adds, "I'm not physically going to harm a single dark hair on your head, Harlow. Not when I'm banishing you out of the city. No longer are you allowed to step foot in Haven Harbor."

Harlow might not be an idiot, but she also doesn't know when to keep her mouth shut. "That's…so unlike you."

She stares at Noah like he's a stranger. So are his friends.

Me? I can't form any thoughts, not when he turns his attention toward me. "Yeah well, I made a promise to someone that I intend to keep."

Gorgeous and fierce, his gaze burns into my skin as his words wash over me. Bathing me in these warm fuzzy feelings that twist me from the inside out.

He remembered.

"But you have a lot of enemies, Harlow." Noah looks back at her, watching the color slowly leave her face. "A lot of people who want to get their hands on you from all the shit you've done and I was just at the top of the list. So you better run and you better hide, you don't have The Underground's protection anymore."

I don't think I've ever seen my sister so pale by the time Noah's done talking. Gone is the anger in her face, replaced by a sense of fear that touches even me. She's being kicked out of the only place she's ever called home and that's worse than any kind of physical punishment.

Which is why Noah did it.

By keeping the promise he made to me many weeks ago, he gets to hit Harlow right where it hurts.

Her hubris.

He's taking away the one thing she can't get back.

Her freedom.

Her home.

And I wish I could make myself feel bad, but for the first time in my twenty-five years, my warm and compassionate heart has turned cold.

"You can't be serious," she finally says, but it's weak. Slight panic hangs onto the edges. Harlow looks scared.

And Noah feeds off it.

He gives her a predator's smile. "A hundred percent." He steps close to where she's still locked in Gabe's arms, pinching her chin between two of his fingers.

Noah brings their faces together. His voice is chilling enough to bring goose bumps to my skin. "If I ever see you or get even the tiniest whiff that you're back, I will find you. And I will end you. I won't give a shit at whom you're related to. Understood?"

My sister doesn't nod. She can't. He has her trapped between his two fingers.

She stares at him, instead. And for several beats, they stay locked in that position until finally Noah lets her go and steps to the side. He gestures toward the door. "Get her out of here."

Gabe and Reeve flank either side of my sister but they take several steps before Noah's voice stops them. "Oh, and Harlow? You have five minutes to get out of this city once you leave this building."

It takes at least ten minutes to reach city limits from here. Harlow doesn't say that. She doesn't say anything as they take her out of the room.

And as she goes, relief settles into my bones with the knowledge that this is finally over.

But that quickly gets replaced with trepidation.

It's over.

Noah doesn't look at me as Harlow leaves the room. Instead he turns to Thea. "And Sam?" he asks, like picking up a conversation from earlier.

"He gave the names of the other people who helped Harlow. They were all the ones involved with the cemetery stunt," Thea informs him while I shiver at the mere mention of that night. I can't sleep in complete darkness anymore. My sister stole even that from me.

"They're on level B2 in holding."

Level B2? "How many floors are in this place?" I ask. It might be a renovated mansion, but there's only so much space a house can have.

Noah doesn't answer, but I've been around him enough to know that he's now lost in his mind. Swimming with ideas.

Thea shrugs. "Enough for everything we need. Remind me to give you a tour sometime."

I nod, but a weight settles in my gut.

Thea talks like I'm still going to be around, but I can't help but remember our conversation at the sushi restaurant.

"What am I supposed to do when this is over?"

"Then you get to go back to your apartment with your cat and return to life as usual."

Well. The time has come. No matter how much I had secretly hoped it wouldn't.

It's finally over.

And I have no idea of where that leaves me.

thirty-three

Sayer

EVERYTHING RETURNS TO NORMAL. OR AS NORMAL AS it gets here in Haven Harbor where art thieves control the city and the rich carry on ignorantly bliss. Everything goes back to normal except for me.

My life.

It's not something I can hit the rewind button on and go back to not knowing. I now walk the streets of this city with my eyes wide open.

A city built on lies, relationships forged by dishonesty.

It's been three days since Noah banished my sister. Three days of him and his friends cleaning up all the messes she made. Three days since I've seen him.

I'm still at his penthouse, but it feels even colder than it did my first night here.

I can't go back there, I think as I walk across campus, leaving my last class of the day sans bodyguards. Now that my sister's banished, I convinced Noah to let me ditch them.

I could call Brin and see if she wants to meet for lunch. Except…I don't want to really be around people right now either.

Without a destination in mind, I let my feet decide the path walking down street after street until I'm in front of a familiar building. My apartment.

The cement steps stare at me in invitation.

I haven't even been on this side of town since finding the letter. Couldn't find any reason to. But I still have my key in my purse. It could be the perfect place to be alone for a couple of hours.

To reclaim a security that was stolen from me.

So I walk up the waiting steps, into the warm entryway. It's a quick trip up the several flights of stairs and before I know it, I'm stepping through the threshold of the apartment I moved into when I was looking for a change.

It looks the same, with some of my boxes still stacked along the far wall.

The door clicks shut behind me as I move farther into the room, running my hand along the wall as I do. I walk to the bookshelf that held the flowers, which still sit there.

No longer are they the fresh and intimidating flowers but dried out and brittle and decaying.

No longer does the sight of them make my blood race.

I was afraid to come back to my apartment because my safety was stripped away. That my skin would crawl and I'd constantly be looking over my shoulder for a threat that may or may not have come.

I didn't come back because I wanted to see where Noah lived. To get closer into his life, his world.

This apartment doesn't feel like mine anymore.

And if I'm being totally honest, it didn't feel like mine when I moved in. Maybe that's why I dragged my feet with unpacking the boxes.

Actually, I can't even remember what I had left.

Might as well get it done now. I'll be back here sooner or later, whenever Noah gets done picking up the pieces my sister's trail left behind. I could go back to Noah's apartment and collect my belongings today. No need to wait for Noah to kick me out.

I could leave today with my pride still intact.

But when it comes to the heart, pride means nothing.

And my heart beats in tune for a man that only wanted me for a pawn. Sure, there have been times where he's said things that have made me question my role in this game he invited me to play. Where he's acted like there's something more between us than the box he originally placed me in.

Which is why I'm not going to go back to Noah's and pack up my things. I want to hold on to whatever part of him that I can for however long I can.

I'll accept whatever hurt comes along.

Because I'm a fool for listening to my heart.

But it's the same heart that finds the paint and canvases in the boxes and doesn't run away in a panic. Who doesn't freeze when picking up a paintbrush.

I decide not to unpack the boxes, after all. Instead I try something I haven't done in a long time.

Running into the kitchen, I grab one of the plates and dash back into the living room where I pull out the easel, stretching it out in front of the window overlooking the busy street and the light shines just right, and place a clean canvas on it. I drop a little paint of every color I can onto the plate.

It feels so natural to dip one of the brushes into the paint and touch it to the canvas. To brush a single stroke of purple.

An overwhelming feeling comes over me. The feeling of comfort and purpose and belonging.

Tears prick my eyes as I continue to paint. A sense of grounding roots deep inside me. Stroke after stroke, color after color. It's been so long, but it feels like I'm coming home. Before I even realize, I've painted the entire canvas.

Nothing concrete, just an abstract of cool and warm colors.

A little taste at what I've missed.

A taste I want more of.

Grabbing another canvas and refilling my paints, I start another. This time with a more definitive vision in mind.

No longer am I able to hold back the tears.

This.

This feels right.

Like I'm fully whole again.

I can't believe I'd denied myself this kind of feeling for so long.

I mourned for so long in all the wrong ways, I was never able to heal. But now I can feel the ache, the hole in my chest start to fill.

My movements become almost frantic as I race to capture the picture in my head, as I chase the feeling it's creating inside me. Painting has always felt like breathing to me and it finally feels like I'm taking my first breath, crisp air hugging my lungs.

I paint until my hand cramps and the sun sinks behind the buildings to make way for the moon.

I paint until I'm speckled with colors.

I paint with tears running down my face.

I paint to heal.

I paint to feel.

I paint to get to know me again.

I paint toward the future I want instead of the past I had.

The painting, when I finally finish, is of happiness.

Hours later, when I can finally drag myself away from my easel, I make my way to Noah's.

The sun has long since gone down. The people out have long since had dinner and are now looking to party. My hands are tight, cramped from holding a paintbrush for so long. I don't mind it. In fact, it's a welcomed pain that I've missed.

My clothes are ruined, covered in an array of acrylic colors. And my entire body hurts from standing in the same position for so long.

But I'm happy. Weightless.

Painting and art has always been a huge part of my life and even though my muscles ache and I'm exhausted, I can't wait for tomorrow. To paint again.

I'm on this cloud as I ride up the elevator to Noah's. A cloud I quickly fall off of as soon as the doors open.

Noah's standing in the hallway, waiting for me. Pan seated at his feet. Both are giving me a hard stare.

"Where have you been?" Noah asks, low. I can feel the energy pounding out of him. He's still but in that stillness lays a man on the cusp of losing control.

I tell myself not to read into it as I step farther into the room, stripping off my coat and scarf and hanging them on the coat rack. "I went to my apartment."

It becomes deathly quiet. Noah looks pissed, so pissed I'm not sure he's even breathing.

"Why?" he finally bites out, a whip cracking in the air.

Oh really? I raise a brow. He's pissed about that? About me not coming back until a couple of hours after I usually do, but he doesn't have to come home at all?

I don't think so, mister.

"Because I wanted to." I march past him and he reaches out, snagging my elbow.

"Because you wanted to?" he repeats, dryly. "Because you wanted to. Of course." He lets out a short chuckle in disbelief. "And you didn't think to check your phone at all?"

Actually, no. I was so caught up in creating, the rest of the world faded away.

My silence only fuels Noah, his face is pinched in anger. He pulls me into him. "You drive me fucking crazy, wanting to go up the wall with worry."

"You were worried about me?" I pull back to stare at his face, his clenched jaw.

The look he sends me makes me wish I hadn't asked.

"I'm surprised you just didn't track me down."

My words send a ripple of disgust through him. He pulls away from me and stalks farther into the room. "You really think I'd do that?"

He doesn't yell but might as well have in the way the words hit me.

"I don't know," I admit, looking down at my hands before forcing my gaze to meet his. "I haven't seen you in *days*, Noah. And it's not like you're an open book when it comes to sharing your feelings! I don't know where we go from here, what we're doing! Or" —now I'm shouting— "how you feel about me."

Noah doesn't say anything, but he motions for me to come closer, to follow him.

I do, with a stampede racing in my chest. I follow him into the living room. And when I do, the first thing I notice is the chessboard with our unfinished game. That's not new. What catches my eye is that there are more pieces missing than when I left this morning.

Only two remain on the board.

A red king and a white queen.

The king lays on his side in front of the queen as if bowing at her feet.

What...

The stampede gets wilder.

I try not to get my hopes up as I turn around to find Noah on his knees watching me.

The sight of him down there constricts my lungs.

"What is that, Noah?" I ask around the tightness in my chest.

"You're not going back to that apartment, Sayer. Not unless you really want to, but I'm fucking hoping you don't. I want you here. With me. For good. I want your crap all over the place, your hair in the damn shower drain. I want *you,* Sayer. I've waited around for you since prep school."

"What?" I breathe, the word barely reaches my ears.

He says so much that makes my knees feel weak, my palms shake with nervous energy. But the words that wreck me the most?

I've waited for you since prep school.

"You don't know the power you've held over me. Have always held over me. You make my life have more meaning than vendettas. More than revenge and anger and all the ways I've lived for all these years." His deep blue eyes are brimming with emotion, alight with emotions he's never dared said. "You make me feel grounded. You make me have another purpose." He crawls to me on his knees and that sight alone as tears prick my eyes. He looks so vulnerable. So open and raw. "I don't want to go another day without you."

He grabs my hands.

They're shaking.

My chest tightens at the sight.

He puts my hands over my heart. It beats strong against my palms. "Every beat I have is for you."

A choked noise escapes me as he keeps talking. "Everything that I am is yours. Everything I have I'll give you. This heart? It's yours. Don't break it. It's a fragile beast."

"I promise," I vow around tears. Happy tears. Healing tears. "Now, stand up. Kings and devils don't kneel."

He doesn't budge. "They do when it's to their queen."

I fall to my knees, then. Pulling his face to mine. Our kiss is slow at first, familiarizing each other and steadily building to ravenous where clothes are peeled off one layer at a time.

And as Noah's unhooking my bra and sliding it off my shoulders, down my arms, he utters a set of words I never thought I'd hear him say. Three little words that destroy me from the inside out.

"I love you," he rasps from the place his lips tease the hollow of my neck. "I never thought I would love anything, but I love you." He cups my face, my shocked, tear-streaked, awed face. "I more than love you, Sayer Brooks. I worship you."

Words I never thought I'd hear, words I never thought I'd get to say back to him. "I love you too," I mostly mouth, my words inaudible with all the elation building inside me.

Noah Kincaid can love. His black beats a little red.

For me.

He loves me.

And I love him.

I survived the blue-eyed devil and came out with his heart.

In all my years I've never felt like I've belonged somewhere more than by his side.

I've spent my life looking for a place I belonged, never to realize it might not be a destination but a person who travels there with me instead.

epilogue

Noah

One Year Later

"**F**UCKING HELL," I CURSE, GLARING AT A SET OF narrow eyes from across the kitchen. "I can't keep doing this."

I'm met with silence and a slow, deliberate blink.

"Really? You have nothing to say?"

More silence.

My eyes cut into slits. "You—"

Before I can finish, they turn and walk away from me.

"Where the fuck do you think you're going? Get back here!" I start after the retreating form when a soft laugh hits my ears.

Spinning around, I find Sayer hugging the doorframe. An amused look on her delicate face. "What're you doing?"

"That cat of yours is out of hand. Look at this!" I swipe my hand over my countertops, holding my palm out so she sees all the white hair left behind by her little shit, who thinks my island bar is a perch for him to sleep. "He has no respect."

One of the rules I had when I couldn't convince Sayer to let Pan go back to living with Reeve, was no cats on the counter. A rule he's steadily broken.

"He's a cat," she reminds me, like that makes a difference. Spoiler: it doesn't.

"So is Hook, but he knows how to behave." I point to the black cat that's sleeping on the cat tree I bought him, not giving a single damn.

Hook is far superior. And I'm not just saying that because he likes me better than Sayer.

He's the perfect creature. Keeps to himself, doesn't shed like a snowstorm, and only scratches at the tree. Unlike Pan, who's made me replace not one but two couches because he decided he wanted to sink his claws into my soft leather.

That's right. This animal hating man now has two cats. All because he loves a girl and making her happy. When she told me she was thinking about getting another cat I told her not a chance in hell, but did she listen?

No. She didn't. The next day she came home with a black kitten in her arms.

"I can't believe you named him Hook," she tells me, still hugging the wall.

"What? Only you can name animals after characters?"

Yeah, that's right. I named him. Staying in theme of what Sayer named her cat after. Thea and Brin thought it was fucking adorable. But what else was I supposed to name him? Hook has a little snaggle tooth that peeks between his lips when his mouth is closed.

It reminded me of a hook.

Sayer shakes her head at me, the amusement growing as she pushes off the wall, walking toward me.

I narrow my eyes. Why is she so happy? Usually, she's not this expressive without at least two cups of coffee.

Leaning against the counter, I take her in. She's still rumpled from sleep, wearing only my hoodie and knee-high socks. Her blonde hair is a tangled mess, her gray eyes still a little dazed.

She's beautiful, my siren.

A year of being together and my need, my desire, my everything for her has grown. Heightened to a place I never knew could exist. There's a lightness in my chest that has never been there before.

Happiness. I'm really fucking happy.

Because of her.

Only her.

I'm still a ruthless, fast-fisted bastard but Sayer brings out this softness inside me that's only for her.

Running a hand up my chest, she presses up on her toes for what I think is going to be a kiss only for her to whisper against my lips, "Where's my breakfast?"

"Delayed." I grab her chin for the kiss she still hasn't given me, but when I try to coax her for more, she pulls away. I sigh.

"Why is it delayed?" She crosses her arms.

"Because of your cat. I have to clean the counters before I can start."

"Don't blame Pan." She sounds slightly deflated, disappointed in my answer.

"It's his fault," I argue, assessing her.

She takes a step away from me. "Well, get to it, Kincaid. I'm hungry."

I watch as she walks out of the kitchen to grab Pan, snuggling him to her chest before I get to work on cleaning all the damn cat hair from the counter and start cooking.

On top of two cats, I now have traditions. It happened accidentally, neither of us even noticed that every Sunday I'd wake up and cook breakfast until one Sunday when I didn't, but Sayer deemed it a tradition so now my ass is always making a feast early Sunday morning.

Surprisingly, I don't mind it as much as I would've before she came back into my life. Especially when her entire face lights up as soon as the plate is in front of her.

I'd do anything to have her face like that all the time.

She's mine. My family. Her and our two cats, though if Pan doesn't shape up with his manners, he's going back to live with Uncle Reeve, who now stops by just to see the cat. Sometimes we've come home to find him here, cuddling Pan.

This is what she's always wanted. A family. People who don't want anything from her except love.

And she has that. With me, with Thea. With Gabe, and hell, even Reeve. She's a part of us now, of our fucked up dynamics.

I still try to keep her out of the illegal dealings as much as I can, to not incriminate her in case anything was to ever go wrong, but when she's on a mission, she'll annoy the fuck out of me until I give her details. So she now knows what I'm doing when I go on extended trips, what's keeping me up late at night.

Everything. Sayer knows everything. All my secrets. All my thoughts.

The only thing Sayer doesn't want is to actually participate in Underground affairs. She graduated from grad school with her masters and is now working at the museum.

"I want to save art, Noah, not steal it," she once told me, almost a year ago. She hasn't been to the holding room at The Underground since the time I brought her there. She doesn't want to know what's there.

She's never tried to change me, to make me stop and I think I fell in love with her more because of that. Because she loves and accepts me just as I come.

Sayer did, however, make me anonymously donate the paintings we still had from when Baron stole from the Haven Harbor Museum over ten years ago.

She's back to painting too. Her old bedroom here is now

her art room. She'd spend an entire day in there if I wasn't here to drag her out.

As for Harlow, I haven't heard a peep since banishing her from the city. I haven't cared to keep track of where she went or what she's doing.

As long as she doesn't cross city limits, I don't give a single damn at what Harlow Brooks is doing. But if one day Harlow gets cocky enough to come back, she'll get all seven layers of Hell raining down on her.

"How's my breakfast coming?" Sayer asks, dragging me out of my thoughts.

I look away from the stove, over my shoulder, seeing her slide into one of the barstools. "You could help, and it'd be done faster."

"I don't cook. I drink wine."

And don't I know it. I had a pretty well-stocked wine collection before she moved in and she went through more than half of it after only six months of living here.

"Well, go open a bottle," I tell her. Every Sunday with breakfast we have bellinis.

"Any special request?"

"No. Just pick whatever."

She nods, looking dejected as she makes the drinks.

What's wrong with her?

I'm about to ask when she hands me a drink and presses a kiss to my chin. "Love you."

"Love you, too."

She smiles and with it the reassurance that everything is fine and I'm being paranoid.

She goes back to the island. Waiting. Grumbling that she's going to shrivel up and die if I don't feed her soon.

Finally, her French toast is done. And her face lights up

like the city's skyline as she cuts into the bread. She's bringing the fork to her mouth when she stops, eyeing me. "What?"

"What?" I parrot back.

"You're staring at me."

"Am I not allowed?" I lift a brow.

"Not when I'm trying to eat. Not like that."

"Like how?" I ask, even though I already know.

"Like you want to eat me." Her cheeks turn slightly pink with her words and I feel my grin turn wolfish. That's exactly how I'm looking at her.

"I always look at you like this."

"I know, but it's really distracting right now."

"Why?"

Without a word, she puts down her fork and slides her hands into her hoodie pocket. When she takes them out, there's something in her hand.

She drops it on the bar between us.

A little velvet black box.

My head snaps to hers. "Snooping in my office again?"

She shrugs, only slightly guilty as I open the box to reveal a beautiful, yet subtle diamond on a simple silver band. The perfect ring to sit on Sayer's finger. Beautiful, yet understated. Big enough for it to shine a kaleidoscope of colors when it hits the light but small enough to not draw everyone's attention.

The room is silent, save for my beating pulse as I stare at the ring. I bought it two weeks ago and hid it in my desk drawer. Deep in the back.

I look to Sayer for an explanation.

She shrugs again. "I was looking for a pen."

I snort, shaking my head, otherwise not saying anything.

"Well?" she prompts.

"Well, what?" I ask.

"Aren't you going to ask me?" She bats her eyelashes.

I level her a look, letting her see all the emotion I usually keep hidden as I grab the box and slide off the barstool. She watches me with elation, adoration.

"Nope." I snap the lid closed and shove the box in my sweatpants pocket.

"What?" She jumps off her stool and follows me around the kitchen.

"I'm not asking you." I go to the sink and start washing the dishes I used to cook.

"What do you mean you're not asking me?" She doesn't sound too happy and I look up to find her glaring at me, hands firm on her hips.

"I mean I'm not asking you today." Maybe tomorrow. But definitely not right now. One of my favorite things is to surprise Sayer and she's already ruined part of it by finding the ring.

I'm going to propose to her when she doesn't see it coming because for the last several months, it's the only thing I can think about. Her. Us. Our future together.

One day I'll get to call her my wife and maybe expand our family from cat children to real children.

Sayer has opened my eyes to a life I never knew I could have. One full of love and companionship and all these things that didn't fit into my cold and orderly life before she came back to town and brought chaos with her.

Not liking my answer, she grabs the hose on the sink, spraying me with hot water. "Oops." She sounds like it was anything but an accident as she backs away from me with a smile.

Without looking away from her, I wipe a droplet away. "Is this any way to treat your future husband?"

"I don't know if I'm going to say yes now."

I raise a brow at her, water dripping down my bare chest. "That so?"

She shrugs, backing out of the room. I start after her and she takes off in a run to the stairs.

Laughing as she does.

I chase after her because I know what it's like to live without Sayer in my life and it's not a feeling I ever want to go back to.

Hearing me approach, she picks up her pace, which causes her to trip on one of the last steps.

I grab her before she can hit the ground, twisting her in my arms and holding her tightly to my chest.

"Got you," I growl into her skin as I bury my head in the crook of her shoulder.

Her nails dig into my back. "Never let me go, Noah Kincaid."

"Don't plan on it, Sayer Brooks."

also by

SARAH E. GREEN

Break Line (a surfer sports romance)

acknowledgements

I can't believe we're here. At the end. The acknowledgements. For so long I didn't know if I'd ever get here with this book. *Under the Lies* is by far the hardest book I've ever written. It tested me, pushed me, broke me, stole from me, but in the end it made me stronger. It put me back together. And I couldn't have made it here without these amazing people.

You, yes *you,* thank you for picking up this book. For taking a chance on it and me. Whether this is your first book by me or you read BL before. I can't tell you how much it means for you to read my words, especially these words. Thank you for reading. And if you've been waiting for another book from me since BL, thank you for being patient.

Jessica and Lacey. The dedication doesn't even begin to cover how much you two mean to me. It's hard to put into words. But I'll try. You're the two people who have read every version of this story and still talked to me after. Because of you (and my sheer stubbornness), I didn't give up. You wouldn't let me give up. Thank you for being the friends I've needed, for putting up with all of my crying phone calls, for putting up with my weirdness and just always being there. The two best friends a girl could have. I love you each to pieces. Never leave me. Seriously. You're not allowed.

Kandi Steiner. You're a ray of fucking sunshine and I don't know if I have all the words to thank you, to tell you how much you mean to me. You're an inspiration, a force to reckon with, and someone whom I've looked up to for years. To now call you my friend and the belief you have in me means so much. More than words can touch. So thank you, for your support, for the laughs and the talks. For the small adventures we've been on. For the writing retreat on the beach and listening to me talk and whine about this story, I'm sorry I'm such a picky eater! Thank you for reading *Lies* and loving my words. But most of all, thank you for your friendship. I cherish it deeply. LOVE YOU TO PIECES!

Jeannine Allison. I don't even know how our friendship really started but now I can't go a day without talking to you. I could go on and on and on about how much you mean to me and how I treasure our friendship but I'm just going to say this: I TOLD YOU YOU'D LOVE HISTORICAL ROMANCE!

Alex. You're a pillar when I need someone to lean on, the reason when I don't see logic. The steady when I feel myself slipping, always telling me I can do this. You're one of my favorite people. One of the strongest and most caring hearts that I know (don't argue with me, deep down you know you have a sweet and kind soul). You make me laugh harder and get me in ways that no one understands. You've put up with my annoying ass for four years, so how about we go another four? And maybe four more after that? 'Cause, you know, I'm a barnacle and you're stuck with me. And because this isn't sappy enough…I love you, frat boy. Thank you for being you and thank you for everything.

To my amazing editors. Becca Hensley Mysoor and Ellie McLove. Holy shit, I love you both. So much. Becca, thank you for giving this book (and me) the ass kicking it needed. You completely saved it. Saved me. You're a magical, magical human who has a gift. Thank you for being on my team! Ellie! Oh my goodness. Working with you has been a dream. Thank you for being amazing. Thank you for making this book polished and as perfect as possible. Your feedback has been tremendous and I can't wait to work together again! Thank you for loving this story (and not firing me lol).

Once again, a huge thank you goes out to Staci Hart at Quirky Bird and Stacey Blake of Champagne Book Design for making my books beautiful from the inside out. You two inspire me, leave me in awe and clamoring for our next project together.

To my PR team, Enticing Journey. You're a dream to work with. Thank you for always making my cover reveals, releases, and tours run as smoothly as possible!

To my amazing betas. Mary, you're a gem I never want to lose. Thank you for always building me up as I try to tear myself down. Jaimi, you're my favorite coworker to bother and get food with. Thank you for taking the time out of your hectic life to read UTL and help me shape the final product. Rachel, your insight saved this book. Thank you for pushing me to get this book just right.

Michelle. Oh Michelle. I'm so glad you came into my life. 2018 was such a crappy year, but you are a bright spot. You are my history loving, wine drinking, *National Treasure* obsessed soul twin. My weirdness digs your weirdness. And I'm so glad to know you.

My family and friends! I'm sorry I'm awful on deadlines. I love you. Forever.

To all my author friends who have made my heart grow so much. Your friendships, your knowledge, your love, your support, they mean so much to me. Thank you for welcoming me with open arms, for believing in me, Krista & Becca Ritchie,

Staci Hart, Autumn Grey, R. Scarlett, Giana Darling, Jessica Florence, Jordan Bates and so many more! I love you all to pieces.

To my favorite little coffeeshop with the cutest pup. I'd never been one for writing outside of my apartment/bedroom/parents house before last summer when I needed a change of scenery to make this book work. I went to this coffeeshop I had only been one time prior and it was everything. Exactly what I needed. Thank you to Kelly and all the fabulous baristas who cheered me on, let me talk plot and rant, and gave me shit for never being done. Well, I did it! And here's too many more projects written in the cutest bunkhouse.

And lastly to the readers, the bloggers, the bookstagrammers, and the book lovers. Thank you for everything you do. For the love you have for books and authors and this community. You make it go round and I'm forever thankful and grateful for you picking up one of my books. You all are rock stars and I'm your biggest fan.

(p.s. if I forgot anyone, know I love you too!)

about the author

Sarah E. Green is a Florida girl through and through; she thrives in warm weather and hides from the cold. When she's not writing at a cute café, you can either find her on the beach, marathoning tv shows, reading, or drinking all the wines and hard ciders with some of her favorite people. She's a lover of history, mythology, and fluent in sarcasm. She's a romantic at heart and is always thinking about what HEA to write next.

Follow her on Facebook:
www.facebook.com/authorsarahegreen

Follow her on Instagram:
www.instagram.com/wordswithsarah

Join her reader group:
www.facebook.com/groups/695086787351048